Drexel

Susan Stastny & David Curry Holmes

ISBN-10: 1469982358
ISBN-13: 978-1469982359

DEDICATION

To John, my beloved husband

~ ~ ~ ~ ~

To my beloved wife Patti, my daughters Dorothy, Betsy and Amy, and my little grandson Aiden. Let me just say "your star is shining - follow it." Love, David, Dad, and Granddaddy

1 A LONG WAY DOWN

Over a bright moonlit sea at midnight, with the lights from shore at Ocean City, Maryland, five miles away and ten thousand feet down flies a twin engine Cessna carrying some unusual occupants, not the least of them a Count Drexel of Sweden, tall and slender with straight, combed-back, thick blonde hair, cold grey-blue lifeless shark-like eyes, a pencil-thin, crooked aquiline nose sporting thick reading glasses, and equally thin, cruel, rubber band-like lips that snapped into a wry smile when he addressed his prisoner that was just coming out of an unconscious state minutes before with an antidote administered by one of Drexel's henchmen.

The prisoner was none other than Senator "Hap" Morgan from South Carolina, who was a key appointed member of the Armed Services Committee who earlier that evening was gambling at a casino in Ocean City with two call girls at his side. Hap Morgan, a large portly man with flush red cheeks and a thick southern accent, was well known on Capitol Hill for his fondness for the ladies of the evening and high-stakes poker. Unfortunately, during his last round of poker he didn't notice one of the women put something in his drink.

Trying to prop himself up from his prone position on the floor of the plane, Drexel gave the nod to one of his men to untie the Senator. Now standing up, the senator was trying to focus his eyes on his captor. "Who the hell are you and where am I?" said the man, puffing, with his cheeks flushed blood red and shaking off the last bits of rope from his hands.

"That is immaterial, Senator," said Drexel, coolly holding what looked like an official Pentagon document with a series of numerical codes on them. Drexel's glasses now sat at the end of his nose so he could look back and forth between the document and the senator. "Senator, if you would be so kind as to point out which of these codes here gives me access to the Pentagon's discretionary spending accounts at the New York Manhattan South Bank, I would be most appreciative," said Drexel, holding up the document to the senator.

"I can't do that, suh; that would be treason!" said the senator, now fully awake and looking around the cabin, not yet realizing that they were already airborne.

"How annoying," said Drexel, turning away from the senator and yelling something in Swedish to the back of the cabin.

Within seconds a figure came from the back of the plane and into the senator's view, which caused the politician to gasp and clutch his chest. "Why, it's me! How is this possible? What did you do to this man?"

"Calm down, Senator. It's not a man at all, but it's the future of your government, or should I say my government, a government not by the people or for the people, but of androids who are only for me and do what I tell them to do," said Drexel, turning to his creation and smiling. Then, turning back to the senator, he forced the document into the senator's hand. "Now point out those codes now!" said Drexel, hitting his forefinger on the document hard enough to almost put a hole in it.

The senator was almost in a hypotonic state as he kept staring at his double. All he was able to do was mutter unintelligibly. Drexel, losing his patience, said something in Swedish, followed by the android picking up the politician with one hand and opening the cabin door with the other to the rushing sound of wind passing the airplane at a hundred and twenty-five miles per hour. The android then thrust the senator halfway out the cabin door, still clutching the poor man by his suit collar and shirt.

"The codes, Senator!" said Drexel, yelling from only a few feet away so as to be heard over the loud howling of the wind.

"Uh -- oh -- uh, it's the first, third, and fifth line of the document," said the terrified man yelling back, now shaking uncontrollably with fright.

"That's better," said Drexel, as he motioned to the android to bring the senator back into the cabin and shut the plane door.

Still shaking, the senator collapsed onto the floor into a fetal position and said in a low tone, "It will do you no good, though."

Drexel, puzzled at this remark, motioned to the android to pick up the man again and bring him to his feet, facing Drexel. "Now what do you mean it will do me no good, Senator Morgan?" said Drexel, looking at the man inches from his face.

"The codes, uh, the codes are only part of the security for online transactions. The other part is a retinal scan by a special camera on my laptop back in my safe at the Hill."

"Oh, that," said Drexel, in a totally unconcerned manner. "We retrieved your laptop from your office yesterday, Senator, while you were busy, shall we say, playing -- oh, what is that quaint American word for skipping school?"

"Hooky," said the android in a southern accent.

"Yes," said Drexel, smiling again. "I programmed you well, Android One, or should I say 'Hap.'"

The android smiled at his creator while Drexel turned his attention back to the senator. "Yes, while you were playing hooky from the armed services session at

.

the poker table, my men, disguised as electricians, went to your office and retrieved the contents of your safe. But that leaves only one thing left to do."

The senator, realizing that he made a mistake in talking about a retinal scan, quickly covered his left eye with his hand. "You wouldn't take my eye, you wouldn't take my eye -- no, not that, please!" said the senator, pleading with his captor.

"I am not a monster, Senator, just a good businessman. Now, if you would be so kind, I'll have your better half do a quick and painless scan of your left eye with his built-in laser and we'll call it a day," said Drexel, motioning to the android to scan the man's eye.

Relieved, the senator uncovered his eye and stood there motionless as the android shot a harmless red beam of light from his left eye into the retina of the senator's left eye. "Done," said the android to his creator.

"Good," said Drexel. "Well, that, as they say, is that, so now, dear Senator, answer me one last question.

The senator, exhausted, leaned his back against the closed door of the cabin, wiping his forehead with a blue handkerchief from his coat pocket. "What do you want to know now?" said the senator, now becoming more annoyed than fearful.

"Tell me, sir," said Drexel, looking at the man and smiling again, "what happens to traitors in your country?"

The senator, puzzled at this question, answered Drexel with a question. "Death?"

"Precisely," said Drexel, as he motioned his android to throw the senator out of the plane.

"No, no, you can't!" said the senator, struggling to break free of the android's grip as the android picked the man up, opened the plane door again, and held the man out of the plane into the rushing wind of the early morning sky. The android turned to Drexel for a second before letting go, as if waiting for an additional order.

"Goodbye, Senator, you have served your people well," said Drexel, as he motioned again for the android to let the politician go, which the android did to the sounds of the screaming senator calling out "nooooo!" as he fell from the plane.

The android stood at the door watching the man fall from the plane, becoming less and less visible in the moonlight until he disappeared altogether into the black abyss of the early morning sea below. As the android shut the cabin door, Drexel asked his creation, "Why did you watch him fall?"

The android said, "I was patterning his screams in my memory banks." "I like his screams," said the android in a matter-of-fact tone.

"Hmmm," said Drexel, thinking aloud, "I did not realize that the self-learning programming had mutated into individual conscious desires."   "Oh, well," said Drexel, looking at his watch, "we have much to do in Washington tomorrow night."

2 NIGHT AT THE EGYPTIAN EMBASSY

Elliott and Pamela Greenwood, the Vice-President and Second Lady of the United States, were guests at the Egyptian ambassador's house two doors down from the Marine Corps commandant's house on Eighth Street and having dinner with the ambassador from Egypt, Ahmir Kazzan, and his lovely wife, Mandisa, along with a small party of friends and Egyptian dignitaries. The dinner, consisting of spinach salad, roasted lamb with rice and an almond glaze, was very pleasant, complete with complimentary toasts of red wine and the usual state compliments all around.

Elliott still had a lot on his mind with his friend and boss, President John Tyler, away in Japan on a trade and goodwill mission. The President wanted Elliott to handle an upcoming scandal involving a former White House aide that was involved in leaking White House secrets to certain members of the press corps. The man was quickly fired, with the promise of criminal prosecution if he told anyone about his misdeeds. So far the scandal had been kept quiet, but Elliott had to figure out a quick response from the White House if and when someone in the press corps decided to go public. He was also nervous about having a smaller than usual contingent of Secret Service about them that night due to the absence of his favorite two agents, Bud and Jim, who were specially requested by the President for his trip to Japan.

Unknown to Elliott was a large black sedan with tinted windows, just sitting with the engine running underneath a sputtering fluorescent street light one block away from the ambassador's house, with several men inside, unseen from onlookers that might happen to pass by. Suddenly, during dessert of coffee and Middle Eastern honey-glazed pastries, one of the agents came over and whispered into Elliott's ear. "Excuse me, Mr. Vice-President, there is a man at the door that says you know him and he keeps on insisting he has to see you. He says it involves something about the press corps, but he won't tell any of us what it's about. What do you want me to do?"

Elliott whispered back, "It's okay, Joe, I'll go see him."

Curious, but somewhat nervous about this unexpected visitor, Elliott stood up and excused himself for a minute from the table. Pamela, sitting next to him, leaned over, tugged on his hand for him to bend down, and then asked, "Is everything all right, Dear?" Elliott gave her hand an affectionate squeeze and said, "Couldn't be better, Darling. I'll be right back, just have to check on something." She gave a weak smile at his answer and turned back around to continue her conversation with the ambassador's wife.

Walking toward the front door, followed by two Secret Service agents, Elliott almost stopped cold with surprise. Through the heavy glass door reflecting the brightly lit porch was a face he instantly recognized, a face well known to him, especially these past few weeks. It was the fired White House aide standing there on the front porch, nervously twitching his face side to side like a rat just coming out of a hole and looking around to see if it was safe to venture out before a cat could get it.

"You!" said Elliott, upon reaching the front door. "We gave you orders to get out of D.C. I don't think you realize the break the President gave you. If it was up to me, I'd have you sitting in an isolation cell in the lowest level of a maximum security prison." Both Secret Service agents, upon hearing Elliott utter those strong words, moved in between the aid and Elliott, but Elliott waved them off.

"I think you'll want to hear what I have to say, Mr. Vice-President. Especially since you will be accepting your party's nomination for president in a couple of months, I think it would be most unwise to sweep me under the rug just yet."

Crawford stepped away from the front porch to keep the conversation private. "Okay, you've got three minutes," said Crawford, pointing at his watch, to the nervous former aide.

"You see, sir, through my connections I know this man that wants very much to speak with you tonight. He can stop any story from being aired or published that he wishes to," said the aide as he looked down the street in the direction of the parked limo.

"I think you are mistaken, sir. No one can do that. Not even media executives have that much power," said Crawford in disbelief.

"Not true, Mr. Vice-President," said the aide. "You see, this man has the majority interest of stocks of all the media that the stories have been leaked to. In other words..." Then the former aide, for no reason, starts to whisper while looking around to see if anyone was approaching them. "In other words, what he says goes."

"Does he have power over all Washington media?" asked Elliott, becoming very curious.

"No, sir, if by that you mean he has power over Everett Gravel, your editor friend at the Washington Evening Star. Anyway, I never talked to any reporter from that paper."

"Well, that's a relief. Well, what exactly does your friend want with me? It isn't blackmail, is it? Because if it is, this conversation stops right now!" said Elliott, as his voice began to get louder and combative.

"No, Mr. Greenwood, not at all. In fact, he admires you and wants to talk to you about contributions to your upcoming presidential campaign. That's all he wants, I swear!" said the aide, holding up his right hand as if he were taking an oath.

"Well, then, if what you say is true, have him meet me back at the Vice-President's mansion. We are leaving this party shortly, and if he insists on seeing me tonight, then he won't mind showing up, say, an hour from now at my home."

"That won't be necessary, sir. In fact, he is just a few blocks away in his limo. He says he has to fly to Europe tonight, but wanted to talk about setting you up a campaign fund tonight," said the aid, pointing to the darkened limo.

Elliott thought a minute and did something that he rarely ever did, which was let his guard down. The thought of a heavy campaign contribution coming his way out of the blue appealed to his sense of need, as already his staff projected a slim start in raising campaign funds due to the President's wishes to postpone the announcing of his candidacy because of the potential White House press scandal. Also the appeal of meeting anyone that had that much power to make the scandal disappear doubled his urge over his reason to go meet this man.

"Okay, let's do it," said Elliott, summoning the Secret Service agents to follow him.

"Uh, sir," said the aid, "your men are, of course, welcome to follow us, but could they keep their distance a bit? It might make this man nervous. He hates guns or anyone that carries them."

"That seems reasonable enough. I can do that," said Elliott, turning to his agents behind him. "Okay, boys, stay back a bit, will you? It'll be okay." The agents grumbled for a few seconds and stayed back as requested, but still followed all the same.

Walking in silence, after a few minutes Elliott began to see the limo clearly under the flickering street light. As they approached the limo, Elliott turned aside and whispered to the former aid, "Uh, by the way, what is this man's name?"

The aid answered quickly, "Uh, I think his name is Drexel. That's it, he goes by the title of Count Drexel."

"Sounds rich," said Elliott to himself, smiling.

A few seconds later a back window rolled down from the waiting limo to reveal Drexel speaking as warmly as he ever could. "Hello, Mr. Vice-President. Won't you join me for a drink, please? My staff told me you like rum and coke with ice. We have much to talk about."

"Don't mind if I do," said the Vice-President, opening the door and getting in the limo.

"Let me introduce myself," said Drexel, as he handed Elliott a drink after shaking hands with the Vice-President.

Suddenly, a few seconds later, the Secret Service agents saw the tinted window rise, making the view of the Vice-President impossible to see. Instinctively they started walking quickly to the limo with their guns drawn. Just as they reached the street side of the limo, they noticed the Vice-President getting out of the limo on the opposite side. The Vice-President held up his hand, saying, "It's all right, boys, we are all finished here. Let's go back to the dinner party."

The agents immediately holstered their guns and followed the VP back towards the dinner party. The former aid walked alongside the VP for a few yards, at which point the VP stopped, handed the aid a thick envelope filled with cash, and the aid took a small bow and went off into the night, clutching the thick manila envelope. As the VP and the agents reached the ambassador's house, one of the agents whispered to the other one, "I thought he was wearing a black suit, not a dark blue one."

The other agent almost seemed perturbed at this remark and said, "Blue or black, what's the difference?

All that matters is that we did our job here tonight. Now

come on, let's get some coffee."

3 GRAVEL SMELLS A STORY

Chief Editor Everett Gravel's office at the Washington Daily Journal had a wide panoramic window showing downtown Washington, D.C., in the background. Gravel was sitting behind a huge, dark, walnut-colored desk with mounds of papers, a medium-sized man with gray sideburns and a lock of salt-and-pepper hair just covering one eyebrow, smoking a cigar and muttering to himself about needing a break on a big story that his 40-plus years of newspaper work and gut instinct was telling him concerning the upcoming presidential nominations. "I'm like a rat smelling a mound of garbage, but can't get my teeth into it because it's behind a thick opaque kitchen door. I need a key, a really, really good key." He pushed the intercom button on his phone. "Mrs. Thomas, send in Emily Patrick, please," he said, snapping the button off.

Seconds later in walks a young woman, tall and slender, looking every bit as young and green as a twenty-four-year-old could that has been thrown into the fast-paced world of news reporting. Her dirty blonde hair tied back with a dark purple bow accented her light gray business suit and green eyes. She had only been on the job four weeks, fresh out of journalism school at Iowa State University, and this job meant a big break. Her small, delicate hands were nervously twitching while holding a fresh note pad and pen. She could barely breathe, much less look at the tough old editor straight in the eye, but she remembered what her father always said about how important it was to be straightforward and never look away from a person that is talking to you, but always look directly at them. "A sign of strength," he would always say.

Here, sit down, young lady. I think I have an important job for you; that is, if you feel you can do it," said Gravel in a paternal, calm manner not befitting his personality. "Emily, if I may call you that," he said, looking at the girl, who gave a brief nod in return, "I have a gift. You could almost say I can see a story before it happens. In the newspaper business it is called 'second sight,' but in my own language I call it survival. If we can't beat the competition to what is about to happen in this town, then we might as well be a shopping guide for little old blue-haired ladies to pick up at the grocery store. You get my drift, right?"

"Y-y-yes, sir," said Emily, shifting in her seat a bit.

"Good," Gravel said, leaning back in his leather chair while picking up some papers off his desk. "It says here," said Gravel, reading the paper that he was holding, "that you were a reporter at your college newspaper and that while there you scored the biggest story in the history of that newspaper. Is that true?"

"Why, yes, sir, Mr. Gravel, I did land the biggest story on the Iowa congressional election fraud of 2008," Emily said in a stronger voice than she used earlier.

"You mind telling me how you did it?" said Gravel, now leaning on his desk, supporting his chin with his left hand.

"Oh, sure, I'd love to! You see, we at the paper got wind of some unusual procedures at the polls during election day from one of the poll workers who said that at the end of the day, before counting the ballots, they sent all the workers out of the room and into another room for a catered dinner that lasted about an hour, and then the workers were taken back into the room to begin counting the ballots. At that time most all of the poll workers noticed that the ballot boxes appeared to have more ballot stubs in them than before they went to dinner, so one of the workers started comparing the stubs as they were being taken out of the boxes to be counted. She noticed that some of the ballot numbers were printed in black ink rather than the normal red ink that was always used. She took one of the black numbered ballots and kept it to show a television news reporter in our town, but he didn't believe her, so then she came to us.

"I took the stub from her and contacted the state printing office in Des Moines, and then I went to the printing office and finally got a chance to speak with one of the pressmen on lunch break. He really didn't want to talk much until I showed him the ballot stub in black ink. In conversation with the pressman, he said that one of the night crew was fired just before they began the ballot run and was replaced by a new guy that no one really knew and that everyone in the press room was mad and rumors were flying around about the night manager having connections with one of the congressional candidates. It turned out that after I did a background check on the candidates that the rumor was true --"

"No need to go on further, " said Gravel, laughing. "I know the rest. It was on the wire, the national news;

hell, I think it was even reported in Timbuktu! That is why I really hired you, young woman. You are a gutsy kid. I had to grab you before some other news organization did when you graduated."

Emily smiled and started to relax a bit and focus on every word her boss was saying. She knew that something big was going to happen to her, but she didn't know exactly what.

Gravel went on. "Emily, something weird has been happening in the Vice-President's inner circle within the last month. People that have been on friendly terms with our reporter, Tom Rogers, who is on his way up here to meet you, suddenly have disappeared and have been replaced by people that seem to have come out of thin air."

"Thin air?" replied Emily.

"Well, that's my term, meaning they have no fingerprints, so to speak. We can't get any background checks on them, where they come from, who they are," said Gravel, relighting his cigar. "Most importantly, why did the VP choose these guys and where did the other bunch go?"

Before Emily could respond, someone politely cleared their throat from behind her. Emily turned to see Tom Rogers, the newspaper's top White House reporter, a southern young man in his early thirties; tall, slender, jet-black hair, hazel eyes, played baseball until he threw out his knee sliding into second base. That changed his whole direction in life from sports to becoming a journalism major.

"You called me, Mr. Gravel?" said the lanky young reporter, continuing to knock on the already open, thick glass-paned door.

"Yes, Tom, come on in," said Gravel, gesturing for Tom to sit by Emily. Tom looked at the beautiful young woman as he sat down next to her, giving her a polite smile, surprised at his own sudden attraction to her. He quickly looked away and hoped she hadn't noticed.

"Well, you two, I want you both to get to know each other real well, as both of you may be working together on the story of the century, so, Tom, this is Emily, and, Emily, this is Tom," said Gravel, motioning toward the young couple to greet each other.

Emily extended her hand to Tom and gave him a gentle handshake, while reeling from the news of what Gravel had just said. She then turned to Gravel and forced her question out. "Story of the century? How? When? Where? Who?"

"Just exactly the questions of a great reporter, Emily!" quipped Tom.

Gravel chuckled a bit and then his face turned serious. "Okay, Emily, Tom has been our main White House reporter for the last three years, making contacts and covering the President and Vice-President along with the rest of the press corps. He is well known and, most importantly, he is a familiar face that the Secret Service recognizes. He is going to be your shadow."

"My shadow?" said Emily, getting more scared than curious.

"Yes, your shadow, young woman. Just hear me out. There has been a large staff shift at the Vice-President's residence within the last few weeks. Some people were fired and some just quit for no reason. The domestic service that the White House uses is desperate for qualified people. One of my closest friends runs this service and is going to have a new employee that I have highly recommended to start tomorrow. Care to guess who that might be, Miss Emily Patrick, undercover reporter?"

4 SOMETHING ODD AT THE VICE-PRESIDENT'S MANSION

It was a breezy, misty, gray September morning at the back gate of the Vice-President's home in Washington, D.C. The three-story, white-painted, brick Victorian mansion shrouded in rolling fog loomed larger than life just beyond the eight-foot black iron-speared back gate. A hint of early morning sunlight was just piercing through the floating grey mass of moisture long enough to give off a few sparkles of red and orange from the leaves of the two rows of sugar maples lining the garden path just yards away from the back screened-in porch. Secret Service agents were beginning a change from the night shift to the day shift as one group of agents walked hurriedly away from the mansion toward their cars, while the other group left their cars and walked briskly toward the mansion. They passed each other without so much as a peripheral glance or an exchange of "hello" or "good morning." This strange action did not go unnoticed by the two figures sitting in a small blue compact car in the press parking space at 34th and Massachusetts Avenue, a stone's throw from the front door of the Vice-President's home.

"See, I told you something was up," said Tom to Emily, as he handed to her the domestic services pass that the newspaper had obtained for her to start her first day in the service of the Vice-President's home.

"I don't understand, Tom. Aren't these Secret Service guys supposed to be serious?" said Emily, putting the pass around her neck and straightening one of her middle brass buttons on her white and charcoal grey wool uniform vest.

"Not that serious!" snapped Tom. "I know how most of these guys operate in the Secret Service. It's like a club. They kid around and joke with each other on purpose to keep things on the light side, especially at shift change. It's sort of a way to keep them sharp and connected. But this," as Tom gestures with his left hand toward the agents, "this is just kind of creepy. I just don't get it."

"Are there any of the old agents left?" asked Emily, as she strained her eyes, looking at the last car of the night crew driving away, thinking that maybe she had missed an opportunity by not writing down a few license plate numbers to check out later.

"Only two," said Tom, as he started to light a cigarette, but stopped when he saw Emily shake her head no.

"I don't want to smell like a chimney. Anyway, you shouldn't smoke. It's bad for you and will make your teeth yellow," she said, as she took the unlit cigarette from Tom's hand and crushed it in the ashtray.

"Just like my mother," said Tom, trying to act upset, but was pleasantly surprised that a beautiful girl like Emily would even care if he smoked or not. "As I was saying, only two Secret Service guys are still left at the house. Their names are Bud and Jim, both on the day shift." He handed her a photograph of himself and the two other men that was taken on a fishing trip last year at the Outer Banks. "You can trust these guys. They are old school. And, by the way, they know about you."

"What! Are you kidding me? Why did you tell them?" asked Emily, as she gazed back at the mansion gate.

"Calm down," said Tom. "Who do you think tipped us off as to what was going on in the first place? Look, don't worry, Jim and Bud want you there. Listen, if something goes south, they will watch your back, not to mention me. I'll be close by. It's okay, believe me."

Emily, feeling more relieved, took the photograph from Tom and studied the two men's faces. They seemed friendly enough. but they appeared to her to possess a hidden quality of a no-nonsense seriousness about them.

To her they would be the type of people that one could turn to in time of trouble.

"Well, it's almost 7:30, time to go to work," said Tom, as he looked at his watch, trying not to stare into Emily's pale blue eyes. "You, uh, better get going," he said, getting out of the car to open Emily's door.

Emily got out and straightened her uniform, then looked at Tom. "How do I look?" she said with a smile.

"Like a real pro who is about to get the story of the century," quipped Tom. Just for a second Tom stared right into Emily's eyes. There was a brief moment of silence between the two of them, and Tom felt the urge to lean forward and kiss her, but then he quickly stopped himself before he got too far into leaning over. Emily may or may not have noticed, but she didn't say. "By the way, Emily, see that window with the green shades open on the second floor?" said Tom, pointing.

"Why, yes. What's so special about that room?" she asked.

"That room is used for escaping from all the parties and social functions that the VP has in the main library downstairs. It's where the younger children of past vice-presidents used to go to get away from all the boring grown-ups and it's now where the VP's daughter, Susan, sleeps when she's at the mansion. Since Greenwood's daughter is usually away at college, that room is basically never used, so if you get in over your head and you can't find Bud or Jim, I want you to get to that room and close the green blinds as an SOS so I'll see it an--"

"Bring the cavalry?" said Emily, with a half smile as she closed the car door.

"Something like that," said Tom, turning to get back in the car. "Just be careful, okay?"

"I will," said Emily, with a fake bravado in her voice as she walked away toward the Secret Service men standing at the back iron gate, thinking almost out loud to herself, "I wonder why he didn't kiss me?"

***

Emily climbed the steep red brick steps leading up to the back kitchen and walked in after producing her credentials to the Secret Service at the gate. The smells of freshly baking bread, coupled with the rushing around of the kitchen staff and the banging of a few dropped pots, as well as the fast whirl of two metal whisks mixing red wine vinegar with olive oil, all seemed to give Emily the impression that one could easily be as inconspicuous as one wanted. A cheerful voice startled her from behind as she dodged a running assistant chef with a sloshing bowl of creamy butter.

"Oh, are you the girl from the agency?" said the voice, as the kitchen noises got louder, thanks to the head chef yelling at one of his subordinates.

"Oh, yes. My name is Emily Patrick," said Emily, as she extended her hand towards a young girl fairly close to her own age.

"Hi. My name is Mara Langston. I'm, well, what you might call an assistant chief of domestic staffing her at the VIPs'."

"The 'VIPs'?" asked Emily.

"Yeah, the VIPs'," said Mara, who was what looked like about half of Emily's size, with a mop of frizzy blonde hair that reminded Emily of her little French poodle, Frou-Frou, that she left at her parents' house before coming to Washington, D.C. "It is a lot easier to say that than the Vice-President's residence, don't you think?" asked Mara, as she started to give Emily a gentle push toward the door leading out of the kitchen.

"Well, I guess so," said Emily, laughing. "Uh, Mara, where do I go to get set up in my duties here at the

Vip's?" asked Emily, now starting to feel a lot better at Mara's friendly manner.

"Oh, I am here to handle all of that," said Mara. "Here, let me take your coat, and follow me downstairs to the lockers and the prep room where I'll explain all of your duties. Say, Emily, are you hungry?"

Emily's stomach had been growling since she stepped out of the car due to being too nervous to eat breakfast that morning, so she actually was starving. "Breakfast would be lovely, but I'm on the clock now, right?" asked Emily, looking at a steaming plate of waffles only an arm's length away.

"Well, yes, you are," said Mara, with her hands on her hips, "but you are no good to us half starved. Tell you what, grab that plate of waffles before we are seen and watch this." Mara waited until the head chef was through yelling at his cowering subordinates and then she shouted, "Chef, where is Mrs. Greenwood's grapefruit and bagel?"

"What!!!" said the chef, exploding in a rapid fire stream of cuss words. "No one told me the Madame wanted grapefruit and bagels! I just can't believe the inefficiency around here!" said the chef, running around the kitchen like a dog chasing its tail, looking for the two phantom breakfast items.

"Now grab that plate of fruit before he sees us," whispered Mara, as the two young women left the kitchen, running for the stairwell like a couple of giggling school girls that pulled off the prank of a lifetime on a crazed teacher.

"What about the VP's wife's bagel and grapefruit?" asked Emily, as she was almost skipping down the steps, balancing the plates of food with both hands, hot on the heels of her new-found friend.

"Oh, she had that over an hour ago," said Mara in a very casual tone. "Don't worry about it. "

***

The basement of the VP's home was the staging ground for all the domestic help. Rows of lockers lined the rosy marble-tiled floor, with a separate shower and a changing room off to the right of the main locker room. The lighted high-beamed ceiling gave the darker, narrow hallways an illusion of space, but when there were more than a few people traveling in the hallway at one time it gave one the feeling of being on an old-fashioned freighter or tramp steamer.

Emily noticed the other staff members briskly passing her in the hallway on the way up the stairs carrying cleaning supplies, small tables, and bottles of wine, indicating to her that they were all preparing for some important event later on that day. Mara was making a bee line for an out-of-the-way small table that was sitting in a tiny room, what appeared to be a large closet space just off the main locker room just one floor directly below the Secret Service conference area. Ushering Emily in, she quickly looked both ways down the hall to see if anyone saw them. The coast was clear. She then closed the small black oak door and, with her finger over her lips, motioned for Emily to hand her a yellow tablet and pen that was on the small rectangular table.

Emily couldn't help but notice the instant transition from the easy-going Mara that she had just met minutes earlier to the serious, secretive Mara that she was now seeing. Mara grabbed the tablet and wrote, "We could be bugged here, will explain after I check everything out." A few minutes went by as Mara searched the room systematically for any electronic listening devices. Not finding any, she then poured them both a cup of coffee and sat down with Emily.

"I know why you are here," said Mara.

Emily almost spilled her cup of coffee upon hearing Mara's blunt statement. "Why, Mara, w-what do you mean?" asked Emily.

"Bud and Jim said they couldn't tell me much, but they said you are here to help and that I could trust you and should help you in any way I can."

Emily relaxed a little bit and started eating her waffle, while offering one to Mara, which Mara took. "Well, you could help me by first filling me in on what exactly is going on around here," said Emily, with her reporter instincts kicking in. "I mean, all this cloak and dagger stuff with the new Secret Service, what's that about?" asked Emily, looking around to see if she could spot imaginary bugs in the room.

"I wish I knew. They aren't a friendly lot, except for Bud and Jim of course, and things have been really tense with the staff since yesterday when they found Mrs. Withers in the wine cellar," said Mara.

"Mrs. Withers?" responded Emily.

"Yes, Mrs. Withers, my boss. She was the chief of staff here at the Vip's for over twenty years, until yesterday morning. They found her at the bottom of the stairs, dead, from what the Secret Service said was a fall. They said she was drunk and tumbled down the stairs."

"Was she?" asked Emily.

"No, of course not!" said Mara. "She never drank coffee, much less anything stronger. Bud and Jim said she was murdered by one of the new agents."

"Oh, come on!" said Emily. "The Secret Service murdering people? Don't you think that's a bit paranoid?"

"It's not just me, but it's also some of the staff that feels this way. Why, two days before her so-called 'accident,' Mrs. Withers said that the VP's wife would not let any of the new Secret Service agents get within ten feet of her, and how Mrs. Greenwood would only communicate with the girl that you have replaced, and Bud, Jim, me, and Mrs. Withers. Now I guess she'll only talk to just the three of us. Also Bud and Jim are never far from her presence. I think for some reason they must feel like she is in immediate danger."

"What happened to the girl that had this job before I did?" asked Emily, getting a little tense.

"Oh, nothing so dramatic as you might think. She decided to go back to school and get her Master's," said Mara, laughing.

Mara's laughter helped break the overwhelming sense of tension for a few seconds that Emily had been feeling since they had both sat down. "Will I get to meet Mrs. Greenwood soon?" asked Emily, looking at her watch, noticing that the morning was slipping away.

"Better than that," said Mara. "The girl that you have replaced was kind of her 'Girl Friday.' Not a secretary, but more of an event or social planner and overall confidant for the VP's wife. You will be like her shadow during the time you are here. I know you'll do fine. You come highly recommended by the agency that sent you over, and I will help you do whatever you need to do to get rid of this dark cloud hanging over this place. Anyway, we better get going upstairs. Mrs. Greenwood is expecting us."

"How nice of Tom and Mr. Gravel to not mention that little detail of my cover. Oh, well, no pressure there," said Emily to herself, as the two women left the room to go up to the Vice-President's wife's office on the third floor.

* * *

Every room on the third floor had a balcony view overlooking the mansion grounds. The hallway ran east to west so that half of the rooms on the third floor could catch the morning sun, while the other half caught the afternoon sun and evening sunset. Mrs. Greenwood's upstairs office, the one at the very end of the hall and to the right of the winding stairwell, had a large double oak door with two Secret Service agents standing outside. Their jackets were off, showing their unsnapped holsters and standard issue .45 caliber rapid fire pistols sticking out of the holsters.

As Emily followed Mara toward the VP's wife's office, she noticed that these two Secret Service men looked older than the rest of the crew of agents. It was obvious to Emily that these men were Bud and Jim. As they approached the door, Mara quickly introduced Emily to the men. Neither man stuck out their hand to shake hers, but Emily could swear that as she passed by them that one of the men winked at her. Mara knocked on the door, and an almost cheerful voice told the two women to come in.

Standing at her desk was Mrs. Greenwood, holding the guest list for the party at 6:00 p.m. that evening that would be given for the Daughters of American Patriots Association, a group of elderly women that was a special favorite of the Second Lady. Emily noticed right away how handsome a woman Mrs. Greenwood was, coupled with a tint of aristocracy about her face. Her black hair, with a few streaks of grey, was pulled back into a bun. She was tall like her husband, with an almost perfect figure, wearing a pink business suit trimmed in a black outline. Her hands were delicate, with long, slim fingers that subconsciously twirled a pencil back and forth as she made one last correction to the list. Then setting the paper and pencil down on her desk, she turned and faced both of the women.

"This is Emily Patrick, ma'am," said Mara, gesturing with her left arm toward Emily.

"Why, how nice to meet you, young lady. I have heard great things about you from your employer. How is that old news-hound boss of yours anyway?" asked Mrs. Greenwood.

Emily was stunned to hear those words from Mrs. Greenwood. "My boss, ma'am?" asked Emily, as she almost sat down in shock in a chair near the front of the desk. Emily thought she was undercover.

Turning to Mara, Mrs. Greenwood said, "Mara, will you excuse us for a couple of minutes, please?"

"Yes, ma'am. I'll be right outside," said Mara, as she left, closing the door behind her.

Then Mrs. Greenwood gestured for Emily to sit down with her on the couch by the east balcony. "I know that this is a bit confusing for you, so please allow me to explain, if you don't mind. You see, your Mr. Gravel and I go way back, long before I even met Mr. Greenwood. We were close friends back in college. Both of us had an intense interest in journalism back then. The only difference was I lost my passion for journalism by my junior year, while your boss stuck with it. He eventually got an opportunity to intern with the New York Times, while I went back to Texas after college to help my parents run their store in Austin. Of course," Mrs. Greenwood said with a pause, smiling a slight smile, "I would have never met Mr. Greenwood had I not gone back to Austin, so all's well that ends well, I suppose."

"So you asked your old friend for help?" asked Emily.

"Yes, I had to," said Mrs. Greenwood. "See, it's my husband. He seems like himself, but he has started acting very distant, almost to the point of being cold. We used to kiss and hug each other even if one of us was going to the store or just out for a walk. When I see him now, the only kind of affection I get is a brief nod and that weird smile, like he doesn't even know me. I first thought it might be another woman, but in my heart I know better, because if that were true he would still be affectionate towards our daughter Susan, but he barely speaks to her as well. Now that she is away at Wesleyan College, she calls me crying because her father used to call her every night to see how her day went, but he has stopped doing that. I just feel like

something terrible has gotten a hold of him, but I just feel so helpless as to what to do," she said, fighting back some tears. Mrs. Greenwood then paused a minute to regain her composure, while Emily was trying to piece this new information together with what Mara had told her this morning.

"But what about the Secret Service? Do you feel as Mara does, that the new replacements are out to hurt you in some way? Because as a reporter I am coming up short on any reason why they would act the way they do, although I'll admit I have seen some strange things this morning," said Emily.

"That is precisely why I asked your Mr. Gravel for his best young reporter, a fresh face that is unknown here. He said you are the best and that I am in good hands," said Mrs. Greenwood, trying to work up a smile.

"I am flattered, ma'am, but wouldn't you want to go to the FBI or another agency and report what you have experienced?" asked Emily, already knowing the answer to that question.

"Who would believe," asked Mrs. Greenwood, "that my head of domestic staff fell down drunk on some stairs and was killed due to some Secret Service plot, or the coldness of my husband, or the strange behavior of the new agents being some sort of conspiracy? No, my dear, you are all I've got! I need something concrete, some kind of hard evidence that something is amiss, and then maybe we can go to the FBI or other authorities."

Just then there was a knock at the door. It was the muffled voice of Mara. "Mrs. Greenwood, the Vice-President has just arrived!"

"Thank you, Mara. I'm coming!" said Mrs. Greenwood, almost shouting. Then she grabbed Emily's hand and whispered, "At the party this evening I'll need your eyes and ears. Please attend and stay close by and watch who gets near my husband."

"I will, ma'am. You can count on me!" said Emily, feeling as if she just made a close friend.

On the lower floor a large entourage came in with the VP. As Emily followed Mrs. Greenwood and Mara down the stairs, she noticed Bud and Jim standing over to one side, silently watching the Vice-President, while the other agents were acting very solicitous over a sinister-looking stranger that had come in with Mr. Greenwood. Emily couldn't help but notice how much interaction the stranger had with the newer agents and how it seemed that some of the agents were taking direct orders from this man. The stranger gave a quick scowl in the direction of Bud and Jim, who were standing at the opposite end of the main foyer and staring back at the stranger with blank expressions.

The Vice-President spotted his wife, walked up to

her and gave her that odd smile, with barely a hug, exactly as Mrs. Greenwood had described earlier. "Hello, dear. I want you to meet someone," said the VP, looking at the stranger all the while he spoke. "This is Günter Bergman, who has graciously donated his time to help me with my campaign."

"A pleasure, madam," said Bergman, as he bent over and kissed her left hand.

Mrs. Greenwood noticed his voice was very cultured, but had traces of a Swedish accent. "Why, err, uh, nice to meet you, Mr. Bergman," she said, fighting the urge to jerk back her hand as soon as he kissed it.

"I don't believe we have ever met before," said Mrs. Greenwood.

"No, madam. I am here on behalf of Count Drexel of Sweden. He is one of your husband's new campaign managers for foreign affairs and has sent me to be of service to your husband. He has taken a great deal of interest in the upcoming election. I am an expert in European affairs and the Count feels I might be of some help to your husband in the debates. I understand we are having a function for some elderly citizens this evening, madam?" asked Bergman, who had just noticed Emily standing a little back of Mrs. Greenwood.

"Why, yes, Mr. Bergman. My husband will be announcing his candidacy for President in a few days at the National Convention and this little function is just one of many down the political road that we are to travel if we are to get the Presidency. And of course you are invited to attend," said Mrs. Greenwood, trying to be gracious.

"Splendid!" said Bergman, who then held up his right index finger in Emily's direction. "Oh, young woman, would you be so good as to get me a drink? And send it to the library. The Vice-President and I have much to discuss this evening." Then, turning his attention on Mrs. Greenwood, he said almost with a smirk, "Madame, we have much to do. If you will excuse us until tonight then?" Bergman then took a brief bow and walked toward the main library off the foyer, with the VP in tow, who had barely acknowledged his wife's presence. Half of the Secret Service also followed them into the library, closing the library door with a loud thud.

"Wow," said Mara, astonished at what she had seen. The king and his court! Don't worry about His Highness, Emily. I'll get him his precious drink. You stay with Mrs. Greenwood."

The VP's wife was crushed at her husband's behavior and would have just sat down and cried right there in the living room, but somehow she gathered her wits about her and headed upstairs to get dressed for the evening. "Emily, you are welcome to try on one of my daughter's dresses for the party. You two are about the same size. Ask Mara to show you where her room is," said Mrs. Greenwood, without turning around as she climbed the stairs.

"Is there anything I can do?" asked Emily, feeling really bad for Mrs. Greenwood.

Mrs. Greenwood never responded, but just kept walking up the stairs.

.

5 A BAD TIME IN LONDON FOR LORD HAWTHORNE

It was a cool, grey, misty, mid-September dawn as two figures strolled through Westminster Hall, unnoticed by the morning cleaning crew just yards away from the men. No one else was around, but they still whispered. The whispers got more rapid with emotion, and then fell back to a slower, easier conversational pace that seemed to echo up to the high medieval vaulted ceiling of the old Westminster Hall.

Drexel had just gotten in from Heathrow Airport, carrying no luggage but a worn leather briefcase that he was clutching to one side. Lord Jonathan Hawthorne, a "law lord" appointed to the House of Lords by the Queen and highly favored to be the next Prime Minister, was looking down at his feet listening intently to Drexel as if he were hanging onto every word. Drexel stopped, looked up at the ceiling, and noticed the massive glass windows welcoming in the morning light. He breathed in a bit, and then exhaled quickly before he spoke. "Imagine, Jonathan, the power of this place. To think that five or so hundred years ago a populace disposed a king or some might say a tyrant, right where we stand."

"You are speaking of the trial and execution of Charles the First, of course," said Hawthorne, pulling a handkerchief from his pocket to clean his glasses.

"Of course," said Drexel, still staring up at the ceiling, "although I find that Charles the First wasn't a tyrant at all, but just an efficient ruler that knew what he wanted. Probably he was more, shall we say, misunderstood?"

"Well, if you call being responsible for the death of thousands of people and the misery of countless thousands more misunderstood, then, yes, I suppose I could agree with you, Drexel. Next you'll be telling me that Adolph Hitler was misunderstood," said Hawthorne, his cheeks flushed and anger rising in his voice.

There was a moment of silence, and then a strange half smile appeared on Drexel's face. "Hitler was not misunderstood, he was just sloppy," said Drexel, clearing his throat, followed by a quick laugh.

Hawthorne, thinking that Drexel was making a joke, followed up with a fake laugh of his own as not to appear to disagree too much with his benefactor, and then he quickly changed the subject. "I appreciate all the financial help and advice you have given me in the past few years," said Hawthorne, as they started to walk again.

"Oh, think nothing of it, dear boy. I know you will make a great Prime Minister when the time comes."

"Then you really think I'll get the position?" asked Hawthorne, looking at his watch.

"It is, as the Americans are so fond of saying, 'in the bag,'" said Drexel, as they both laughed. Then Drexel's tone turned serious. "Look, you have the endorsement of the Queen and a large portion of many ML's in the House of Lords and many MP's from the House of Commons. You have done wonders on your committee appointments, especially your work on the Council of

Europe in unifying the counsel on important matters like combating terrorism and cutting through the red tape of individual's rights versus the state's right to investigate and prosecute suspected terrorists. You're the perfect man for these troubled times," said Drexel, putting his hand on Hawthorne's shoulder.

Hawthorne felt relieved from Drexel's reassuring tone and looked at his watch again.

"Your breakfast briefing with the Prime Minister?" asked Drexel.

"Why, y-yes. How did you know?" asked Hawthorne.

"Oh, I'm just good at what I do," said Drexel in a casual tone, which by now had stopped whispering. "Here, take this briefcase with you. I want you to study some things that will help you in your future job as the new Prime Minister, as well as a private letter to the PM. Don't bother looking at it right now. Just peek at them when you sit down for breakfast. I'll call you tomorrow to get your impression on how the conversation went."

Hawthorne was almost overcome with emotion at his perceived benefactor's confidence in his future. "Yes, I'll be glad to do that. I'll make it our first order of business," said Hawthorne, as he took the leather bag from Drexel's outstretched hand.

"Good. And, by the way, where are you and the Prime Minister meeting this morning?" asked Drexel.

"We are meeting at the PM's favorite pub, the Blue Heron, just around the corner from the 'tube' station," said Hawthorne, as he tucked the bag under his arm and shook hands with Drexel.

"Oh, yes, I've heard of that place, small and over-decorated," said Drexel. "Maybe I can suggest a few interior design changes to the owner some day."

"I suppose you could," said Hawthorne, as he turned to go out the side door exiting onto Victoria Street, muttering to himself, "What an odd chap that Drexel is."

***

The Blue Heron was a small pub frequented by many members of both houses of Parliament and a special favorite haunt of the Prime Minister. It sat right by a London subway or "tube" station just two blocks from West Minster Hall, and by 7:00 a.m. it already had clientele lining up for an early breakfast. In a small back room sat the Prime Minister and Lord Hawthorne, sipping their coffee and waiting to be served their meal. Half the crowd outside the propped-open light blue door of the pub was still waiting to be seated.

Lord Hawthorne's foot hit the leather case as he pushed his chair away from the table to get more comfortable. He was suddenly reminded of his promise to Drexel and he picked up the briefcase and sat it on the table in front of the Prime Minister. "Minister, my benefactor, Count Drexel of Sweden," has taken a personal interest in my political career and has a letter for you that he says is of great interest."

The Prime Minister raised one eyebrow, showing a look of mild amusement on his face, and said, "All right, Lord Hawthorne, let's have a look and see this letter of great importance."

Hawthorne then unsnapped the brass clasps on the

leather briefcase and opened it. Suddenly there was a brilliant flash of light, followed a half a second later by a terrific explosion, blasting apart the small dining room and one third of the back of the pub. Bodies and body parts flew everywhere, mixing in with glass, brick, plaster and wood. Like a stepped-on ant hill, people that were able were pouring out of the pub, collapsing all around the front entrance. The Prime Minister was thrown against the pub's west side, now a crumbling brick wall. He died instantly. Hawthorne was thrown in the opposite direction, passing through the pub's stained glass window depicting the pub's namesake of a large blue Heron standing amid a bunch of lily pads floating on an even bluer pond. He landed on the sidewalk across the street from the pub, near death, but for some reason was still breathing.

Ambulances poured into the immediate pub area from all directions, while the police tried to restore order, keep the crowd back, and direct ambulance traffic, until someone in the pub shouted out to the crowd, "The Prime Minister is dead!" Then all pandemonium broke loose, with the crowd and the police running in all directions and some civilians and members of Parliament and the House of Lords running around in circles screaming, "The PM is dead, the PM is dead!"

Unnoticed, over by the sidewalk, a mysterious ambulance of a different color than the standard red and white ambulances of London snuck in a back way and picked up Lord Hawthorne and put him on a gurney, sliding him into the green-bodied vehicle, and rushed away towards London's downtown trauma center. Passing back over the Thames River, just minutes away from the trauma center, the ambulance stopped near a cement guardrail and two EMTs opened the back of the vehicle. When there was no oncoming early morning traffic, they took the decapitated body of Lord Hawthorne and threw him over the side, his body sewn up in a weighed-down white burlap sack. Seconds later a splash was heard, and one EMT asked the other, "What about the head mate? When do we dump that?"

Responding, the other EMT said, "Naw, not an issue. 'E said we can dump it in the hospital waste bin when we get there. They crush their garbage in about an hour. No muss, no fuss, eh? No one will ever know it's 'em. Let's go, mate, the doctor is getting nervous."

6 THE VICE-PRESIDENT A PRISONER ON GOTLAND

On the southern rocky windswept coast of the Swedish island of Gotland, in the middle of the Baltic Sea, lies a medieval limestone castle of the Swedish Count Drexel. It sits high on a jagged cliff, surrounded by massive razor-sharp volcanic rock. There's only one way in or out of the fortress and that's by a small cobblestone road that runs through a narrow barbed wire gate sandwiched between sixty-foot-high walls that run all the way around the castle.

The large black Leer jet landed on the moonless night at a private air strip at the north end of Gotland, ten miles from Drexel's castle. A small contingent of Drexel's men awaited their leader as the jet rolled up to several helicopters that were to take Drexel and his most recent prize back to the castle over the island's rocky and barren terrain.

Drexel was somewhat nervous at Elliott not responding to the antidote of the heavy tranquilizer first administered to him back in Washington, D.C. After spending a day at his secret residence outside Washington, D.C., trying to revive his captive, Drexel had decided to head for Gotland where he had his own medical team waiting to work on the Vice-President. As soon as the plane stopped and the portable ramp lowered, he quickly stepped off the plane, barking orders to his men in Swedish. Elliott still laid unconscious in the very back of the jet, strapped to a portable gurney.

"Are you sure Dr. Goteborg is fully prepared, Captain?" asked Drexel to one of his aides, while looking back at the jet.

"Yes, sir, all is ready for your arrival," said the captain.

"Good, very good. Now get the Vice-President off the jet and into the back of my helicopter. Hurry now, time is of the essence!" said Drexel, as he rapidly walked over to his helicopter and took the microphone of the helicopter's radio. "Gotland Two, this is Gotland One, do you hear me, over," said Drexel, as he pushed the two-way radio button.

"Gotland One, this is Gotland Two. We receive

your transmission and await your orders, Master," said the voice at the other end of the transmission.

"I need to know the progress of my brother, Olaf, and his flight from Dubai with all his passengers, over," said Drexel, leaning in a little closer to the radio due to some varying static noises.

"Gotland One, this is Gotland Two. Your brother is in the air and on schedule with a full load of guests, sir. They will be arriving at the island in four hours' time."

"Good," said Drexel, as he gave in to a quick smile. "Go ahead and send the welcoming party for the guests in about an hour and a half at the landing strip. I want to make sure these guests are comfortable and happy. Make sure their rooms are ready with champagne and caviar and flowers. I want every luxury we have at their disposal. Do you understand, Gotland Two?"

"Yes, Master -- err I mean Gotland One, we understand. All will be ready. Gotland Two out."

"Excuse me, sir," said the captain, running up behind Drexel. "He is off the plane and coming this way on the gurney."

"Good, Captain. Carefully load him up in the back and make ready for takeoff!" said Drexel, as he got into the passenger side of the helicopter while watching his men load Elliott carefully into the cramped quarters of the helicopter.

Twenty minutes later at Drexel's castle was a medical team, headed by Dr. Goteborg, pouring out of the castle's front entrance into the spacious limestone-bricked courtyard in response to the thunderous sound of the whirling rotors of the landing helicopters. The doctor approached Drexel's helicopter first with a medical team. Drexel, now almost in a panic, jumped out of his craft while it was still in the air, hovering a few feet from the ground, and headed for the doctor, screaming, "I thought you said the tranquilizer would wear off in twenty-four hours! It now has been almost two days and he still is unresponsive! I have a very important client showing up in under four hours' time to see my newest and best achievement and now all I have to show them is an unconscious man lying in a fetal position! Do you realize this could cost me my largest investors? Do something,

Doctor! Do something now!" said Drexel, as he grabbed the doctor's white lapel coat with both his fists, yelling at the hapless doctor only inches from his face.

The doctor, who was quite alarmed at the VP's reaction to the drug, dared not say his fears out loud to his employer, but instead outwardly remained calm and retreated into the type of language that doctors often do when faced with the unknown. "Don't worry, Count Drexel, I'll have my staff take him to the viewing room and we'll start him on an intravenous antidotal drip. He should be up and around and ready to be viewed and questioned by your investors," said the doctor, not really believing what he was saying, but hoping against hope that he could bring the VP around before Drexel's guests would be at the castle, all wanting to see if Count Drexel's claims of replacing the Vice-President of the United States with a perfect replica were true.

Drexel seemed somewhat calmed at the doctor's fake reassurance and released the man's lapels and walked toward the front entrance saying, with his back to the doctor, "Good. Have it done. I'll be in the viewing chamber, and keep me informed. And, Doctor?" said

Drexel, as he stopped and turned to face the medical practitioner.

"What, sir?" responded the doctor, with a lump in his throat.

"Don't disappoint me," said Drexel, as he turned back around and walked toward the castle.

The doctor lost no time in getting Elliott off the helicopter and onto a rolling gurney while barking orders to this staff, "Get him down there in the viewing room and start him on a water and glucose drip as soon as possible. I want him to flush what's left of that drug out of his system!"

The staff quickly obliged and rolled Elliott into a side door of the castle and onto an elevator that went down to the bottom level below the main dining hall that led into a spacious room with a dark glass ceiling. The room had whitewashed walls, a ruddy oak-planked floor, with various Persian throw rugs strewn about the room in a random fashion. Several tall, skinny reading lamps hovered over a feather down brass bed that was situated in the middle of the room, along with a nightstand that sat by the bed which had a carafe of expensive red wine, with various types of cheeses and breads arranged in a symmetrical pattern on a small silver platter sitting precariously on top of the tiny nightstand. The spacious room seemed almost cozy, if it were not for the curious fact that the bed was set in the middle of the room for some unknown purpose. Elliott was placed onto the brass feather bed, while nurses brought in an IV pole with a bag of the water and glucose-mixed formula. A needle was soon placed into Elliott's arm and the formula began cruising through the VP's veins.

***

In his state of apparent unconsciousness, as the formula was entering his body, Elliott began dreaming. It was a vivid dream back when he was seventeen and a civic air scout flying with his old instructor, Captain Bob Waller, formerly of the Army Air Corps of World War II. This was the flight right before Captain Waller, or "Cappe" as many of the boys called him, would give permission to Elliott to fly solo the following week. Flying at ten thousand feet in a twin engine Cessna, the sky was ice blue. Cappe was testing the young scout's ability to handle the small plane by constantly questioning the boy on many different aspects of the instruments of the plane as well as any fears he might secretly harbor about flying solo. Elliott showed no fear so far in the flight and seemed to answer every question perfectly that was thrown at him as both of them flew on.

"You're doing well, kid," said Cappe, as he winked at the boy, "but now I want you to head into that cloud bank over to our left and let's see how you do flying blind."

Young Elliott was very nervous at that order, but did as he was told and flew the small plane into a massive white and grey cloud bank, which was like flying the plane into a giant ball of dense floating cotton. With zero visibility, the young Elliott was a bit shaken, which Cappe fully expected. "I'm flying blind, Cappe! I can't see. What do I do?" asked the young pilot.

"No, no, kid, this is your flight now. You tell me what you are going to do. But first I want you to answer some questions that will help you out of a tough situation like this.

"Okay. I'm listening," said the boy.

"Good," said the veteran pilot. "First answer me this, are you still flying level?"

"Of course," said the boy, somewhat surprised at such a question.

"Good. Then you aren't going to crash and die any time soon," said Cappe. Now answer the next question. What direction does your compass say?"

Young Elliott looked at his floating compass on the instrument panel which read north by northeast. "I'm flying north by northeast," Cappe.

"Good!" said the old pilot. "Now, young scout, tell me about your fuel consumption. How much fuel is left and how much flying time do you have?"

Elliott noticed that he had over half a tank. "Half a tank and about three hours' flying time," responded Elliott.

"Excellent!" said Cappe. "Now, one last question. What direction was the cloud bank before we flew into it and how many minutes have we been flying in this soup?"

"That's easy," said the boy. "We have been in here only about ten minutes and we haven't changed directions at all yet, so the cloud bank must be north by northeast."

"So with all that information that you just came up with, you now tell me what you are going to do," said Cappe, looking at the boy with a blank expression so as not to coax any answer out of him.

"Well," said Elliott aloud to himself, "I have three hours of fuel, which is way more than enough time to fly out of this mess, since we have been in here only ten minutes. I am not losing any altitude, so I am on the same line of flight that I was on when we came in here, and I haven't changed direction from north by northeast. So..." Then Elliott paused and looked at his instructor. "I've got it! All I have to do is turn around and fly in the opposite direction at south by southwest for ten minutes and I'm out of the clouds!"

"I knew you would get it, kid. Now let's get out of here," said Cappe, patting the boy on the back.

***

Suddenly Elliott woke up. His eyes still somewhat fuzzy, he looked at the dark ceiling and, feeling something on his arm, he slowly realized that he was attached to an IV. For a minute he just lay there muttering to himself, "I'm flying blind, Cappe. What do I do?" Then he began a dialogue with himself, speaking out loud. "Okay, I'm still alive and in a comfortable bed," he said, as he rolled over to see the night stand. "I see some food, so wherever I am, they must want me to eat to stay alive, so they're not going to kill me." Then, feeling a little stronger, he sat up and looked around the room with no windows. "I must be, in some strange way, a guest or a prisoner, but which?" Then his memory began to come back of him sitting in the limo, and the last thing he remembered seeing was the strange smiling face of his host, until he felt something prick his arm. "Okay, it's got to be a prisoner, but why?" he asked, as he felt even stronger, sitting up more and yanking the needle out of his arm, while still looking around the room.

***

Meanwhile, one floor directly above Elliott was Drexel's guests, all from rogue states in the Mideast, Latin America, Africa, and the Far East, sitting in a circle around a one-way, thick viewing glass floor, looking down at the Vice-President, all applauding Drexel who was standing off to the side and taking a small bow of appreciation. "You see, my friends, I have done the impossible, and you can, too, in all of your own countries, with my help of course. All I ask is, shall we say, a percentage of your vast profits that you will make controlling every leader of your own governments. Just think of it - my droids as your own personal private bankers! You tell them how much money you want and in a relatively short time the money shows up in your offshore accounts that I have already set up for you!" said Drexel, winking at Dr. Goteborg who was standing over in the corner of the room and looking extremely relieved at seeing the VP revived from his unconscious state.

"Too good to be true!" said one of the guests from South America. "How do we really know this is the real Vice-President and not some imposter?" asked the man, pointing down at Elliott who was now beginning to get out of his bed and walk around.

"Yes, how do we know this is real?" asked another man from the Middle East.

Now a small verbal rumble began to arise around the room from all the guests murmuring to themselves at possibly being taken in by this scene taking place below them.

Drexel's smile disappeared for a second or two, being displeased at not being totally trusted, but his smile returned as he said something to one of his aides in Swedish who then quickly handed Drexel what looked like a remote control of some sort. Drexel pointed the remote control at the wall behind them and within a second or two a large white screen dropped down. On the screen was a scene of the White House Oval Office, and sitting next to the President of the United States was the droid, impersonating the Vice-President, with the Secretary of the Navy and the head of the Federal Reserve sitting on the right side of the droid.

The guests gasped all at once at seeing the live feed. The eye camera, being operated by a VP droid Secret

Service agent was standing at a door at the opposite end of the Oval Office, purposely focused on a newspaper lying on the table, showing that day's date. Next, Drexel brought out from his coat pocket a small pocket computer and he typed something on the tiny keyboard that he held in his hand. The next scene that showed up on the screen was the Vice-President, seated at the table, excusing himself and walking out the side door of the Oval Office on the pretense of going to the restroom, followed by the droid replacement of the Secret Service agent. Then the next scene was the Vice-President standing by the mirror in a White House restroom, looking into another portable camera that he had sat on top of a hand blow dryer just opposite of him and only a few feet away.

"Can you hear me, Mr. Vice-President?" asked Drexel, loud enough for all his amazed guests to hear.

"Yes, Master," was the response from the droid in the exact voice of the Vice-President, which was met by thunderous applause from all of the guests sitting in the room.

"Would you, Mr. Vice-President, show our dear guests that you are one of my best creations?" asked Drexel gleefully, while rubbing his hands together and watching the guests transfixed on the screen.

"Of course, Master," said the droid, removing one of his eyes as easily as if removing a pair of glasses and holding it out close to the camera.

Suddenly the room exploded into applause, with shouts from all the guests of "I'm in, and here is my bank draft for whatever you want!" as they rushed up to a grinning Drexel to give him their money.

"Patience, patience, dear friends," said Drexel, holding up his hands. "Please sign up and hand your money to our accounting staff in the next room where you will then receive your offshore bank account information and your own order forms for whomever you wish to be duplicated," said the evil genius, as he looked down through the glass viewing floor at a fully recovered Elliott, although still somewhat bewildered and walking around the room to see if there was some way of escape. "No escape for you, my little gold mine," said

Drexel, as he snapped closed his pocket computer and gave orders to his men to take Elliott to the room in the tower of his castle and followed his guests into the next room.

7 ELLIOTT AND DREXEL MEET FACE TO FACE ON GOTLAND

Two days later, after his guests had left the island, Drexel decided it was now time to go see his important guest, who by now had recovered from the effects of his ordeal and was safely ensconced in his impeccably appointed cell.

In a cramped room on the south tower overlooking a bright morning seascape, Elliott Greenwood sat at a small wooden card table. Bent over, with his hands covering his face and rubbing his temples, his salt-and-pepper hair matted and oily and his grey suit wrinkled, with one pocket slightly torn, his face gave the appearance of a man who hasn't slept much, if at all, in the past several days. A meager breakfast of oatmeal, cold coffee, and sausage sat untouched. The only thing that didn't look worn about him was his lapel pin shaped like the American flag that was fastened to his suit collar. Behind him he heard the door open, but he didn't bother turning around to see the visitor, and just kept staring at the black varnished table top.

"You haven't touched your breakfast, I see," said the tall, thin, well-dressed man, looking at his watch more than once.

"What's the point, Count? You're just going to kill me anyway. For all I know, this was supposed to be my last meal," said Elliott, with a bit of defiance in his tone.

"Oh, you Americans, always so dramatic and predictable. Do you really think I would have stolen you away from your posh limousine in Washington, D.C., and brought you thousands of miles away to my humble home just to kill you?" asked Drexel, taking out a cigarette while motioning to some figures standing near the door to leave.

"Not afraid of the Vice-President of the United States, are we?" asked the man, now standing up to face his captor.

"Um, no, not really," said Drexel, lighting his cigarette while taking out another one from his pack and offering it to the Vice-President, who then took a long step over towards Drexel and grabbed it. "You see, Elliott -- err, may I call you Elliott?" asked Drexel. The VP nodded his approval, letting the count light his cigarette. Drexel made a motion for the VP to sit back down, while grabbing another chair from the table for himself. Continuing, he said, "Ultimate power has no enemies, does not know fear, does not have any worries or cares that the vast majority of the human race experiences every day. Power is its own being. Imagine, if you will, a population of people that can experience total peace of mind and purpose without the fear of want, no need of emotional ties, the stress of relationships, the worry of, oh, what's the word --"

"Love?" interjected the VP, sarcastically.

"Well, love could be one of those stresses, I suppose," said Drexel, "but more importantly than, say, love would be freedom from want. Imagine never having a financial burden or a worry. Imagine all your needs met. Only power gives you that.

"Okay, I've got to ask," said the VP, "who gets this ultimate power?"

"Why, only those who could control it, of course," said Drexel.

"Meaning you?" asked the VP, already knowing what his captor was going to say.

"Yes, of course me, and, umm, a few others scattered

here and there around the world, but yes, mainly me," replied Drexel.

"And then who would you use this ultimate power on, as if I couldn't guess," said the VP, folding his arms.

"Why, everyone else in the whole world, Elliott. All the rest of the world has to do is just submit to this power and never have another worry for the rest of their small, insignificant, little lives."

"Humph," said the VP in disgust. "World domination, you know, has been tried ever since the time of Alexander the Great, right up to Adolph Hitler. It's never worked and it never will!"

The calm, composed face of Drexel drew a little tight and signs of annoyance could be clearly seen as his complacent smile turned into a slight frown. "Well, all of those in history were trying to impose power on the world by external means, forcing one's will on human beings from an outside force, thereby arousing them to resist and struggle against that same will. What I propose is changing and controlling human beings from the inside."

"From the inside?" asked the VP. "That's impossible! No one can do that. History has also shown how it has been tried by oppressive governments like the communists in Russia and China in their "re-education" slave labor camps and all they ever got from that was a lot of dead people."

"As I said, from the inside, as you will shortly see for yourself," said Drexel. "People in general will follow leaders that they choose. In other words, if they think that they have the right person to follow of their own choosing, like the lemmings that they are they will follow and won't rebel. Of course, any good leader has to make independent decisions on his own without consulting the electorate on his every move. So sometimes the leaders have to think for the people, and if the leaders think like I do, so much the better. Then who really needs the people after all?"

"So what you're saying," asked the VP, while looking straight into the ice blue eyes of Drexel, "is that if you plant your own people in positions of leadership, then you can control the people, right?"

Drexel, showing a little sign of exasperation in his breath, answered the VP, "Over all, yes, but there are some exceptions, and those exceptions can be eliminated and replaced by more people of the right sort."

"I'm sorry, Count," said the VP, "but I'm just not following your line of reasoning. What do you mean by the right sort?"

There was a brief second of silence from Drexel. Then the VP heard Drexel speak some sharp words in the direction of the hallway in what must have been Swedish. "As I said, Elliott Greenwood, Mr. Vice-President of the United States who will be running as his party's Presidential nomination in a few weeks, I want you to meet someone that will be very familiar to you and most definitely the right sort of people that I'm thinking of," said Drexel, as his wry smile began to return to his thin lips.

From out in the hallway, and through the door, walked in a man that sent a shockwave up and down the spine of the VP. The stranger's appearance was uncanny in his likeness to the VP, even down to the slightly noticeable scar that the VP had on the left side of his face that he got in a car accident, shortly after being married, when he and his wife were driving home from their honeymoon in Florida, swerving to miss a deer that darted into the road and forcing them to hit a ditch, cutting his jaw on some flying glass. "It can't be," he said. "I refuse to believe this! You can't be serious! You'll never get away with this. He can't be me!" said the VP, flushed with emotion.

"We already have gotten, as you say, away with this, Elliott. Mr. Greenwood here," said Drexel, gesturing to the new arrival, "has just returned from a campaign strategy meeting with the President yesterday. Right now, back at the White House, they just think he -- uh, I mean you -- took a few personal days off to rest up before you are officially nominated for the President of the United States."

The VP sat down, having all the strength of his legs evaporated upon this amazing news. A few minutes of silence went by, and then the VP regained some of his composure. "My wife! Yes, my wife, she will find out! As I said, he can't possibly be me or know the things I know. That will be your undoing. Do you understand me?"

The strange droid-man just stood there expressionless, as if waiting to hear a directive from Drexel as to an appropriate response to the VP's remarks. Drexel suddenly turned serious. "You are correct, Elliott, he doesn't know what you know. Therefore, you will have to teach him everything about your private life before he returns to Washington, D.C., and your wife."

"I won't do it, never, never, never!" screamed the VP, as he lunged for the stranger, grabbing the man by the shoulders, then pummeling him with his fists. The android just stood there, silent, until Drexel gave him a nod. The man picked up the VP by his shirt collar with just one hand as easily as someone might pick up a wadded piece of paper. Then Drexel said something in Swedish and the stranger put him back down just as easy.

"Who or what are you?" asked the VP, stepping back from his double.

"He is an android," said Drexel, "that I created in your likeness. Basically it's a better version of yourself, without the frailty of the human body, and it obeys my every command through the main program that I created in his core computer, or you could say his primary brain."

"Primary brain?" asked the VP, forgetting the magnitude of the moment and now becoming curious about this machine that looked like him.

"Yes, Elliott," said Drexel, in a gleeful tone, only too eager to brag to his most prized victim about his creation. "You see, I have moved beyond mere circuits and static computer parts to more fluid minicomputers flowing in his artificial bloodstream, all carrying out every bodily function that a human being has, all controlled and coordinated by the primary computer in his head. With this fusion of nano and large computers, he can make independent functioning and human response decisions on his own. The only thing he can't do is go against my wishes."

"And just what are your wishes?" snapped the VP.

Drexel, without a word, produced a picture of the VP's wife and daughter and gave it to the android, which then slowly tore the picture into shreds while grinning menacingly at the VP. "Need I say more?" asked Drexel, walking over to the android and putting his hand on its shoulder. Turning to the VP, he said, "Elliott, it's time to brief the future President of the United States on his personal life. Any objections?"

The VP went over to the table and plopped down,

feeling totally defeated, knowing that he would have to betray his country in order to save his wife and daughter. In the back of his mind he eased his conscious a little by telling himself that he would play along for now, but somehow he would stop Drexel. But now was not the time to cross him. "Okay, hot shot, you win. Send your boy over here and I'll fill him in," said Elliott.

"Good. Glad you see it my way, Elliott," said the evil genius. "You two have your little chat while I catch a plane to London. It seems there is a Lord Hawthorne in Parliament that needs my attention. He's going to be the next prime minister, you know."

8 ESCAPE FROM GOTLAND

The lower floor of Drexel's castle contained a well built twenty-by-fourteen-foot jail cell, complete with open-spaced steel bars facing the stairs coming from the first floor and main entrance of the castle. The basement floor was a dull institutional blue ceramic tile where every footstep could be heard by Elliott Greenwood of the comings and goings of his android guards who treated him dispassionately, as if he were some pinned-up animal needing only food and water, but no exchange of conversation or compassion. In the back of the cell was a wall made up of stone and masonry, with a small iron-barred window overlooking the courtyard and Drexel's fleet of five Huey C3 model helicopters, almost the same type of helicopters that Elliott flew as a pilot back in Vietnam, but with some more modern modifications in the fuel tanks and fuselage.

Elliott would stay up most of his nights staring at

those helicopters and trying to formulate an escape plan, but nothing as yet came to his tortured mind. His worries about his wife's and daughter's safety almost consumed his only waking thoughts, not to mention his android double being nominated for the President of the United States. If not thinking about his family, he would then turn his attention back to the helicopters and take notice of when Drexel's pilots would often fly them. Usually one or two of the Hueys would be used at about 6:00 a.m., and would finally return to base around noon for refueling and maintenance. This did not make sense to Elliott, unless they were going for some sort of supplies, but he never saw anything being unloaded, so he then assumed that these helicopters were airborne the whole time they were gone, possibly on some sort of air patrol, scouting out a large area away from the castle for unwanted visitors perhaps, or the like. Because of this logic, he then assumed that these model Hueys probably had about six hours of fuel, as did the Hueys he flew during his Vietnam days.

With that conclusion fixed in his mind, he started

to think about his next obstacle, the guards. As androids go, they weren't a talkative bunch, but seemed every bit as human as his clever counterpart did and just as dangerous. Elliott decided that this night, when dinner came, he would try to get any kind of reaction he could out of the android guard just to see what effect it might have on it. Maybe there is some sort of weakness I could discover, he thought, as he heard the footsteps of the nightly guard approaching his cell, carrying his dinner tray. But something was different about these footsteps. They were quicker, more natural, less mechanical and staccato-like than the ones he always heard before. From his cot against the left stone wall just out of sight of the cell door, Elliott got up to see who this new guard might be. Just as he stood up and made a few steps toward his cell door, a face appeared that was actually pleasant and relaxed, holding his dinner tray.

"Why, hello, Mr. Greenwood," said the guard, wearing a pilot uniform. "I brought you dinner."

"You speak English and you're not one of them," said Elliott, relieved to finally talk to somebody."

"No, I'm very real. Your guards are, shall we say, being refitted for other tasks at the moment," said the pilot, as he bent down to slide the tray under the door, and then turned to leave.

"Wait, please don't go. You see, I'm just, uh, just kind of cut off from the world here. Could you perhaps stay a few minutes, just a few minutes?" said Elliott, as both his hands grasped the bars.

The pilot at first looked perturbed at this request until his eyes caught a ring on Elliott's left ring finger. He then froze his gaze on the gold and ruby ring with the silver propeller etched into the shiny crimson stone. Elliott, for a second, looked puzzled at the pilot's staring, but then he suddenly noticed the same ring on his new guard's finger. Elliott was taken aback. The Knights of the Air was a sacred brotherhood of young men that, when joined, brought the new members into a world of duty and honor, bound by their oath to help all those who suffered oppression as well as promote virtue through flying.

"I can't believe it! This is beyond coincidence!" said Elliott, extending his hand through the bars.

The pilot grasped Elliott's hand. "You're the first Knight of the Air I have made contact with since I started flying for my brother some years back," said the young pilot.

"Your brother?" asked Elliott, as he grabbed a wooden stool and slid it up to the bars, while his newfound comrade grabbed a rickety wooden guard's chair and pulled it up to the steel bars as well.

"Why, yes, my brother, the Count," replied the pilot. I am what you might say the black sheep of the family. My brother never felt the need to think of me as anything but a failure, even though I'm a damn good pilot, thanks to the Knights of the Air who our father made me join when I was fifteen. When did you join, Mr. Greenwood?"

"I was fifteen as well, although that was back in the late 1950s. But my father said it's either the Knights of the Air or the Boy Scouts, and I always wanted to fly, and I hated camping, so the choice was easy," said Elliott.

Both men laughed at Elliott's response. Elliott felt he had finally found a true ally and friend since his kidnapping. The men talked on into the morning like old friends, despite their age difference.

"Oh, I forgot, my name is Olaf. I guess I could be a count as well, but I hate the pretension," said Olaf, pulling his collar up a bit to keep his neck warm from the cool breeze blowing through the cell's barred window.

Elliott felt relief at being able to just sit and talk to a friendly face, almost causing him to forget his escape plans for a moment.

Olaf suddenly looked at his watch. It was 4:00 a.m. "Well, Mr. Greenwood, I guess we better get started."

"Started?" asked Elliott.

"Yes, started on getting you out of here," said Olaf. "I can't leave a brother knight in this awful place, can I?"

"But your brother, what would happen to you if he found out?" asked Elliott.

"Leave that to me," said Olaf, as he produced a key, unlocking the cell door. "Just thank the gods that we have a crescent moon this morning rather than a full one. We have only a half an hour before the guards go back on schedule. This is the perfect time to escape. Could not have been better if you planned it, Mr. Greenwood."

"Call me Elliott, friend," said Elliott, still feeling that this was some kind of dream.

"All right, Elliott. Just one question. Can you fly a Huey?" asked Olaf.

"Uh, I can manage," said Elliott, grinning.

"Good," said Olaf, taking off his jacket. "Put my jacket on. In the dark it will be hard to tell who is who in case you are spotted. Now here is what you need to do..." Olaf told Elliott about the route out of the castle, up the stairs, straight on to the right, to the side door that leads to the courtyard. "The Hueys are already fueled and ready to go. I recommend you head for London. It is only four-and-a-half hours away by air at 255 degrees south by west. You understand, Elliott?"

"Perfectly," said Elliott. "But, Olaf, I have to ask you about these androids of your brother's. Is there any way you can tell them apart from humans? Because I've sat here for days and I can't figure out any difference at all."

"You mean you haven't figured it out yet?" asked Olaf.

"Figured out what?" asked Elliott.

"Their eyes, they don't blink but every forty-five

seconds, unlike humans who need to blink every two to three seconds. My brother is still working on that problem as well as a few other problems that I could tell you, but now time is running out!" said Olaf.

"Now that you mention it --" said Elliott, interrupted by Olaf holding up his hand.

"No more time to chat, my friend. I need you now to go ahead and hit me hard on the jaw by your cell door," said Olaf, bracing for a punch.

"Hit you?" asked Elliott, taken aback. "No way! I can't do that!"

"You have to in order for this escape to appear genuine," said Olaf. "After all, I can't just tell my brother I let you out. Anyway, the most he would do to me is shake his head and yell at me and tell me what a total incompetent failure and disappointment I am to the Drexel name, but he won't hurt me. Of that I'm sure."

"I hate this," said Elliott, pulling back his arm,

getting ready to sock his newfound friend in the jaw.

"Not as much as I do!" said Olaf, bracing himself. "Now do it!"

Elliott let fly his fist, landing squarely on Olaf's right jaw bone, which sent Olaf flying, bouncing him off the cell door and landing on the tile floor, out cold. Bending over his friend, he checked Olaf to make sure he didn't get a concussion by opening his eyelids and looking at his eyeballs to see if they were rolled back into his head. "Good," he thought, "he's fine, no concussion. Best get out of here."

Gently putting his friend's head back down on the floor, he put Olaf's jacket on and ran up the stone steps to the main room on the first floor. No one was about in the main room. To the right was the door that led out into the courtyard where the Hueys were all fueled and ready to go. Double checking for any signs of life, he took a deep breath and headed for the door. "So far, so good," Elliott thought.

Suddenly there appeared two pilots carrying coffee and coming in from the courtyard, speaking Swedish. They were tall men, taller than Elliott. One was apparently telling a funny story to the other one, who started to laugh until he saw Elliott only a few feet away from them, off to the side. Instantly Elliott threw himself into the two men, knocking them down, spilling their hot coffee everywhere. One of the men yelled out something in Swedish, sounding like the word "alarm." Elliott wasted no further time on the men, who were struggling to get up. He sprang out the entranceway, running to the Huey on the far left of the courtyard, pulling his jacket over his ears, when he saw some guards running at him. Yelling the word "alarm," Elliott pointed to the main room where he had just been. The guards apparently were fooled into thinking he was one of the pilots. They passed him and headed for the other two men who were now up and stumbling down the steps into the courtyard.

Jumping into the open cockpit of the Huey, he hit the starter button which started the engine and rotors.

He then slammed and locked the cockpit doors and pulled back on the Huey's joystick, which sent the engine into a high-pitched whine and the rotor blades into takeoff mode. Just then the sounds of gunfire came from the two guards, while the recovering two pilots ran to their Hueys, getting ready to give chase. Elliott pulled back full throttle, sending the Huey airborne fast, leaving behind the courtyard and the castle and flying into the night air. Luckily the guards' shooting didn't hit the helicopter, but his luck would still have to hold out against the other two Hueys getting ready for takeoff on the ground, especially if they were carrying 50-caliber machine guns like his Huey had.

Elliott looked down at his controls that were all lit up. "Almost like my car's dashboard," he said to himself, smiling. Then, checking his on-board navigation positioning compass, he turned the helicopter around until the needle pointed to the direction of London at 255 degrees south by west, and pushed his joystick as far as it would go to give him the fastest speed possible. With the castle behind him and growing smaller and smaller with every passing second, he was starting to feel really good about his escape, until he caught a glimpse of the other two Hueys' running lights that were about two miles behind him, one flanking his left and the other on his right, closing in fast. Just then he saw the flash of lights coming from the front of the helicopters, which could only mean one thing - machine gun fire!

"Let's see if these guys can out-fly an old combat pilot," said Elliott to himself, as he turned off all his running and cabin lights, leaving his helicopter totally in the dark, making it virtually invisible in the air. Then, going into fast descent mode, he dropped down several thousand feet below the other two helicopters and slowed his speed down enough to see them both pass over him, heading in the same direction as he had been just a few seconds before.

"Okay, these guys are about to get a lesson in tactical combat maneuvers. I hope they can swim," he said to himself. Elliott then shot his Huey straight up in the air and came in fast about a hundred yards behind the two helicopters that were still holding a straight course east. Swinging his Huey from side to side, he then pressed the red button on his joystick, which let fly a thousand rounds of 50-caliber machine gun bullets per four seconds. Suddenly there was an explosion on the helicopter to his left, which sent it crashing down in flames into the dark abyss below. The next thing he heard was a voice in broken English crackling over his cockpit radio, apparently from the other pilot in the Huey that was in front of him and to his right.

"Don't shoot, am breaking off my pursuit, don't shoot, don't shoot!" said the shaky voice, clearly unnerved by what had just happened.

"All right, young man, calm down, calm down. I am not interested in murder. Just drop back and you won't get hurt," said Elliott, feeling bad at having to shoot down an inexperienced pilot, even though he could have easily been the one crashing into the sea in flames a few minutes earlier.

The other helicopter flew off and headed back toward the castle. Elliott saw his running lights trail off in the distance and then finally disappear into the night. "I hope he thinks up a good story for his superiors as to my escape," said Elliott, smiling to himself, as he turned his cockpit back on. His compass bearing corrected to 255 degrees south by west. He finally relaxed a little bit, grateful for his escape and grateful to Olaf pledging that when this was all over he would again meet up with his friend and reward him for his valor. "Now on to London," he said to himself, as he searched for some on-board food rations that all Huey helicopters were known to carry.

9 LONDON ESCAPADE

It was seven a.m. and the Huey was still making a bee line for the English coast. Earlier that morning Elliott turned his craft south-southeast from the North Sea, swinging his helicopter toward the English Channel where there was a private airport just outside of Dover. This secret airport was widely used by foreign dignitaries that needed a quick way in and out of the country, allowing the dignitaries and others to avoid the long lines through customs at either Heathrow or Gatwick airports. Elliott himself, upon occasion, and members of the diplomatic corps, used this airport as a convenient spot for brief meetings with various members of the British government. The only problem now was that without any identification of any kind, no one would accept him as the Vice-President of the United States or, for that matter, even as an American citizen, not to mention the problem of his escape, being discovered at any time by Drexel's men. He knew that Olaf would buy him as much time as possible, but sooner or later word would get back to Drexel and then the hunt would begin to find and capture him at all costs.

.

With these thoughts swirling in his head, his thinking started drifting to his beloved wife and daughter, remembering their last time together at dinner and how he promised both of them that they would all spend more time together as a family. Those brief happy thoughts somehow stiffened his resolve to get back to them as quickly as possible. A plan began to form in his mind. First he knew that he would somehow have to land his craft away from the main part of the airport and avoid any contact with the British authorities. Next he would have to get in contact with the one person that he could trust in all of England, Reggie "Reggs" Barlow, a close friend deep within in MI5 whose cover was that of an ordinary cab driver.

Reggie was the driver that always gave the Secret Service the slip when Elliott came to London and wanted just to have a drink or two in a real English pub as a private individual, not as the Vice-President of the United States. Reggie knew how to drive through the narrow London backstreets at break-neck speed and would often brag to Elliott how many minutes it would take to "lose the blokes." His record stood now at four minutes from

Elliott's last visit two months ago. After finding Reggie, Elliott decided that he would contact his old political ally, Lord Hawthorne. Lord Hawthorne would be his ticket out of the country and back to the States without being noticed by any officials, British or American.

The sun was well up now and starting to turn the chalky white cliffs of the British coast into almost pinkish frosting, like mounds of earth rising up from a pale green ruffled sea in the distance. A voice came crackling over the Huey's multi-band frequency radio: "Unidentified aircraft, you are now entering British royal airspace. Please identify."

Elliott had found earlier the helicopter's code book and had the correct call numbers and codes that he needed to enter the country. "Yes, one-niner. Niner-five requesting vectors and permission to land at Tremble Downs backfield, if possible. This is Sweden 5776892, Drexel Eight. No passengers, just pilot, on urgent business, over," said Elliott, flipping the button to the off position.

"Yes, of course, Drexel Eight. Welcome to England.

Sending the vectors now. You may set down at Backfield Seven," said the airport tower.

"Roger that, Tower. Also have request for driver highly recommended to us by American Government named Reggie Barlow. His number is in the registration book. Please have him at Backfield Seven as soon as possible, over," said Elliott, crossing his fingers and holding his breath as he waited for a reply.

A few minutes of radio silence went by as the cliffs of Dover grew larger and larger. He was only twelve minutes from the airport now, and, if Reggie wasn't there, to avoid detection he would have to set down and run from the helicopter as fast as he could toward a ten-foot-high barbwire fence. Reaching the fence, he then would somehow have to scale the fence and head for London on foot, a prospect that seemed too unpleasant to dwell upon just yet. And now he was starting to fly past the cliffs of Dover.

The radio suddenly came alive with sounds of static and then a voice from the tower was heard. "Drexel Eight, we have contact with said Reggie Barlow and he replied that he and his wife are leaving for New York on vacation tomorrow and he is off duty, over."

Elliott gave a huge sigh of relief and smiled, saying, "Tell Reggs that Stinky" - a nickname that Reggie gave Elliott after a night of drinking in a local pub where afterwards Elliott stumbled into a small horse manure pile after leaving the pub - "is flying this crate and kindly requests the pleasure of his company, over."

"Roger that, will convey, over," said the tower.

Forty-five seconds of radio silence went by and then the tower came back saying, "Drexel Eight, your driver will be there in ten minutes. You may now vector to Backfield Seven, over."

"Roger that, Tower, and making my turn now. Thank you and out," said Elliott, starting to feel a ray of hope at succeeding in getting home.

The helicopter started descending at an angle towards the airport. He was flying now several hundred feet over the British countryside's patchwork of fields and narrow roads. Off in the distance he noticed a small blue car speeding towards the back entrance of the airfield, kicking up a lot of sand and gravel in its wake. "That has to be Reggs," Elliott thought.

Now over Backfield Seven, he gently set the helicopter down without so much as a bump onto the ground. The car he saw just moments before was now headed directly towards him like a wild boar charging through brush. Elliott didn't have long to wait now. The car came to a screeching halt just inches from the helicopter. A large man got out with flaming red hair and a twisted, winding mustache to match, wearing a green checkered shirt and brown wool pants. Were it not for the fact of his hair and clothes, Elliott and this man could have passed as brothers in their looks and overall frame and stance.

"Bloody hell, Stinky, what are you doing by yourself in a Swedish aircraft? Are you on the run from a jealous husband or did you rob the Bank of England!" asked Reggs, as he gave his old friend a big bear hug.

"Nothing like that, my friend. Lots to tell you. Let's get in the car and get out of here," said Elliott.

"Blimey! You are on the run!" said Reggs, as they both climbed in the car and sped out of the airport.

Heading toward the main highway to London, Elliott filled his friend in on all that had happened to him since his capture and how Drexel planned to use his small army of androids to take over the government of the United States as well as harm his wife and daughter if he did not cooperate. Hearing himself relaying every detail to Reggs, the story seemed unbelievable even to Elliott, like something from a horror movie. No telling what his friend was thinking.

"This is incredible," said Reggs, as he wiped a smudge from the windshield with one hand, still driving and trying to sip his coffee with the other hand. "And poor Pamela and Susan! Do you really think this bugger will actually hurt them now that you've escaped?"

"I have to think now, now that I'm on the loose. He is very calculating and careful in all that he does. I feel that if I hadn't escaped, he would have done away with them anyway since they probably know too much already. But knowing this Drexel, he still may use them as bait to recapture me. So as long as I stay free, I feel they will be safe," said Elliott, looking at his watch, noting that it was a little after 9:00 a.m.

"Well, you can count on me, mate, and if I see one of those android buggers over here I'll give 'em what for, eh?" said Reggs, giving Elliott a wink.

"That's what I'm counting on, old friend," said Elliott, grabbing Reggs's coffee and taking a sip for himself. "Listen, Reggs, I really need to find Lord Hawthorne this morning. Any chance he may be in Parliament today?"

"You didn't hear then, did you, Stinky," said Reggs, swerving to miss another oncoming car.

"Hear what?" asked Elliott.

"His Lordship was in a pub bombing and was rushed to the hospital at Parkside several days ago."

"He, uh, he's not dead, is he?" asked Elliott, feeling a lump rising in his throat.

"Oh, no, mate, but it's real strange, though. No one

except his personal physician and a few others that don't work at the hospital has been allowed to see him. Everyone else has been kept away."

"Is that what the news people over here say?" asked Elliott, relieved that Hawthorne survived.

"No, mate. I have a good friend that's a male nurse at Parkside. He said that Lord Hawthorne has his own personal bodyguards standing outside his room at all times. The bodyguards even take the food into his Lordship. Doctor's orders, they say," replied Reggs.

London was only an hour-and-a-half away. Elliott was quiet for a while as he listened to Reggs who had changed the subject by talking about his wife and her annoying family, as well as his trip to see his wife's American cousin in New York, where they were promised a night on the town which was to include a Broadway play and a fancy dinner. A few more moments passed and Elliott asked his friend," Reggs, listen, Lord Hawthorne is the only one that I can trust in the government to not let my secret out about me being over here. Is there any way you could ask your nurse friend to sneak us into his hospital room? I know Hawthorne is the only one that can get me home possibly by late this evening!"

Reggs was quiet for a moment, contemplating the request, which was a good sign and meant that he was scheming. He then beamed a big smile and said, "Of course, mate, we'll get you there! I have never let you down before, have I?"

"No, thank God, Reggs, you haven't. Thank you," said Elliott, leaning back into his seat, shutting his eyes for a few minutes' rest while Reggs drove on.

***

It was now 11:00 a.m. London morning commuter traffic was dissipating. Reggs did what he does best and navigated the fastest route into the city, headed to Parkside Hospital, which was just in the shadow of the not-too-distant Parliament building that sat across the Thames River. Reggs swung his blue car into the loading zone in the back of the hospital. Then he pulled out his magnetic sign with the word "Courier" on it and attached it to the driver's side door. "Just so they don't tow your old mate's pretty car away, eh?" Reggs said, nudging his friend to wake up.

"What? Are we here?" asked Elliott, yawning.

"You needed the rest, mate. Just let you go on sleeping I did, but now we'd better get down to business. You stay put for a minute and I'll go inside and arrange to get you in with my nurse friend. Be back in a few," said Reggs, as he headed for the delivery entrance of the hospital.

Elliott finished up the last of the coffee which had grown cold, then took a comb that Reggs had in his glove compartment and combed his matted hair, straightening his shirt collar and running a finger over his teeth and wishing he could find a toothbrush somewhere. It seemed like an hour that he had sat there in the loading zone, but really it had been only a few minutes when his friend finally returned, carrying a large bouquet of flowers in both hands.

"It's all been arranged. Here, look in the backseat and put that jacket on," said Reggs, sitting down the bouquet and helping his friend get the delivery jacket on.

Then Reggs grabbed a hat from the backseat also and handed it to Elliott, who was now standing outside the car. Reggs, stepping back to admire his work, said, "Blimey, you look right smart," and picked up the unwieldy bouquet of flowers to give to Elliott.

"Where did these come from?" asked Elliott.

"I liberated them, mate, from somebody who probably didn't need them," said Reggs.

"Who wouldn't want these?" asked Elliott, as he took the flowers from Reggs.

"A dead man!" said Reggs, now walking towards the delivery door. "Now come on, mate. It's show time!"

***

Once inside the hospital, Elliott waited while his friend walks over to the service elevator doors and talked to someone who apparently was his contact. Reggs then called Elliott over to meet his friend and discuss the plan. Then all three of the men stepped into the large elevator and went up to the top patient floor where Lord Hawthorne's room was located.

Getting out of the elevator, Reggs thanked his friend profusely, then turned to Elliott and whispered, "Okay, mate, follow my lead. Once I get rid of these goons, you head straight into the room. Got it?"

"What about the other staff, like the doctor or his nurses?" asked Elliott.

"Taken care of, mate. Everyone is taking lunch down in the cafeteria. Only the goons are on duty at present. Now let's go!" said Reggs, now walking towards Hawthorne's room.

Elliott quickly moved in pace with Reggs, following closely behind with the large bouquet of flowers. As they neared the guards, Reggs suddenly shouted as loud as he could, "Flowers from the Queen! Flowers from the Queen! Make way for flowers from the Queen!"

The guards appeared stunned and almost paralyzed by the strange behavior from Reggs. "Vhat do you vant?" asked one guard in a heavy Swedish accent.

"We are bearing flowers from the Queen herself. Out of our way, you heathen Swede!" said Reggs, motioning Elliott towards Hawthorne's hospital door.

"Vee vill take those!" said the other guard, still looking very rattled.

"Do you want me to call the Queen's guards now, my good man?" barked Reggs? Leaning over to whisper into the guard's ear, Reggs said, "You know we still chop off the heads of foreigners in the Tower of London who offend our Queen?"

"No!" said the guard.

"Oh, yes, we do!" Elliott joined in, trying out his best British accent.

Before the guards could respond, Reggs shouted out, "Queen's guards, Queen's guards, take them away!"

If the guards weren't convinced before, they were now, with this bit of improvised drama. "Three minutes. You have three minutes," said the guards, quickly opening the door to Hawthorne's room. Reggs bowed toward his friend to go on in while he stayed outside with the Swedish guards.

Entering the room with the flowers, Elliott saw his friend, Lord Hawthorne, standing by the window looking out onto the hospital courtyard.

"What was that noise?" asked Hawthorne in his upper class British accent.

"Jonathan, how are you? Are you okay? Shouldn't you be in bed?" asked Elliott, sitting down the bouquet on the nightstand by Hawthorne's hospital bed.

"You may address me as Lord Hawthorne, sir!" said Hawthorne, turning from the window, clearly perturbed at being addressed by his first name.

"But it's me, it's..." But before Elliott could identify himself, he froze. Something just didn't seem right about his old political friend. Sensing something was terribly wrong, he reverted back to his delivery character that he had been playing and, picking up the bouquet, handed Hawthorne the flowers, all the while watching his face, especially his eyes. "Incredible! He hasn't blinked!" thought Elliott, realizing that time was running out and the guards would soon come in. "These are for you, Lord Hawthorne, from our Queen, in hopes that you will get better soon," said Elliott, slowly backing towards the door.

"Tell Her Majesty that I appreciate her thoughtfulness and I will be back in Parliament in a few days," said Hawthorne.

Elliott bowed and said, "Yes, Lord Hawthorne," and quickly turned around and left.

Outside, Reggs was giving the Swedish guards a lesson in British etiquette when Elliott politely intervened with a quick hand motion, trying not to raise suspicions, causing Reggs to quickly end his squabble with the guards and head down the hall towards the elevator with Elliott.

"How was your friend? Is he going to help you?" asked Reggs, as they reached the elevator doors.

Elliott whispered into Reggs ear, "He's one of them!"

"Blimey, how'd you know? Did he recognize you?" asked Reggs.

"I'll explain on the way to the car, but no, thank God, he hadn't a clue as to who I was. I guess Drexel is still having him briefed. Let's get out of here!"

10 THE "THIRD BRAIN"

Back at the castle, Drexel received word from one of his men that the Lord Hawthorne android had just left Parkside Hospital on his own without telling anyone, but left a note with one of Drexel's men to give to his creator which read, "Feeling much better, have to go now to meet the Queen at the Fleet Street Charity Auction tonight, need a haircut and new suit." When his men radioed Drexel, hearing this strange news immediately caused the evil genius to fly into a rage and run out of the castle and into the courtyard, followed by his brother Olaf, both making their way to an awaiting helicopter that would fly them to London, rather than using Drexel's private Leer jet which was currently down for maintenance.

Climbing into the cockpit, Olaf prepared for takeoff while listening to Drexel bark orders over his cell phone to his hapless men still combing the hospital grounds, but finding nothing. "You mean there is no trace of him anywhere?" screamed Drexel, with his veins popping out of his neck.

"No, sir," Drexel's man replied. "As I said earlier, he just vanished from the hospital after breakfast this morning. The second watch was just coming upstairs when they noticed a half-eaten plate of scrambled eggs and sausages and..."

Before Drexel's man could finish his sentence, Drexel went into a tirade of oaths sprinkled in with various commands. "You all are idiots! I thought I could trust you fools with one simple task, but you can't even do that right! What am I paying you for? My garbage droids have more brains than you men! So listen and get this through those thick skulls of yours: get the rest of the watch crew together and get over to Number 17 Fleet Street and surround the whole premise before tonight's event. I want that droid stopped! He is in no condition yet to see the Queen. Fail me again and I'll personally have your heads stuffed and mounted in my trophy room! Do I make myself clear?"

Before the poor berated sergeant in Drexel's army could answer, Drexel switched off his cell phone. Olaf had the helicopter airborne and was looking towards the left side of the windshield, trying not to look at his brother, which would only give away his wide grin due to finding his brother's reactions comical.

"Why are you so quiet, Olaf?" snapped Drexel, who could only see the back of Olaf's neck.

"Nothing, brother," said Olaf, trying to regain his composure. "Just getting some altitude. We'll land in a few hours at the usual airfield outside London. Here, grab a beer from the cooler behind my seat. It might make you feel better. By the way, I didn't know droids ate anything."

"Yes, well, my droids can eat in a very limited fashion. My droids have been retrofitted with a small cavity that can be filled and emptied. It still needs to be refined, but it will have to do for the cocktail parties and dinner parties where my droids will have to appear like normal guests.

At this, Drexel started a brand new tirade. "At least I think Günter can handle things for me in Washington with the Vice-President droid."

Olaf experienced a moment of resentment at this reference to Günter Bergman, who had been with his brother for years and had his complete trust and confidence and the thing Olaf wanted most from his older brother, respect.

"Also, my dear brother, beer is for commoners," growled Drexel, as he reached to grab a beer anyway. "But since this morning has been a disaster, I'll take just one to settle me down."

"Good," said Olaf, as he stopped grinning and handed his brother a bottle opener. "Tell me, brother, what went wrong with this particular droid? I thought he was supposed to be one of your best creations."

"He was -- err, I mean is -- well, you know what I mean," said Drexel. "This Hawthorne droid had one feature all the other droids never had and --"

"You mean the third brain?" interrupted Olaf. "I heard you speak of this before with your scientists as I was flying all of you to America two months ago where we planted the Vice-President droid in Washington, D.C."

"Yes, the third brain, my best improvement, I thought, up until now," said Drexel, finishing his beer and unconsciously grabbing two more beers, opening both and handing one to Olaf while taking the other one for himself.

Olaf rarely saw this side of his brother. As their parents were dead, they only had each other for family. Drexel, the older sibling, had always been the serious one, never laughing and never entering into a relaxing conversation with anyone, unlike the one they were having now. Olaf knew his brother's moods. He always felt that if his brother had not been rejected in his youth by the beautiful Countess Marguerite Van Stephenson when both were in their twenties and both rich - in title only, not wealth - that his brother would have been a different man. But the beautiful countess chose money over Drexel's brilliance and married a rich duke from Sussex, leaving Drexel bitter and hardened toward life and anything British.

After their parent's death, Drexel had to sell off most of their family's assets to pay back massive loans his father made two years before his death to the Bank of

London. Olaf felt that was yet another reason that motivated his brother to despise the English. After the rejection by the countess, Drexel threw himself into creating wealth by any means he could. Usually he lent his services to rogue nations who paid the young genius any amount he wanted to develop advanced weaponry that their rivals couldn't even dream of, all the while amassing great amounts of wealth for himself, while sending his younger brother to the finest flight schools all over Europe.

Olaf knew that every trace of his older brother's contact with humanity would soon vanish when on the evening of the tenth anniversary of the very day that Drexel's marriage proposal was rejected by Countess Marcia that he, by accident, walking in an open upper passageway of the castle that evening, spotted Drexel standing on the rocky cliffside of the castle below. Olaf saw his brother ripping up his former beloved's picture that he always carried next to his heart and letting the wind take the pieces out over the cliff face and into the blackness and depths of the raging sea. Watching his brother complete this private ritual, Olaf felt a shiver down his spine, knowing that his brother would now solely focus on his own twisted destiny and never again try to fit himself into any type of relationship with human beings.

Olaf always suspected that his brother was attracted to the emotionless, mathematical predictability and logic of his androids and liked avoiding any warm human feeling and emotion at all times, but this brief moment of candor and goodwill from his brother was refreshing and continued as he sipped his second beer.

"You see, brother," Drexel continued, "I had the idea of a third brain months before we did away with the troublesome Lord Hawthorne. I wanted a method that would allow my droids to learn about themselves in the role of their human counterparts that didn't involve the complicated process of kidnapping and extracting vital information by force from the victims, then programming that information into the droid later. It's too messy, too inconvenient, and too expensive in planning and executing."

"But isn't the purpose of the Hawthorne droid to get

close to the Queen in order to kidnap her?" asked Olaf, as he swung the craft to the right to avoid a flock of seagulls.

"In this case, yes," Drexel said, "due to the impossible security surrounding the Queen, but I wanted a test case like the Hawthorne droid to be more independent of my programming, more self-aware, capable of actually forming his own identify, more --"

"Human?" interjected Olaf.

"Yes, more human," Drexel agreed," but I'm afraid his third brain took control of the programming of his second brain and now he is like a loose cannon running all over London doing who knows what with whom as the real Lord Hawthorne! And then of course there is another feature…"

"Another feature?" asked Olaf. "I'm still trying to remember what the first two droid brains are for."

"Here, pay attention, for I'll only say this once, Olaf," said Drexel, grabbing his third beer, much to a surprised Olaf, who was about to mention to his brother that a third beer might not be a good idea, but quickly deciding just to keep quiet and fly. "Think of an android's brain structure as that like the structure of a human brain," said Drexel, popping the top of his beer with the bottle opener and taking a long gulp, wiping the foam off his mouth with his sleeve.

"With you so far, brother," said Olaf.

"All right," said Drexel. "First your subconscious mind controls the nervous system, organs, and functions of your body. That is what the basic programming in the droid does, thus the name 'first brain.'"

"That seems simple enough," responded Olaf.

"Then," Drexel said, taking another long gulp of his beer and burping, "then the second brain, like the learning and reasoning faculty of the human brain, allows the androids to learn from experience and reason, thus as the android experiences the lives of their human counterparts, eventually they can, on their own, reprogram their memories and actions to reflect more of the character than what I am able to originally give them."

"Like all the droids you have in place so far?" asked

Olaf.

"Yes, exactly, except for the Hawthorne droid who has the third brain," said Drexel, putting his empty bottle down on the cockpit floor and closing his eyes as if he were about to go to sleep.

"And the third brain is what?" asked Olaf, becoming very curious about the whole matter and also glad to see his brother had calmed down to a state of drowsiness.

"The third brain, or should I say the Hawthorne brain," said Drexel, yawning and stretching his arms, "achieves a conscious state where the droid becomes the character of his human target through intensive learning before assuming his identity. This, as you recall, involves months of having the droid assume various domestic roles to get close to his target, such as when we had the droid replace Hawthorne's masseuse back at the Parliament Club six months ago. Remember?"

"Yes, I do remember," said Olaf. I also remember we had the Hawthorne droid disguised as Lord Hawthorne's barber about three months ago."

"Exactly, Olaf. And do you know why?" whispered Drexel, now almost in a twilight state of sleep.

"Because no one talks more about themselves than to their barber or their masseuse?" asked Olaf, already knowing the answer.

"Exactly!" said Drexel. "The thing is, though, I never dreamed that once the droid totally converted to his human subject that his third brain would subconsciously block out my ability to control him." By now Drexel had positioned himself in his seat to where his back was facing his brother and his head was on the headrest. A few minutes later Olaf heard his brother snoring, apparently in a deep sleep.

"Sleep on, dear brother, and take your rest, for we shall have the morrow," whispered Olaf to himself, paraphrasing a quote from Shakespeare's play Henry the Fifth as he set his navigation system for the private air field just outside London.

11 OLD HAUNTS FOR THE HAWTHORNE DROID

It was a rare sunny morning in London and the Hawthorne droid was out and about, walking toward the Parliament Club after deciding to get a steam bath and shower and shave, not conscious of the fact that water running over his body would totally destroy his circuitry and basically turn him into a crumpled heap of gears and gadgets. Wearing a pair of plain woolen grey pants, a white shirt, and black leather shoes which he had found in the hospital, he couldn't understand why he didn't remember being dressed the way he was, nor why he didn't have any money in his wallet, but felt the Parliament Club several blocks down would be the best place to go to get ready for that night's charity function as well as catch up with some of his friends on what was going on in that day's legislative session in the Parliament building, which was only two blocks from the club.

Walking on the sidewalk of a bridge that crossed the Thames River, he looked out at the sun glistening off the surface of the water, seeing the various barges and tugboats moving up and down the river. Staring out at this peaceful scene, he scarcely noticed the passing crowd of pedestrian traffic walking by him just a few feet away. His mind seemed only to think of meeting the Queen that night, and it bothered him somewhat that he didn't know why he was so eager to get close to her. Something was tugging at his brain, but he couldn't put it into words. It was almost like seeing an old friend's face, but forgetting their name.

The android was so engrossed in his thoughts that he didn't hear the footsteps running toward him and the words being shouted at him in a language that he felt he once knew, but now only sounded like babbling. Running up behind him, the three men yelled in Swedish, "Stop! You must get back to the hospital now! Come with us immediately!" The three men then grabbed his arms, tugging and pulling on him, but he just stood still and looked surprised at the behavior of these three strangers.

"I say there, you stop that nonsense this instant or I shall summon the police, do you hear?" said the droid, now addressing the men.

One of Drexel's men answered in Swedish, "You must come with us now or your master will be displeased," tightening his grip on the droid. A crowd was starting to form, shocked at these men attacking what looked like an innocent passerby just walking on his way to work. One woman shouted, "Eh, Alfie, call the police!" Another member of the crowd shouted, "Let's get 'em, mates," pointing directly at Drexel's men. But before anyone could do anything, the indignant droid shouted, "Unhand me this instant, do you hear!"

Then, as effortlessly as if someone was tossing a wadded up piece of paper, the droid threw one of the men clinging to his left arm into the air and over the side of the bridge, then quickly proceeded to do the same to the man holding onto his right arm. Only a few seconds passed when splashing noises were heard as Drexel's men hit the surface of the water eighty feet below the bridge, both still alive and just missing a passing tugboat. The third man, alarmed at seeing his two comrades being dispatched so easily, let go of the droid and turned around to start to run, but not before the droid could pick up the man by his collar and kick him like a football into the air, landing the terrified attacker ten feet up in one of the maple trees that lined the bridge's sidewalk. A few seconds later the man, dazed but conscious, shimmied down the slender tree and ran off down the street to a cheering crowd.

A reporter passing by from the London Channel 5 News Team, on his way over to cover Parliament that morning, pulled his van over to the side of the bridge and got out, running with his cameraman over to where a large crowd had now formed and was clapping, as Lord Hawthorne took bows and waved. Many in the crowd rushed the reporter once they saw the camera lights on, telling him of the amazing feat that Lord Hawthorne single-handedly did.

The reporter told his cameraman to keep filming while he rushed over to the droid, who was still waving to his admirers, and with his microphone in hand and being almost out of breath he asked, "Lord Hawthorne, can you tell us what happened to you this morning?"

The droid, feeling pleasure at all the attention, looked straight at the camera and started talking in a casual manner of how the morning events came about, receiving exclamations of "wow" and "how exciting" and "weren't you scared?" to which the droid replied very matter- of-factly, "Not at all. I was just protecting the good citizens of London by getting rid of that type of riff-raff," at which point the crowd, now having grown five times its original size and blocking all lanes of traffic, burst into loud applause and cheers. After more waving and bowing, the droid said, "Now, if all of you will excuse me, I must get going over to the Parliament Club. Thank you all and goodbye."

The crowd, not wanting to give up the heroic moment, began collecting behind the droid as if he was the head of a parade. They kept following the droid, clapping and cheering, as he continued his way across the Thames. The news reporter ran back to his van and started a satellite feed to his news station. Every morning he presented live news of events as they happened. The story went electric all over London by the time the droid made it to the Parliament Club for his steam bath and shower. He was met by his own party that had heard the news and had come streaming out of the club, and members from both the House of Lords and the House of Commons were also fast on their way from the Parliament building just two blocks away to meet the new hero.

"Jonathan, old chap, just heard the news! You are out of the hospital and doing some kind of hero business?" asked one familiar member.

"Barney, old friend, good to see you," replied the droid, who had remembered him from his earlier training with Drexel. "I was just about to go in to freshen up and come over to the House of Lords this morning, but I think I'm in need of a decent suit to wear. Any idea where I could get one this early? I know there are a few shops that I have accounts at, but I can't seem to remember where."

"No time, old chap," replied Barney. You need to get onto the floor right now. With the election only weeks away, you could ride this hero business right into Number 10 Downing."

"But -- but my shower and shave and clothes," protested the droid.

"Nonsense, lad! I'll have my tailor come over right away. You can change into something better in a few hours, but let's go," said Barney.

The droid forgot about the shower and complied with his friend request and calmly followed Barney into the House of Lords while the crowd behind him continued to follow and cheer him on.

12 "GRABEN SPINNEN"

The helicopter landing had gone as smooth as all the others Olaf had previously done at the private London airstrip, so smooth in fact that Drexel didn't wake from his sleep. A dark limousine pulled up to the helicopter and two sheepish-looking men got out, almost shaking with fear at what Drexel might do to them since they had allowed the Hawthorne droid to leave unnoticed from the hospital, not to mention their failed attempt at apprehending him on the Thames River bridge.

Olaf hopped out of the cockpit and greeted the two men. "Drexel is asleep, so let's not wake him yet. Has the droid been found?" asked Olaf.

One of the men replied, "Please, sir, would you come into the limo and see what's on the television? We have something to show you before you wake up your brother."

Olaf's face expressed confusion upon hearing this strange request, but he quietly complied and got into the limo, only to see a live broadcast from Parliament featuring the main speaker, none other than the droid Hawthorne! The men also proceeded to tell Olaf about their earlier encounter with the Hawthorne droid on the bridge. Trying to remain expressionless, he got back out of the limo and proceeded to give orders to the men to escort his sleeping brother to the limo. "Take him to his hotel room and, whatever you do, don't let him see any TV until I can talk to him first!"

The men complied by lifting the unconscious Drexel into the limo, and then it sped off to the downtown luxury hotel where Drexel always stayed on the top floor when he was in town. Watching the limo leave, Olaf then went into a small airport shed where he always kept a gassed-up motorcycle for emergency purposes, and after several tries at starting the bike, it finally fired up and he headed off to downtown London and the Swedish Embassy.

Upon getting into the embassy, he requested an audience with the ambassador, and since Olaf was from the family of Drexel, his name got him an immediate response from the ambassador himself, who came into the embassy waiting room to meet him.

"Ah, Count Drexel the younger!" said the ambassador, walking over to shake Olaf's hand.

"Thank you for seeing me, Ambassador Fergusson," said Olaf. "It is always nice to see you." Jumping straight to the point, Olaf continued, "This is kind of an emergency. Is there any way you could get my brother and I invitations to this Fleet Street charity auction tonight? It would mean a great deal to my brother.

The ambassador was silent for a minute, but then smiled and said, "Of course! Anything for the house of Drexel! Apparently this event has become the most desired place to be this evening with the Queen herself being there and the new popularity of that Lord Hawthorne who will also be attending."

"Oh? I hadn't heard," said Olaf, as casually as he possibly could.

Walking to a nearby desk and telephone, the ambassador buzzed his personal secretary and within minutes the secretary appeared from an outer office with two sealed invitations wrapped with red official-looking ribbons and handed them to the ambassador. "Here, my boy, take these," said the ambassador, handing the invitations to Olaf, who then took a brief bow of respect and shook the ambassador's hand, thanking him profusely.

"It is I who should thank you, young count," said the ambassador. These invitations were originally for my wife and I, but we haven't had a night off at home in weeks. Please take them and enjoy, and give my best to your brother."

"Thank you, sir, I will," said Olaf, tucking them into his coat pocket. After again shaking the ambassador's hand, he left the embassy and made a quick stop at an apparel shop, purchasing two tuxedos for the night's charity auction at the fashionable London Night Club 17 Fleet Street, then headed straight for the downtown Hyde Park Hotel which was only minutes away.

***

The room was still spinning when Drexel heard a knock at the door. Groaning, he said, "Yes, yes, come in whoever you are." Drexel's head felt like it was killing him and he didn't know where he was.

Olaf opened the door, holding the two tuxedos. "Get dressed, brother. We have a charity function to go to tonight. I'll explain in a few minutes!"

Drexel, still dazed and confused, was experiencing his first ever hangover from the beers he had consumed earlier that morning in the helicopter. Olaf carefully informed his brother about the new-found fame of the droid Hawthorne by explaining how their men tried to grab the droid on a bridge over the Thames River as he was walking towards the Parliament club and how quickly the droid dispatched Drexel's men by throwing two over the bridge rail, while making the third airborne into a nearby tree. All three, Olaf said to Drexel, survived and were back at base awaiting further orders. The one thing Olaf wanted to explain to his brother was that there was no possible way now to stop the Hawthorne droid because he was surrounded constantly by the press and new-found fans everywhere he went.

Olaf was expecting his brother to fly into another rage like the one he had earlier that morning, but instead Drexel calmly took the tuxedo from his brother and, without saying a word, laid it on his bed, grabbed some fresh scented hotel soap and a towel, and went into the bathroom to take a shower. Olaf took that as a good sign, as in the past when his brother was in deep thought he would get very quiet and go about doing some mundane chore, all the while his brain churning at high speed. Olaf decided this was a good time to go to his room and change as well.

Thirty minutes later Olaf returned, all dressed up, only to be met by his brother in the hallway outside of his room, struggling with his black bowtie as if it was some great mystery as to how to get it tied properly. "You know, in America most teenage boys going to their high school prom can do this in about one-hundredth of the time you are taking, brother," said Olaf, grabbing both ends of the stringy black object and undoing the double knot that Drexel had just made.

"Well, Olaf, most teenage boys in America were not double majors in physics and mechanical engineering at Stockholm University by the time they were fifteen either," smirked Drexel, as Olaf finished up a proper bowtie knot perfectly snug against his brother's neck.

"There, all done," said Olaf. "Now let's get going. The sedan is waiting. And, oh, by the way, you aren't going to do anything bad to those three bunglers of ours, are you? They did do their best."

Drexel smiled a quick smile. "Well, earlier I was going to have them eliminated, but then I remembered that labor, even incompetent labor, isn't cheap, so I'll let that feeling pass for now. So let's go meet the Queen, shall we?"

"I am all for that, brother." Any idea on how we are going to fix the droid at the auction tonight in a room full of people?" asked Olaf, pushing the elevator down button, waiting for the door to open. "I didn't want to bring it up, but I have noticed that you don't seem at all worried about this evening."

Drexel didn't say a word, but reached into his coat pocket, producing a small silvery round metallic object no larger in diameter than a quarter and held it out flat in the palm of his hand. Olaf leaned his face in closer to the object to inspect the tiny detailing etched into what appeared to be a very soft metal ball. Suddenly the ball transformed into an eight-legged spider-like creature and jumped onto Olaf's face just as the elevator door opened. A woman who was getting off the elevator screamed as she saw Olaf swatting at his face and yelling "get it off, get it off!" The woman ran out of the elevator and down the hall as Drexel, for the first time in a long time, actually bent over laughing as he watched his brother dance around the hotel hallway, hitting himself as he tried to kill the metallic creature.

Laughing, Drexel said, "I'm sorry, Olaf, but I can't help it. You look so ridiculous!" Drexel then touched a button on his watch which turned the spider into a soft round ball again, causing it to drop off Olaf's face and fall down to the floor, where Drexel quickly scooped it up and placed it back into his pocket.

"What was that?" gasped Olaf, trying to calm down, straightening his shirt collar and his bowtie, then pulling out a comb for his hair, now feeling a little sheepish for reacting to one of Drexel's inventions in such a manner.

"That, dear brother, is what I call 'graben Spinnen,'" said Drexel, as he pressed the down button on the elevator again after having missed the last ride.

"I'm sorry," said Olaf, with sarcasm rising in his voice, "but my German isn't up to par right now. You'll have to explain that term to a lesser intellect like myself."

"Drexel rolled his eyes and said," 'graben Spinnen' is German for digging spiders."

"I'm listening," said Olaf, now becoming curious.

"You see," continued Drexel, retrieving the rounded object from his coat pocket again, holding it up with his right hand like a jeweler showing off a large diamond with pride, "there is a type of spider in southern Bavaria that I named my invention after that makes its living tunneling for its prey. It doesn't catch insects using webs like other spiders. This species feels for vibrations in the ground that are made by its prey, moves into position underneath its prey, and before any bug or beetle can get away it shoots its stinger directly into its prey's belly, thus catching and dissolving its dinner much faster than other species of spiders."

"Impressive. But you said spiders. I see only one,"

said Olaf.

"You are observant, little brother," said Drexel. "These spiders are always pregnant, thus stepping on one as I have done in the past produces hundreds of smaller spiders running and escaping from its dead parent!"

"So we have to squash this thing somehow?" asked Olaf. "I'm still confused."

"It's quite simple," explained Drexel. This little metallic ball dissolves into a light viscous transparent liquid in; let's say for instance, alcohol. Once it enters the droid's catch basin, within minutes this viscous liquid solidifies and reforms itself into hundreds of smaller creatures like the one you just experienced. Then these tiny creatures disseminate throughout the droid's body. In this case they will disseminate towards the neuron connections running from the second brain located at the back of the skull to the third brain located at the front of the droid's skull. Then they will sever all electrical neurons running back and forth between the two brains, thus putting the droid back under my immediate control, with no harm to the droid and no memory of any activity that the third brain controlled. Once done, they will exit the droid through various openings, such as the ears, mouth, or nasal cavities."

"How long does this take?" asked Olaf, feeling slightly nauseous at having come into contact with his brother's invention.

"Fifteen minutes at the most," said Drexel, looking at his watch.

"So all we have to do is spike the droid's drink somehow and hope no one notices these things running out of the Hawthorne droid's head?" asked Olaf, just as the elevator door opened.

"Precisely. But these things are so small that I doubt if anyone could tell. Besides, I have a plan to get the droid off to the side and away from the crowd so as not to take any chances. So here's to our success!" said Drexel, as he patted his brother on the back and jumped onto the elevator.

13 CLUB 17 ON FLEET STREET

It was a perfectly cool, clear evening, with faint traces of a fading pastel blue sky interlaced with crimson red, feather-like circus clouds hovering like a huge clear colorful tarp over the most historical and beloved city in the world. The Club 17 Fleet Street was only a five-block drive through the flower and produce market district of London. Olaf asked his brother if he would mind him letting the windows down so he could enjoy the drive more. Drexel's earlier good mood had seemed to vanish once they got into the limo. Even Olaf couldn't understand these sudden mood swings. Drexel just sat there staring straight ahead, not saying a word, but gave a quick roll of his right hand like some monarch giving his half-hearted approval to a request from a lowly subject. All the same, Olaf was glad he did and lost no time in rolling down the two back windows to let in the pungent fragrances of pomegranates, melons, periwinkles, roses and violets. All these items mixed into a perfumed watery soup as the bits and pieces of leftover wares from that day's market sales were hosed down on the gray cobblestone streets by the vendors busily cleaning up for the next day's work.

"You are quite the romantic," remarked Drexel, sporting a frown as he came out of his trance-like state, looking sideways at his brother.

"Oh? So you don't believe in romance, do you, brother?" asked Olaf in a half-mocking manner.

"You know she was the only one and there will never be another," responded Drexel, now staring straight ahead again.

"Well, then, brother, this conversation is rather pointless, isn't it?" replied Olaf, as he leaned over closer to the window to partake in the night air again.

"Stop that!" said Drexel, slamming his right fist into the black leather headrest of the empty seat in front of him. You are doing that to try to get me to think about her. I just know you are!"

Olaf, now losing his good nature, fired back at his brother. "It's not all about you, Your Highness. Some of us have our own torches to bear, like mine, if you are interested --"

"Well, I'm not interested in the slightest," interrupted Drexel, trying not to conjure up the image in his mind of the only woman he ever loved.

A few moments of silence hung between the brothers like a heavy, wet, black curtain. Both men, however brief, were lost in the past and didn't wish to remain there too long.

"Who was she?" asked Drexel, trying not to appear too curious, of which he really was.

"The ghost that haunts me is in Paris, or was," said Olaf, taking a picture out of his wallet and handing it to his brother.

"Pretty enough, I suppose," said Drexel, flipping the picture back at his brother. "Poor, too, I bet."

"Oh," said Olaf with a sigh, as he put the picture back into his wallet, "she had some money, but she insisted that if we were going to be together that I would have to quit jet-setting around and settle down with her in Paris."

"Well, why didn't you?" asked Drexel in a defensive manner, already knowing the answer involved him and his brother's loyalty to him.

"What, and let you run the world without me?" said Olaf with a wink, trying to lighten up his brother's mood. But before Drexel could respond, Olaf said, "Oh, look, we are already here at the club!"

***

Seventeen Fleet Street had its red carpet rolled out in between tall, black iron, well-lit Victorian gas lamps that were emitting wide streams of yellow-white light, illuminating on many eager faces in the crowd already lined up on both sides of the carpet to see and cheer on the Queen. Usually the British monarch would arrive last, as had been a tradition at any major function involving her presence, thus all the guests could greet her with applause as well as a few fortunate guests who could actually kiss the royal hand and exchange a few pleasantries. This night was a little different, as the Hawthorne droid was the head of the welcoming committee instead of the acting Prime Minister who was away on a brief holiday in Bermuda.

The welcoming party was standing just off the curb where Her Royal Highness would soon pull up in her bulletproof limo with its black tinted windows and her royal protection service guards riding on specially built running boards, straddling both sides of the vehicle. Drexel wanted no part of the limelight and ordered his driver to pull into a nearby red brick alley that was beside the club where they wouldn't be noticed.

"Do you think 'she' will be there?" asked Drexel in a wistful manner, while looking out of the back window of their limo at the Hawthorne droid who was now shaking hands with some fellow House of Lord members that had just arrived.

"'She' who?" responded Olaf, knowing full well who his brother meant.

"Don't play with me. You know who I mean," growled Drexel, still watching the crowd.

"Well, if you mean Marguerite, then yes, no doubt she will be at the club tonight, along with ninety-nine point nine percent of all British Royalty. This is the event of the year and you know all royals like to see and be seen."

"I should have had that fat philandering husband of hers disappear a long time ago," said Drexel out loud to himself.

"And do what?" said Olaf, feeling the heat rise in his face. "Tell her of your little schemes of world domination through your droids and sweep her off her feet to Gotland to live in a drafty old castle in the middle of the Baltic Sea?"

"You don't understand!" snapped Drexel, turning around to face his brother. "I could give her everything she could ever want and more than even in her wildest dreams! Besides, she doesn't have to know everything about me."

Suddenly the Royal Guard Band stirred up its rendition of "God Save the Queen" as the Queen's limo pulled up to the curb to a cheering crowd. Drexel's worst fears were unfolding right before his eyes when he saw the Queen get out and extend her hand to be kissed by the fake Lord Hawthorne, who immediately afterward offered his arm to the Queen to escort Her Majesty inside.

"Tell me this is not happening!" screamed Drexel. "One false move in front of the Queen and all my hard work will vanish in an instant!"

"Don't worry," said Olaf, getting out of the car. "The driver said there is an employee entrance at the back of the club. We would probably have an easier access to the Queen and the droid coming from the back of the club rather than fighting our way through the crowd."

"Good thinking, brother!" said Drexel, getting out of his side of the sedan and following Olaf around to the back of the club.

***

The 17th Fleet Street Club's appearance seemed to match its name. The inside looked like an early 1930's speakeasy off some side street in Hollywood. Plush red leather chairs were evenly placed around small round tables with fresh white linen tablecloths held in place with red, green, blue and yellow twisted depression glass vases filled with fresh cut violets or daisies, all bathed by flickering candlelight wicks floating in bulbous mason jars full of red wine-colored wax. Various blinking colored neon-shaped faces of 1930's movie stars and other well known personalities of that era adorned the whitewash surrounding walls. Personalities such as Clark Gable, Vivian Lee, Bette Davis, Ginger Rogers, Fred Astaire, Mae West, Errol Flynn, W.C. Fields, and ending with the Marx Brothers, were all looking down toward the center stage where the band members were wearing dark 1930's style pin-striped suits, white spats, and dark-colored shirts with white ties, busily playing "Night and Day" by Cole Porter. Above the band was a large banner strewn across the width of the club saying "Welcome to the Annual 17th Fleet Street Charity Auction."

A large unoccupied table just a few feet from the stage was roped off from the public for the Queen and her accompanying party to sit and enjoy the evening's festivities. The room was already packed with London's elite society as well as those of lesser means who somehow, maybe through personal contacts of the club's owner or one of its employees, were able to grab a few tickets and, for an evening at least, pretend to be one of high society's fellow members. As the Queen entered escorted by the Hawthorne droid, the band, as if on cue, suddenly stopped the Cole Porter song and went into a straight rendition of "God Save the Queen," in which all the audience in the club stood straight up on their feet at their tables, in silence, while some bowed as the Queen passed.

Drexel and Olaf made it into the kitchen at the back of the club, looking through the swinging door's rounded glass windows, dodging waiters as they streamed in and out of the kitchen's galley way. "Watch out, mate!" yelled a waiter, holding two trays high above his head, just missing bumping into Drexel.

"This is intolerable!" said Drexel, ducking from the waiter. "I can't see a thing. Too many people are blocking our view. Plus I don't see any vacant tables."

"Not a problem," said Olaf, disappearing around the

corner and then coming back a few seconds later with a small extra table he saw tucked away in the corner of the spacious kitchen. "There is a space just to the left of the front stage where we can sit this table down and observe the Queen and the droid."

"Good thinking again, little brother!" said Drexel, as he grabbed the other side of the small table to help Olaf carry it.

Both men hurried unnoticed through the crowd, who were too busy watching the Queen be seated alongside the Hawthorne droid than to pay them any attention. Drexel and Olaf then quickly placed the table about twenty feet left of the kitchen door. Finding two folding chairs conveniently leaning against the wall of an adjacent walkway leading out to the club's veranda, Olaf snatched them and handed one to his brother, wherein both sat down. A waiter coming out of the kitchen, noticing their bare table, sent over another waiter with a tablecloth, candle, and flowers, plus two complimentary drinks from the club.

"I don't like scotch and water," said Drexel, frowning

as he tasted his drink.

"Can't you be happy about anything, brother? Look, we are close to the droid and it seems that the Queen finds him as charming as the original. I think you might come out on top of this one, so can we be a little bit more positive about the future?" remarked Olaf, casually looking around the room to see if Marguerite had shown up.

"I'll be positive when I have that droid's neurons turned into spaghetti," said Drexel, starting to smile a bit as he took another sip.

A club manager showed up at their table holding a fistful of tickets. "Gentlemen, may I see your invitations, please? The bidding will start in a few minutes."

"How does this work?" asked Olaf, handing the man their two invitations.

"It's all by number, sir," said the manager, handing Olaf and Drexel two large white cards with black numbers on them. You just hold your number up when you wish to bid and shout out an amount of money you wish to pledge. That is about it. The process is simple really, and remember it's all for charity."

"Thank you," said Olaf. As the man turned to leave, Olaf whispered to his brother, "Are we bidding on anything tonight?"

"Of course not!" Drexel said. "Now, quiet! I'm thinking abut how to get near our target. Having the droid so close to the Queen changes everything. I will have to be extra careful on this one."

"Of course, brother, you are always careful," said Olaf, half listening, having just seen Marguerite out of the corner of his eye, sitting quietly with her boisterous husband just eight tables away.

"What's wrong with you, Olaf?" asked Drexel. "You look like you've seen a ghost!"

"Uh, maybe I have," said Olaf, shifting his seat over more towards the Queen's direction so his brother wouldn't see the love of his life sitting just a short distance away from them.

"Here, Olaf, order another drink, say gin and tonic.

That should dissolve our little spider friend easy enough while I think of an excuse to offer it to the droid in front of the Queen before the bidding starts."

"Sure thing, brother. I'll be right back," said Olaf, jumping out of his seat and trying not to look in the direction of Marguerite.

Less than a minute later Olaf returned with a gin and tonic, complete with a small red parasol sticking out of the glass. Olaf was sensing his brother was coming out of his dark mood now that he was able to focus on the droid and not if Marguerite would show. "Uh, brother, once we get the droid, what say we get him out of here right after he drinks his drink," whispered Olaf, as he handed Drexel the gin and tonic. Drexel was already taking the "graben Spinnen" out of his pocket, then dumped the little round object into the alcohol and watched it immediately dissolve, blending in with the clear liquid.

"That's the plan, Olaf," said Drexel. "See that hallway where we got the chairs from?"

"Yeah. So what?" answered Olaf.

"That will be our escape to the balcony. Once I get him away from the Queen's presence, I'll offer him a toast, and as soon as he drinks it I'll lead him out to the back balcony. Once his third brain dies, I'll order him to come with me, until we can figure out how to get him back into the Queen's presence," said Drexel, getting up from the table. "Wish me luck, brother!"

"Good luck," whispered Olaf, as he watched his brother walk towards the Queen's table.

***

The Queen was sitting around her table with the American and French ambassadors as well as the Hawthorne droid, who had just told another joke, making the Queen laugh for the third time that evening. Suddenly she stopped laughing as she saw Count Drexel approaching her table so deliberately.

"Your Majesty," said Drexel, bowing deeply, "You may not remember me, but --"

"Oh, Count Drexel, of course I do! I never forget a face," responded the Queen, extending her hand, which

Drexel gently but eagerly took and planted a quick kiss on.

"Your Majesty has me at a disadvantage. I seem not to remember us ever meeting," said Drexel, straightening up his stance after bowing.

"Well, permit me to remind you of our first meeting, young man. It was when I attended a dinner at the Swedish ambassador's house. You must have been at least ten or so."

Drexel was really thrown off at the Queen recognizing him from his boyhood. "But, Your Majesty, how --"

"You look just like your father, that's how," interjected the Queen. "My, you are the spitting image of that dear man."

Drexel, grateful to hear any stories about his father, paused in his response after hearing the Queen allude to his father as a "dear man," thus leading to a brief awkward moment of silence.

"Oh, where are my manners," said the Queen,

gesturing to the French and American ambassadors sitting on her left. "This is Francois Gerard, the French ambassador, and Bill Jones, the American ambassador, and of course you know our man of the hour, Lord Jonathan Hawthorne."

"Gentlemen, it is a pleasure," said Drexel, bowing to all three men, with the men nodding their heads in response. "Actually, Your Majesty, it is Lord Hawthorne I was hoping to speak with briefly on matters concerning both our respective countries, if I may be so bold as to borrow him for a minute --"

"I say, old boy, is that gin and tonic you are holding? I can smell it from here," said the Hawthorne droid, interrupting before the Queen could respond to Drexel. "I thought this place only served that dreadful scotch and water."

"Actually, your Lordship, I brought it over for you," said Drexel.

"Capital!" said the droid, taking the drink from Drexel's hand before Drexel could stop him and downing the drink in one gulp.

"My, my, you are passionate, Lord Hawthorne!" said the Queen, putting her hand to her mouth to cover her brief laughter.

"All in a day's work, Your Highness," responded the droid to further laughter from the table, while Drexel just stood there expressionless, almost in shock.

Two seconds later came the announcement by the club manager, who was standing on the stage, that the auction would now begin. The Queen was so excited about the night's events that she asked Drexel if she and her party could be excused, meaning that Lord Hawthorne would not be going anywhere for the moment and that it would be no use contesting the matter. Drexel had no option but to respect her request. Bowing, he quickly left the Queen's presence and retreated back to his table to work out an emergency plan with his brother.

"What am I going to do now? That idiot droid gulped the drink so fast I couldn't stop him!" Drexel exclaimed to his brother as he sat back down at the table, nervously looking at his watch.

"I thought you said those spiders would exit undetected," replied Olaf, trying to think of a way to calm his brother down.

"Normally, yes, but the most powerful monarch in the world is sitting three feet away from a droid meltdown!" said Drexel. "Even if the Queen and the guests at the table don't see these things exit, they will certainly notice the droid's behavior. There is a second possibility that he may just shut down altogether, if we are lucky, but if he reverts too fast to the second brain, another possibility exists that he might think he is in some sort of danger and then go through a defensive status and enter into a lethal attack mode."

"You mean he could kill the Queen?" exclaimed Olaf, who was now beginning to panic. "Why didn't you think of this before?" Olaf was just incredulous that his brother would not have thought things through more carefully.

"I did think of it, brother, but my planning required my presence with the droid when he came to. Not in my wildest dreams did I anticipate that I would not be with him when he woke up," Drexel said."

Drexel looked at his watch again. They now had only twelve minutes before the droid would be separated from his third brain. The brothers were so involved in their plight that neither of the men heard the auction taking place right in front of them until Drexel heard the name "Duchess of Sussex," followed by a loud round of applause. "Marguerite!" said Drexel out loud, as he turned around to face the stage, suddenly becoming transfixed, watching the woman that had been burned in his mind ever since he laid eyes on the beautiful, tall, slender brunette years before in his youth.

Standing before the audience on the stage was the Duchess, dressed in a black sequined, strapless evening gown, wearing a white rose on the left side of her wavy black hair that hung loose about her alabaster white shoulders. Her piercing turquoise blue eyes were looking out into the audience, but apparently had not noticed Drexel, who was like a hungry cat stalking a bird, watching her every move.

The club manager standing next to her announced,

"The Duchess has kindly offered to auction for charity tonight a song that she will sing for all of us at the highest bidder! Shall we start the bidding at, say, one hundred pounds?"

There was a brief moment of silence from the audience, as no one expected something like a song to be auctioned. Drexel frantically fumbled around for his numbered card. Finding it in his left pocket, he held his number up high and was about to make a bid when the android shouted, "Number Twenty-three bids a hundred and ten pounds!" much to the delight of the crowd, who applauded wildly at the novelty bid.

"Are you out of your mind?" yelled Olaf to his brother amidst the loud applause. Look at the time. We have only ten minutes left!"

Drexel totally ignored his brother as he shouted out, "Number Forty-five bids five hundred pounds!"

The crowd gasped, and then applauded even more at such a handsome offer. The droid, looking annoyed, held his hand back up and yelled, "Number Twenty-three bids one thousand pounds!"

Some people in the audience got so excited that they stood up and yelled "Bravo, bravo!" while others just cheered. Even the Queen was caught up in the moment and gave the Hawthorne droid a quick friendly flick on the shoulder with her rolled up program book.

Olaf again tried to get Drexel's attention. "This is madness, brother! Obviously the droid has somehow ingrained his emotional patterns from your subconscious mind's affection of Marguerite. In effect, he has, or thinks he has, affection for the woman you love, Drexel!"

Olaf's words rang clear in Drexel's mind, bringing him back to reality and a sense of euphoria at the accidental discovery of the possibility of the third brain somehow picking up memories or emotions of human beings. Stunned at the infinite potential of future droids, Drexel stopped his bidding war against the fake Lord Hawthorne and sat down.

"Olaf, my brother," said Drexel, sounding like his old self again and grabbing Olaf's shoulders with both hands affectionately, "you may have single-handedly given me a new lease on life with your casual conversation! Think of it, my droids being able to read human minds and program themselves to be like their human counterparts without months of training!"

"I didn't exactly say that, brother. And, by the way, we have eight minutes left," said Olaf, pointing at Marguerite as she picked up the microphone to sing.

"Huh? Oh, yes, of course," said Drexel, retrieving his thoughts from the clouds. "Don't worry. I think I have a plan. Let's first hear her sing, though." Drexel then became transfixed again at the sight of Marguerite and her sequined dress sparkling under the hot stage lights.

Olaf just rolled his eyes skyward and turned his chair around to get a better view of Marguerite on stage. As Marguerite thanked the audience for their kind applause, Olaf noticed she had lost all trace of her Swedish accent since having married and subsequently residing in England. Her delicate frame and facial features gave away her French lineage from her mother's side, the Countess du Bois of Burgundy, rather than her father's more solidly stout build that was common among Swedish country gentry.

She approached the front of the stage, panning the audience. Seeing the empty chair of her husband at their table, she frowned slightly, thinking that he was probably off chasing some waitress or barmaid. She then scanned the audience again and directly rested her gaze on Drexel. Their eyes met. Drexel felt a lump in his throat. His whole body went limp, so much so that he had to prop himself up with his left arm on the small table top, and he never lost eye contact with her except to blink. Olaf didn't notice Drexel's reactions. He was just staring at the droid, watching his every move and looking for signs of the "graben Spinnen" at work in the droid's body.

Marguerite cleared her throat, then thanked the Queen for her presence, also thanked the Hawthorne droid for his generous contribution for her song, and then announced, "This song is for someone tonight very dear to my heart and they are in the audience, and this song is very appropriate for the club since it was written in 1933 and first performed at the Cotton Club in Harlem in America."

Drexel, thinking that she was referring to her husband, just shut his eyes and winced, thinking, how could she possibly love this fat, bloated, philandering, dim-witted, Duke of Sussex!

"Maestro, if you please," said Marguerite, gesturing to the band leader.

The band started an overture that was very familiar to Drexel. As a matter of fact, he knew this tune by heart! He slowly opened his eyes, thinking, is it possible? Could it possibly be?

Marguerite then began singing, "Don't know why there is a sun up in the sky, stormy weather..."

"It can't be!" said Drexel, jumping out of his chair. "That's our song!" Turning to his brother, he said loud enough for half the audience to hear, "Olaf, she means me! She loves me!"

There was some laughter and applause coming from the tables near Drexel and Olaf, as some of the audience found Drexel's reactions endearing, while Marguerite kept staring at Drexel as she sang, and even gave him a weak smile. Olaf was in shock at seeing his brother in this condition and whispered at him through clenched teeth, "Sit down! You are acting like a lovesick school boy. Let me remind you that we have six minutes and ten seconds before the Queen is dripping in 'graben Spinnen'!"

"You are right, of course," said Drexel, as he tried to compose himself, sitting back down. He was so weak in the knees he could barely stand anyway.

"And your plan? What about your plan?" whispered Olaf.

"Don't worry, it's all under control, dear brother," said Drexel. "Now let her finish her song."

Marguerite's voice carried Drexel's mind back to where they first heard that song on a cruise ship that was bound for Greece. In the middle of the Mediterranean, on a moonlit night, the ship's orchestra played that song from the ballroom below deck and the music was piped all throughout the ship. Marguerite and the young Drexel danced up on the top deck, overlooking a calm sea that shimmered so much in the moonlight that it appeared that the whole surface of the Mediterranean was strewn with sparkling cobalt blue diamonds. That was the night that Drexel first told Marguerite of his love for her, and she responded that she loved him and would ever be true in her heart to him.

As Marguerite finished the song, the Queen and the rest of the audience stood up and cheered, while Marguerite bowed and gestured to the band leader, causing him to bow in return. The club manager walked out on stage, clapping all the way, and gave Marguerite a brief hug. Then taking the mike, he announced, "As shown on the program, ladies and gentlemen, there will be a thirty-minute intermission. You are all more than welcome to come up front and dance as the band keeps playing. Thank you!"

The audience members applauded again as chairs were pushed back and people started heading towards the stage to dance. Olaf, looking at his watch said, "Well, brother, you never cease to amaze me. We have less than five minutes. Now seems our chance to grab the droid."

"That's the plan," said Drexel, smiling. "And I plan to talk to Marguerite after we take care of this droid. I'll need you to go over there and tell the droid that he has a call from the Swedish Ambassador and he is to follow you into the cloak room by the kitchen, while I go ahead and set up…"

Before Drexel could finish his sentence, he noticed Marguerite was not returning to her table, but walking directly towards him. As she passed by the Queen, she bowed, while the Hawthorne droid stood up and excused himself from the Queen's presence, then walked over to Marguerite. Taking her hand firmly, he said, "May I have this dance?"

This caught Marguerite totally by surprise, but because the android had paid so much money for her song that night, she succumbed with a half-hearted smile and accepted his offer. As the two began to dance, Marguerite gave a quick glance towards Drexel as if to apologize. The couple worked their way to the center stage area where they were the center of attention.

"Now what?" said Olaf, looking at his watch. "We are just about out of time, brother. Your Marguerite could be in danger within two minutes' time!"

Drexel didn't respond at first because all of his senses were focused on Marguerite and her protection. Staring intently at the Hawthorne droid and Marguerite, he then said, "Olaf, meet me in the cloak room. I'm going to stop this now." Drexel started walking over to the dancing couple, withdrawing a small input computer drive from his pocket as he crossed the floor, knowing he had only about one minute left to do something.

Marguerite felt the droid's light dancing hold on her tighten to where she could hardly breathe. "Lord Hawthorne, you're hurting me. Please stop!" begged Marguerite.

The droid said nothing, moving about more like a drunken man fumbling in the dark than a British lord dancing. Drexel made it up to the couple and, placing his hand on the droid's shoulder and trying to make it appear that he was assisting Lord Hawthorne, quickly jammed the small input device through the droid's skin below the back of the neck, hoping Marguerite couldn't see what he was doing.

"Aslund, he is hurting me!" said Marguerite, who was

the only one in the world that referred to Drexel by his first name. Even Olaf didn't call him Aslund.

"Don't worry, Marguerite, I'm here," said Drexel. "I think our Lord Hawthorne has taken ill and thinks he'll fall if he lets go of you. Let's try to walk him over to where he can lie down in that room across from the stage. Afterwards, please wait in the club for me while I get him some help. I have much to say to you."

"And I you, my darling," Marguerite said, still wincing in pain from the droid's death grip on her. Suddenly Marguerite felt her whole arm itching, like something was crawling all over it. Looking up at the droid's face, she saw thousands of tiny spider-like creatures oozing out of the droid's nose and mouth. She was so shocked at what she saw that she wanted to scream, but the droid's grip grew even tighter to where she couldn't breathe at all.

Drexel, panicking, grabbed a carafe of ice water from one of the tables and poured it down the droid's back, causing the droid to let go of Marguerite, who by now was almost faint, but managed to make it to a nearby chair to catch her breath, while Drexel grabbed the droid and pushed it the rest of the way into the cloak room where Olaf was waiting. The droid immediately started disintegrating into a heap of smoking skin and circuit boards. Fortunately the droid was far enough away from the crowd that most of the guests hadn't noticed anything was wrong, and those guests that did see the droid slumped over before he entered the cloak room thought that Lord Hawthorne may have had too much to drink, so they just went right back to dancing and chatting.

Out of sight from everyone, Drexel, with Olaf's help, moved what was left of Lord Hawthorne onto a small cot towards the back of the secluded room. "Did you have to destroy him?" asked Olaf, not noticing that Marguerite had recovered and was standing just a few feet behind them.

Drexel, seeing Marguerite, walked over to her and asked, "Are you all right, my darling?" As Drexel tried to put his arm around her bare shoulders, she pushed his arm away, still staring at the smoking heap lying on the cot. "Aslund, what have you done? Is that one of your toys?"

Drexel looked at his brother and motioned with his head for Olaf to leave the room while he talked to Marguerite. Olaf quickly exited, gladly leaving the couple alone to talk.

"I know you probably won't understand or believe me as to what I'm about to tell you, Marguerite, but do you trust me?" asked Drexel.

Marguerite stood there for what seemed like a whole minute of silence, looking into Drexel's ice blue eyes. Then she relaxed her expression a bit and responded, "You know I always have and always will, but you are right, I really don't understand this at all. Is this something to do with some secret government project?"

As evil and as bad as Drexel had become, one good character trait he still carried was that he couldn't directly lie to this woman he loved, but in his heart he knew that he couldn't tell her the whole truth. He thought that maybe one day, if after they ever got back together, he could reveal his whole plan, but this was not the time, so he kept his answers to her questions in the realm of half truths and in very general terms. "Yes, my dearest, it is a secret project that involves many governments, but I can't tell you much more. I've been sworn to secrecy. Can you forget what you have seen tonight?" asked Drexel, not knowing what he would do if she said she couldn't.

"Yes, I'll keep your secret, of course, Aslund, because I have a secret of my own that I must tell you."

Drexel breathed out a sigh of relief, knowing she would be true to her word. Also he was inwardly overjoyed at the thought that she was probably going to confess her love for him, and already in his mind he was formulating a way to ask her to leave her husband and come away with him. "Any secret you give me, I'll keep until I go to my grave," he said, as he embraced her, drawing her close to him.

Marguerite, looking into Drexel's eyes, said, "I know you are hurt at me turning down your proposal of marriage, but back then we were both very poor and --"

"I was hurt beyond comprehension and still can't understand why you chose him over me," interrupted Drexel.

"It wasn't a choice, my darling. I had to find a way to provide for my baby."

"Well, of course a duke would have the money and then some to provide for his child," said Drexel, now thinking of ways he could have her husband killed off.

"No, no, dearest, you don't understand. Our baby had to have a real home and real security so she could grow up to her highest potential in life."

Drexel stood silent, sifting through Marguerite's words. "Uh, Marguerite, are you trying to tell me..." But Drexel couldn't continue. He couldn't get the words out.

Marguerite reached into her clutch purse and pulled out a picture of a beautiful young woman in her early twenties who looked somewhat familiar to Drexel. Taking the picture from Marguerite, he couldn't help but notice that the woman's eyes and nose resembled his.

"Aslund, darling, I want you to meet your daughter, Shellie," beamed Marguerite. "She is twenty-three and brilliant, a graduate student in the very top of her class at MIT in America, majoring in robotics!"

14 EARLIER BACK AT THE HOSPITAL

The back of the London hospital loading dock was the perfect way of escape as Elliott and Reggs got off the service elevator and started to head for the car. Elliott was still in shock at his discovery that his old political ally, Lord Hawthorne, was an android, and he couldn't shake the nagging thought in the back of his mind as to what to do next about getting home and rescuing his wife and daughter from the clutches of Count Drexel.

Suddenly Elliott noticed his friend Reggs freeze at the top of the loading dock stairs, his right hand extended straight out to prevent Elliott from moving any farther. Reggs was staring at the back hospital driveway where two black limousines had pulled up to a screeching stop and six men jumped out all at the same time, wearing long winter wool coats and black sunglasses. Two of the men looked like they were carrying some sort of automatic weapon after a quick breeze blew one side of their coats open, revealing large leather shoulder holsters and the butts of guns. Four of the men ran up the stairs, just barely missing Elliott and Reggs by a few feet. The other two men with the guns stayed by the limousine. Luckily, the four men that just passed by had paid no attention to Elliott and Reggs but just headed straight for the passenger elevator and jumped on.

Reggs just shook his head and said, "I think, mate, we've been found out. Here, throw this on." Taking two lab coats from out of one of the laundry bins, Reggs pushed Elliott around the corner of the loading dock and well out of sight of the two remaining gunmen. "I'll take the other one," Reggs said, as he grabbed the other coat.

"So what's the plan?" asked Elliott, struggling to get his arms through the tight sleeves of the orderly's coat.

"The plan is, mate, to just follow me to the car and nod at everything I say," said Reggs, as he rummaged through several trash bins, finally pulling out a large white box with a red medical hazard sign on the side. "Perfect!" he said, heading for the stairs with the box.

Elliott, a little confused, but by instinct had learned to trust his resourceful friend, just followed right behind Reggs. Walking quickly down the stairs and heading toward the car, Elliott noticed that the gunmen were looking intently their way. "I think we are becoming an object of interest," whispered Elliott.

Without hesitation, Reggs blurted out loud enough for the gunmen to hear, "All right, mate, we'd better hurry because those bleeding kidneys have to make it to Heathrow in forty minutes!"

Hearing Reggs' statement, one of the gunmen just shrugged, turned back around, and fixed his gaze again on the loading dock, but the other gunman stared at Elliott and Reggs until they finally reached Reggs' car. Then he also turned his attention back to the loading dock and started talking to his companion.

"Looks like we made it. Good plan, Reggs. Thanks," said Elliott, as Reggs hurriedly backed the car out of the hospital lot, then turned left down a narrow side street that emptied into a major London downtown thoroughfare.

"I guess this means that Drexel knows you are here, mate," said Reggs, taking out a cigarette and offering one to his friend.

Elliott politely rejected the cigarette and just sat there quietly thinking for a few minutes as Reggs made his turn onto the busy London turnpike. Finally he said, "I can't be seen getting on a commercial flight. Who knows how many people Drexel has here in London? And I couldn't sneak onto a freighter heading for the states because that would take too long. I guess, old friend, I seem to be out of options for the moment."

Reggs just smiled at his friend and then started to laugh.

"What's that for?" asked Elliott, a little perturbed at his friend's levity.

"Oh, nothing, mate. I was just thinking about how you would look with a red moustache," responded Reggs, still laughing.

"A red moustache?" exclaimed Elliott, more confused than ever.

"In case you haven't noticed, mate, we could be, with a little work, almost twins, or at least brothers."

"So what's your point?" prodded Elliott, becoming

more interested.

"My point is," said Reggs, as he turned off the turnpike and headed for Sunbury, a London suburb where his home was, "that you are going to America on a British Airways flight at 11:00 a.m. in the morning, landing in New York, Mr. Barlow. The only real problem with this trip will be Mrs. Barlow," he said, still laughing. "But here, let me explain..."

Reggs explained his plan to Elliott, who at first thought it all too impossible to work, but the more Reggs kept talking about how he could make his friend into almost a perfect image of himself, the more Elliott seemed to calm down and listen. "So let me get this straight, Reggs," said Elliott. "You can fix me up to look like you and I can use your passport to get on a plane with your wife that's going to New York so she can visit her sister, and then I can use your brother-in-law's car to get to Washington, D.C. to rescue my wife and daughter?"

"Something like that, mate. Anyway, once I explain this to the missus and she makes a call to her sister in

New York, it will be fine. Eh, what do you think?" asked Reggs.

A few more minutes went by in silence while Elliott thought about what his friend had proposed. Then he looked over at Reggs and said, "I like it! It's absolutely brilliant, but I can't ask you to give up such an expensive trip on my account."

"Listen, mate," said Reggs, "the last bloody thing I want in the world is to go and sit with my missus and her sister in New York while my brother-in-law shows me his collection of bird-watching videos. Naw, you are doing me a service! And I've got a spot picked out by a small lake in Scotland where I'll drink my beer, fish, and enjoy some peace and quiet for the first time in many a year. The only catch is..."

"Is what?" asked Elliott.

Reggs sucked in deep and continued, "Well, the only catch is if you come to the U.S. as me, you will have to leave the U.S. as me, or I'll get in trouble with the authorities, both British and American. Do you think you can do everything that you need to do in a week's time before the missus has to return home?"

"Listen, my good friend," said Elliott, "once I make things right, I'll fly your wife home in Air Force One!"

"I'll take that as a yes, then," said Reggs, smiling.

***

The drive to Reggs' suburban home in a quiet cul-de-sac in Sunbury took only forty-five minutes. Upon arriving at Sunbury-on-Thames, Elliott was immediately taken aback at how quaint and peaceful the little suburban village was. It was hard to figure out why a man so outgoing and gregarious as his friend Reggs was would want to live in such a place so unbefitting his personality. Rows of small whitewashed two-story homes with dark wooden criss-crossing beams lined the oak tree-strewn narrow streets. Sidewalks were everywhere, as well as many mothers pushing baby carriages and children riding bikes as school had already let out for the afternoon. The Barlow home was like all the rest of the homes in the area, with one exception. Instead of whitewash, Mrs. Barlow was partial to a robin's egg blue wash, which drove the homeowner's association on South Bend Street crazy for years. But it showed the independence and the individuality of the Barlow household.

Reggs pulled his car onto the right side of the driveway since Mrs. Barlow's car was sitting on the left side with the trunk wide open, exposing several suitcases that had already been packed. Evelyn Barlow was making another trip to the car with several wrapped gifts for her sister and brother-in-law when she noticed her husband with a stranger parked in the driveway. Turning to Elliott, Reggs said, "Best let me talk to her first, mate, before we make the introductions." Getting out of the car, Reggs said, "Eve, love, come inside for a minute. I have to tell you something," ushering his wife back into the house.

A few minutes went by as Elliott sat there drumming his fingers on the dashboard and aimlessly playing with the tuning knob on the car radio until he heard this shrieking coming from the Barlow house. "You want me to do what!" screamed Evelyn, as her husband tried to calm her down before the neighbors could hear.

Several more minutes of dialogue ensued between

Reggs and his wife as he tried to reassure her that letting the Vice-President of the United States impersonate him on their once-in-a-lifetime trip to New York was of highest national importance. "It could even protect the Queen herself," pleaded Reggs. "Just think, love, you might single-handedly save Britain from being taken over by these robotic blokes!"

Evelyn stood still for a moment and then, as if she had been in a trance, suddenly turned her attention to the man in their driveway. She opened the door and walked out to where Elliott was sitting and extended her hand and said, "Hello, Mr. Vice-President. My name is Evelyn Barlow, and it will be a pleasure to assist you in any way we can. Please come inside and let's have dinner. Then we'll see how to make you look like my husband."

Sitting at a small table in the kitchen, Reggs filled Elliott in on every aspect of personal information about himself that he could think of while Evelyn prepared dinner. "You were born in Surry. You come from a family of six children and all but two are dead --"

"I'm sorry to hear that," interjected Elliott.

"Let's stay focused, mate," said Reggs. Handing Elliott his passport, he continued, "Now, you have never been to the States before, as you can see by my passport, but you have traveled extensively through Europe, and you served two terms in the British Army, stationed in Gibraltar, as a radio intelligence officer."

"That's how we met," interrupted Evelyn. "He was a sergeant and I was a nurse at the base hospital. One day he came in so sick and pathetic. I fell for him right then and there!"

"That's fine, love, but we really need to stay on task here," said Reggs, with a bit of impatience in his voice.

"Ohhh, excuse me, Mister Big and Important Advisor to the Vice-President of the United States, but you left out one tiny little detail that might be useful to Mr. Greenwood here," quipped Evelyn.

"All right, love, I give up. You tell me the tiny little detail I left out," said Reggs, as he sat back in his chair and crossed his arms.

"He is a Yank, Reggie! He doesn't talk like you, my

dear. If he says one word at customs in either country, he'll give himself away, don't you think?" asked Evelyn, as she set down the mashed potatoes.

"She's absolutely right," said Elliott. "I could never sound English. Heck, I have trouble speaking without my southern accent coming into play every now and then."

"Well, as your traveling wife and ad hoc nurse," said Evelyn, leaning over and putting her hand on Elliott's forehead, "I would say, love, that you have a nasty case of laryngitis. Cough for me, my dear."

Elliott faked a couple of coughs and the three of them burst into laughter.

***

At 6:00 a.m. everyone was up in the Barlow residence. Reggs was busy trying to find one of his suits that would fit Elliott. Evelyn died Elliott's hair red the night before and now she was giving him a haircut to match that of her husband. All had to be on their way to Heathrow in forty-five minutes so as to get into international check-in on time. Elliott had had nightmares and didn't sleep well at the Barlow home. He kept dreaming about his wife and daughter being tortured by Drexel personally and that he was powerless to stop him. Thankfully, the sun came up early, with the birds singing, and his memories of the past night faded over breakfast and pleasant conversation with the Barlows.

Reggs finally found a good-fitting suit for Elliott and Evelyn finished trimming his sideburns. "There, almost perfect," Evelyn said, standing back to admire her work. "Well, almost," as she started to frown.

"What's wrong, love?" asked Reggs.

"Look!" she said, pointing to Elliott's face. "You tell me!"

"Oh, right," said Reggs, as he pulled the red fake moustache out of his coat pocket and started to attach it to Elliott's upper lip. "Went by Jimmy's Trick Shop last night and got this while you were taking a nap, old man. It is a perfect matching color for my own hair, if I do say so myself," he said, as he adjusted the moustache. He then stepped back to admire his work. "Blimey!" said

Reggs and Evelyn at the same time.

"Your own mother wouldn't know," said Evelyn.

"It's like looking in a mirror," whispered Reggs to himself.

"So it's good then?" asked Elliott, who just wanted to hear some extra reassurance from his hosts and friends.

"It's good enough, old man," said Reggs, slapping Elliott on the back. "Let's get going!"

***

The drive to the airport was quiet. Reggs drove Evelyn was sitting next to him in the passenger seat, while Elliott was sitting in the back behind Evelyn. Evelyn and Elliott were feeling somewhat tense, and given the dangers of being caught at British customs, Drexel's men and androids spotting them, getting through American customs unnoticed, and getting away from Kennedy International Airport in New York without being spotted added an air of deadly seriousness about their future well-being. Reggs, on the other hand, was quite cheerful and even started to whistle a bit, which annoyed his wife to no end.

"How can you be so upbeat about everything?" asked Evelyn, as she gave her husband a quick jab with her left elbow.

"Oww! That hurt, love," said Reggs, as he handed his wife a piece of yellow paper.

"What's this for?" she asked.

"It is a number to call if you get into trouble," said Reggs.

"I've never seen this number before," said Evelyn. "Is it a work number that I don't know about?"

"Something like that, love. Just put it in a safe place, will you?" urged Reggs.

Evelyn tucked the small piece of paper into her inner coat pocket and reached over to hug her husband's left arm.

The airport loomed up fast. Reggs drove over to the international terminal baggage check-in and said, "All right, you two, it won't do for the world to see two Reggie

Barlows at one time running about, so it's time for me to say goodbye."

Reggs stayed in the car while Elliott jumped out to grab the luggage from the trunk. Evelyn and Reggs hugged each other and said some private words, causing Elliott to stay put at the back end of the car until Evelyn got out of the car and headed for the luggage check-in counter. Elliott then walked over to his friend and shook his hand hard through the car window. "I can't thank you enough, old friend. I owe you everything. How can I ever repay you?" said Elliott.

"You can't, mate. Just look after my girl and remember that number I gave her. If someone so much as sneezes suspiciously near you both, call that bloody number. You got it?" said Reggs.

"Elliott, looking puzzled, asked, "Is there something you aren't telling me, Reggs?"

Reggs just laughed and then, without a word, stepped on the gas and left the terminal.

Elliott caught up with Evelyn at the baggage check-in

counter and then they both went into the main terminal, getting into the line for customs and security. While waiting in line, Elliott looked around the airport, trying not to be obvious, but just seeing if anyone was looking back at them or showing any unusual sign of interest towards them. Nothing so far, he said to himself.

"Do you have your passport ready, Mr. Greenwood? Because we are next," whispered Evelyn.

Elliott coughed loudly, as if on cue, and then shook his head yes.

The customs agent took Evelyn's passport first. "Business or pleasure, mum?" asked the agent.

Evelyn, being very cool and collected, said, "Pleasure. My husband and I are visiting my sister in New York. We will be in the States for a week or so."

"Very well, mum," responded the agent, as he stamped the passport and handed it back to Evelyn. Reaching for Elliott's passport, the agent asked again in almost a machine-like tone, "Business or pleasure, sir?"

Elliott just coughed and handed him the passport.

Evelyn quickly interjected, "My husband has laryngitis, but, yes, he will be visiting with me at my sister's too, of course."

The agent took the passport, looked at the picture, and stared hard at Elliott, who was now forming beads of sweat on his forehead. He could feel the wax adhesive on his mustache beginning to come loose from the light perspiration on his lip. Coughing again, he used his closed fist to cover his mouth, gently pushing against the mustache at the same time. It worked. He felt the mustache adhere again.

"All right, sir, you both may proceed to security. Thank you and have a safe trip," said the customs agent, gesturing them towards another long line.

"Thank you, sir," said Evelyn, grabbing Elliott's hand like she would grab a child's hand to lead him on, as Elliott heaved a quiet sigh of relief. They both went through security with no problems and headed for the moving sidewalk that led to the terminal ticket gate. It was 10:30 a.m. Once they got to the gate, they both sat down to wait until it was time to board.

"Hungry, Mrs. Barlow?" asked Elliott. "I saw a bagel and coffee shop just around the corner.

"Shhh!" whispered Evelyn. "You are not supposed to talk, remember? And, yes, that would be lovely. Thank you."

Elliott coughed lightly, covering his mouth again with his hand, and quickly whispered, "I'll be right back."

Walking over to the bagel stand, Elliott continued looking around to see if anyone looked suspicious. Everything appeared normal. People were rushing about, minding their own business, and not one person even gave him more than a peripheral glance.

"Would that be all, sir?" asked the attendant, handing Elliott a bag of bagels and two coffees. Elliott had, minutes earlier, written down his order on a piece of paper, ending it with the word "laryngitis." Elliott weakly shook his head yes, and then reached over to gather a few creams and sugars for their coffees. This is all too easy, he thought to himself as he collected the condiments.

Suddenly, behind him he heard fast-paced footsteps.

Quickly looking around, he saw two well-dressed men running to the ticket gate where Evelyn was sitting! Holding the bag of bagels in his teeth and a coffee in each hand, he walked cautiously back toward the gate, watching the two men carefully. The men then rushed up to the ticket counter, expressing loudly to the ticket agent that they were running late and were afraid of missing their flight. "Easy Elliott, easy boy, just a false alarm," Elliott said to himself, as he casually walked up to Evelyn and handed her a coffee and the bag of bagels.

A few minutes later the boarding sign came on and everyone began walking down the portable ramp to the British Airways Boeing 727. "Can I have the aisle seat?" whispered Evelyn. Elliott shook his head yes as they boarded the plane.

Having missed a good portion of the previous night's sleep, Elliott, once seated beside Evelyn, fell into the first deep sleep since his capture. Several hours went by as the plane made its way through the hazy ice blue sky that hung over the frigid waters of the North Atlantic below. The beverage sign came on and the flight attendants started making their rounds.

Evelyn gently nudged Elliott and said, "Sorry to wake you, but would you like something from the drink tray?" All Elliott could muster up was a slight groan as he turned himself towards the cabin window, his back now facing Evelyn.

"There is something else, Mr. Elliott," whispered Evelyn. "Those men sitting across the aisle from us are the same ones that were running late. They have been staring at you for over an hour!"

Elliott, by some internal engine in his body, suddenly snapped fully awake. Staring out over the ocean, a terrifying thought sprung up. He then rolled himself over to face Evelyn, trying to pretend he was still asleep. After another minute of silence, hoping he had fooled anyone that might still be staring at him into thinking he was asleep, he whispered, "Tell me, Mrs. Barlow, were those gentlemen blinking at all as they watched me?"

"Well, now that you mention it that was the odd thing about it, Mr. Elliott. I don't think they were!" said Evelyn. Stealing a quick glance towards the two men and noticing their attention was now focused out the cabin window, she bravely continued and said, "There was also something else strange about them…"

"What's that?" asked Elliott.

"Before they started staring at you, they were up and down the plane, pretending to go to the bathroom a lot, and when they would walk past us, they appeared to be sniffing the air, almost like bloodhounds! Eventually they stopped walking back and forth and sat back down in their seats and haven't stopped staring since," said Evelyn.

"I don't believe it," said Elliott to himself. "It must have been the ticket agent that sent them. The androids don't recognize me in my disguise, so they are sniffing the air? For what? Possibly my DNA? I don't believe it," thought Elliott.

Tossing a few ideas around in his head, Elliott finally whispered, "Evelyn."

"What, Mr. Elliott?" replied Evelyn.

"Call the number that your husband gave you, please. I need to talk to him," said Elliott.

Evelyn, sensing that they were in trouble but not knowing why, tried to calmly pull the piece of yellow paper out of her coat pocket that her husband had given her. Dialing the number on her cell phone, she then handed the phone to Elliott.

The phone rang only once before Reggs picked up. "Reggs, we've got androids on board," said Elliott.

Reggs was silent for a few seconds and then said, "Okay, mate. You hang on tight to my Evelyn and once you land, head straight for customs. Don't stop for anything, and I'll take care of the rest!"

"Got it, Reggs. Elliott out." All Elliott could do now was try to keep them both calm.

"Is there something wrong, Mr. Elliott?" whispered Evelyn.

Mustering up as much steadiness in his voice as he could, Elliott said, "It's all right, Mrs. Barlow. Just hang on tight to me when we land and walk fast. All right?"

"I can do that. You just tell me what to do," said Evelyn, as she put the phone number back into her coat and tried to calmly stare out the airplane window like the rest of the passengers. She knew all she could do now was trust the Vice-President and her husband.

***

A few hours later Elliott sat almost defiantly straight up in his seat. The seatbelt sign had come on to prepare the passengers for landing. With an occasional sideways glance he had noticed the androids weren't staring as intently at him as they had been previously. Elliott thought to himself that the androids must feel their target is secure, so the need to constantly stare at him was unnecessary.

Within minutes the plane landed smoothly at Kennedy Airport and was rolling up to the gate. It soon stopped, and after the customary preparations were made by the crew, the passengers began to disembark off the plane and head towards customs.

"Okay, Mrs. Barlow, let's go," said Elliott, firmly holding onto her arm as they stood to disembark.

"Those men are almost right behind us, Mr. Elliott,"

whispered Evelyn.

"That's okay, Mrs. Barlow. Let's just focus on getting into the terminal. And, remember, walk as fast as you can!" said Elliott.

Both Elliott and Evelyn walked through the narrow tunnel into the terminal with the androids closing in fast from behind. Fortunately, there was a lot of people mingling about that were hindering the androids' progress, but as the couple walked towards the customs gate the crowd of people started thinning out, and after another few moments of fast walking only a handful of British citizens were walking beside them.

The androids had now caught up to the couple and were within arm's reach of Elliott's neck! The customs gate was now only several yards away. One of the androids who was now standing directly behind Elliott poked his hand into his pocket as if he were carrying a gun and was about to say something to Elliott when all of a sudden from around the restroom corner came a voice! "You best don't want to be doing that, mate," Elliott heard the man say to the android. Four other men quickly surrounded the two androids, all wearing long black trench coats.

"Who are you?" asked one of the androids in a British accent.

"Friends of the couple you are trying to get a hold of, mate, and I really suggest you follow my men here or we may have to ship you back to your masters in pieces," said the man.

Not wanting to be exposed for what they really were, the androids complied, especially after seeing four automatic weapons pointed at their heads along with four separate open containers of water in each agent's hand.

Watching the androids being escorted away, a relieved Elliott, holding onto Evelyn who had since fainted, turned his attention to the stranger and asked, "Who are you?"

"Never mind, mate. Let's just say some old friends of your friend Reggs," said the man.

"CIA?" asked Elliott.

"Lord, no," said the stranger. "The CIA is probably infected by now with these droids. Let's just say we used to work for Queen and country. Now, obviously there is a change in plans because of the droids so if you'll help me with the missus, we'll get you both through customs so you can be off to D.C. straightaway and Mrs. Barlow can go on safely to her sister's."

15 THE VICE-PRESIDENT DIDN'T BLINK

Tom Rogers knew he needed to hurry and get to the Vice-President's home after getting a call from Bud and Jim saying something was up. All they could relay to him in their hushed phone call was that they needed him to watch what was happening outside the VP mansion while they kept tabs on what was going on inside the mansion. They informed him that the party was in two hours and the Daughters of the American Revolutionary Patriots would soon be arriving en masse to have their annual function at the VP's home.

Tom was at his desk searching for his palm-sized tape recorder which he never went anywhere without when Mr. Gravel stormed into his office and yelled, "Rogers, just where do you think you're going? I have the Mayor's conference over at City Hall that needs covering in about an hour, so get over there before I find a new star reporter!"

Finding his tape recorder under a pile of fresh news copy, Tom popped the recorder into his coat pocket and then looked up at his boss through his reading glasses that were halfway down his nose and said, "Boss, Bud and Jim called and said something was up at the VP mansion. The VP is back and he's with a whole new bunch of friends. Something's gotta be going on!"

Gravel pulled out an unlit cigar and started chewing on the end, which was something he did when he was worried. Another reporter suddenly came running up behind Gravel, almost out of breath, and whispered something into Gravel's ear. Looking at Tom, Gravel said, "Okay, hot shot, get your butt over there! I just heard the VP is giving an announcement tonight and I want you to get an exclusive. I'll get somebody else to cover the Mayor. And listen, keep watch over Emily. If anything happens to her or to Mrs. Greenwood, I would never forgive myself."

As Tom was headed for the door, Gravel said, "Oh, wait a minute, I have something for you." Tom waited by the door until Gravel returned from his office with an object in his hand that took him by surprise. "Here, kid,"

Gravel said, as he tossed the object toward him like he was tossing a softball. "You'll probably need this," said Gravel, enjoying Tom's expression of shock.

"A Snub-nosed .38?" asked Tom, catching the pistol with both hands. "Boss, I don't have a permit for this. Are you kidding?"

Gravel just turned and headed back to his office, yelling over his shoulder, "Neither do I, kid. Now get going!"

With no time to argue, Tom put the small pistol in his coat pocket, grabbed his fedora, and headed out the door. As he was driving towards the mansion, his worries over the pistol soon faded as he started daydreaming about Emily. By the time he hit Seventh and Broad Street, just blocks away from the VP mansion, he and Emily were married and already on their honeymoon in Sanibel Island, Florida, a favorite spot of his that he had visited since he was a kid, with fond memories of sailing and snorkeling in the warm gulf waters. "Mrs. Emily Patrick Rogers!" he kept muttering to himself as he looked into Emily's clear blue eyes in his imagination.

Suddenly he heard a loud screech, followed by honking and cussing. "Damn, I ran a stop sign!" huffed Tom. "Didn't see that one coming. Better focus, Tom, old boy."

Minutes later he pulled up to the front of the mansion. As he reached for his phone to call Bud, his phone suddenly rang, startling him. "Tom, it's Bud. Are you here yet?"

"Yeah, man," answered Tom. "I'm right outside. What do you need?"

Bud warned, "Just stay put for now. I have Jim watching the library and those new agents. None of this makes sense. Secret Service protocol calls forth all newly arrived agents to meet with agents on staff for briefing. These guys are just standing around like a bunch of amateurs doing nothing. It's nuts!"

"Okay," said Tom. "Listen, have you seen Emily and Mrs. Greenwood about? Gravel was concerned."

"Yeah; they're fine," said Bud. Mrs. Greenwood is changing for the party and Emily is snooping around with this staff kid named Mara. She's cool and is in the loop as well. We asked them to check out anything suspicious and report back to us."

"Sounds like a plan," said Tom. As he was about to hang up, he said, "Bud, wait. Another Secret Service car just pulled up. Hold on, will ya?"

"Will do, partner," said Bud. "Standing by."

Tom watched as the large black Suburban town car pulled up to the front gate. Two agents got out and opened the back passenger door. A young woman who appeared to be in her early twenties stepped out, carrying a small suitcase and a yellow book bag. One of the agents offered to carry the items for the woman, but she refused, looking quite defiant. The two agents then ushered the young woman up the sidewalk, walking close to her, one on the left side of the girl and the other on the right.

Recognizing the young lady, Tom lifted the cell phone back to his ear and said, "Bud, it's Susan, the VP's daughter! Does that make sense? Harvard hasn't let out for the semester yet, I don't believe. What do you think is going on?"

"This just gets stranger and stranger," said Bud. "Don't worry, man. We'll check it out. I'll let Mrs. Greenwood know that she is here. You still stay put now, okay?"

"Okay," answered Tom, "will do. But keep an eye on my girl, will ya?"

"Emily?" asked Bud, chuckling.

"Yeah, Emily," said Tom, now feeling a little embarrassed.

"Okay, you got it, lover boy. Bud out."

***

"Darling!" shrieked Mrs. Greenwood, as she came running down the stairs with her arms open, followed closely by Bud. "What an unexpected surprise! Didn't know Harvard had let out yet."

"Hi, Mom," said Susan, as she dropped her bags and hugged her mother. "No, I'm still in session, but Daddy called me and said that he needed me home for some important reason."

That's odd, thought Mrs. Greenwood. "He didn't tell me about it," she said, as she looked over at the library door which was still shut.

"He said he had some kind of announcement to make to the press and he wanted me to be there and standing by you both when he did it," Susan elaborated. "Daddy's okay, isn't he, Mom?"

"I think so, honey," replied Mrs. Greenwood. "Come on upstairs and I'll have some lunch sent up and we can catch up before the party we are giving here tonight."

"Okay, Mom," said Susan, handing her bags to Bud. Bud gave Susan a quick kiss on the top of her head as he grabbed her bags. He then turned around and gave the new agents a hard stare. "You boys just sit here and don't move," ordered Bud, as he followed the women upstairs.

The new agents seemed a little taken aback by such a direct order, but mechanically sat down on some chairs in the foyer, staring blankly at the opposite wall.

Bud escorted the women to Susan's bedroom, and

then he and Jim took their revolvers out of their holsters, took the safeties off, returned their guns to their holsters, and guarded the bedroom door. While Susan and Mrs. Greenwood chatted and ate their lunch, Bud and Jim stayed silent, both in deep thought and wondering what the night's events would hold in store.

***

Six-thirty p.m. came fast and the guests had begun arriving, as well as various teams from the TV news and press corps, who were all being ushered into the garden where the kitchen staff was busy setting up a buffet-style dinner onto various sizes of tables that had been spread about among the lush green grass-carpeted outdoor sanctuary. TV cameras went up over the rose bushes while the various reporters were busy positioning themselves near where the Vice-President would be soon speaking over by a stone wall next to a statue of John Paul Jones, the father of the U.S. Navy.

The little old ladies of the Daughters of the American Patriots were buzzing through the house, ogling all the various paintings and antiques and making comments on either how lovely they were or how they had something better at their house. All were asking about the VP and his wife and where they were. A few of the old women had noticed that some of the Secret Service agents were acting like the stoic Queen's guards at Buckingham Palace in London and began giggling and entertaining themselves by making faces at the agents to see if they could get them to change their blank expressions.

Inside the mansion, Mrs. Greenwood and Susan were busily getting ready for the events in their upstairs quarters. Hearing a small knock on her door, she opened it to find Emily and Mara, who were back from their spying exploits and already dressed for the party.

"Come in," said Mrs. Greenwood, as she ushered the two girls in and quickly closed the door.

Susan looked surprised at seeing Emily in an outfit that she had left at the house before going to school, but thought it best to stay quiet about it and wait for an explanation.

"Susan dear, this is Emily. Emily, this is Susan, my

daughter. Emily has recently joined the staff and has already been a big comfort to me. She will be attending tonight's festivities with us and needed a proper outfit." Turning to Mara, Mrs. Greenwood asked, "Mara, could you help Susan get dressed while I speak to Emily alone?"

"Yes, ma'am, of course," said Mara, as she nodded to Emily as if they had shared some big secret. Focusing her attention on Susan, Mara said, "Good to see you, Susan. Come with me and I'll get you fixed up."

Susan could feel tension in the air, but couldn't quite put her finger on it. Before following Mara to the door, she smiled at Emily and said, "Nice to meet you, Emily."

Mrs. Greenwood took Emily's hand, almost like two old friends greeting each other, and both of the women sat down. "You look like the cat that swallowed the canary, dear. Tell me what you have found out," said Mrs. Greenwood.

Emily couldn't wait to start talking. Her reporter instincts were coming into play as she began to lay out in orderly fashion the events of the afternoon. "Mara took me to a secret attic room right above the library. We could see everything through an empty heating grate just above the bookcase next to a table where your husband and that Bergman fellow were sitting."

"Yes, I know that room," said Mrs. Greenwood. "I had meant to have it sealed off for security reasons. Anyway, could you hear what was going on?"

"Perfectly," said Emily. "This Bergman was reading a long speech to your husband, and after he read it, he had your husband repeat it back word for word, and it seemed to me it was without a single mistake!"

"That's real strange," said Mrs. Greenwood. "Are you sure that he wasn't reading it off a teleprompt that was out of your view? There is one in the library that Elliott practices on."

"Yes, I know. It was directly behind your husband. And the whole time he was staring at this Bergman and he didn't..." Emily paused, not quite sure how to describe it.

"Didn't what, dear?" asked Mrs. Greenwood.

"Well, he didn't blink at all. I swear! I kept staring at

your husband's eyes. They were almost blank, like he was in a trance. I tell you, he didn't blink not once for what felt like ten whole minutes while he repeated this speech! I always look at a person's eyes while they talk. It's a good way to read people," Emily explained.

"Well," sighed Mrs. Greenwood, as she sat up straight in her chair, "Elliott is either drugged, hypnotized, or something else that I can't think of at the moment, but one thing is for sure, he is not himself. Anything else you can tell me?"

"Yes," said Emily. "It's that Bergman person. When he wasn't giving that speech to your husband, he was ordering those agents around like they were his own personal staff, while your husband just sat there silent, doing nothing."

"He *is* drugged or in a hypnotic state!" said Mrs. Greenwood. "Elliott would never sit still and let anyone, except the President of course, throw orders around in his presence."

Mrs. Greenwood tried to compose herself after hearing all this news, while Emily put her arm around the

VP's wife to comfort her. "What would you like me to do, ma'am? I am here to help in any way I can," assured Emily.

A few silent moments went by as Mrs. Greenwood sifted through her thoughts. "Emily dear, I think I have a plan to snap my husband out of this state he's in."

"And what's that, ma'am?" asked Emily.

"Get Susan and Mara and have them in the garden as fast as you can," replied Mrs. Greenwood. "I want you and Mara seated as close to me and Susan as possible. Mara is in charge of the staff, so no one would object to the seating arrangement. I'll have Jim and Bud just behind us for extra protection. I'll fill them in on my plan on the way to the garden. I don't want to alarm my daughter, so I'll just tell her not to bother her father for anything because he is not feeling well and is under a lot of stress and not quite himself today."

"All right, Mrs. Greenwood. I'll see you downstairs," said Emily, as she got up and went to find Mara. Let's hope no one gets hurt, Emily thought to herself.

***

Thirty minutes later, with the clock striking 7:00, everyone was told to be seated as the VP would be coming out of the library and making his entrance with his family at any second. The Marine Corps band was already set up to the left of the garden doorway ready to play the VP anthem as soon as the Second Couple made their entrance.

With the guests now seated, the VP came out of the library, followed by Günther Bergman and his agents. Mrs. Greenwood had previously come downstairs, with Bud and Jim walking closely behind her. The Vice-President stopped on cue at the stairwell where his wife was waiting and extended his arm to her, but did not so much as look at her nor say anything to her. He just kept staring straight ahead towards the garden entrance! Mrs. Greenwood took her husband's arm and started to walk with him, all the while glaring at Bergman, who was trying to follow the couple as close as possible.

After a few steps, Mrs. Greenwood stopped and turned around, stared directly at Bergman and said, "He is still my husband and you are not invited."

Bergman was taken aback at this statement. He had had the impression that the VP's wife was a weak person and could be manipulated, but things appeared to be different. He decided to stop following the couple, especially since Bud and Jim were now motioning for him and his agents to stay where they were, revealing their holsters by pulling back on their suit coats. Bergman held up his right hand and signaled his men to stop as he reluctantly watched the couple continue on towards the garden.

***

The sounds of applause were heard as the VP and his wife entered the garden. The Marine Corps band struck up the Vice-Presidential theme 'Hail Columbia' as the couple made their way towards the head table. Mara, Susan, and Emily were already seated, but stood up with the rest of the guests as the second couple walked in their direction, waving at friends in the crowd and shaking extended hands as they walked. The TV cameras were on as well and a lot of flash pictures were taken as the couple was seated.

With the guests still applauding loudly, Susan, who was seated on the other side of her mother, leaned over and shouted, "Hi, Daddy! I missed you!" But her father barely looked at her. He just kept waving to the crowd in an emotionless and mechanical-like trance. Susan, with tears forming in her eyes, tried to quickly focus again on the guests, hoping her eyes would dry up and not draw attention to herself.

Soon the applause died down and the VP stood up to a small podium next to his chair. Smiling, he started to give his speech. "Welcome, Daughters of the American Patriots!"

More applause erupted as a sea of little old ladies stood up, sporting all sorts of flowered hats and waving and banging their water glasses on the white linen dinner tables, some taking out their dentures to whistle, while others were trying to wave to the TV cameras as the cameras panned the audience.

As the applause died down, the VP continued. "I am privileged here today to give you wonderful women the news that I will seek the nomination of my party for the President of the United States of America!"

The audience exploded with a riot of excitement and even stronger applause. A few of the women were overcome with emotion and fainted, causing members of the staff and some of the Marine Corps band members to come running to their aid and fetch smelling salts for them.

During this melee, Mrs. Greenwood saw her chance to put her plan into action and hopefully snap her husband out of this state of mind that he was in. Mustering up all the courage she had, she stood up next to her husband, offered him a glass of ice water to help clear his throat, and, pretending to let the glass slip, she spilled the contents all over his shirt. But her husband acted like he didn't even feel the cold water! He just kept smiling and waving at the crowd as if nothing happened.

Feeling utterly defeated and not knowing what else to do, Mrs. Greenwood started searching for a napkin to help with the spill. As she reached out to dry his shirt off, she noticed that smoke began rising from his shirt!

Suddenly his mouth became twisted and his face contorted. His eyes closed and he fell to the ground.

Screams and gasps gripped the crowd. At the same time, Bergman's agents started running towards the VP. Bud and Jim made it to the VP first, but Bergman's men poked hidden guns into their backs, causing them to back off. Mrs. Greenwood tried to get near her husband, but was pushed back and secured by more of Bergman's men who had jumped out from behind bushes. Fearing for her daughter's safety, Mrs. Greenwood turned her attention toward Susan, but it was too late. She too was being held by agents. Emily and Mara had tried to fight them off, but to no avail. All the girls were surrounded.

Bergman then entered the garden and walked up to the podium, motioning to his men to take Mrs. Greenwood and the three girls back into the mansion. Tapping on the podium microphone, he motioned to the audience and said, "It's all right, everyone. Everything is under control. Please stay where you are. The VP has had a grueling week and needs rest, that's all," he said, smiling in an eerily surreal calm manner.

"Who you are?" shouted one reporter.

"Me?" asked Bergman, with a tint of false modesty. "Why, I am an emissary from Count Drexel of Sweden to assist in Mr. Greenwood's campaign, and I'll be happy to answer any question you may have."

With no warning the press corps rushed to the podium, shouting all sorts of questions at Bergman. "One at a time, one at a time," said Bergman, holding his hand up.

As the press corps settled in with their recorders and notepads, an agent walked up to Bergman and whispered in his ear. "What are we to do with them, sir?"

"Bergman beamed a wicked smile and whispered back, "Take Mrs. Greenwood and the three younger women and lock them up in one of the upper rooms. Tie everyone up. I'll prepare their doubles later."

"And the two agents?" asked the android.

"Drug them both and put them in the basement. They may be useful to the master later," said Bergman.

"As you wish," said the droid.

***

The women were all taken at gunpoint and forced upstairs. The agents chose Susan's bedroom to throw all the women in, then sat them down in chairs and tied them all up. One agent quickly pulled down the blinds so their activities weren't visible from the street.

Outside, Tom had fallen asleep in his car while waiting for the event to end, hoping he could meet Emily in private and maybe even get an exclusive interview with the Vice-President. Something caused him to suddenly awaken, almost like a feeling of dread. Yawning, he tried to regain focus, and quickly looked at his watch and said out loud "Whoa! How long had I been asleep?

16 THE PINK POODLES

The sun had almost set over the newspaper office where Gravel was working late. Chewing on his last cigar and staring at his phone, he forced himself to focus on the view out of the large bay window overlooking Capital Avenue in Washington, D.C. The streets below looked almost lifeless and empty, with only an occasional taxi zooming by or a slow moving street sweeper meandering past the newspaper office. His cup of coffee was cold and black, like his mood. No one had dared to knock on his door since his employees learned long ago to never bother him when he wants to be alone.

He turned off the TV after seeing the VP press conference several hours earlier, convinced that his initial feelings were correct about something being very wrong at the VP mansion. No contact at all from Tom Rogers about Emily or Mrs. Greenwood. A sense of heaviness overcame him, causing him to sink further down into his large wingback leather chair. Leaning over his desk, he rested his elbows on the glass desktop, propping up his head with both hands, as he ran his fingers through his salt-and-pepper hair. Suddenly the phone rang. Jolting straight up in his chair, he snatched the phone before the second ring.

"Gravel here!"

"Lewis, it's Elliott," said a faint voice barely above a whisper.

"Elliott, I saw you pass out and hit the floor on national TV. What is going on over there?" asked Gravel.

"Okay, Lewis," said Elliott, "I just want you to sit down and listen to what I'm about to tell you. Can you do that?"

"I am sitting," grumbled Gravel, "and frankly real sick of it. Now tell me, Elliott, are you okay? Pamela contacted me last week and said she was worried about you and that these new people you have surrounded yourself with have been making her nervous. I got so concerned that I sent some of my best reporters over to the mansion to check things out, but haven't heard anything back from them, and frankly I'm getting really worried."

"I'm okay and I understand," said Elliott, "but just simmer down a minute. What I have to tell you may seem fantastic, but you gotta believe me. Everything depends on it!"

Gravel, taking a deep breath, let out a long sigh. "I am a newspaper man. I'll believe anything you say, Elliott, especially if there is a possible first-run story for me in it," he said, quickly laughing to try to interject a little levity in the conversation. "So, yeah, go ahead, buddy. I'm all ears."

"Okay, my friend, here goes," said Elliott. "First off, what you saw tonight wasn't me."

"Whaaat?" said Gravel, his voice booming so loud that the people in the outer press room stopped what they were doing and looked towards his office.

"Just hear me out," said Elliott. "I'm running out of

minutes on this damn phone card. Okay?"

"Yeah, okay, okay," said Gravel, as he sat back down in his chair.

Elliott continued. "As I said, what you saw wasn't me, but an imposter controlled by a man named Drexel. He is trying to infiltrate every level of our government and control us like puppets. What the imposter says and does is only at the whim of this Drexel guy."

"You mean this imposter is some sort of zombie or something?" asked Gravel, still trying to take it in.

"Something like that, but worse," said Elliott. It's an android that can look, act, and talk like any person this Drexel wants!"

"You mean it's a machine of some sort?" asked Gravel.

"Exactly, but a very dangerous machine that is a lot stronger than any human. And it can learn as well, which makes it almost invincible and undetectable."

"I saw this invincible machine fall down on TV after

your wife spilled something on his shirt. Maybe she discovered a weakness of some sort," said Gravel, waving at a passing copy boy outside his office who was holding up a coffee cup as a sign for a fresh cup of coffee.

"You saw my Pamela on TV?" asked Elliott, with a lump in his throat.

"And your daughter as well," said Gravel. "Susan and one of my reporters and another woman were sitting just a few yards away from yourself -- or I mean the android."

"Thank God they are okay," said Elliott, with a sigh of relief.

"That means he must need them for his cover," said Gravel.

"I hope you are right, Lewis," said Elliott. "That would buy me some time."

"Time for what?" asked Gravel. "And, by the way, where the hell are you calling from?"

Looking at his watch, Elliott said, "No time to

explain. Only a minute-and-a-half on this phone card. Listen, Lewis, I'll be in D.C. in several hours. What I need is a place I can hide out until I can figure out my next move. Any ideas?"

"Yeah. You can use the condo over in Fredericksburg. The key is under the mat," said Gravel.

"You mean your ex-wife's condo off Leafwood and Broad Street?" asked Elliott.

"Yeah, that's the one," said Gravel. "But don't worry, she's in California visiting her mother." Before Elliott could hang up, Gravel added, "Hey, listen, don't you think you'd better let the President in on this android stuff?"

"I would if I could trust any of the Secret Service or CIA, Lewis. Looks like for right now, buddy boy, I'm pretty much on my own."

"No, you're not!" snapped Gravel.

"What do you mean by that?" asked Elliott, a little surprised at Gravel's outburst of emotion.

"Because you've got me," assured Gravel. "Look, things will be clearer in the morning. Get over to the condo. The fridge is stocked and that place is real quiet and peaceful. I'll drive over and pick you up in the morning. You have a way to get there, I hope?" asked Gravel.

"Roger that," Elliott said. "It seems I was able to get a car. Listen, I am really in your debt here. I can't thank you enough."

"No, you can't," said Gravel, who always felt uncomfortable receiving or giving any kind of appreciation or gratitude for doing the right thing under any circumstance. "So forget it." With Gravel's last statement, the phone card ran out, then nothing but silence on the line.

***

The back lot of the airport where Elliott had been ushered by the last remaining MI5 agent seemed safe enough from any interference or from any potential danger. The car parked a little over twenty-five yards away was a small subcompact that had been offered to

Elliott by the agents on the direct order of Reggs. Elliott gratefully took the keys, and then the agent handed him a money clip containing close to eight hundred dollars, all in twenties, and something else. "Reggs said all of his staff carries one. He thought you should, too," said the agent, handing him a black and gold Glock 9-millimeter automatic pistol with three extra clips of ammunition.

"I am not MI5," said Elliott, as he gratefully took the gun and the ammunition.

"Neither are we, officially mate," said the agent with a wink and a grin. "Listen, mate, you'd better get going. Pretty soon the word will be out that you are still on the loose, and then more of whatever those things are will be coming after you."

"What are you going to do with those androids that tried to jump us back there?" asked Elliott, stuffing the gun and money into his coat pocket.

The agent just pointed to a propeller-driven private plane taking off on a side runway. "I'd say those fellas are now on their way to meet Reggs and have tea and biscuits and of course a long conversation. Hopefully for their sakes it won't be one-sided," said the agent, laughing.

Elliott smiled, took the keys, and pressed the unlock button, sending a small honk from the subcompact to signal that the car was now unlocked. Shaking the agent's hand, he said, "Well, I won't ask your name as I know you wouldn't give it to me anyway. Sure wish you would come to D.C. with me. I could use the help about now."

"Can't, mate," said the agent. "Have to go and make sure Mrs. Barlow has a pleasant stay here in your country. One can't be too careful. Anyway, Reggs said you are a fairly tough bloke. Just remember to shoot a little to the right of the target. Those Glock Nines carry a wallop."

"Wallop," parroted Elliott, feeling the gun in his coat pocket. "Thanks, young fella, I'll remember that," he said, shaking hands again with the tall stranger.

"Cheers," said the agent, walking off.

"Cheers," responded Elliott.

To Elliott's delight the small car was a stick shift with an inboard GPS and mapping system that would come out of the dashboard with the flick of a switch. There were also small posted sticky notes pasted over various unusual looking buttons that were in no way standard features. One note read, "Whatever you do, Elliott, don't touch this." Another two notes sitting on top of two red buttons that protruded out of the dashboard next to the cigarette lighter read, "If you get into a jam, use this for the front; use this one for the back." Elliott smiled and thought to himself, someone has been watching too many spy movies.

In the back seat was a change of clothes and a thermos of hot coffee, as well as a couple of ham and cheese sandwiches, which Elliott made quick use of both by pouring the coffee into a waiting Styrofoam cup and unwrapping one of the sandwiches.

Driving out of the parking lot, Elliott caught the "K" loop to the expressway south of Washington, D.C. Feeling tired, but relaxed, especially after he had eaten his meal and had started on his second cup of coffee, he began to think about the day and how lucky he had been to get even this far. Exiting off the "K" loop, he merged onto I-95 South and began seeing his first of many toll booths.

"Darn," he said to himself, "I don't have any quarters." Pulling up to the first booth, he pulled out one of the twenties. "Sorry, buddy, I don't have any change," Elliott said, handing the attendant the twenty dollar bill.

The attendant barely even looked at Elliott, but mechanically handed Elliott back his change in ones. The toll gate went up and Elliott drove another ten minutes until he hit the next toll booth, and then the next one and the next one. Finally running out of change from the first twenty dollar bill, Elliott pulled up to his fifth toll booth and handed the attendant another twenty dollar bill, but noticed something was very different about this attendant. As Elliott handed the man his money, the attendant looked directly at his face, emotionless, not blinking! Elliott felt a cold chill come over him. Had he been spotted? Not waiting for his change, he gunned his car and threw it into second gear, crashing through the toll gate. Seconds later he was up to seventy miles an hour and looking behind him for any sign of a chase.

"So far nothing," he said to himself, as he pulled out his Glock Nine pistol and laid it on the seat beside him. A few minutes later he saw the last toll booth between him and Washington, D.C. Instead of going through the gated lane, he slowed down and pulled his car over into a pre-paid lane which would at least allow him to get by the toll booth without smashing through another gate. Passing the toll booth, the road looked fairly clear, so he sped up to eighty miles an hour, moving over to the middle lane.

A few minutes later he happened to look up into his rearview mirror to see two large tractor-trailers speeding up behind him. "They must be doing a hundred and twenty," he thought, as he floored the accelerator, pushing the little car up to a hundred. "Not fast enough, old boy," Elliott said to the car, as he veered it all the way to the left-hand lane to avoid hitting a small pickup truck going only fifty miles an hour.

The two large tractor-trailers were closing in fast. Suddenly machine gun fire came from the truck closest to Elliott's car, hitting the trunk, with some bullets breaking the rear window, going through the passenger seat, and hitting the dash. Elliott wanted to return fire, but at this high speed he would be forced to take his hands off the steering wheel to use the pistol. Instead, he had to stay focused on his driving, so he just kept weaving his car back and forth, hoping to be less of a target.

The second tractor-trailer was now closing in on Elliott and started to open fire. "Well, old friend," looking at the sticky notes the agents had left, "I would call this a jam," said Elliott. Ripping away one of the sticky notes, he pressed the little red button. Suddenly a spray of small miniature heat-seeking missiles hissed out from under the back of the car and found their targets seconds later, sending up billows of flames, smoke and tires where seconds before there had been two large trucks.

"Maybe I could work for MI5 unofficially after all," said Elliott, smiling to himself as he threw his car out of fifth gear and down-shifted to slow the car down, blending in with the other traffic on the expressway going south. As he slowed the car back down to seventy miles an hour, he started noticing a strong smell of gas that seemed like it was coming up through the floorboard.

"Oh, no, they hit the fuel tank!" he said, as he watched the needle on the fuel gauge fall towards the empty mark. Seeing a green highway sign advertising a truck stop and restaurant at the next exit, he headed for the off ramp. Reaching the top of the ramp on a small hill, he briefly stopped at the stop sign and looked back to see if there were any more vehicles following him.

"Coast is clear. That's good I think," he said out loud as he made a right turn, spotting the truck stop about a tenth of a mile away. Hopefully he could grab a quick meal and a new phone card and then he would take a look at his vehicle.

***

The truck stop was a good choice for Elliott to blend in. He had parked his car off to the side, in between a large RV and a tour bus. His small blue compact car was well hidden. People were streaming in and out of the restaurant, some with their hands full of gifts or toys that they had bought from the tiny gift shop inside, hauling their goods to the tour bus, some escorting children or loved ones back to their cars. There were too many people to notice him or who he was.

Before he could get out of his car, Elliott noticed a

particular group of tourists that were getting off the bus parked next to him. They were all women dressed in some sort of club uniforms consisting of pink blazers, white ruffled blouses, pink slacks, white tennis shoes, and all wearing plain pink caps. Something seemed very familiar about that group of women. It wasn't until he saw the last woman get off the bus that he suddenly recognized the group and her. It was Jenny Spalding, president of the Pink Poodles Ladies Club! They had visited the White House on their annual tour almost exactly one year ago. Her tall, five-foot-eight-inch slender frame sported a pink dyed beehive hairstyle tied up in a pink and white polka-dot ribbon, all stuffed under a fluorescent pink baseball cap showered in glitter, with the word "President" emblazoned in a solid hot pink glitter glaze, projecting an unforgettable sight that had been burned in Elliott's mind over a year ago when he first met her and her club briefly in the White House foyer. "I even had a nightmare about her once," said Elliott to himself, as he shivered, turning his face away from the horrific sight and gazing in the opposite direction, waiting for the women to get past him and into the restaurant.

Elliott then put on his gray sport coat, tucking the Glock Nine in a side pocket, and walked into the restaurant, grabbing a complimentary newspaper at the checkout counter. He then found a seat at the opposite end of the dining area from where the Pink Poodles were gathered. "It's like watching a gaggle of pink human flamingos," he said to himself, shaking his head in disgust as he opened the paper in order to hide his face, waiting on his food order to arrive.

"Would you like a refill, sir?" asked a waitress, waiting to pour Elliott a fresh cup.

"Why, yes, please," he said, sliding his cup towards the waitress. "Um, tell me, ma'am, how far is it to D.C. from here?"

"Not far at all," said the waitress, pointing to the expressway. "It's about eighty or so miles south from this exit, and an easy ride, too, unlike what I just heard happened to the poor people coming in on I-95 a few miles north of here."

"What do you mean?" asked Elliott, trying to maintain a blank expression, looking directly at the waitress and hoping to sound as casual as possible.

"Oh, the massive wreck, sir, just an exit or two up the highway. I heard two tractor-trailers ran into each other and are blocking all lanes southbound," she said as she poured Elliott a fresh cup of coffee.

"Imagine that!" said Elliott, trying to look surprised and taking a sip of coffee.

"Yes, sir, imagine that," the waitress said. "Will there be anything else, sir?"

"No, ma'am. Thank you. Keep the change," said Elliott, handing the waitress a twenty dollar bill.

"Why, thank you, sir! Your breakfast was nowhere near that, but I appreciate the tip!" said the waitress as she almost snatched the bill out of Elliott's hand.

A small rumble of chairs could be heard as the women from the Pink Poodles Club pushed away from their tables after having finished their breakfast and were making their way towards the gift shop directly behind where Elliott was sitting. Elliott quickly put the paper back up in front of his face and pretended to be reading it in order to remain unrecognized by any of the women, especially the president. When they had all made their way past him and he could hear them making comments about which souvenirs they would like, he relaxed a bit, putting his paper down again.

Outside the restaurant window he immediately noticed two well dressed men in grey suits and red ties, wearing sunglasses, looking over his bullet-ridden car. One of the men bent down and looked as if he was feeling the underside of the vehicle for some sort of device. Both men's movements were very natural and free form, but droids, Elliott knew, could easily mimic the movement of people. But seeing these men moving and twisting their bodies with such ease halted the notion that they were droids in Elliott's mind. Droids would move in a more stilted fashion.

"They must be Drexel's goons, but how did they find me?" Elliott said out loud as he slowly got up from his chair and headed into the direction of the crowded gift shop, not worrying anymore about being recognized by the president of the Pink Poodles Club, but certainly worried about being spotted in the middle of the less crowded restaurant.

"Got to talk to Lewis again", he thought, as he grabbed and paid for a half-hour phone card. Taking the card, he slipped into the rear of the gift shop, unnoticed, to a pay phone by the back restrooms. He then quickly dialed Lewis Gravel's number, only to be met by Lewis' answering machine.

"Damn, what do I do now?" he said, as he hung up the phone, now watching the front door for the two men to come in and start looking for him at any second.

Over by the greeting cards stood Jenny Spalding, thumbing over card after card on the twirling rack, humming some tune. Thinking for a second, Elliott had an idea that just might get him out of the truck stop without being spotted by these two men. Walking straight up to Jenny, he stood directly behind her and could hear her muttering something to herself about finding the perfect souvenir card for her Aunt Edna in Pittsburgh that lived alone with her nine cats.

Clearing his throat, he said, "Excuse me, ma'am." The woman, a little startled but curious as to who wanted to speak to her, turned around and looked at Elliott, face to face. "You may not recognize --"

Before Elliott could finish his sentence, the woman's expression exploded with excitement and she started jumping up and down, her bouncing beehive hair throwing off the sparkling pink cap that hung onto her head with one small hairclip. "Why, you are Vice-President Elliott Greenwood! I can't believe this, me and the Vice-President having a conversation right here in the middle of -- of --"

"Maryland," Elliott interjected dryly, while he brought his finger to his lips, hoping she'd get the point.

"Yes, Maryland," responded Jenny in a hushed tone, taking the hint, while looking around to see if anyone in her club had heard her. They hadn't.

Elliott whispered, "I may have need of you and your club's assistance, ma'am. It is of the utmost urgent national matter. Can you help me?"

"Why, yes, sir, anything you need, anything at all!" whispered Jenny, standing wide-eyed at attention like a soldier. "What do you need?"

"First, can you tell me where your group is headed?" Elliott asked.

"Yes, Mr. Vice-President --"

"Please, call me Elliott," said the VP, smiling.

"Why, yes, of course, Mr. -- I mean Elliott. And please, you can call me Jenny. We are headed to Washington, D.C., for our annual tour of the White House. We met once, you know," she said, slightly blushing.

"Yes, yes, I remember, Jenny," said Elliott, thinking how he could ever forget. "And I'm glad you are headed to D.C. You see, I have these two bad men following me and --"

"Where?" interjected Jenny, looking around the gift shop.

"No, no, please don't look around," begged Elliott, gently taking her hand and kissing it to get her to face him again. "They are outside for now."

Jenny's face became flushed, but the trick worked and she became calm and attentive.

"You see, Jenny, I am alone with no Secret Service help and my car is broken down," explained Elliott. "I must get back to D.C. as fast as possible. Is there any way I can ride with all of you back to D.C.?"

"Of course you can, Elliott, but..."

Elliott's eye caught the two men as they were coming through the front door, apparently looking around for him. Fortunately, she and Jenny were well hidden, thanks to the many large gift displays. Jenny had stopped talking in mid-sentence when she saw Elliott's face tense up and then immediately drops his gaze to the floor.

"They are inside the store now, aren't they, Elliott?" asked Jenny, sounding more serious and in charge than she had just moments before, finally realizing the nature of the situation.

"Yes, Jenny, but I think they are moving toward the restaurant," said Elliott, as he stole a glance and followed the men with his eyes as they walked towards the open dining area.

"Well, then, we will have to make you one of us very quickly so they won't see you!" Jenny said. "Stay here, Elliott, and watch the Pink Poodles in action!"

Jenny's take-charge attitude startled Elliott for a moment, but before he could ask what she intended to do, Jenny quickly turned and walked over to some of the ladies in her club who were standing by the crafts section of the gift shop. Seconds later, the once noisy group became very quiet and all eyes were now staring back at Elliott. Jenny then took a large pink blazer off one of her more hefty members, as well as a pink cap off another, and started walking back towards Elliott. He noticed the other women who had been previously staring at him now starting to scatter throughout the shop like little bees, whispering to other members who were mingling about, filling them in on the details of their rescue scheme.

"Here, Elliott," said Jenny, placing the pink blazer over Elliott's jacket, resting it on his shoulders, and then reaching up to put the pink cap on his head. "This should help."

"What's going on?" asked the confused VP, looking around, watching as all the club members started towards him from all parts of the store, surrounding him like some giant pink escort, while one Pink Poodles member remained as a lookout just out of the sight of the men who were still conducting a search of the restaurant area. Suddenly the lookout waved her arm, signaling for the other women to escort Elliott out of the store.

"It's okay," Jenny said. "Those men just sat down at a table. Apparently breakfast wins over looking for you," she said, grinning. She tugged on his pink jacket sleeve and said, "Let's go."

"I feel ridiculous," moaned Elliott out loud, as he became the center of a long silent moving pink line heading out the door.

As he was walking with the women towards the bus, Elliott took a sideways glance at the restaurant and its two occupants who had sat down and were being waited on by the same waitress that had waited on him minutes before. Their faces were buried in their menus, and so far they had not looked up.

Jenny, walked by his right side while trying to shield as much as she could of her new famous friend. Whispering through her teeth and trying not to move her lips she said, "Have they seen us yet? How are we doing?"

"So far so good," Elliott whispered back, now looking straight ahead, intent on making it to the bus.

"Maybe you're mistaken about these two men," said Jenny, as they reached the open doorway of the tour bus.

"No way; they are the bad guys all right. Here, look at that dark blue sedan sitting in the parking lot twenty feet from my car," said Elliott, pointing.

"Yes, I see it. But so what?" asked Jenny.

"They always travel in those exact same types of cars. And do you notice something else?" asked Elliott, now pointing at the driver's side door of the sedan.

"Yes," said Jenny, "I see what looks like --" then she paused and her voice quivered "-- bullet holes?" But she already knew the answer to her question.

"Yes, exactly, bullet holes," answered Elliott. "They must have ricocheted off the pavement from the machine gun fire when some other people were chasing me earlier. Funny thing, though, I never saw this car after me, only the tractor-trailers."

"Machine guns? Tractor-trailers? Bullet holes?" asked Jenny, grabbing the railing on the steps of the bus. "Mr. Vice-President, let's get on board now!"

***

The bus quickly filled up with the Pink Poodles and their newest member. Jenny made a quick introduction to the bus driver, telling him their new passenger was a very important guest, but she couldn't reveal his identity. The bus driver seemed not at all to care, but just muttered something about getting paid for it anyway and went back to his sports magazine while he waited for the women to board.

Jenny seated Elliott in the seat across the aisle from hers over the objection of some of the members who wanted the VP to sit next to them. The oldest and loudest member, Doris, was particularly vocal about wanting the Vice-President to come back and sit with her, but was shouted down by Edna, the treasurer, who said, "Knock it off, Doris; you haven't even paid your dues yet, so no dibs on the hunk."

Doris, indignant at Edna's announcing out loud in front of everybody that her dues weren't paid, shouted back while shaking her fist, "Well, I would have, Edna, but you took forever to cash my last check and I forgot about it, which caused my checking account to bounce, costing me three hundred dollars!"

Instantly an argument ensued, not only between Edna and Doris, but other members who were quick to take sides, some stating Doris was right or Edna was right, and all of them seemed quick to forget about Elliott sitting in the front of the bus, which was just fine by him. He took off the pink blazer that was still wrapped around his shoulders and slumped down in the plush seat, winked at Jenny across the aisle, and pulled the pink cap over his eyes and tried to go to sleep. Jenny leaned forward and told the bus driver to never mind the noise and she would pay him a little extra for his inconvenience, to which the bus driver smiled and nodded, closed the bus door, and pulled the vehicle out of the parking lot and onto the expressway, heading south to Washington D.C.

***

For thirty minutes the ride went smooth and uneventful. The members had all quieted down, with a few mutual apologies being exchanged, but none between Edna and Doris, who just sat in their seats quietly while angrily glaring at each other. Elliott was now snoring loud enough to be heard throughout the bus cabin, but no one dared try waking him since they all knew that he must need the rest after his adventures of running from what they all were now calling "the bad men."

The bus was at cruising speed when suddenly there was a loud popping sound followed by a rapid "bump, bump, bump" sound coming from the back of the bus.

"Oh, no," moaned the bus driver. "We must have blown a tire. I better pull over at the next exit just up the way here." Elliott shot up out of his seat when he heard the bus driver making his plans to stop and asked Jenny to tell the driver not to stop just yet while he ran to the back of the bus to look out of the window. Sure enough, when he got to the back window, he saw just ten feet away from the right side of the bus the same two men in the dark blue sedan who were at the restaurant, and now they were shooting at the back tires!

"Damn! They must have gotten my description from that waitress," he said, pulling out his Glock semi-automatic pistol. Then he shouted, "Everyone get down now!"

Kicking out the back window amidst the screaming and shouting from the club members, including the driver, Elliott opened fire at the fast moving car, missing the occupants, but putting holes into the roof of the sedan. The return fire from the sedan sprayed the whole bus with bullets, blowing out most of the windows and sending glass everywhere. A stray bullet even hit the driver in the right shoulder, causing the bus to swerve violently and cross three lanes, ending up in the far left lane and sending cars leaping off the expressway and rolling into the grassy median.

Jenny jumped up and helped the driver regain control of the bus by grabbing the steering wheel and keeping it steady. The driver bravely said, "Here, just get a rag and put a pressure point on the wound while I keep driving." Trying to reassure Jenny that he was okay, he added, "And, by the way, I'm getting extra for this, right?"

Jenny winked and said, "You betcha, cutie," as she slid off her red silk scarf and wadded it up, pushing it hard against the wound in his shoulder while giving him a quick kiss on the top of his head.

Doris, knocked to the floor by the sudden swerving of the bus, reached up and grabbed her oversized purple and gold cloth purse from the seat and opened it, exposing a large 45-caliber standard Army issue pistol.

Edna shouted, "Doris, we told you before never to bring that thing on our trips again!"

Doris shouted back, "Shut up, Edna, I am saving your oversized backside!" She reached down into her purse, producing a clip, and shoved it into the receptacle of the pistol. As she got onto her feet and ran, crouched down, to the back of the bus where Elliott was trying to eject his used clip, she hollered, "It's lock-and-load time! Go Army! Step aside, sonny, and let the retired First Sergeant Doris Kowalski, United States Army Marksman Corps, show you how it's done!"

Before Elliott could object, she pushed the VP down into a seat, and then stood directly in the doorway of the rear end of the bus, holding the 45-caliber in both hands with arms out, taking aim at the car now only a few yards away.

Having seen a new head pop into view, Drexel's men started firing directly at her, knocking off her grayish-purple wig, revealing her short gray hair under a hairnet. But unfeigned and not moving an inch, Doris kept steady aim at the two men, firing two quick shots in succession, killing them both instantly, at which point their car went out of control and caught fire, rolling off the steep right bank of the expressway and crashing into a clump of trees and exploding into a huge fireball of orange and red flames.

Elliott, amazed at what he'd just saw, stood up and grabbed Doris, giving her a bear hug and saying, "You are incredible! I'm putting you in for the Congressional Medal of Honor when all this is over with!"

Doris, taking her pistol barrel up to her lips and blowing away the smoke, replied, "No thanks, sweetie; I already got one back in '74."

Meanwhile, up front, the bus driver had started feeling queasy and was close to passing out when Jenny grabbed the steering wheel again and told him to help her pull the bus over and get it stopped. Ambulance and police sirens could be heard as they came off the exit ramp just a quarter of a mile ahead. When the bus was finally stopped, Jenny noticed a small black helicopter landing a hundred feet away with a British flag on the side. She called Elliott to the front and asked him if that was more trouble, to which Elliott replied, "No; I think my ride is here."

"Well, then, Mr. Vice-President, I think you had better get going," said Jenny. "I know you don't want to be around when the police and the reporters get here."

"That's true enough," said Elliott, "but first I must do something." Then, standing at the front of the bus, he yelled, "Ladies, may I have your attention, please!"

All the women, who were trying to find their seats again, became quiet so that Elliott could speak.

"I want you all to hold up your right hand and repeat after me," said Elliott.

The women, still somewhat dazed from the preceding events, obediently held up their right hands, ready to repeat what he was about to say.

Elliott continued, "All right, repeat after me. I swear..."

The women all said at once, "I swear..."

"... that what has just happened never really happened, and I, your Vice-President, was never here."

The women repeated what Elliott said word for word and then waited in silence for the next round of words, but Elliott only said, "Congratulations, ladies! You may put your hands down now. You are all now honorary Secret Service agents under my staff and command. Thank you all and goodbye!" With that,

Elliott jumped off the bus and headed toward the waiting helicopter.

***

"Thought you were in England, you liar!" said Elliott to his friend.

"Naw, mate. My boys took the droids all right, but I wanted to stick around just in case you got in over your head, and it looks like you did a little," laughed Reggs.

"You bugged my car, didn't you, Reggs?" asked Elliott, in full appreciation of what Reggs had done.

"And your gun, too, mate. But after seeing all that carnage on the highway, you weren't that hard to track, making those bugs pretty unnecessary. C'mon, let's go rescue your wife and daughter."

The helicopter lifted off the ground as all the police, firemen, and ambulances surrounded the bus. As they flew away, Elliott took one last look at the events below him and watched Jenny helping the bus driver into a waiting ambulance. "What a great gal she turned out to be!", he thought.

17 THE BLINDS ARE CLOSED AT THE VICE-PRESIDENT'S MANSON

It was late at the Vice-President's mansion. The sun had already set and was replaced by outside security lights surrounding the house and grounds. All the dignitaries, members of the press, and the entourage of the Daughters of the American Patriots had long left the garden party. Günther Bergman and a few of his men had taken the VP android and had left as well, going to the airport to board his private plane that would take them back to the lab in Gotland. Günther realized that he had to get this new creation back to the lab before any more of Drexel's prized droid's complex circuitry could corrode due to the water that the VP's wife had thrown on it earlier that evening. The rest of his men could stay with the women they had tied up and secured until he gave them further orders.

***

Tom didn't know how long he had been asleep. He was in his car, parked on a side street and totally unnoticed by anyone. His tape recorder was still on where earlier he had been taking notes on who went in and out of the mansion. Looking at his cell phone, he noticed it had been accidentally set on vibrate, which was not good. Suddenly his tape recorder started automatically rewinding and the high-pitched whirling noise jerked him farther out of his sleepy state.

"I can't believe it!" Tom said, annoyed at his falling asleep, trying to see his watch by the street lights' glow overhead. "That's what I get for not stopping and getting a thermos full of coffee before coming here."

Tom looked at his cell phone again and discovered that his battery was dead, and he then remembered he left the charger back at the office on his desk.

"Aww, just great! Old Man Gravel will bust me down to writing obits for not reporting in," he said to himself as he splashed some water on his face from a half-empty bottle of water.

Drying his face off with his sleeve, he yawned and took out a small pair of binoculars and started panning around the Vice-President's home, trying to see any signs of movement. Except for the outside lights and the downstairs foyer lights, he saw little else. He then panned towards the upstairs windows of the huge monstrosity of a home and noticed they were all dark. Making another quick sweep with the binoculars, a dim light caught his eye that he didn't notice the first time coming from one of the upper level windows. His insides started quivering. This was the signal that he and Emily had earlier agreed upon. The light was coming from the VP's daughter's bedroom window and the blinds were closed!

"I don't believe it!" he said out loud, as he furiously fumbled around for the small 38-caliber pistol that Gravel had given him earlier in the evening. "If anything happens to her, I'll never forgive myself," said Tom, thinking about Emily as his hands finally found the butt of the pistol wedged under the passenger seat. "Thank God," he whispered, as he hastily put the gun in his coat pocket and quietly opened the car door.

No one was patrolling on the grounds that Tom could see, so he walked straight up to the tall, black iron picketed fence. A convenient overhanging oak tree limb jutted out past the fence which Tom eyed, trying to size it up to see if it would hold him. Tom carefully inspected the fence for any type of trip wires or sensors that might be in place to set off an alarm. Seeing none, he jumped up and caught the tree limb with one hand while putting his left foot on a crossbar of the iron gate. He then pushed himself higher until he caught the limb with his other hand and pulled up both legs, wrapping them around the rough bark of the oak tree and started moving forward over the top of the fence like an inchworm moves across a leaf.

Passing over the fence and only eight feet from the ground, he was about to let go of the limb and drop to the ground when suddenly he heard what sounded like several sets of footsteps walking toward him. The gaits of those steps were slow and not rushed. Tom stopped all movement and just hung there on the limb like an opossum would while trying to evade an enemy.

The footsteps grew louder and he could hear muffled voices that sounded like they were speaking in a language he couldn't understand. Then the footsteps stopped and the voices were coming from directly under him! Because he was hanging upside down, he couldn't see what was happening just a few feet below him. He tried to stop his breathing so he could hear every nuance of movement from the men below. His heart was now pounding alarm and fear into his brain. Just then he heard a click. Was that a gun, thought Tom, as he felt his heart almost stop.

What seemed like an eternity later, but was only seconds, he heard puffing sounds followed by the familiar smell of cigarette smoke. The two men below him were puffing away and laughing at something that was said between them in their foreign language. When he heard the clicking noise again, he realized it was the closing of a cigarette lighter.

After a few seconds more the men moved on, their footsteps growing fainter and fainter. The fear left Tom as fast as it had come and his body became limp with relief to the point of almost losing his grip and falling, but he managed to compose himself and hang there totally motionless until he couldn't hear the footsteps any longer. Swinging his legs down first, he then dropped silently to the ground and hurried to the limestone brick wall of the VP mansion that was some thirty feet below the dimly lit window with the shades drawn.

"No nice tree limbs here," he thought to himself as he looked up at the window.

Tom started looking around for the nearest entrance point into the house. Finally he noticed an open basement window not far away that had what looked like an old coal chute running through the middle of it. "Perfect," thought Tom, as he quickly headed for the chute.

Thankfully this part of the house was unlit, and he kept close to the wall of the mansion, blending in with the shadows as he crept towards the chute. Upon reaching the window, he looked down into the blackness of the chute, took a deep breath, and, grabbing the metal top of the chute, jumped into the tube-like structure, sliding down the chute like a lumpy sack of coal. It didn't take long to reach the bottom, landing feet first on the dark concrete basement floor in a cloud of coal dust.

Coughing, he wiped the coal dust from his face with his coat lapel and looked around. The basement was cool and spacious, with a high ceiling and four other outside basement windows that had beams of light shining down through them from the security lights outside, offering enough light to help him maneuver. Looking around for a way out of the basement, he noticed something peculiar at the opposite end of the large room. Creeping slightly closer for a better look, it appeared to be two figures slumped down on the floor next to a door, which probably was the exit he needed. Cautiously he walked towards them, training his gun on the motionless figures. When he reached them, he looked straight down at them, horrified at what he saw. In the dim beam of light he recognized one of them to be his friend Bud, who was tied up and appeared to be in some type of trance-like state. Quickly he pulled out a small pocket knife that he always had with him for the purpose of sharpening pencils and furiously started cutting at the ropes that were tied around Bud's hands and feet.

Bud let out a small moan when Tom tried to move

him.

"Bud, it's me, Tom," he said, as he patted his friend's face.

Bud, as if half asleep and barely able to move, started to mutter something. "They drugged me and Jim - must get help - too weak to move - save them." Then Bud stopped talking and rolled over on one side and quit moving.

"Save who, Bud, save who? Come on, old friend, speak to me," begged Tom, gently shaking the large Secret Service agent.

A few seconds went by and Bud, weaker than before, barely whispered, "Mrs. Greenwood and the others, they're being held prisoner upstairs in the daughter's room. Secret passageway to upstairs from room next door," he managed to say before finally passing out, and this time Tom couldn't revive him.

Tom knew the drugs wouldn't wear off anytime soon, so he quickly untied Jim and then left them both to go find the secret passageway. Putting his ear to the basement door, Tom listened for any movement. There was only silence. Luckily there was no lock on the door, so Tom gently turned the old-fashioned brass door knob and slowly pushed the door open, looking straight down the basement hallway to a small red door to the left. That had to be the room Bud was talking about.

Opening the door wider, Tom looked both ways down the hall. The coast was clear. He then quietly closed the door, making only the sound of a small muffled click as the door closed shut, and headed for the next room. Standing outside the red door, he listened again for any sounds coming from inside. No sound. He then gently opened the red door and quickly went in, closing the door behind him.

Looking around, he saw it was a small room with a refrigerator, a small sink, a coffee maker, and a plain rounded table with what looked like some leftover birthday cake loosely covered in foil. A lit lamp on a small stand stood off in the corner by some sort of opening in the drywall, revealing the brick of the outside wall of the mansion. In the middle of the opening was a wooden ladder that seemed permanently fixed in place.

The ladder appeared to have been there for a very long time.

"That's gotta be it!" said Tom to himself as he headed towards the opening.

Grabbing the rungs of the ladder, Tom looked up and saw beams of light coming in through various cracks in the upstairs flooring. Quietly he started his accent up the ladder, wondering how he would find an opening that would leave him unnoticed as he moved about. Five minutes into his climb he began to hear the sound of female voices, whispering. The voices seemed to come out of thin air and from no particular direction. From what he could tell being suspended forty feet up on a ladder in mid air, he could be near where the women were being held captive, but in the dimly lit vertical crawlspace he couldn't make out any opening. Climbing a few more steps, he suddenly stopped. One of the voices he could hear whispering was that of Emily and her voice seemed to be coming from just beyond a brick wall only inches in front of him!

Excited at hearing Emily's voice, he tapped on the

brick wall with the metal end of his pocket knife and said, "Hello, Emily, is that you? It's me, Tom. I've come to get you out of here."

A brief moment of silence went by, and then the whispering voices increased in pitch and excitement. One of the voices, what seemed like that of an older woman, seemed to dominate the conversation, and Tom could hear her saying, "Pull the lever by the fireplace, dear, and stand back."

Suddenly there was a scraping sound as the brick wall opened up, exposing a brightly lit room and revealing the four captive women. Three of the women were standing just a few feet from Tom, while the fourth was sitting down in a green armchair with a white folded napkin over her forehead, her feet propped up on an antique footstool, and smiling at their rescuer.

Tom quickly left the ladder and stepped into the room. Emily couldn't restrain herself and ran over to Tom, throwing her arms around him and burying her face in his coal dust-covered jacket and saying, "I knew you would get here, I just knew it," almost sobbing as she said it. Then realizing what she was doing, she stepped back in embarrassment, trying to regain some of her composure, and said, "I mean I'm glad you are here. I, uh, have lots," she paused for a second to clear her throat, "of things to report back to you and Mr. Gravel."

Tom was thrilled that he saw this side of Emily, which he knew unmistakably, revealed that deep down she had strong feelings for him. The other women kind of nodded to each other and smiled at Emily, knowing she was obviously in love with this fine young reporter.

"I too am glad you have come for us, young man, but you will have to forgive me for not standing up. My ankle was badly twisted during our capture," said Pamela Greenwood.

"That's true," said Susan, the VP's daughter. "My mother is in no condition to walk, much less attempt an escape from this place, and I can't leave her."

"Nor will I," said Mara, bringing over some freshly brewed tea for Tom from a small microwave that was sitting by a tiny sink in the corner of the room. "Madam is in no condition to go anywhere. Here, sit down and we will bring you up to speed on what has happened."

Mara motioned for Tom to sit down in a chair by the fireplace, and everyone, especially Emily, filled him in on what had happened over the past evening's activities. Tom, taking sips in between each story that grew more and more incredible, finally drained his cup and shook his head in disbelief at the accomplishments of Drexel.

"Why can't we just go to the police or FBI or even the CIA?" asked Tom, which was followed by a chorus of "No!" from all four women.

"Not while my husband is in the hands of this Bergman person or his boss, Drexel," said Pamela Greenwood. "I don't know where he is or what he will do to my Elliott, but you can be sure that these people are dangerous and have probably infiltrated the Secret Service, and may already have agents in the CIA and FBI. Just get back to your boss, Mr. Gravel. He is a smart man and knows many insiders in Washington. He'll help me and he'll find the right people to rescue us. Poor Bud and Jim, I hope they are still alive."

"They will be fine, Mrs. Greenwood," said Tom. "I

found them in the basement not more than a half hour ago. They will just have to sleep off the drugs that Drexel's men gave them, though." Grabbing Emily's hand, Tom added, "Don't worry, we will be back to save you and everyone and we'll find your husband."

Mrs. Greenwood seemed to relax and smile a bit, feeling comforted at Tom's reassuring statement.

"We?" asked Emily. "What do you mean by saying 'we' will be back? If Mara and Susan won't leave Mrs. Greenwood, how could I?"

"Because Tom needs you, dear, and I need you to go and help him figure out how to save us all," said Mrs. Greenwood.

If Emily was relieved at Mrs. Greenwood's statement, she didn't show it, feeling as she did that somehow she was leaving her new-found friends who were still in danger while she runs to safety. But dutifully complying with Mrs. Greenwood's request, she put on her coat and grabbed some notes that she took in Susan's room during her brief capture.

"All right, Mrs. Greenwood, I'll go, but under protest. We will get help and bring you all to safety."

Mrs. Greenwood hugged Emily and said, "You and your young man please be careful."

"He's not my young..." started Emily, but stopped herself in mid-sentence and turned away, blushing and trying not to smile.

Tom wanted to give Emily a way out of an obviously embarrassing moment, said, "We had better get going. Is there another way out than through the basement?"

"Yes," said Mara. "If you continue up the ladder, you will see a private walkway going all the way across the house to another ladder. That ladder takes you directly down to the other side of the mansion and then to a private exit way that is covered in ivy that leads directly out into the garden, fifteen feet or so from an unpatrolled opening in the gate. Once you're through the gate, you step directly out into the street and to safety."

"Simple and direct," said Tom, walking over to Mrs. Greenwood. "Madam," said Tom, gently taking her hand

and kissing it, "We will return, this I promise."

"I know you will," said Mrs. Greenwood weakly. She then leaned back in the chair and closed her eyes.

Tom and Emily headed for the ladder. He had Emily go up first in the event she slipped on the rungs and he had to be there to catch her. Before he stepped out onto the ladder to follow after Emily, he motioned for Mara to come over to where he was, away from Mrs. Greenwood and her daughter, so as not to alarm them. Curious, Mara walked over to him, and he reached into his pocket and showed her the pistol and whispered, "Do you know how to use this?"

Mara beamed a wide smile and whispered back, "My father was an FBI agent. I could shoot before I could ride a bicycle."

"Good," he said, handing her the gun. "This is just in case," he said, as he turned around to grab the ladder.

"Just in case," she whispered back. "Good luck!"

***

Just as Mara had said, the ladder went straight up to an overhanging catwalk that was independently hung from the ceiling so anyone using it could safely walk across it without making any sounds on the ceiling rafters below. Both Tom and Emily quickly made it to the other side of the house and down the ladder to a small bricked archway leading straight out into the garden. No lights were present on that part of the house, thus making it an easy walk to the secret opening in the gate, through some thick hedges, and stepping right out into the street.

"My car is just a block away," whispered Tom to Emily, who had just taken off her shoes so as not to make any sounds on the pavement.

"Good," said Emily. "The sooner we get to your car, the sooner we can call Mr. Gravel."

Tom sheepishly replied, "Uh, that, uh, might be kind of hard to do. I kind of let the battery die on my cell phone and the charger is back at the office."

"You what!" said Emily, loud enough to attract the attention of two agents who were standing unnoticed on the other side of the fence.

Tom, looking out of the corner of his eye, saw the two men approaching them. He quickly thought of a plan, knowing that now he was unarmed and he couldn't outrun them, especially with Emily having just taken off her shoes.

Before Emily had a chance to see the men coming towards them, Tom turned to Emily and whispered, "Do exactly what I do."

Before Emily could respond, he took her in his arms and gave her a passionate, long kiss, with Emily's eyes wide open in surprise and his mouth muffling her protests. Seconds later, she closed her eyes and her muffled voice went silent as she gave in and her arms encircled him, totally forgetting about the approaching agents.

Still kissing Emily, Tom looked up and saw that the agents had turned around and were heading back on their regular route. His plan worked! Once he was sure all was okay, he gently pushed away from Emily, who clearly wanted to continue kissing him, tightening her hold on his neck. He then kissed her again and said, "We had better get going; the agents are gone."

Emily, still in a daze, said, "The what -- who -- oh, yeah, the agents," as she let Tom go, picking her shoes up off the ground that she had dropped in surprise when Tom kissed her. Still not clear about what he was talking about, she asked again, "What agents?"

"The agents that were walking towards us," said Tom.

"Oh, *those* agents," she said, trying to act as if she really knew what he was talking about. Putting on her shoes, she said, "I guess we had better get going."

The brief walk to the car was silent. Both Tom and Emily didn't feel the need to talk about anything. They just held hands, not looking at each other. Upon reaching the car, Tom unlocked Emily's side first, and Emily, without even looking back at the mansion, whispered, "Oh, look, agents!" and threw her arms around Tom and started giving him a long kiss. Tom, just to be sure, looked up towards the mansion grounds and, seeing nothing, closed his eyes and kissed her back passionately, encircling his arms around her waist tightly and running his hand through her soft blonde hair. Pulling away for the second time, he whispered in her ear, "We had better get back. And, by the way, I love you."

Emily didn't seem at all surprised when she heard these words come out of her mouth in response as she was about to get into the car. "Yes, Tom," she whispered back, "I love you, too. I really, really do."

18 DREXELS NEXT VICTIM - THE QUEEN

Drexel and his younger brother, Olaf, stood alone in the highest tower of Saint Magnus Cathedral in the Orkney Island Scottish town of Kirkwall, which sits directly across the bay from Balfour Castle. Looking through his telescope past Balfour's walled gardens and almost at the edge of the heavily oaked woods Drexel could see Lord Hawthorne's private helicopter that Olaf had flown the Hawthorne droid replacement in with the night before.

The Hawthorne droid was waiting at the front of the castle for the arrival of the Queen's royal helicopter that would be landing in about fifteen minutes if it was on time, at which point the Queen would retire that morning to rest up for an afternoon of horseback riding with Lord Hawthorne on the castle grounds. The Queen felt it important to get to know Lord Hawthorne on a personal basis, seeing that he would most likely be voted in as the new Prime Minister next month, and the horseback ride through the Orkney Island of Shapinsay, on the Balfour

Castle grounds, gave the Queen the opportunity to combine business with her favorite pastime of being out in the fresh air in this beautiful setting. Here on this quiet island the Queen could at least feel some peace from the hectic pace of Buckingham Palace, while at the same time privately form some sort of bond with a future elected leader of the British people.

Back at the cathedral, Drexel, like a general, was directing his men that were hidden on the other side of the Balfour Castle grounds to be ready to handle the capture of the Queen and to deal with her private royal security staff. Drexel was getting extremely nervous at this new mission of his creation. To Drexel this would be his greatest accomplishment, kidnapping the Queen and replacing her with a droid right under the noses of her own security guards without leaving any trace of suspicion!

He had earlier forgiven his brother for letting Elliott get the best of him back on Gotland and escaping. Olaf had let his brother keep on believing, as he had since they were children, that he was a bungler and generally incompetent and that he had truly been overpowered by the Vice-President. But Olaf was still the only person in the world that Drexel trusted besides Günther Bergman and, as such, they were the only two men in the world that had the courage to speak their minds on matters of importance to Drexel.

As they stood at the cathedral tower, Olaf, speaking in Swedish, said, "Honestly, brother," as he took the telescope from Drexel to look out at the castle, "I don't like this business at all. I hope you understand that this is the most powerful and well loved figure in the world."

"And the richest, don't forget the richest," said Drexel, squeaking out a broken high-pitched laugh as he took the telescope back from his brother so he could keep his eye on the droid who was still standing in front of the castle.

"So it's about money, then," said Olaf, frowning at his brother.

"Umm, well, in this case the money can't hurt. After all, she *is* the richest woman in the world," said Drexel, setting down the telescope and pulling up a chair, watching his brother grab a coffee pot on a nearby bench and pouring them both a cup of coffee.

"That's my point, brother," said Olaf. "There are easier ways to get large sums of money to fund your operations than trying to do something as dangerous as this."

"Yes, but you are missing the point, Olaf," said Drexel, now turning serious. "Think a minute, dear brother, of all the world leaders the Queen comes in contact with."

"I don't follow your logic," said Olaf, putting a herring on a stale cracker left for them by one of the monks earlier that morning.

"That is why I am where I am and you," said Drexel as he rolled his eyes, "are where you are." Look, the Queen gives private audiences with just about every leader in the world, except the President of the United States, whose secret service stay so close to him that he is never really alone, even with the Queen." Then Drexel paused for a second to check his watch.

"All right, I am beginning to understand a little bit.

Go on, brother," said Olaf.

"Well, even you probably can figure out the rest, how easy it would be to schedule an audience with, say, the President of France or Russia or even the Premier of China! All we have to do is know in advance who is coming so that we have time to make ready a droid replacement of anyone we wish, and it's all done within the privacy of the Queen's chambers and no one would ever be the wiser," said Drexel, starting to cackle again at his own cleverness.

"Makes sense," said Olaf, pondering it over in his mind. "Uh, you, of course, are not going to do away with the Queen, are you?" he asked, looking straight into Drexel's cold blue eyes.

"No, of course not," said Drexel. "I need her alive. That woman has over three generations of British secrets tucked away in her royal brain. As a matter of fact, that's where you come in, brother."

Me?" said Olaf, starting to feel really uncomfortable at where this conversation was going with his brother.

"Yes," said Drexel, as he stood up and walked back over to the tower window in order to scan the castle grounds again. Turning back to Olaf, he continued, "You are to take personal charge of the Queen once you fly her back to Gotland. Make sure she is comfortable in every way and that she understands that I have complete power over her and that if I so desire any information from her, she will either give it to me or..." Drexel paused, letting his thoughts drift to the repercussions he would make the Queen suffer if she became disobedient.

"Or what?" asked Olaf.

"Or someone in her precious royal family dies the instant she refuses me any information that I desire!" growled Drexel, turning his back on his brother and raising the telescope again to his eye. "So you had better get going to the other side of the island, Olaf. That blue fishing boat down at the pier below us will take you back to Hawthorne's helicopter on the back of the island. And this time..." Drexel paused again and turned to face his brother, who had started putting on his leather flying jacket. "And this time, Olaf..."

"Yes, brother?" responded Olaf.

"This time, dear Olaf, try not to let a prisoner overpower you when you bring in their dinner, even if the prisoner is an 88-year-old woman!" Drexel cackled, then gave his brother a wink.

Olaf shrugged, gave a weak smile back at his brother, and headed silently out the door, thinking to himself that if there was any trace of humanity still left in his brother's soul that he may have just seen a tiny glimmer of it in that quick wink. As Olaf walked down the spiraling cathedral stairwell, he comforted himself in one major part of his brother's plan, and that was he would have personal charge of the Queen and could protect her from any of Gotland's staff or droids, and he swore to himself then and there that he would make it his mission in life to find an opportunity to rescue her and get her back to England when the opportunity presented itself. But now no such opportunity was apparent.

***

The wobbling roar of the Royal British RAF Wessex helicopter quickly replaced the placid musical chirping of the Shapinsay island song birds heard a few minutes earlier as it flew over Balfour Castle's front lawn, blowing away what was left of the morning fog hanging low on the freshly cut dew-soaked dark green Bermuda grass. Five men, all wearing side arms and military style waistcoats, jumped out of the helicopter seconds before the craft gently touched down only yards away from the Hawthorne droid, who just stood there on the front stone steps of the castle, waiting to become the familiar personage of the now dead Lord Hawthorne, his eyes fixed on the stepladder that had been immediately hooked onto the open doorway of the helicopter where the Queen herself would soon appear.

Slowly and deliberately the Queen, the object of Drexel's desire, wearing a blue-gray tweed dress ensemble, stepped onto the small stepladder, holding onto the rail with one hand and her rounded-brim pink straw hat with the other. Her medium-gray hair pulled neatly back into a bun revealed a strong, yet pleasant, feminine face that sported an aquiline nose and a wide grin as she looked up through her thick black glasses at the immobile droid Hawthorne.

Drexel had worked especially hard on his most advanced model, programming every conceivable fact he knew of the British protocol on how a lord should act and talk in front of the Queen. With this Hawthorne droid model, Drexel wanted perfection in every detail of thought and action, almost to the point of making the droid human.

The Queen approached with her royal protection service men at her side, one of whom gave the Queen his arm as a gesture of love and respect, as if the royal woman was his own elderly mother, while at the same time looking at the droid that stood before them in suspicion. The droid stood still, as protocol dictated, until the Queen was within ten feet of him, and at that point the droid took a deep bow and uttered, "Your Majesty," taking the Queen's extended arm and briefly kissing her white gloved hand.

"Lord Hawthorne, how nice to see you." Pausing for a minute, the Queen looked in the direction of the stables down the hill and to the left of the castle's small red bricked bakery. With excitement in her eyes, she asked, "Are you ready for a romp this afternoon?"

"Yes, Your Majesty. I do believe that the stable staff has your favorite horse, Wind Rider, saddled and ready to go at your pleasure."

"Wonderful!" said the Queen, "but first let's you and I have a little morning repast in the east room with that gorgeous view of the sun rising over the sea. I find such inspiration in the sea. Don't you, Lord Hawthorne?"

"Yes, mum, of course. All true Britons love the sea and are bound to it," said the droid, as if on cue.

"Well spoken, young man," said the Queen, turning to her royal guard as she approached the castle's front entrance where the household staff was already lined up and ready to bow as soon as she set foot on the castle foyer. "Gerald, you and the lads can take a breather; as you can see, I am in good hands. Why don't you all go down to the stable and have them saddle some fine mounts for all of you while I confer with Lord Hawthorne here," she said. Then, turning to the droid, she whispered in his ear, "They really hate to be separated from me, even for an instant!"

"Yes, mum," said Gerald, who was the officer in

charge of the five men, still eyeing the droid. "We'll be only an instant away if you need us, mum." The lead officer then turned around and reluctantly headed towards the stable, followed by his men, muttering to himself aloud and within earshot of the droid's keen ears, "Mates, there is something not right with that Hawthorne bloke, not right at all!"

***

Morning quickly turned into the afternoon as all the remaining morning mist and fog burned away to reveal rolling hills and pastures, some of it being hemmed in by four-foot-high slate stone walls that stretched as far as the eye could see, following narrow packed dirt roads as they meandered throughout the island. Horse trails and foot paths also wound in and out of open pastures and deep woods, some trails coming to an abrupt stop as they dead-ended upon high limestone cliffs that dropped hundreds of feet straight down below to a sea crashing its foamy fury on large jagged boulders.

Promptly at noon a line of well groomed Andalusian horses from the castle's stables were all saddled up and waiting for the Queen and her party of guards, as well as the droid Hawthorne, at the front entrance.

"Please inform Her Majesty that all is ready for their ride this afternoon," announced the stable master, holding the reins of the Queen's favorite horse, Wind Rider.

The Queen finally came out first, as protocol demands, followed by the droid Hawthorne and three of her royal protection guards who are required to give the Queen some privacy by riding fifty yards behind her at all times and to only approach her if she so wishes.

"Lord Hawthorne, I have been on horseback for eighty of my eight-eight years. Do you think you can keep up with me?" asked the Queen amidst the muffled laughter of her guards as she was being helped up onto her horse by the stable master.

"Missing the joke entirely, the droid dryly responded, "Why, yes, Your Majesty, I'll do my best."

"Well, then, young man," said the Queen, as she took the reins of her horse, "watch and learn! Tally Ho!" The

Queen shook the reins and thumped her riding crop on the horse beneath her, making the horse go from a full stance position to a respectable trot in a matter of seconds, followed by the droid and the three royal guards who kept back from the couple at their respectable pace.

"You ride well," said the Queen, as the droid finally caught up with her, riding now parallel to Her Majesty.

"Thank you, Your Majesty, as do you," said the droid. After a few minutes of riding in silence beside the Queen, the droid said, "Your Majesty, may I suggest a different path to try rather than the one we are now on?"

The Queen thought for a moment and then, looking at the droid, said, "By all means, Lord Hawthorne! I am feeling a wee bit adventurous this morning. Lead on!"

The droid then rode out ahead of the Queen, leading her on a path that took them away from the open pasture and into the thick oak woods.

Following closely behind and seeing that they were headed towards the tree line, the Queen said, "I say, Lord Hawthorne, this path is unknown to me. Are you sure we can safely ride in there?"

"Perfectly safe, Your Majesty," said the droid. "I'll stay in the lead, if you don't mind, and all you need to do is follow me closely.

"I will, Lord Hawthorne, but mind you I wish to open Wind Rider's gait a bit and these woods are too confining, so before long let's go back out into the open," the Queen requested.

"A few minutes more, Your Majesty, and all will be well," answered the droid, as he turned sharply towards the right, leading them off the path they were on and onto another path, briefly disappearing from the Queen's sight.

Searching for the droid as she continued her course into the dark woods, the Queen yelled, "Hello, Lord Hawthorne, I can't see you. Are you there?"

"I'm just ahead of you," the droid yelled back. "Keep coming. Why, Your Majesty, I think I see open pastures just ahead of us!"

"Well, it's about time," said the Queen, who had

begun to feel a little alarmed at being so alone in the darkening woods. Her faithful guards, who before could be easily seen, had vanished from her view, causing an uneasiness to grow inside her.

Continuing on, a few more tense minutes passed and there was still no sight of Lord Hawthorne. Finally, the Queen's temper started to flare. Yelling into the emptiness in front of her, she said, "Really, Lord Hawthorne, I --" Suddenly the Queen pulled back on her horse's reins, seeing something ahead that made her think she was losing her mind! On the narrow path in front of her was a woman, sitting on the same type of Andalusian horse that she was riding on, a woman that looked exactly like her, right down to the kangaroo leather riding boots and her diamond-studded hair pin given to her by her husband on their fiftieth wedding anniversary!

"Who are you? I say, who are --" Before the Queen could finish her question, she felt a tiny prick on the side of her neck, and then there was darkness.

Drexel's men quickly appeared from the bushes that lined both sides of the narrow path, catching the Queen as she fell off her horse, unconscious. Doubling back, the droid rode up to the men and said, "Take her immediately to the helicopter as the master has commanded, and hurry, get out of sight, I hear her men coming up the trail!"

"Yes, sir!" said one of the men, placing the Queen on a stretcher and hurrying off towards the direction of the helicopter, silently disappearing into the thick woods.

After the men were out of sight, the droid turned toward the other woman and bowed, saying, "Your Majesty, shall we go back to the castle now?"

"Why, yes, Lord Hawthorne," said the Queen droid. "I have much to do when I get back to Buckingham Palace, much to do!" And with that, the fake queen took the lead and headed back down the path towards Balfour.

***

Off in the distance, back at the cathedral, Drexel watched Lord Hawthorne's helicopter rise up into the air and slowly turn out to sea in the direction of Gotland. Smugly he said to himself, "Game set and match, dear

Queen. I always wanted to rule this little island of England." Grabbing his telescope, he walked down the tower stairwell, feeling the joy of total victory.

19 THE QUEEN IS ABDUCTED

Olaf quickly took the helicopter up, with the Queen still unconscious and lying on a field cot only a few feet behind him in the middle compartment. One solitary guard from Drexel's castle sat a few feet away from the monarch, making sure she didn't spill off the cot in the event of sudden bumpy weather.

Olaf set the course for Gotland, taking the most direct route over the North Sea, which could possibly mean rough weather ahead. He secretly wished he could just turn the helicopter around and head for Buckingham Palace and the English authorities, but he knew well that his brother had far too much control of the government, and besides, he thought, who would believe him? Also the possibility of the drugs wearing off before he got the Queen to Gotland bothered him greatly. How could he explain to her what happened? Or worse, what if she started pleading for him to help her? If she did that, he knew for sure he couldn't refuse the elderly monarch and would try and most likely fail at getting her back to British authorities. He knew deep down that at present the safest course of action would be to go ahead and get her to Gotland where he could make her comfortable and where there was medical staff if the need arose. Besides, he thought, even my brother would keep the Queen alive if not just for her invaluable information on the operations of the British government, then at least in case his empire started to crumble and he needed a supreme hostage for his quick escape.

With those thoughts churning around in his head, he turned his craft eastward towards the North Sea and Gotland. For three hours the trip was uneventful, with Olaf turning back to the guard every now and then, asking how the Queen was doing. The guard would always give the same answer of "still out, Captain." Three quarters of the way to Gotland, the afternoon sky was getting cloudier, flying at ten thousand feet. Becoming more alarmed because he was losing visibility, Olaf went to twenty thousand feet to get a better view and monitor the ship-to-shore radio traffic for a weather report. Over the static he heard that an unusual polar front was sliding down from the Arctic Circle, creating an unstable air mass over most of northern Europe, and that soon gale force winds would be blowing in from the northeast at about sixty to seventy miles per hour. His helicopter was currently flying about a hundred and fifty miles per hour, which meant that the gale force winds would soon begin to push him sideways somewhat, reducing his speed down to a hundred and ten miles per hour.

That wind would cost me another forty minutes in the air, Olaf said to himself, noticing that his fuel gauge was sitting a little over a quarter of a tank.

"Captain?" said the guard.

"What is it, Bjorn?" asked Olaf, a little annoyed at being interrupted from his continual monitoring of the weather reports.

"It's starting to get bumpy back here. Should I strap the Queen in her cot?"

"No, no, don't do that!" said Olaf. "Strapping her in might cut off her circulation. Grab as many cushions as you can and set them around her body, then scoot the cot against the wall and lean with your back against the cot.

That should steady her somewhat. And Bjorn..."

"Yes, captain?"

"Put your parachute on," said Olaf. "It is going to get real rough in about twenty minutes or so. There is a bad storm front coming in." Olaf paused for a few seconds and said, "Just in case, son."

"Yes, sir, but what about the Queen?" said the young sergeant.

"If you can manage it without stress on her arms or chest, get a parachute on the Queen, but most likely if we have to bail, one of us will have to carry her down with one of us."

"Err, yes, sir," said Bjorn. "I'll do what I can, sir."

"That's a good lad," said Olaf. "Now throw me my parachute."

The young sergeant lost no time in tossing a parachute to the front cabin, with Olaf catching it and quickly sliding the parachute onto his shoulders while trying to hold firmly onto the helicopter joy stick which, due to the increasing winds, was becoming harder to maintain control of. Some minutes passed and the visibility went from a manageable eighty percent down to almost zero. A heavy wall of thunder clouds started to envelope the helicopter with strong updrafts, followed by a loud staccato of hail pelting the metal craft like bullets hitting a tin can. The craft was soon lit up with an artillery barrage of lightning in quick succession of flashes, with cannon-like thunder drowning out the noise of the helicopter's engines and almost drowning out the voices of the two men shouting back and forth to each other.

"How far is Gotland, Captain?" yelled the sergeant, bracing himself against the cot as hard as he could with the Queen still sleeping amidst the chaos of the tiny helicopter cabin.

"Too damn far, I think, and I don't have enough fuel to go around this storm. We'll have to keep flying in a straight line," shouted Olaf," with his eye on the fuel gauge, which now appeared to be a little above the empty mark. "My instruments have gone out and this storm is eating up our fuel! We'll have to take her down to eight thousand feet. Hopefully it will be clear enough to get our bearings."

"Yes, sir," responded the sergeant, checking to make sure his parachute was on tight.

At that moment he noticed a slight movement from the Queen. "Uh, sir?" said the sergeant.

"Kind of busy, boy. What is it?" asked Olaf, as he descended through the storm almost at a forty-five degree angle, seeing nothing but boiling gray masses of clouds passing by his cockpit windshield.

"The Queen, sir! She's awake!" yelled the young soldier over the roar of the storm.

"She's what?" said Olaf, taking a quick look over his shoulder. But before the soldier could respond, Olaf watched as the Queen rose up and hit the young man as hard as she could with her fist while trying to get off the cot. Despite that, the sergeant was still trying desperately to keep her pinned down so she wouldn't bounce all over the shaking cabin.

"You monster!" shouted the Queen, as she continued

her struggle with her captor, now turned guardian.

"Keep her steady!" shouted Olaf, suddenly seeing a clearing patch of sky coming up in front of him, revealing just a few miles away the rugged coast of Gotland. "Thank God my calculations were incorrect, he said to himself as he leveled off his craft, steering to the upcoming rocky coast on the front side of the island.

Suddenly a loud clap of thunder, sounding like it was just a few feet away from Olaf, boomed all through the cabin, knocking out the Queen and the sergeant, who both fell unconscious to the floor, followed by a sickening high-pitched whine of the engine slowly winding down in sound until there was nothing to be heard but the sound of the whistling wind blowing around the doomed aircraft which was now falling rapidly toward the cold sea.

Olaf dashed back to the unconscious pair and started shaking the sergeant and slapping his face in an effort to wake him up. "Bjorn! Bjorn, wake up! We're falling! We have to bail now!"

There was no response from the young soldier.

Seeing a water bottle in a compartment above the young man's head, he quickly grabbed it and threw the remaining contents in the man's face, reviving him to consciousness. Olaf grabbed the sergeant and carried him over to the side door of the aircraft. Standing him up, he opened the panel door, letting in the wind and rain, which helped the soldier come to his senses. The young man weakly nodded in agreement.

"We are almost to the island! Jump!" commanded Olaf. He then pushed the young man out, while grabbing his rip cord for him. Olaf watched as the parachute safely opened and the soldier started his descent. Then, almost cat-like, he turned and grabbed the Queen in one fell swoop, throwing her over his shoulder, and in two leaps he was out the door of the falling helicopter, completely clearing the plunging aircraft before opening his own parachute, still roughly three thousand feet above the stormy sea.

The wind was terrific. It took the parachute and caught it like a sail, blowing it towards the island's jagged cliffs. Olaf could see Bjorn's bright orange parachute directly below him, now headed straight for the cliffs, with no chance of escaping death. And worse, it looked like the soldier was out cold again, hanging from his parachute like a rag doll!

An idea came quickly to Olaf's mind. They were now only several hundred yards away from the island, so he thought instead of trying to go above the cliffs, he would aim for a small strip of sandy beach that was at the bottom of the cliffs, hoping that would be soft enough for them to land on. Knowing the odds of hitting that small beach would be almost impossible, he still had to try.

Balancing the Queen on his shoulder with one hand, he grabbed his service knife with the other and cut several of the main cords to his parachute, letting out some of the air, causing him to fall fast enough to catch up with the sergeant's parachute. Touching the top of the parachute with his feet, it allowed him to push some air out of the young soldier's parachute, making him fall faster to the sea and closer to the beach, which was now yards within their reach. Still too high, he cut several more cords, which allowed more weight on the bottom parachute, causing the unconscious soldier's feet to touch the top of the sea surf. Seconds later the sergeant's parachute landed on the sand, dragging the sergeant across the sand and coming to a stop at the base of the jagged rocks. Olaf cut three more cords and dropped ten feet, landing onto the beach himself, still upright and still holding onto the unconscious Queen. They had made it!

As exhausted as he felt, he knew none of them would get far in this weather. Looking around, he spotted a small cave at the base of the cliff which looked like it would make a safe shelter from the wind and rain. Steadying himself, he quickly carried the Queen to the small cave opening and gently put her down, leaning her against a dry sandbar. He retrieved what was left of his parachute and wrapped it around the unconscious monarch several times, which provided her some insulation from the cold and would help prevent her body temperature from dropping any further.

Next he turned his attention to the sergeant who was lying prone on the beach some yards away, his parachute still flapping wildly in the wind. Leaving the Queen, he ran over to his comrade and called out, "Bjorn, are you all right? Falling down in the sand beside him, he noticed the young man was beginning to show signs of life.

"Yes, sir, I think so," said Bjorn, trying to stand up. "Nothing is broken, but I have a terrible headache."

"Easy, son. We'll get you back to the cave and then I'll go get help," said Olaf, helping Bjorn to his feet.

"No need for that, Captain," said Bjorn. Reaching into his pants pocket, he pulled out a small black waterproof case, unzipped it and pulled out a small hand-held radio. "I thought it might be useful, so I stuffed it into my pocket before I put on my parachute," he said, holding up the radio to a delighted Olaf.

"I'm glad I saved your life!" said Olaf, winking at the young sergeant.

Taking the radio, Olaf switched the dial to an SOS frequency that would start sending out an automatic distress call. Within seconds he could hear the series of steady beeps. "Come on, young hero, let's get you to the cave and out of this weather. We should be picked up in fifteen minutes or so," said Olaf, guiding Bjorn towards the cave.

It wasn't very long before a swarm of small helicopters landed on the small beach. The castle's medical team jumped out first, running towards Olaf who was standing outside the mouth of the cave, waving and pointing to the occupants inside.

"Be careful of the Queen. She had a very rough flight and she is still unconscious," Olaf said to the medical team as they rushed to put the Queen and Bjorn onto stretchers.

"We thought you had crashed at sea," said one of the pilots as he shook Olaf's hand.

"We almost did," said Olaf, looking back out at the horizon and rough surf.

"Well," said the pilot, "that was a neat bit of flying. How you bailed out in a storm and made it back here alive is a story we all at the castle will be telling for some time."

"Don't count on my brother regaling my exploits about the castle," said Olaf, accepting a cigarette from the pilot as they walked back to an awaiting helicopter.

"You would be surprised," the pilot responded, leaning over with a cigarette lighter to light up Olaf's cigarette.

"How's that?" asked Olaf, taking a long puff and blowing it out the side of his mouth to avoid the wind blowing it back in his face.

"Well, I just got a message a few minutes ago from your brother saying that you have risen up a notch in his already high opinion of you and that one day he may even let you run all the operations here at Gotland!" Olaf laughed, as did the pilot, almost beaming with pride as he opened the side panel of the helicopter while placing his jacket over Olaf's shoulders.

Before Olaf got into the helicopter, he took one last long puff of the cigarette, looked around at the sea that had almost been his watery grave as almost a badge of remembrance of his most recent deeds, and then flicked the cigarette onto the beach, saying quietly to himself, "I always assumed that honor would go to Günther Bergman, but if it is to be a contest, I'll have to try to come out on top. I have always thought that Gotland needed a new change of management." Then he got into the helicopter and took off.

***

The next morning was as quiet and beautiful as the previous day had been gray and stormy. The morning sky had broken out into a glut of small puffy white clouds, reflecting the faint rose-colored morning sun's rays as a small army of seagulls flew about the diamond-sparkling sea looking for their first meal of the day.

In a room at the top of the castle keep was one high-arched lead crystal glass window with a view that looked out over all the courtyard of perfectly mowed grass, interlaced with large gray and flat cobblestones. This opulent corner of the castle was now the Queen's new quarters at Gotland. Her high-canopied, solid oak bed with double down mattresses were surrounded with various Swedish tapestries of ancient Viking exploits hanging down from the rough hewn castle stone walls, interlaced with paintings of Drexel's ancestors all in various poses befitting nobility.

The Queen noticed that some nobles were on

horseback, some were pointing off in the distance, while some were just standing there looking complacent or arrogant, or both. One painting in particular was of a modern noble that wore a gray business suit, with a know-it-all smirk that seemed to leap out from the painting and demand the viewer's full attention. Then suddenly a memory flash acting like a lighting rod filled her mind with the image of the same Count Drexel that she saw earlier some weeks ago at the Club 17 on Fleet Street. "Count Drexel"?" she gasped out loud.

"That would be my brother," said a voice from the doorway, as Olaf politely knocked on the bedroom door that was standing slightly open. The Queen had been up for several hours with an array of medicines and hot tea at her beside. Her rosy complexion, unlike her white chalked face the night before, had returned. She had a nurse sitting on the other side of her bed watching her every move, and was basically acting more like a chambermaid than a professional nurse, retrieving anything the Queen wanted.

Now staring at Olaf, the Queen answered, "You must be the young man who saved my life," as she pulled the collar of her blue robe closer to her neck.

"Yes, Your Highness. We both had a rough night," said Olaf, still standing in the doorway, waiting for the Queen to give an indication of permission that he was allowed to enter the room.

Still staring at Olaf with a puzzled look on her face, the Queen finally said, "Oh, where are my manners. Please do come in and sit down by me here," as she pointed to a thatched wooded straight-back chair near her bed. "I have many questions to ask, and for some reason I feel I can trust you."

Olaf silently gave a quick bow and obediently sat down in the chair beside the Queen.

"You must forgive my staring, young man, as I ascertain that my glasses are now at the bottom of the sea?" asked the Queen.

"Probably so, Your Highness," said Olaf, offering to refresh her cup of tea.

Shaking her head no to Olaf's offer, the Queen asked, "Then if this old gray head of mine understands this situation I am in, am I to assume that I am being held as some sort of prisoner?" Courage showed on her face, but her insides trembled in fear, knowing the answer she would hear.

"Not mine, I assure you, Your Majesty. I am, though, unfortunately, the brother of your captor." Then Olaf paused, looking at the Queen, who remained almost expressionless at the news he was telling her. "However, I swear on my life to you that I will let no harm come to your person while you are here!" said Olaf, tempted to take another bow, given his awe of her dignity and her very presence.

"Well," said the Queen, "I trust that I have a friend and ally here in this strange place. And, by the way..." The Queen paused and pointed towards Olaf, expecting him to reveal his name.

Olaf understood the gesture and replied, "Olaf. My name is Olaf."

"Well, young Olaf, can you tell me where exactly we are?" asked the Queen as she pointed to the window.

"We are on an island in the Baltic Sea, ma'am, not too far from Sweden," said Olaf, as he produced an old wrinkled map from his pocket that showed the island and its distance from Sweden. Olaf found the Queen to be very direct in her questioning and he quickly understood that she was a person of no nonsense, expecting direct answers. It was probably a necessary trait for her position, being the defender of her country.

"Then I expect your brother wants something of me, then, Olaf," said the Queen, taking the map out of his hand and studying its contents.

"Yes, he does!" said a voice behind Olaf. Drexel barged into the room without any pretense of respect, walking over to the end of the bed and looking at the Queen with contempt.

"Remember your promise, Olaf," whispered the Queen, as she stared directly into Drexel's pale blue eyes.

Before Olaf could answer, Drexel grabbed a foot stool, waved the nurse out of the room, and sat down, saying, "Oh, you needn't worry about your safety, Your Highness," he said with sarcasm as he stood up and gave an exaggerated bow to mock the old woman. "I would never harm you, as you are way too valuable a prize to be hurt in any manner, but --"

"But *what,* you coward?" snapped the Queen, her cheeks turning fiery red.

Laughing, Drexel continued, "But if you don't behave, my dear Bonnie, Prince what's-his-name might have a nasty polo accident at the club or your young grandsons, princes that they are, might suddenly disappear from visiting their "grandmum" in her lovely country mansion, never to be found again, and, oh, wouldn't you make a lovely grieving widow at your husband's funeral after his plane crashes in the Scottish highlands --"

"That's enough, brother!" shouted Olaf, standing up with his fists clenched. "You are speaking to the Queen of England and you are dishonoring our family name."

"Oh, sit down, Olaf. I have to leave anyway. You have done me a great service in getting the Queen here, but don't test my patience. My goals are far bigger than any brotherly feelings we might have, so don't get too much in the way or you might find yourself at the bottom of the sea with the Queen's glasses."

Sensing Olaf's surprise, Drexel continued, "Yes, I was eavesdropping, brother. And as to the family name, well, it was the British bankers that ruined our father and sent him into a mental hospital and to his untimely death, so you might keep that in mind next time you wish to pledge your loyalty oath to the Queen."

Then turning his attention to the Queen, he said, "Madam," giving another fake bow, "until we meet again in how you English people say a fortnight, and I will have some really good questions for you and you will give me some really good answers, I'm sure."

"Olaf, you stay here and attend to Her Majesty all you want to, and please emphasize to her that cooperation with me is her only option!" said Drexel as he left the room, slamming the door behind him.

Olaf looked at the Queen's shocked face, stepped over to her bed, kneeled down by her side and said, "Your Majesty, command me and I will obey."

"The Queen looked down at the kneeling Olaf and squeaked out the words, "Olaf, I want to go home."

"Then home you shall go," said Olaf, standing up and taking her hand to kiss it. I must leave for a bit, but I will return and get you out of here long before my brother comes back." Turning from the Queen, he spit at his brother's picture on the wall. "I'll send the nurse back in. Goodbye for now!"

"Goodbye, sir knight," said the Queen with a weak smile. Then she closed her tear-stained eyes to go to sleep as Olaf quietly left the room.

20 REGGS AND ELLIOTT TO THE RESCUE

Coming at a high altitude over the Potomac River in Washington, D.C., on a pitch black, moonless night, were two marble black helicopters flying in perfect formation so close to each other that through the reflection of the cockpit lights the crew of each helicopter could see their comrades in the other craft making ready their parachutes for the upcoming jump.

Suddenly a quick burst of static could be heard, followed by an unknown voice barking orders over the radio. "Unidentified aircraft, this is Air Force Washington Command. You have two seconds to turn around or you will be shot down by two approaching F-16s on your flank and coming up fast."

"I thought you had gotten us clearance, commander?" asked a very nervous MI5 pilot as he prepared to veer off his target.

"Nonsense, mate. You just let ol' Reggs handle these

buggers." Reggs patted the young pilot on the shoulder while pressing his microphone button. "This is code clearance 555 on a training mission rescue. Do you copy, Air Force Washington Command?"

There was a few seconds of nervous radio silence, followed by the familiar voice that was just heard seconds before, except the tone was more conciliatory. "Yes, sir, we have confirmation on the highest level. You are free to proceed. Good luck."

"Roger that, mate. Over and out!" said Reggs, as he switched the radio button off. He then gave a thumbs up sign to the other helicopter.

"How did you do that, sir," asked the young pilot.

"In this town it's not what you know, mate, but sometimes who you know," laughed Reggs.

"*Who* you know, sir?" asked the pilot, beginning his turn toward their target.

"That radio silence was compliments of our friend the Vice-President taking control of the situation on the ground at the Pentagon," explained Reggs.

Turning around to the members of the team squatted down in the cabin behind him, Reggs said, "Okay, mates, drop zone in four minutes. Everyone got their secret weapon?"

"Not funny, sir," grumbled a soldier named Herbert as he held up a water gun they had purchased the day before at a local suburban Washington, D.C. discount store. "Honestly sir, I don't fancy risking my life" - pointing at his water soaker rifle that was complete with pump action plastic pink and blue grips - "over some kid's toy against real danger, sir." There was a muffled agreement in the form of "hear, hear" echoed from Herbert's comrades.

Reggs never really got mad in front of his men, especially before a dangerous mission, so instead of yelling, his cheeks turned fiery red as he let out a low growl, snatching the water rifle out of Herbert's hands and holding it up high for all to see. "Listen, mates, if any of you want to give me back this *toy*, as you call it, go ahead, but before you do, you might want to consider this." Then, taking the water gun, he pointed it at Herbert and barely squeezed the trigger, producing a short blast of water to Herbert's face, watching Herbert react the way Reggs expected him to.

"Hey, what did you do?" asked Herbert, wiping his face with his jacket sleeve as the rest of the men chuckled.

"Are you a droid, mate?" asked Reggs, with a totally blank expression on his face.

"You know I'm not!" Herbert shot back, turning red in the face with embarrassment.

"What if you were a droid? Would you be just sitting there like a jackanapes wiping water off your face, or would you be a crumpled up heap of circuits?" Reggs waited for the obvious answer.

"Heap of circuits, sir," Herbert responded weakly.

"Right then," said Reggs, tossing the water rifle back to the man.

Letting the mood in the helicopter cabin turn serious, Reggs said, "Mates, we just have one shot at this and I want every one focused on this one hundred and one percent." Then, taking out a cigarette, he paused while Herbert leaned over and lit it for him. Reggs took a puff and continued. "Miss Patrick, if I may remind you of what she told us back in briefing, said the women are being held in the northwest side of the mansion. Unfortunately, that's where all the trees are and we can't land near there, not to mention that everyone, with the exception of a few of Drexel's men and the two Secret Service agents tied up in the basement, are droids. So as Team One in the other chopper lands in the garden behind the mansion, I need some volunteers to land with me on the roof top. Who's with me?"

There was some surprised grumbling among the men before one spoke up. "That wasn't in the briefing, sir," said John, squatting next to Herbert.

"I know, lad, I know," answered Reggs, "but something in this playbook just wasn't adding up and now I think I finally know what it is."

"What's that, sir?" asked John, who quickly added, "And, by the way, I'm in, sir." Most of the other men joined in by saying "me, too" and "count me in." Herbert remained quiet as he took the cigarette out of his commander's mouth and drew a few puffs on it himself. Throwing it on the aircraft's metal floor, he used his boot heel to extinguish it before speaking. "You are not leaving me out either, sir. I'm in, too."

"Good, lads!" said Reggs. "Now, as to what I figured out, once we got airborne I thought about something Miss Patrick said about how the droids behave or might behave."

"Behave, sir?" asked John.

"Yes, John. Miss Patrick said the night of the big press conference, once all hell broke loose after the droid VP had water thrown on him by his wife, that she heard Bergman utter the words 'inga doda.'"

"So?" asked John, waiting on Reggs to explain.

"Well, Miss Patrick looked it up in a Swedish dictionary and it means 'no kill,' which tells me that these droid buggers start killing humans as a programmatic reaction to any signs of trouble. So --"

"Which means", Herbert interrupted, "that we've got to get to the captives within minutes of landing or the droids, without Bergman or Drexel there to command them, otherwise, will automatically start killing them."

"Precisely, lad," said Reggs, turning his attention to the ground beneath them.

"Thirty seconds to drop, sir," yelled the pilot.

After scanning the site beneath him one last time, he said, "Okay, lads, the roof is the only dark spot on the mansion grounds. Everything else is lit up. Let's go!"

Suddenly both helicopters let their side doors open and fourteen figures all seemed at once to melt into the blackness five thousand feet over the quiet Washington, D.C. neighborhood where the Vice-President's wife, daughter, and Mara, their faithful employee, were being held in a corner room, otherwise known as the VP's daughter's old bedroom.

The VP mansion sat at the end of a cul-de-sac and was surrounded by smaller Victorian homes built around the turn of the late nineteenth century, complete with fake gas-lit lamp posts and high iron rail gates with sharp edges which could prove to be decorative death traps to anyone landing with a parachute, not to mention the power lines that entwined through the neighborhood or the many large oak trees.

All fourteen figures, dressed in black and looking more like ninjas than MI5 commandos, shot down through the night at a hundred and fifty miles per hour, approaching from the southwest side of the mansion where the spacious gardens were located. Within minutes all the parachutes opened, causing their speed to slow to thirty miles per hour, still much too fast for an urban night landing. But with only four hundred feet to go, they had to make it work.

***

Pamela Greenwood loved looking out at the gardens, even at night with the grounds lit up. The gardens were full of roses and daffodils, with quaint stone walkways meandering their way throughout the lush garden grounds. The only hindrance were the ceramic white statues of garden nymphs, cherubs, and deer, something she detested and meant to have replaced as soon as they moved into the mansion, but never got around to it. But now even they gave her comfort as she stared out at them and their almost magical appearance from the corner room in the mansion which had become her prison.

It was ten o'clock in the evening and Mara and Susan were making hot cocoa in the microwave to sooth Pamela's headache. Mrs. Greenwood was a strong woman and wasn't so much worried for herself or her daughter's safety, given that they were really of no possible use to this Count Drexel, but her thoughts rested on her husband and his whereabouts and whether he was even alive, let alone would he be able to come rescue them.

Susan sensed her mother's feelings as she handed her the steaming cocoa. "Mom, Dad's okay. I just know it. And you know it. He'll stop at nothing to get to us. Remember when I was at camp and my canoe tipped me and my friends into the lake? Dad ran and jumped thirty feet into the air, swinging from a vine and dropping into the lake from the high bank above us, singing the camp song as he swam toward us to make us laugh so we wouldn't panic."

Pamela let herself break into a smile as she remembered that day, while seeming to look off into the distance as she took a sip of her cocoa.

"And Mom, Dad saved us all, even Lizzie Bitterman who couldn't even swim. Lizzie thought that Dad was so funny and she kept laughing as she hung onto the upside-down canoe while Dad pushed us all to the shoreline." Susan was glad to see her mom smile.

Pamela Greenwood leaned back in her armchair, holding her cup and saucer, and closed her eyes. Her tense facial features relaxed, causing the rest of her body to follow in the same manner.

Mara, the Greenwood's employee, was touched by the story that Susan told and began to think of her own family as she walked over to the window, looking out through the tree branches and to the mansion grounds below. Then suddenly, with no warning, appeared a man just a few feet from the window, swinging back and forth like a pendulum, dangling upside-down from what looked like a bunch of kite strings that were attached to the surrounding trees! He was dressed in a black sweater, black pants, a black knit cap, and had a pistol on his side. He was holding what looked like a large squirt gun and appeared to be smiling. It was the strangest sight she had ever seen in her life!

Getting the sense it wasn't one of Drexel's men or his droids, she threw open the window, but before she could speak, the man in black said, "Uh, excuse me, miss, but I suppose you are one of the women who needs rescuing?"

Mara let out a small yelp of excitement, causing Susan and her mother to both run to the window to see what was going on. "Pull him in!" whispered Mrs. Greenwood, trying not to draw the attention of their guards outside the door.

Grabbing a fireplace poker, Mara tried to snag the upside-down man by the parachute strings. The man tried to help by swinging his body towards the direction of the window, bumping against the shutters once or twice, but eluding the girls' grasp. But the third try with the poker was successful and snagged the parachute cords directly above his head, giving the man a second or two of momentum in order to swing his body directly at the window, where he caught the window sill with both his legs. For a few seconds he hung there motionless, half his body in the window and the other half hanging like a puppet caught up in its own strings.

"Err, miss, reach and grab my knife from its sheath and hand it to me and I'll do the rest," said the man.

Mara, still grasping the fireplace poker with one hand while the other two women also held onto the poker, reached over towards the man's thigh and unbuckled the top strap, pulling out the man's service knife. She handed it to him and he immediately cut the strings above his head, causing him to drop flat against the side of the house while his legs were still draped over the window sill and now were supporting his full weight.

"Pull him up!" Pamela Greenwood said, as she let go of the poker and rushed over by Mara, who was pressing against the man's legs so as not to let him slip away and fall. Susan, leaning out the window, reached down and grabbed the man's right arm while her mother grabbed his left arm, and together they pulled him through the window where he spilled onto the bedroom floor. After regaining his composure, he stood up and, with a slight bow towards Pamela, introduced himself. "We are all here, ladies, to rescue you."

"You aren't CIA or American Secret Service, are you?" asked Pamela, extending her hand to shake the young man's hand.

"No. We are a special branch of MI5, ma'am. Your CIA and Secret Service are as of now, shall we say, indisposed due to possible droid infection. By the way, I'm Herbert."

"I'm Mrs. Greenwood and this is my daughter, Susan, and our friend, Mara," replied Pamela, gesturing towards the other two women. "By any chance is my husband with you?"

"No, ma'am," said Herbert. "He was at the Pentagon helping us get clearance to fly in here, but I am sure he is only minutes away and coming here as fast as he can, ma'am."

Pamela's heart filled with excitement at the good

news that her husband was alive and headed their way. "How many are there of you?" she asked.

But before Herbert could answer, machine gun and pistol fire could be heard from the back of the mansion, followed by footsteps that sounded like they were coming from the roof right above them.

"I think we all better get going," Herbert said. But before he could barely finish his sentence, the bedroom door was kicked in and two droids stood there, fixing their gaze menacingly on the three women who now tried to hide themselves behind Herbert.

"No kill order!" thought Herbert to himself as he dove for the water rifle that he had dropped on the floor as he was being pulled through the window. The two droids quickly lunged at the women, grabbing Susan, while Pamela repeatedly hit one of them with her fists and Mara tried to fight the other one off with a footstool. Finally she threw the footstool at the droid with all the force she could muster up, but he just caught it and broke it in two with one of his hands, all the while smiling at her. He then grabbed her by the throat and started choking her.

"Inga doda!" shouted Herbert at the droids. The droids immediately stopped what they were doing, released their grasp on the women, and turned their attention on Herbert with a look of confusion on their faces at hearing that order that only their Master would command. Standing their motionless, it gave Herbert just the few seconds he needed to lift his water rifle and blast the droids with water, hosing both of them down. Immediately the droids started to crumble into a steaming mass of circuitry, dropping to the ground, convulsing into humanoid-sized heaps at the feet of the terrified women.

At that moment two more figures appeared in the doorway, at which point Herbert let loose with a second blast of water, but this time to no effect!

"They are human! Drexel's people!" shouted Mara. But before they could run, the soaking wet men, with smiles on their faces, drew their guns and shot Herbert three times, hitting him once in the stomach and twice in the shoulder, sending him flying backwards and into the stone fireplace, where he fell, motionless, barely alive.

Then the two men, as unemotional as Drexel's droids, aimed their Glock Nines execution style at the three women who had huddled together in a nearby corner. Just as they were ready to pull their triggers, there was a loud blast of machine gun fire followed by a man crashing through the window who was holding onto a rope with one hand and a Thompson submachine gun that was from Mr. Gravel's 1930's gun collection in the other hand, sending Drexel's men flying out of the room and into the hallway, dead, with twenty or so rounds in their bodies.

"Daddy!" cried Susan, as she ran towards her father.

"Elliot!" yelled Pamela, running towards her husband. All three just stood there, hugging each other.

Elliott made himself pull away from his family long enough to shout out the window, "Reggs, man down."

From the roof Reggs yelled down to Elliott, "I'll get my chopper and a medical team down here right now." As Reggs went for the helicopter, more of the team appeared at the doorway, some rushing towards Herbert, the fallen hero, and others towards the women and the Vice-President.

"Sir, all droids are disposed of and all of Drexel's men are either captured or dead," the sergeant said.

"Good job, Sergeant," Elliott responded. "Will you please escort the women down to the limousine out front while I see to that young man who just saved my family's life?"

"Aye, sir, it will be our pleasure," said the young British agent.

"I'm waiting for you, Dad," Susan said. With that, she kissed her mother and watched the agents escort Pamela and Mara out of the room. She wasn't about to leave her dad again. She didn't want him out of her sight.

Elliott walked over to the wounded agent who was lying unconscious on the floor. Two of the man's team members were pressing wadded-up towels against his body to slow the bleeding down from the three wounds until the medical unit arrived. Another team member stood close by, relaying the events by radio to their command.

Leaning over the wounded agent, Elliott kissed the top of Herbert's head. Then, taking off his 1974 West Point class ring, he handed it to the agent who was standing close by and said, "Tell this young man when he comes to that this ring now belongs to him and that I owe him a debt that I could never repay."

"Yes, sir, I'll do that, sir. We'll see that he pulls through. He's as tough as they come, sir."

"Thank you," replied the VP.

Turning, Elliott offered his arm to his daughter so he could escort her to the waiting limo. As they left the room, Susan looked up at her dad and said, "Just like at camp, Dad. You came swinging in to save us all."

"You know what, baby girl?" said Elliott, looking down at his daughter. "And I always will. Now let's get out of here."

21 SECRET TUNNEL UNDER MADISON SQUARE GARDEN

New York was alive with the events of the Presidential Nominating Convention. President John Tyler had just arrived in the city and had his Secret Service staff escort him to his special suite at Madison Square Garden. He needed to freshen up before he would give that night's opening speech, introducing his friend, Elliott Greenwood, as the presidential nominee for their party. He was annoyed at Elliott for not being at the Garden before he got there so the two men could sit down and talk strategy before going out on stage. The President had recently met his friend's new campaign manager, Count Drexel, whom he had a natural distaste for. Even though Drexel continually assured the President that his friend and candidate would arrive at the Garden early, he really didn't believe the man, and for some unknown reason he felt Elliott was in trouble, but he couldn't quite put his finger on it.

Meanwhile, Reggs, after the rescue of the Vice-President's wife and the rest of her party, had some of his men go up to New York and get his wife safely back to England while he stayed behind to assist Elliott with the rest of his men. Mrs. Barlow was not too happy about cutting her visit short with her sister, but she always knew instinctively to trust her husband's wishes if danger was around.

Now at a hotel five blocks down from Madison Square Garden at 42nd and 5th Avenue, near the New York City Public Library, Elliott left his wife in their room with Mara and Jim, while he sent Bud to meet up with the four MI5 agents already at the Garden, warning them not to do anything until they heard from him and Reggs. Then he went downstairs to the coffee shop to meet up with Tom, Emily, Reggs, and Gravel to discuss how to stop Drexel's plans for that evening.

"I tell you, I don't like it. I don't like it one bit, Reggie!" said Gravel, who lately had become a big fan of MI5. Reggs tried to keep his patience while taking small sips of coffee, trying to get used to the American flavor of it, but now wishing the waiter would bring him more cream to help hide the taste.

"Don't like what?" interrupted Elliott, as he came into the shop from the elevator lobby, pulling up a chair at the end of the large red booth his four companions were sitting in. "Coffee, please," he said to the waitress behind him at the counter.

"Don't like the setup at the Garden," said Gravel. He then started to take out a cigar and light it, but changed his mind when he noticed the frown on the waitress' face. Putting his lighter back into his pocket, he just chewed the cigar in his mouth. "Hell, we don't even know if the President is not one of them."

"He's not one of them," said Reggs.

"Well, why not?" asked Elliott, taking his coffee from the waitress.

"Because," said Reggs, "if the President was an android, then why would Drexel waste time with the VP when he could concentrate on the President and the seat of true power and not have to go through all this charade of getting the Vice-President elected. Makes sense, doesn't it?" Reggs waited on everyone's response, noticing Tom had wrapped his hands around Emily's hands and was kissing them.

"You two stop that!" growled Gravel. "I won't have my two star reporters acting like they are, uh, what's the word…"

"In love, mate?" said Reggs, while winking at Emily.

"Something like that," muttered Gravel, as he took his now wet cigar and hid it in a napkin under the side of his plate.

"Did I hear you say two star reporters?" piped in Emily with a look of surprise.

"Quit while you are ahead, kid," quipped Elliott, giving Emily a friendly smile as he answered his cell phone that had started to ring.

"Yeah, Bud, what's up?" After a moment of silence from Elliott's end, the VP followed up with several "uh-huhs," then followed those with, "Well, that could be useful; okay, you stay with the Brits and we'll meet up in twenty minutes by the tunnel."

Emily looked at Tom and mouthed, "Tunnel?"

Hanging up, Elliott then looked at everyone and said,

"Okay, gang, let's move. I'll explain on the way."

***

Madison Square Garden was all lit up on the outside, with big search lights beaming in all directions, and masses of delegates from every part of the U.S. were arriving by bus or limo as they were dropped off into a maelstrom of reporters and curious onlookers. The process of nomination and speeches by the head delegates would begin in about two hours, proceeded by the opening speech given by the President, who then, to thunderous applause, would call the Vice-President out from the side of the arena to receive their party's official blessing as the candidate for the office of the President of the United States.

Across the street from Madison Square Garden, in a darkened alley, waited Bud and the four British agents. Drexel and his men were lurking around the side arena, much to the annoyance of the President's Secret Service agents, who were uncomfortable at the strange and distant behavior of these new unknown Vice-Presidential agents.

Bud and his men were soon interrupted by the arrival of Elliott and company, all a little out of breath, but very excited at the plan that Elliott and Reggs had formulated since the cell phone conversation with Bud twenty minutes earlier.

"Bud, thanks for the info, but are you sure the android is unattended?" asked Elliott.

"Yes, sir, " answered Bud. "That Drexel fella was so upset at the possibility of something going wrong with the President's staff that he grabbed practically all his people and sent them upstairs to the arena."

"Practically all, mate?" asked Reggs.

"Well, sir," said Bud, "he does have two men just outside the locker room door where the android is plugged into some kind of machine, or at least was when we saw him a few minutes ago."

"You actually saw him?" whispered Tom, his

reporter instincts kicking in.

"Well, yes, sir. This tunnel here," Bud said, pointing to a side door that had steps leading down about fifty feet to a passageway under 42nd Street, "was used by a lot of celebrities that used to sneak into the Garden back in the sixties and seventies, but was sealed off back about twenty years ago when Public Works ran a new gas line into the Garden's westside boiler room. It was re-opened by management of the Garden, but hasn't been used much since. It leads to a glass door on the side of the same locker room that the android is being kept in."

"My staff knew about this tunnel for a while now, thanks to one of my people giving us the heads up about it," said Elliott. Unanimous muffled sounds could be heard from the British, followed by Gravel, Tom, and Emily with quiet cries of "Here, here!"

One of the British agents then whispered into Reggs' ear, handing Reggs a black bag.

"All right, everyone, let me ask, would anyone like some protection?" Reggs held up several Glock 9's as well as two Smith & Wesson .38 caliper six shooters.

Gravel grabbed one of the guns and carelessly started twirling it like a professional gunman would in a western movie.

"Uh, mate," said Reggs, "that's loaded, okay?"

Gravel stopped twirling the pistol and, feeling a little sheepish, quickly stuffed the gun into his coat pocket.

"I'm okay," said Tom, and Elliott followed up with the same, both patting their pockets where their pistols were concealed.

Suddenly, a small voice squeaked out, "I'll take the Glock Nine!" Emily grabbed the gun, much to the surprise of the group who all at once were looking at the short, pretty blonde reporter.

"Why are you all staring at me?" asked Emily. "After all, I am a southern girl from Valdosta, Georgia. We do more down south than just sip sweet tea and rock on the front porch," she added with an exaggerated southern drawl. Emily then popped out the clip of the gun to check how much ammo it had, and then popped it back into the gun like she had done it hundreds of times. She then placed it in her handbag.

"Okay, here is the plan," said Elliott, waiting for everyone to gather around. "First, we need to know if the two guards in front of the locker room are androids or human because brute force or even guns may not stop them if they're androids."

"How do we do that?" asked Emily.

Looking at Emily, Elliott said, "That's where you come in, Miss Delegate to the convention from Valdosta, Georgia. Now, everyone, this is how it will go down..."

***

All the members of the team made it through the tunnel without incident. Elliott was the first to reach the glass door off to the side of the tunnel, while the others stood still only a few yards away waiting to get the signal from him that it was all right to proceed further on.

Peeking up from the bottom of the door to the main glass window pane, Elliott saw no activity except for the android, the spitting image of himself, just like Bud had said, off in the corner asleep, plugged into some sort of computerized charger. No one else was around, but he could see through the thick mottled glass pane of the front locker room door the shadows of two men standing in the hallway.

Waving his hand, he then gave the "okay" signal to proceed with their plan. Everyone else moved forward while Elliott crouched and waited. A few minutes later he could hear the sounds of Emily speaking loudly in her exaggerated southern accent.

"Hey, y'all, I am the delegate from Georgia and I am so lost. Could you handsome men be so kind as to point me to the main area of the convention?"

Waiting a few more seconds in silent anticipation, Elliott finally saw the two men's shadows fade out of view. In what seemed like an eternity but was only another minute or two, he heard from around the tunnel corner the panting voice of Reggs in a loud whisper, "They are human all right, mate. Come on, you are up next!"

Elliott nodded at Reggs and followed him to the front hallway, where he saw the two men laying on the floor, knocked out by Reggs, and Tom comforting Emily, who appeared to be a bit shaken as she was explaining to Tom how one of the men had tried to make a pass at her.

Reggs must have seen Elliott's look of surprise because he quickly said, "They aren't dead, mate. I just shot them with a 12-hour dose of tranquilizer. We at MI5 sometimes like our enemies alive and talking. But now it's your turn. Are you sure you can handle that android bloke on your own?

"No problem, Reggs. I've seen these things before. I'll dispose of the android, take its place, and wait for Drexel's men to take me upstairs. Pray they won't notice I'm not the droid. And you better get going. Besides I don't think Drexel is using his androids as errand boys on this one because if he had he would not have earlier put his human goons down here to guard my double. So I think I'll be safe enough from detection."

"I agree, mate. My men and I better get going. We will be in place when the fireworks go off, though!" said Reggs, as he turned to Tom and Gravel. "Can you two Yanks get these guys hidden and meet us at the top of the stairs in two minutes?"

"Sure, no problem, mate," Tom said in his new British accent as he and his boss started dragging the unconscious guards into a closet in the adjacent locker room.

Elliott then told Bud to get Emily out of there and find some place safe because it may get "pretty rough in a few minutes around here", but Emily fired back, "Look, Mr. Vice-President, I'm in this as far as you men are, so I am not going," giving Bud a look that told him he better not escort her anywhere.

Bud just shrugged and looked at Elliott, who said, "Okay, Miss Reporter, but just stay close to Bud. He's the best there is at protection. Now get going all of you!"

Tom and Gravel had finished with their task of hiding the men and quickly joined the group. All of them rushed up the long stairwell, leaving Elliott by himself with the assignment of destroying the android.

A real sense of conflict and terror went through Elliott as he approached the android. Not only did the android look exactly like him, but even in its sleep mode it breathed heavy breaths just like a human would, making him wish for a split second that he didn't have to destroy this near-human version of himself.

Taking out his pistol, he focused on the android's ear, the only vulnerable spot on the machine of which a bullet could penetrate through the titanium metal in order to reach its brain and destroy its processing center. Walking within inches of the head, he held up the nozzle of the gun to the ear of the machine, and just when he was about to pull the trigger, the android's eyes opened!

Startled, he jumped back from the android, watching the android's head turn towards him. Reacting on instinct Elliott quickly sprung into action and swung the gun up again and opened fired on the android's head, missing each time. The android lost no time in pulling itself off the recharger and heading toward Elliott. Elliott then ran and grabbed a nearby office chair and threw it at the android, trying to trip it up, but it didn't work. Next he threw some wooden benches, but the android caught them and broke them in half with his bare hands, still making its way toward Elliott with a menacing smile on its face.

Elliott knew he only had one bullet left in the chamber, so he aimed carefully at the droid's ear. The android jerked its head to the left at the same moment Elliott pulled the trigger, causing the bullet to fly past its head, slightly grazing its face. Elliott then threw the gun at the android and turned to run for the door, hoping maybe he could reach his friends in time and get them to come back and help him destroy the machine.

Almost making it to the door, Elliott tripped over a broken piece of wood from one of the benches and fell to the floor. The android quickly caught up with him and with amazing strength picked Elliott up off the floor and threw him over by a shower stall where he hit the ground and slid into one of the showers.

Before Elliott could recover, the android was back on top of him, picking him up again and grabbing him by his throat. As the machine started choking him, it looked into Elliott's eyes and said, "Any last request, Elliott Greenwood?"

Elliott, swinging his arms wildly at the droid and

trying to grab anything close by to hit the droid with, finally caught hold of the cold water shower knob behind him. Gasping for breath, he croaked out the words, "Yeah, you piece of garbage, how about a shower," and with the last of his strength he turned on the faucet. The android, feeling the water, suddenly let go of Elliott's neck and started to jerk and twist as it fell to the ground, sparks flying from every area on its body. "A little present from my wife," said Elliott as he turned up the faucet as far as it would go, watching the android crumble into a massive heap of wire and circuit boards. "And now on to your boss," growled Elliott, as he dragged the dead android and hid him in a back shower stall, covering him up with a shower curtain.

The locker room was now a mess, and if Drexel's men came back down and saw the guards missing and the destroyed locker room, then Drexel would be on high alert and Elliott's friends would be in danger. Thinking fast, he quickly went back to the android and took off its smoldering brown tweed suit from its mangled body. Squeezing the water out of the jacket, shirt and pants, he then turned on the hand dryer by the sink, which quickly dried the shirt and tie. The tweed jacket and pants weren't fully dry before he realized, looking at his watch, that he'd better get out of there before Drexel's men showed up. He put on the android's suit, which was almost a perfect fit. Although the suit had a few burn marks on it, as well as did the shirt, they would have to do. There was no more time to waste.

He ran out of the locker room and to the stairs just in time to hear Drexel's men coming down to get him. Elliott started climbing the stairs to meet the men, deterring them from the sight in the locker room.

"Hey, shouted one of the men, what are you doing out on your own? Where is Charlie and Gant?"

Elliott had to think on his feet. "Oh, they went upstairs earlier to find a part for my charger which stopped working ten minutes ago, and I was on my way up to ask the master what I should do," he said, in a perfect replica of the android's voice. Funny, Elliott thought, that now he's impersonating the android who was impersonating him. Rather ironic how the tables were turned.

The men seemed to accept his explanation of events. "Well, you'd better come with us," said the escort. "It's almost time for the President's speech."

As they reached the top of the stairs, Elliott could hear the crowd roar throughout the whole Garden as the speaker introduced John Tyler, who within just a few minutes would be calling Elliott to come out onto the podium and speak to the delegates. One of the men who had escorted him up the stairs quickly walked over to where Drexel was standing and whispered into his ear. Then Drexel started coming towards Elliott, swearing in Swedish and shaking his fist at his "perfect" creation. Elliott quickly glanced around and spotted Reggs and the rest of the crew who were staying close by and off to the side, thanks to Bud's connection with the head of the President's Secret Service division, before he turned his attention back to Drexel.

"You know better than to ever wander off by yourself!" hissed Drexel. But before Elliott could respond, Drexel continued, "We will deal with this stupidity after the convention. Now, how much power do you have? Can you get through the speech at least?

You *must* speak, do you understand?"

"Yes, my master," said Elliott, exactly like he had once heard his double respond to Drexel when he was in Gotland.

"Good. Then come stand over here at the entrance and I'll let you know when you are to go out onto the podium," barked Drexel.

Drexel walked with Elliott to within yards of his old friend, the President, and obediently stood at attention. The President was giving his speech, totally unaware of all that was happening around him. How he wished he had time to let his friend in on what was going on, but he knew it would sound just plain crazy. No, he said to himself, I'll just have to play along until the time is right.

Suddenly he heard John Tyler calling his name and heard the crowd roar and applaud, waiting for his appearance. Drexel gave him a slight nod, and Elliott walked out onto the stage in the middle of Madison Square Garden and hugged his old friend, the President. The President hugged him back, all the while smiling, but talking through gritted teeth. "Where the hell have you been? I can't even get five minutes' time with you without that new campaign manager of yours saying you are sick or off somewhere. And where is Pamela? She is supposed to be here with you on this night of all nights!"

"Sorry, boss. I have a lot of explaining to do. We'll sit down and I'll explain everything when this convention is over tonight."

"I'll take you up on that," the President said, now shaking Elliott's hand and waving at the crowd. "I'll be sitting right behind you while you speak. Now go get 'em!" yelled Tyler with enthusiasm, waving again at the crowd and patting his old friend on the back. He then sat down on Elliott's left, directly behind the podium.

Elliott turned and faced the crowd. "My fellow Americans!" he said, waving at the thunderous crowd who was chanting his name over and over again, "Elliott for President, Elliott for President!" Waiting for the crowd to calm down, a terrible thought suddenly came to his mind concerning Drexel's plan. Why hadn't he thought of it before! Drexel wanted Elliott to be President all right, but right now, at this very time, not later! Drexel hadn't been able to get close enough to the President until this particular night. It was all starting to make sense. Drexel had men fanned everywhere throughout the Garden for the sole purpose of keeping the President's Secret Service off guard so that an assassin could easily kill him as soon as Elliott received his party's nomination for President, thereby not only having the immediate control of the Presidency, but control over the White House for possibly the next eight years!

Still smiling, still waving at the crowd, Elliott turned towards the President and said, "Don't stand up, Johnny. We have a major problem."

Tyler, very puzzled, sat still, staring at his friend, wondering what was going on. But he saw how serious Elliott was and he knew he could trust Elliott, so he did as he said and stayed seated.

Elliott had an idea. Since Drexel's men were scattered everywhere and Reggs, Bud, and the rest were close by, he would make his move, which would bring Drexel out into the open and distract his men. Turning his full attention back to the crowd, he raised his hands as if to signal for the crowd to be quiet, but before they could obey his gesture, he quickly clutched his chest and fell to the floor, just like his double had done back some weeks before. He knew it was going to be political suicide and would destroy any chances of getting a nomination if he fell in front of the public again, but this could save his friend's life and get Drexel at the same time.

When Elliott hit the floor, Drexel came running out, just as Elliott knew he would. He knew Drexel would do anything to salvage his chance of getting his android nominated.

"I asked you about your power, you stupid fool!" yelled Drexel, grabbing Elliott's coat and ignoring the President entirely and all his men who were now running toward the stage.

Elliott, pretending to be unconscious, immediately opened his eyes and pushed Drexel away from him. Jumping up onto his feet, he looked at Drexel and said, "I guess you won't be seeing Gotland for a very long time!"

Drexel's mouth dropped wide open as if he'd just

been given the surprise of his life. Assessing the situation quickly, he made a mad dash for the stairwell with a few of his goons following behind him, while Reggs, Bud, and the other Secret Service agents took chase.

John Tyler made his way over to Elliott and put his arm around his friend. "You okay, Elliott?"

"I am now, old friend," patting the President on his arm. "How about a drink?"

"Yep," said Tyler, "I think we could both use one. And I could use an explanation."

As the two men walked off the stage, with the audience in complete chaos, they met Reggs in the stairwell, who was just returning from chasing Drexel and his men.

"He got away, didn't he?" asked Elliott.

"Yeah, mate, he did, but don't worry, we'll get him, sure enough. But we have a bit of a problem," said Reggs.

"What's that?" Elliott asked, afraid to hear the answer.

"Well," said Reggs, "the Queen is not blinking!"

22 THE QUEEN IS A DROID?

Elliott listened while Reggs explained how Drexel disappeared after running down the stairwell while a few of his MI5 crew, along with Bud and a few other Secret Service agents, were still down in the lower floors of Madison Square Garden looking for the evil genius and his droids. Elliott, at first greatly relieved, was now deeply concerned at Reggs' earlier report that the Queen of England wasn't blinking. Certainly that was a sure sign that the Queen had been replaced by a droid.

As they entered a private guest suite to escape the pandemonium of the press corps, staff, audience members, and various party officials who were all still running around the Garden trying to make sense of the events after their Vice-President fainted, Elliott quickly introduced Reggs to President John Tyler. Then all three men sat down on tall bar stools at the suite's built-in private bar. Two agents stood guard outside the door, making sure no one entered the suite. Reggs volunteered to serve as bartender, taking the President's and Elliott's order while pouring for himself his favorite drink of rum and Coke.

They both brought the President up to date on who this Drexel character was and how he was attempting to achieve world domination by using his droids as replacements for all the various world leaders. John Tyler was incredulous at not having been informed by his close friend, the Vice-President, of all that was going on.

"How could I, John?" asked Elliott, shrugging his shoulders. "If the situation was reversed and you had told me that some maniac was running around all over the world replacing heads of state with androids, hell, you would have had me locked up. Besides, he had Pamela and Susan at the time, and I wasn't even sure that you or your staff wasn't one of them!"

The President was silent for a moment, digesting all that he had been told, then sat his drink down on the bar and said, "Yeah, Elliott, if he'd had my wife and daughter I would have played it close to my vest, too. But why didn't our people pick up on this? Someone in the FBI or CIA might have at least heard of this guy."

"That's the point, Mr. President," said Reggs,

refreshing the President's drink. "I believe our people at MI5 have been what we call infected, and the same could be true concerning your people. The agents I have here are the only ones that I can truly trust. Now it has come to light that our own dear Queen is a droid! If I went back to London and told my superiors at MI5 what has happened, well, let's just say that good 'ole Reggs here might suddenly come down with a case of invisibility, and wouldn't that make the missus mad. No, sir, as you have well said, we have to play this close to the vest."

The President smiled at Reggs' candor and started to say something, when suddenly a voice came over Reggs' hand-held radio. "Sir, you had better get down here at the tunnel in the basement. We have a situation!"

"On my way, mate," said Reggs, snapping the radio button off and reaching for his gun.

"I'm coming with you," said Elliott, quickly downing his drink and slamming the shot glass down hard on the wooden bar as if to emphasize his anger and determination at capturing Drexel.

"Me, too!" said John Tyler, quickly drawing a

negative response from both Reggs and Elliott.

"Sir, we don't need an army of Secret Service getting in our way down there. Please stay up here, and we'll report back as soon as we find something," pleaded Elliott, placing his hand on his friend's shoulder. He knew John Tyler could be stubborn, but he hoped this wasn't one of those moments.

Before the President could respond, Reggs piped in, "Here, mate -- uh, I mean, sir -- take this and you can monitor what's going on by keeping the frequency on 412." Reggs handed him his hand-held radio after turning the dial to the correct frequency.

This seemed to settle the President down, and they knew they had won the argument of having him stay put while they went to see what was going on in the same tunnel that had been used earlier by Reggs, Elliott, and the others to get into the Garden.

"Okay, boys, you win," said the President. "I'll stay topside, but let me know if you run into trouble and I'll bring down every agent I've got."

"Thanks, John, we'll do that," said Elliott.

"Yes, thank you, sir," echoed Reggs, as both men rushed past the President and out the door.

***

Elliott and Reggs hurried down the stairs they had earlier used that evening to sneak into the Garden. At the bottom of the stairs, just off to the right of the entrance of the tunnel that went under 42nd Street, were Tom and Emily. Upon seeing Reggs and Elliott, they made quick hand motions, waving them over to join them. Emily, very excited, was the first to speak.

"I was the first to see them, sir!" she whispered as the two men approached her and Tom.

"See who?" asked Elliott, trying to peek around the corner and look down the half-lit tunnel.

"Drexel and three droids," said Emily. I saw him sneaking out of a hidden room nearby when I came back down here to get my tape recorder that I had dropped earlier. Tom was with me at the time and he ran to get Bud and the others."

"So we have them?" said Elliott, starting to beam a broad smile.

"Not quite, sir," answered Tom. Pointing in the direction of the tunnel, Tom said, "You see, he is threatening to have his three droids self-destruct if we get any closer to him. He is claiming that his droids could blow up half the Garden and kill everyone inside if we try to capture him."

Reggs said, "He's bluffing. That twisted bloke wants to live as bad as anyone else. He wouldn't kill himself over a botched escape!"

The sound of rapidly approaching footsteps could be heard on the concrete floor. Elliott put his fingers up to his lips to tell everyone to get quiet. Reggs looked around the corner to see one of his agents coming towards them, breathing heavily as if he had run a long distance and couldn't catch his breath.

"Gawd, it's good to see you, sir!" said the British agent, barely able to talk.

"Calm down, mate," said Reggs, patting his agent on

the back. "Take a few more breaths and let me know what's going on."

The agent, clearly out of shape, breathed deep for about a minute and then spilled his story. "We 'ave him alright. All of our guns are on him and those bloody droids, but he is daring us to get closer. He's laughing at us and says he wants to speak to Mr. Greenwood, so I came back to get him, and of course you, sir."

"Well," said Elliott, "let's not keep our guest waiting. Tom, you and Miss Emily are welcome to come with us and get the story of a lifetime if you'd like. And Reggs, you --"

As Elliott turned to speak to his friend, he discovered that Reggs was well on his way down the tunnel, followed by the hefty out-of-shape agent. Elliott turned back to the couple and said, "Well, kids, what are you waiting for?" Not waiting for a response, Elliott took off into the tunnel.

Tom was very conflicted about having Emily go with them. Taking the tape recorder out of her hand, he said, "Look, why don't I take this one and you go upstairs and warn everyone to get out of the Garden?"

"Good try, lover boy, but I'm sure the other agents got the word out already to evacuate the building, so I guess you are stuck with me on this one," said Emily.

Knowing he couldn't change her mind, Tom said, "You are such a pain when you are right," and then gave her a quick kiss on her forehead and handed her the tape recorder back.

"Come on, I'll race ya," said Emily, as she turned towards the tunnel.

***

About halfway in the middle of the dimly lit tunnel, directly under a sewer manhole that led to a traffic light some sixty feet above them on 42nd Street, was Drexel, standing still with a very calm expression on his face, almost bordering on a look of boredom, as if he were waiting on a cab. In front of him were his three droids, acting as a shield between the agents and their master, just like he had taught them. All guns had been trained on the droids, with strict orders from Bud and the watch commander of the British agents to hold their fire.

Drexel's face started growing a thin, wide, crescent-shaped grin upon seeing the approaching familiar face of his hostage-now-turned-foe, Elliott Greenwood, who was running behind Reggs and the other MI5 agent. Emily and Tom quickly brought up the rear, showing up just as Reggs positioned himself directly in front of his men while the watch commander informed Reggs on what had happened. Bud quietly took the Vice-President aside and told him of the current situation, starting with Drexel threatening to give his droids a self-destruct order that would destroy most of Madison Square Garden if he was prevented from escaping.

"Why, hello, Mr. Vice-President and guests," said Drexel, making an exaggerated bow from the waist up. Looking towards Emily and Tom, he said, "You two in the back there do come closer into the light so I can see all of you."

Emily and Tom stepped forward toward Elliott so they could be seen by Drexel.

With an amused look, Drexel said, "Well, well, if it

isn't that annoying reporter who discovered my little secret at the Vice-President's house, and her friend. How do you do my dear? I hope I can let you discover another one of my little secrets in a few moments. What would you think of that?" asked Drexel, now looking at his watch.

"I, uh, don't know what you mean, sir," said Emily, showing fear for the first time with a trembling voice, which made Tom put his arm around her and draw her closer to his side.

"All right, Drexel," began Elliott, but was cut off in mid-sentence by the Count who was holding up his hand like a traffic cop.

"That's *Count* Drexel to you, sir," said Drexel, who was starting to frown for the first time.

"Okay, *Count* Drexel," said Elliott in an exaggerated manner. "You don't really expect us to believe you would kill yourself and all these people here just to make an escape which I believe you could have very easily done an hour ago, do you?"

"You have me, Mr. Vice-President, pegged, as you Americans say," said the count, now smiling again. "Yes, my dear Elliott, I did so want to show you a new side of my droid toys. Because of all this work I've been doing, I would like a little recognition for my genius outside of a world of my own making. After all, being called Master all the time by my droids does get a bit weary. But make no mistake; I will destroy everything here if I choose, so you might want to tell your British friends in the corner to lower their weapons. I think one or two of them are getting a bit too eager." Drexel made sure everyone knew who he was talking about by glaring directly at Reggs, who had just pulled back on the trigger of his Glock.

"Reggs, what are you doing?" whispered Elliott out of the side of his mouth.

"I can pop him, mate; I know I can," whispered Reggs back. "Look, he isn't holding controls of any kind, which means he has to use his voice to give those things a self-destruct order. I could turn him off like a light switch!"

"The self-destruct order is initiated at the sound of a

gun going off or any other sudden movement, my foolish British friend," said Drexel in a very dry manner, to the surprised expressions of Reggs and Elliott who didn't think Drexel could hear them.

"Yes, I can even hear you whisper," Drexel continued, taking out a chip from one of his robot's ears. "You see, some of my droid parts can be integrated into the human body. I made this little gem --" Drexel held up the droid ear microchip with his right hand "-- to fit into my inner ear over a year ago. I can even hear a worm crawling on the ground a hundred feet away. Who knows, maybe one day I'll insert my whole brain into a droid body for myself so I can be immortal."

"That's a mental image we could all do without," said Elliott in disgust as he spat on the ground.

"Well," said Drexel, snickering, "I see that my welcome is wearing thin, so I think I better

go --"

"What about the Queen?" asked Reggs, interrupting Drexel's exiting speech.

"The Queen? Whatever do you mean, sir?" asked Drexel, showing signs of losing his composure for the first time by the deep crimson red color of blood that was now rushing to his cheeks.

"We got you dead to rights, mate. She's a bloody droid, isn't she, just like those three," accused Reggs, pointing at the droids that stood before them.

Drexel was becoming very unnerved and wanted to ask how they knew, but caught himself. He dared not let them know their suspicions were right. It would thwart his plans.

Trying to keep from shaking with rage, he screamed, "I don't know anything about your precious Queen, but if you think I have her, come find her and get her back! And because you have insulted me, maybe I'll take Miss Reporter with me as well! Try to stop me and I'll blow us all up! I need someone to document all my life's work anyway, and since she's has shown such an interest in me in the past, she'll do just fine! Right, Emily?" With those words Drexel signaled with his forefinger for Emily to walk over to him.

"No!" yelled Tom back at Drexel. "You can't have her!"

"Tom," said Emily quietly, as she gently pushed away from him, "he'll kill us all in the rage that he's in. Let me go. It will be okay. There will be another time, I promise."

"She's right, Tom," said Elliott, giving Emily a quick hug. "He won't hurt her. He has no reason to because she's not a threat. But in his state of mind now, if we don't let her go he will blow us all up, I'm afraid. We'll get her back, I swear, Tom," said Elliott, looking Tom straight in the eye.

Tom, visibly shaken, resigned himself to losing his new-found love and gave her one last hug, saying, "You know I love you, don't you?"

Emily, with a tearful voice, responded back with "I love you, too," as she picked up the tape recorder and started walking slowly towards the droid and Drexel.

"Hurry, young woman, I'm not a patient man," warned Drexel.

Emily walked straight past the droids and stood by Drexel who, without looking at her or even acknowledging her presence, stood and faced his opponents one last time. "Remember what you see here and know what kind of intellect you're facing." Then, turning to Emily, he said, "Say goodbye to your friends, Miss Reporter. We have to leave now."

Before Emily could respond, Drexel muttered something in Swedish to the droids, grabbed Emily, and then simply vanished before their eyes without a trace, leaving Reggs, Elliott, Tom, and all the agents looking at each other, not believing what they had just witnessed.

"Nobody move," said Reggs. "It could be a trap!"

"Don't think so, Reggs," said Elliott. He then motioned for his men to retreat back to the beginning of the tunnel.

Satisfied that Elliott was probably right, Reggs gave his agents a similar order. "All right, blokes, you all follow the Americans back into the building as well. It looks like the show is over for now."

Walking over to Elliott, Reggs asked, "What do you think that Drexel chap did to make everyone disappear like that?"

"He hasn't disappeared as yet, Reggs," said Elliott, looking back into the tunnel.

"You mean he is still there?" asked Reggs, looking into the tunnel as well.

"In a sense," said Elliott. "You see, I think Drexel has figured out what our CIA has been working on over the last twenty years."

"What's that mate?" asked Reggs, as he put his gun back into his shoulder holster.

"It's called a reverse hologram," said Elliott

"A reverse *what*, mate?" asked Reggs.

"A reverse hologram," Elliott repeated. "Instead of using a hologram to project an object that is not really there, Drexel is somehow using his droids to inversely project an object away from the physical space it occupies, leaving nothing for the eye to focus on except empty space."

Elliott pulled out a cigarette from his pocket and offered one to Reggs. Although Reggs had promised his wife he would never smoke again, he gratefully took the cigarette and lit his and Elliott's with a handy pocket lighter. Under these circumstances, breaking a promise not to smoke was the least of his worries.

"Clever bugger, that Swedish bastard," said Reggs, blowing smoke rings as they walked, trying to make sense of what he just saw Drexel do. Then he added, "By the way, mate, you sure let that young Emily go rather easily. I thought you and Tom would put up a fight."

"Oh, in a way I did, old friend," said Elliott, fumbling in his pocket and pulling out a small round, metal object for Reggs to see. "You see, I stuck a bug under her coat collar as I gave her a hug. Bud gave me several of these earlier this evening to keep just in case I got close enough to Drexel or one of his droids. Looks like I did, in a way."

Reggs laughed. "If you don't want the President's job, you might want to work for MI5 and me. The pay isn't much, but you see all the fun we have."

"I might just do that, Reggs. Now, let's get upstairs and see where Drexel is headed to," said Elliott, as the two men entered the basement of Madison Square Garden.

***

Several blocks away, on 42nd Street, five figures emerged from the tunnel and disappeared into the dark alley. A black limousine sat with its engine running. They got into the limousine and sped off into the night...

23 EMILY RADIOS FOR HELP

Emily Patrick watched her captor through her guest room window as he left his castle again by helicopter for another mysterious meeting in some far-away country. With Drexel gone, this left her totally free to roam the property and to ask anything she wanted or see anyone she wanted on the castle grounds as long as she stayed away from Drexel's secret lab in the west tower basement.

Thinking back to their earlier conversation before Drexel left, he had told her, "Explore my castle and read my philosophical writings and notes I have made about myself and the future of the human race. I want the world to be able to get to know the real me once I start running it, of course. So, Miss Patrick, I leave all that I own in your capable hands. Just one rule, though..."

"Outside of keeping me here against my will?" quipped Emily in a sarcastic tone, which only produced a small pained expression from Drexel.

"Yes, outside of that, Miss Patrick," responded

Drexel, in his low, monotone voice.

"Let me guess, stay away from your secret lab in the basement, or some such nonsense as that?" Emily wished she hadn't made that last comment about "nonsense". She could tell she had pushed him too far.

Drexel's face became flush red with anger and his veins were sticking out of his neck, but his desire to have his story told professionally helped him control his temper. He did however take her hand and, tugging slightly on her arm, walked her across the dining room hall to a large, high ceiling window where he proceeded to point to a solitary crooked, round, stone tower that stood precariously high above the rocky cliffs and sea below. To Emily it looked as if a strong wind could blow it all down any moment, but to Drexel it was the birthplace of all his best and brightest ideas.

Answering her last comment, Drexel said, "It's not in the basement, my dear, but over there," still pointing. "And I would appreciate it very much if you didn't go near it because then my two droids by the door there would have to instantly break your beautiful neck."

Following Drexel's pointing forefinger with her eyes, Emily saw the two droids standing at the forbidding, impossibly thick, black oaked, iron-rimmed door." Trying to maintain her composure, she slowly swallowed and remained silent.

"Do I make myself clear, my young miss?" asked Drexel, releasing her arm almost as quickly as he had grabbed it earlier.

"Perfectly," gulped Emily, as she kept her eyes fixed on the menacing tower, trying to avoid Drexel's gaze.

Drexel then gave a quick bow, followed by a rubber band smile that instantly snapped back into a serious frown as he turned to leave the dining hall without saying another word.

Emily bravely called out to Drexel before he disappeared, "How are you paying me, Count Drexel, in dollars or krona?"

Without taking the time to turn back around, Drexel responded, "Neither, Miss Patrick, but in lives and possible freedom for yourself. Do a good job, Miss

Patrick, and live." Then he exited the dining hall as silently as a slithering snake.

***

Now watching his helicopter fade from view, it made her feel a bit safer, although Emily wasn't phased in the least by Drexel's veiled threats. She knew his giant ego was so wrapped up in telling the world his story through her writing that he wouldn't dare harm her. She also knew that Tom, Mr. Gravel, the Vice-President, Reggs and his men would stop at nothing to get her back. The only problem running through her mind was how and when they would be able to do it.

Seeing a telescope by the window, she thought she would try to scan the horizon for any clue of where she was, but the view from the dining room hall all only offered a quiet courtyard below and a vast, empty, unknown blue sea with not even a single seagull or ship. "A fat lot of good that did, Emily, ole' girl," she said to herself, as she half-heartily spun the telescope around with her forefinger, then walked over to the table and picked up Drexel's notes and started thumbing through the well worn yellow-tinted pages.

"He sure does fancy himself," Emily muttered out loud, her voice echoing off the vaulted ceiling as she read about Drexel's fifteen-year master plan of world domination and how each droid would be in all key positions of power in all the governments of the world by the end of those fifteen years. The vast portion of the human race eventually would be reduced to performing menial work and living like domesticated animals in massive slave labor camps set up in desolate third-world countries, while a smaller contingent of humans loyal to Drexel would be middle managers, themselves living in the industrialized cities throughout the world and doing more complicated tasks, but even they would be under droid control. And controlling the droids, of course, was Drexel himself, the ultimate supreme ruler of the entire planet.

"This guy is crazy!" Emily said in disgust as she tossed the notes back onto the dining room table, scattering the handwritten yellowed paper everywhere. "I've got to get out of here."

Hearing a commotion outside, she walked over to the dining room windows and looked down. Some hundred feet or so below in the courtyard were two men hauling boxes in hand-trucks. One of the men was yelling and cussing in Swedish at the other man as they moved their load across the cobblestone path that led straight towards Drexel's secret lab. As the men got closer to the tower, Emily watched as the two androids standing at the tower entrance moved aside, allowing one of the workmen access to what looked like a small box located near the door. Hoping the object was what she thought it was, she dashed back to the telescope and aimed the lens directly at the small box. She could make out a keypad, and the workman was starting to punch in the secret code!

"One, two, three, seven, six," Emily said to herself, as she watched the two men enter the lab. She then repeated it to herself again, "one, two, three, seven, six," as she ran back to the table to write it down before she forgot it. "Oh, where is that pen!" she said in frustration, shuffling through Drexel's notes. Finding no pen, she spied some burnt charcoal in the fireplace on the opposite wall. Rushing over and snatching a piece of charcoal, she scribbled the code onto one of Drexel's notes that she had earlier subconsciously wadded up and put in her pocket.

"There!" she said in a triumphant voice, as she gently folded the note and put it back into her pants pocket. Leaving the dining room hall, she patted the note hidden in her pocket as if she had just found a treasure map worth millions and muttered to herself, "Okay, Mr. Drexel, you may be a genius, but you just let the cat into the cage with the canary. I'm going to find out just what makes your world tick, sir!"

***

Emily turned into the long, narrow hallway that led back to her guest room that Drexel had provided in order for her to do her work. She hoped to retreat there and formulate a plan to break into Drexel's secret lab. Just before reaching her room, she narrowly missed bumping into a domestic droid holding a silver breakfast tray with coffee, crescent rolls, and jam.

"Good morning, Miss Patrick," said the droid in

perfect English. "I was just on my way to bring you breakfast and to tell you that the master requests you to meet our new guest, the Queen, at lunchtime today."

"The *Queen?*" asked Emily in surprise at hearing such a strange request. "The Queen of what, Sweden? What do you mean?"

"No, ma'am," said the droid, as he opened the door to her guest room and quickly set the breakfast tray on a small table. "Why, the Queen of England, of course. She is our guest, and the master has arranged for you to meet her. He's quite sure her kidnapping will serve as a wonderful demonstration of his power and he would like you to include it in your writings."

Now I have heard everything, Emily thought to herself as she followed the droid into her room and sat down; allowing the droid to tuck a napkin under her chin like a professional waiter would at a five-star hotel. Next he set the table, poured her a cup of coffee, and offered her a crisp newspaper.

"London Times, Miss?" asked the droid. "It just came in this morning."

"Sure, why not," said Emily, resigning for the moment into this role assigned to her of an imprisoned pampered guest. "And while you are at it, give me two creams and one sugar. And, if you don't mind, could you butter a couple of those crescent rolls, Mr. -- Um, what is your name, Jeeves the Butler or something?"

"Oh, no, miss," said the droid, buttering the last crescent roll and placing it before her on a small blue china plate. "I am Droid Twenty-Two of the domestic staff. I do not have a name."

"Well, Droid Twenty-Two of the domestic staff," said Emily, "you do now. I think I will call you Jeeves!"

The droid paused briefly, and Emily thought she saw him give a slight nod of approval at hearing his new name. Then, as if on cue, he picked up the empty tray and bowed to her, saying, "Would there be anything else, miss?"

"No. Thank you, Jeeves. I'm fine for now. I'll just sit here, sip my coffee, and read the paper. But thank you, though," said Emily.

The droid, silent for a second, walked to the door, turned, and gave a deep bow to Emily. "No, miss, thank you. I'll come back in two hours to show you to the Queen's chambers."

Emily would have sworn she sensed a tone of gratitude from the droid at having been given a name, but then quickly dismissed it as her own imagination. "Surely droids don't have the capacity of being grateful, do they? Strange how they were so life-like." She almost said aloud as she starred at Jeeves for a minute looking for human traits behind that programmed smile of his.

"See you then, Jeeves," Emily said as she picked up the newspaper and started reading the headlines. "Hmmm," she murmured, looking for any news from America. "Lord Jonathan Hawthorne elected Prime Minister of England. How about that? Now, where have I heard that name before..."

After half-heartedly scanning through a few more articles, Emily realized she was growing tired in light of the morning's events and thought she would lay down on the bed for a quick nap. After closing her eyes for what seemed like only minutes, she was awakened by a gentle knock at her bedroom door.

"Miss Patrick, it is noon. Please come out and follow me to meet the Queen," beckoned the droid.

"Be there in a second, Jeeves," Emily answered, yawning. Still fully dressed, she rushed over to her bathroom mirror, brushed out her hair, changed into a fresh yellow blouse, and grabbed a tape recorder provided to her by her host as an aid in doing her writing.

"Okay, all set," Emily said to Jeeves as she rushed out of her room, giving Jeeves a wink, to which the droid automatically responded by returning a wink of his own. "Let's go meet Her Majesty!" she said, still not really believing it was the true Queen, but was curious all the same.

The Queen's chamber was on the opposite side of the castle, but still facing the same courtyard that Emily saw from the dining room windows. The droid, Jeeves, and Emily were silent as they took the five-minute walk through the long winding corridors, passing many of the domestic staff of droids who were busy cleaning various artifacts that lined the hallways or waxing the black marble floors that honeycombed the castle walkways.

As they passed by the other droids, Jeeves just kept looking straight ahead, not acknowledging any of them as they went about performing their menial duties of the day. Emily didn't think much of it, but still thought it strange that this droid who showed her such attention and kindness would turn a blind eye and not even acknowledge his fellow creatures.

"Well, here we are, Miss," said Jeeves, as he knocked at the Queen's bedroom door.

Emily heard an elderly woman's voice in a very refined British accent respond with a "Do come in."

Upon entering the Queen's quarters, Emily noticed a woman with a stately air about her wearing a comfortable-looking plain green cotton dress and pink house slippers sitting at a table by a small window that overlooked the courtyard. She was being served lunch for two by another domestic droid who didn't talk, but just placed the food on the table and poured the Queen some freshly squeezed lemonade.

The Queen's soft gray hair was pulled back into a tight bun. Her complexion was fair and her cheeks had a natural pinkish blush to them. Her piercing blue eyes had a stark commanding presence, not at all showing age and weakness, but emitting an inner strength of purpose and character. This was no frail woman in her eighties, Emily thought to herself, or some sort of droid imposter, but an embodiment of all that was noble of the British people.

Emily's doubts disappeared at once. She felt immediately this woman's genuineness and being an American didn't stop her at all from taking the deepest bow she ever took in her life and uttering the words, "Your Majesty!"

"There, there, young woman, do come over and sit down. I think that this little lunch they have prepared is for the both of us. Besides, I am thrilled to have some company. All they do around here is serve me meals and bring me odds-and-ends to make my visit more comfortable, but for what purpose I am still in the dark about. Anyhow, it's a delightful lunch, as you can see, of roast beef and pheasant. Not as good as I get at home, but passable, considering our situation here."

Emily quickly took a seat across the table from the Queen. Turning to the droids, the Queen said, "Would you both mind leaving us for a bit while we chat and eat our lunch?" To Emily's surprise, both Jeeves and the other droid bowed and left without protest.

The Queen lowered her voice a little and said, "Ah, now that we are alone, let me ask you something."

"Yes, of course, Your Majesty," replied Emily.

"Oh, you don't have to call me that, young woman. My friends call me Betsy. It's a nickname I've carried ever since I was a school girl. And what is your name, by the way?"

"Well," said Emily, "I'm Emily Patrick from Georgia and my nickname -- well, I really don't have a nickname, but my father has always called me "Emms" ever since I was little and he still does that today, so I guess --"

"Well, Emms," the Queen interrupted as she extended her hand, "It's a pleasure to meet you. Emms is a fine name!"

Emily took the Queen's hand and gently shook it,

saying, "And it's a real pleasure to meet you, Your Maj -- I mean Betsy."

As the two ladies proceeded to eat their lunch, the conversation was fairly light, centering mostly upon what hobbies the Queen enjoyed and what Emily did for a living.

"A reporter?" asked the Queen in surprise. "I should have known since you did come in with that little tape recorder. Were you going to interview me or something?"

"Oh, no, Betsy," Emily said, causing herself to blush at using the Queen's nickname. "This is for note taking. Count Drexel asked me, or should I say is forcing me, to write his memoirs. I guess that is why he kidnapped me from America."

At the mention of Drexel's name, the Queen rolled her eyes in disgust and said, "Oh, him. So that's another thing we have in common, we are both being held here by force. I'm so sorry dear." Emily asked, "What do you think of this Drexel, Betsy?" changing the pleasant tone of conversation.

"I think," the Queen began, patting the sides of her mouth with her napkin, "that he is a tortured soul that has committed the unspeakable crime of kidnapping an old woman from her home."

"You mean kidnapping the most powerful monarch in the world!" responded Emily with indignation at the thought of what Drexel had done.

The Queen smiled at Emily's response and said, "Yes, something like that, although I could almost feel sorry for him when my people come to rescue me. I feel it won't be too long now, and I can tell you this, Emms, my lads in the MI5 branch of my government will not be too kind to Drexel when they get here."

"You mean they probably will kill him?" asked Emily.

"I'm afraid so," the Queen responded with a sigh. "These young men are fiercely loyal to my safety and consider any attack on my person lethal to the attacker."

"Well, I am sure Lord Hawthorne, the new Prime Minister, will pull out all the stops in looking for you," said Emily casually as she took another bite of roasted pheasant.

"Lord Hawthorne, the new PM? Oh, no, dear me!" uttered the Queen.

"Why, yes," said Emily. "I just read it in the London Times this morning. My servant droid brought the paper to me at breakfast." Sensing the Queen's agitation, she asked, "Is something wrong, Betsy?"

"There could very well be something wrong," said the Queen in surprise, now remembering the morning of her kidnapping and how she, before passing out, had seen her double on horseback staring at her with a menacing smile on her face. "Oh, dear me," she said again, staring straight out the window. "Oh, dear me, I totally forgot! How could I have forgotten that awful, awful morning!"

"That morning?" asked Emily.

"Yes. When I went horseback riding with Lord Hawthorne earlier that morning, he led me deep into the woods, off of my usual path, and I was trying hard to keep up with him, ready to scold him for separating me from my guards, until..." The Queen paused for a second, catching her breath, as that fateful morning's memories washed over her troubled face.

"Until what, Betsy?" urged Emily, hoping the Queen would continue. "What did you see?" Emily reached across the table and took the Queen's hands in her own as the Queen continued to stare out the window.

"Until I saw myself on another horse smiling back at me. Then I must have fainted or something and the next thing I recall is waking up here in the castle." The Queen then looked at Emily, trying to read Emily's face after what she had just told her. It still sounded so unbelievable.

"Oh, I see," said Emily, less surprised than she thought she would be. "It was a droid replacement. Now I understand. They made a droid to replace you, didn't they, Betsy?"

"I suppose so, Emms. Maybe this means help isn't coming after all if they aren't even aware I'm missing. I suppose we really are on our own." The Queen sighed again and stared out the window, trying to hide the fear that was rising within her at the thought of her predicament.

Picking up on the Queen's distress, Emily offered, "Oh, I wouldn't say that, Betsy. You see, a few weeks ago some of your MI5 people and our own party of secret service, including our very own Vice-President Greenwood, discovered what Drexel was about to do and we gave chase to him in New York, but he got away, kidnapping me in the process. So knowing my friends, I think help is definitely on the way. The only problem is if they can find us. Do you have any idea where we are, Betsy?"

The Queen, encouraged by her new friend's words, walked over to the window and beckoned Emily to join her. Pulling open the window pane, she said, "Emms, take a deep breath, my dear, and tell me what you smell."

Emily leaned out the window and breathed in a deep breath. "All I smell is the salt air of whatever sea that is out there. What do you smell, Betsy?"

"Well, Emms, what I smell is the Baltic Sea," answered the Queen, taking another deep breath of the sea air.

"The Baltic Sea? How can you tell, Betsy? I thought salt air was salt air. Don't all seas smell the same?" asked Emily.

"Oh, maybe to you Americans, young woman, but remember I am a monarch over a nation of seafaring people going back thousands of years. I have sailed in every sea and ocean of the world in my lifetime and each sea has its own distinct smell. This particular one has that oily fish and salt air combination that can only be found in the Baltic! In fact," the Queen started, forgetting her unhappy mood, "I dare venture to say we are off the coast of Sweden or on an island in the Baltic not too far away from the Swedish coast!"

"Hmm, that would make sense because Drexel is Swedish and is bound to own some important property in Sweden. Betsy, you are amazing!" responded Emily to her new-found friend's observation.

"Nothing amazing about it, dear Emms," said the Queen, now laughing and feeling a big weight being lifted off her shoulders.

A few moments passed by as the women continued

to stare out the window silently at the sea and the vast courtyard, both deep in thought.

Emily broke the silence and said, "Betsy, do you feel up for a bit of adventure this afternoon that might help our rescue situation?"

"Emms, I am game for anything that gets us out of the clutches of this Drexel person," answered the Queen. "What do you have in mind?"

"Well, you see," explained Emily, "I have a way to get into Drexel's secret lab over there." Emily pointed to the crooked rocky tower that loomed ahead. "I think maybe I could find some sort of radio or some device to use to summon help, or at least that's what I'm hoping. The only problem is those two droids standing guard in front of the entrance. I think I have a way of distracting them, if you will help me."

"I am all yours!" said the Queen. "Let me change into my walking shoes and I'll follow your lead."

"Great!", replied Emily. Looking around the Queen's room, Emily asked, "Um, could I borrow that small jacket of yours hanging up in the corner over there?"

"Certainly. I have several of them," said the Queen. "But it's not cold outside, Emms. In fact, it feels rather pleasant."

"It's not for the weather, Betsy, but for something to hide *this* in." Emily then held up her tape recorder for the Queen to see.

"Oh!" said the Queen, smiling. "I see. Yes! Please, by all means, take it."

Emily quickly grabbed the jacket and then walked over to the Queen while she was changing her shoes and whispered her plan into the Queen's ear just in case there were any listening devices planted in the suite. The Queen, after hearing the plan, silently squeezed Emily's hand as a gesture that she understood and approved.

"All set, Betsy?" asked Emily.

"All set, Emms!" said the Queen, giving a quick thumbs up.

"Good. Let's summon some help." Emily motioned for the Queen to ring a small bell that would summon the domestic droids into the room. Seconds later, Jeeves and another droid appeared at the door.

"Is there anything you need, Miss Emily?" asked Jeeves.

"Yes, Jeeves," replied Emily. "The Queen wishes to go for her walk in the courtyard today. Could you accompany us outside?"

"Yes, of course," said Jeeves. "Ready when you are, miss." Jeeves then turned to the other droid and dismissed him, which is exactly what Emily hoped he would do.

"Good!" said Emily. "Let's go."

***

Both Emily and Jeeves carefully walked with the Queen down the flight of marble stairs to the main floor, going only as fast as the Queen was able to. Everyone was silent until they reached the ground floor, when Emily stopped and asked Jeeves a question.

"Jeeves, I'm trying to learn Swedish while I'm here. Could you perhaps say a few sentences in Swedish that I could practice on today? I would really appreciate it."

"That's a most admirable ambition, miss. Certainly I would be glad to help you learn our language," said Jeeves, escorting them both out into the courtyard.

"Great. Thanks, Jeeves," said Emily. "Let's try a silly phrase that I could remember. How about something like 'The Queen has escaped and the master has ordered you to go find the Queen at once'? Emily watched the droid as he seemed to play it back in his mind and she couldn't tell if he was going to fall for it or not.

"That *is* a silly phrase," said Jeeves, as Emily fumbled for the hidden tape recorder and switched it on. Looking as if he was still digesting the words, he finally continued, "But if it will help you learn Swedish, I'll comply." Emily let out a quick sigh of relief. She didn't realize she had been holding her breath.

The droid uttered the phrase with feeling, pronouncing every syllable in crisp, clear Swedish, "The Queen has escaped and the master has ordered you to go find the Queen at once!"

Emily quietly shut the tape recorder off, then repeated the phrase back to Jeeves in Swedish, and thanked him for helping her. "I'll practice it over and over, Jeeves," she said. Emily then gave a slight nod to the Queen, signaling her to go forward with her part of the plan.

Clearing her throat, the Queen said, "Um, Jeeves, is it?"

"Yes, Your Majesty?" responded the droid.

"I have changed my mind about the walk. Would you be so kind as to accompany me to the library and read me some Dickens? My eyesight is not so keen this morning and it would be delightful to have someone read to me today."

"It is my pleasure to serve you. Please follow me this way." Jeeves gestured for the women to follow him back towards the castle.

Emily said, "Um, Jeeves, I will walk by myself today. You two go ahead without me."

Jeeves bowed and said, "Very well," and turned to lead the Queen to the library. The Queen stole a quick glance at Emily and mouthed the words "good luck" before following the droid.

Watching the Queen and Jeeves disappear from sight, Emily clutched the tape recorder still hidden in her pocket and started towards the tower. I didn't expect *that* to go so smooth, Emily thought to herself. Apparently Drexel's droids weren't capable of picking up on deceit, which worked well to her advantage at that moment. But now she had to focus on the next phase of her plan. She still needed some good luck and hoped all the droids had shortcomings like Jeeves did.

Reaching the front entrance of the tower that hid Drexel's secret lab in it, she bravely walked straight up to the two droids who were now looking blankly at her as she approached.

"I have a message for you. Listen." Emily took out the tape recorder and turned it on, waiting for the droids' responses. And it worked! The two droids, without a single word or hint of expression, left their post and hurried off towards the main part of the castle, well out of sight of Emily. Quickly she keyed in the code on the keypad and waited for the secret lab doors to open.

"I'm in!" she said, rushing through the doors before they could close again. Once inside the lab, she stood still for a moment and waited on her eyes to adjust to the darkness. She was finally able to see a small, dimly lit tunnel-like entranceway that led down a flight of stairs. It eventually opened up into a large domed room that looked like it could have been Frankenstein's lab in the black-and-white movies she watched sometimes when she was younger, but this lab was filled with the latest that technology had to offer. Half-completed droids of every type and size were everywhere. Some were only in their skeletal stage, while others were fully formed, waiting only for activation.

Emily noticed in the center of the room a glass cylindrical encasement filled with a viscous liquid bubbling up around yet another android. Walking closer, she could now see that the droid was halfway covered in what appeared to be real human tissue on his arms and legs. How eerily real everything looked. She thought she could even see veins and arteries where the "skin" hadn't yet enveloped the machine. But what she saw next was something she didn't expect. Looking up at its face, the droid was the image of Drexel himself!

It took her a moment to realize the gasp she heard had come from her own throat. After catching her breath, she wondered, was Drexel planning to transfer himself somehow into a droid? Mesmerized at the sight before her, she finally made herself tear away from the grizzly image and remind herself of why she was there. She had to find something in the lab that could be used to send a message, a stress signal, or a SOS, whatever she could get out.

Walking between and around the droids gave Emily a creepy feeling, like she was in a morgue filled with disemboweled corpses. "Focus, Emms," she heard herself whisper. "They're nothing but machines."

On the other side of the lab was a long glass case holding dozens of fully formed androids, their eyes staring blankly out at her. Walking closer to the large case, Emily held her breath as she gazed into each one of their faces, halfway expecting one to move. These were replicas of all the world's famous leaders and politicians. She recognized most of them from her work at the newsroom. There were also several famous movie stars, with every detail of their flesh perfectly sculpted.

As she was trying to grasp in her mind the impact this would make on the world if Drexel was allowed to follow through with his sick plan, she made her way down to the end of the glass tomb and froze in her tracks. In front of her, perfect in every detail, was an image that caused shivers to go up and down her spine. "No way," she muttered. "No way!" It was a droid of her!

Emily could feel her legs wanting to buckle. She closed her eyes for a moment and tried to regain her composure. She couldn't faint now. She had to save herself and the Queen. There was no time for weakness.

Making herself open her eyes, she looked again at the droid. It was like looking at herself in a mirror. "He had no intention of letting me go!" she yelled, stomping her foot on the concrete floor. "Damn him! Just damn him!"

she said, looking away, trying to hold back the tears that were now welling up.

Sensing that too much time had gone by since she snuck into the lab, Emily pulled herself together and forced herself to keep searching for something, anything, to get her and the Queen out of this dreadful, deadly predicament. Her eyes fell on some charts and graphs that were crumpled up on a nearby table. They appeared to be schematic drawings of the lab. Flipping through them, she ran across a detailed diagram of a radio that had an antenna running from the basement all the way up the tower and to the roof!

"That's gotta be it!" she said, tracing her finger on the diagram to a square drawing, what looked like a small radio room at the top level of the tower. There were also some numerical codes scribbled on the drawing, but she couldn't read them and assumed they were in Swedish. "I've got to try," she thought, and grabbed the drawing, heading for the stairs that led to the top of the tower.

***

The climb was exhausting. It took her a full ten

minutes to reach the top of the winding staircase. At the top of the stairs was a small metal walkway that wrapped itself around the outside of the tower, allowing one to get a 360-degree view of the sea and Gotland itself.

"So we're on an island," she said, looking out and seeing all of Gotland. Off in the distance she could see the outline of a large body of land. "The Queen was right after all. I bet this *is* the coast of Sweden," she thought to herself. "If this was another moment in time, I could appreciate the beauty, but now is not that time."

Turning her attention back to the tower, she noticed a small room with a long aluminum antenna sticking out of it. This must be the radio room I saw on the diagram, she thought. Opening the small green wooden door, she spotted a large black radio console, and behind it was a huge map of the world that was lit up in various places by what looked like thumb tacks with tiny lights on the end of each one. It didn't take long for Emily to surmise that they probably represented where Drexel had managed to plant his droids. Below each lighted thumb tack was a numerical code. Looking at the drawing she brought with her, she noticed the codes written on it were the same kind as the ones on the map. The radio dials also had codes written on them. "These have to be frequency settings for Drexel's droids," she thought.

Studying the world map, something near London caught Emily's eye. It was a small emblem of a jet and below it was another numerical code stamped in red. "It has to be an airport Drexel uses," she said to herself, so she switched on the radio, turning the dial to the matching frequency for the airport. The crackling noise of static came over the radio speaker. Emily switched on the microphone and quickly said, "Mayday, mayday, this is Emily Patrick from the Washington Star Newspaper. I am a news reporter being held prisoner somewhere on an island in the Baltic Sea near the coast of Sweden. Mayday, Mayday. Over."

Nothing but white, empty noise for what felt like minutes. Then the radio came alive again with static, followed by an angry voice in a thick British accent. "Now see here, miss, this is a private airport frequency used only for air traffic and not some American tourist's idea of a prank. And how did you get this frequency anyhow? Over."

Emily couldn't give up now. "This is not a joke, tower, and I am not carrying on some kind of prank. If you could call my boss in America at the Washington Star, 612-458-8976, he can verify my story and send help. Over." Emily hoped the seriousness and desperation in her voice carried over to the man on the other end of the line. She needed him to believe her and she didn't know how much time she had to convince him.

"I will do no such thing, young woman, and furthermore --" Then she heard nothing but silence, followed by what sounded like a scuffle and the man saying something like "how dare you, sir," and then dead silence again.

Great, thought Emily. But suddenly a very familiar and warm voice came over the microphone. "Emily, this is Reggs. Looks like you hit the jackpot today, Miss American Star Reporter. We have been stationed throughout the country monitoring all private radio traffic in Europe, trying to track you down. Our radio tracker has you coming from a general area on the island of Gotland, but we were hoping to get a more precise fix. Now we have an exact fix thanks to your transmission!

You really have us worried. Drexel, I take it, must have a base there. Over."

"Reggs! Oh, it's so good to hear your voice, Reggs!" Emily thought she really was going to cry now, but she gulped it back and continued, "And yes, Reggs, he does. It's some sort of fortress or castle at the end of the island. Over."

Reggs paused for a second before continuing. "Emily, dear, this is a very delicate situation and I need you to get away from the radio the instant you answer me one question," commanded Reggs.

"Yes, Reggs. Please go ahead. Over."

"Is the Queen with you on the island and is she in good health?" asked Reggs.

"Yes, Reggs, she's here and in perfect health! But both of us are in danger, real danger. When can you get here? Over." Emily looked back towards the radio room door, glad to see she was still alone.

But Reggs didn't answer her last question. All he said was, "Now, as fast as possible, get out of there before you are discovered, understand? Over."

"Yes, Reggs, of course," Emily said. Then she yelled into the microphone, "And please tell Tom I love him!"

Emily heard Reggs say "Tom is here in London, so I'll tell him; now get out of there!" before she turned off the radio, heaving a huge sigh of relief, not yet noticing the menacing figure that was now standing behind her.

"You are much too much trouble!" the droid said in Swedish, grabbing Emily and dragging her through the doorway. With one quick motion he had her lifted over his head and was walking toward the edge of the metal walkway!

"What are you doing!" Emily screamed, as the droid carried her closer and closer to her doom. She kicked and squirmed as hard as she could, but she was no match for the droid.

The droid, now standing at the edge of the walkway, held her in mid air. Looking down, she could see the jagged rocks below her and hear the loud waves crashing against them. She knew it was too late for her, but maybe

Reggs could still save the Queen.

Feeling the droid loosen his grip on her as he was about to throw her to her death, she closed her eyes and waited for what she knew was coming. But just at that moment something yanked her backwards, out of the clutches of the droid, and she opened her eyes just as she hit the metal walkway and found herself rolling. Seeing the edge of the walkway coming at her again, she grabbed the railing and stopped herself. Looking up, she saw Jeeves just as he was throwing the guard droid off the tower!

"Jeeves, you saved me! But why? You are a droid made by Drexel," said Emily.

"True enough," said Jeeves, "but I'm programmed to serve you. Besides, I like having a name. Now come on, miss, let's get back to the castle before anyone else finds you here."

Looking one more time at the ragged rocks below them, Emily asked, "But won't Drexel be curious about the missing guard droid?"

"No, not at all," said Jeeves. "I'll turn one of my domestic staff into the guard droid and adjust his programming. They really are not programmed to be too bright, you know. Anyway, Master Drexel is far too busy to notice a minor adjustment in personnel."

"I'm sure glad you're on my side," said Emily, reaching to give Jeeves a hug.

"And I'm glad I finally have a name!" said Jeeves, as he gently picked up his mistress and carried her down from the tower to safety.

24 DREXEL GOES TO MIT SEES MARGUERITE

New York's Grand Central Station was busier than ever. Drexel and Olaf waited patiently to board the train to Boston so they could then rent a car and drive over to MIT to meet an old colleague of Drexel's, Dean Anderson. Anderson was Dean of the School of Robotic Science at MIT. With the Queen and Emily safely stashed away at Gotland, Drexel had talked Olaf into traveling with him to MIT. Drexel's real reason for seeing his old friend was to find out more about his daughter, Shellie, who coincidentally was introducing her thesis proposal that afternoon to her faculty advisory staff as well as some fellow classmates and anyone else that would be interested to attend at the small lecture room that was located in the basement of the School of Robotic Science.

Olaf, still reeling from the news that he was an uncle, was unusually animated that morning, barely able to finish his coffee and Danish he purchased from a vendor at the train station. Drexel, for the first time in his life, was feeling excited as well, to the point of elation, about the possibility of seeing this child of his, although there was the understanding that at present he could not reveal himself to her for fear that the shock would be too much for Shellie, not to mention damage his newfound ties with Marguerite if she ever found out that he went to see his daughter.

Unknown to both Drexel and Olaf, a couple had boarded the train for Boston some fifteen minutes earlier and was seated in the dining car, pausing in their arguing long enough to order breakfast. Once the waiter left, they went back to their heated exchange, punctuating their whispered conversation every now and then with clearly audible phrases of "how dare you say that!" or "you insensitive brute!" The last comment came from the irate woman, who was ready at any moment to toss her hot tea into her clueless husband's face.

"Marguerite, I never understood this coddling of yours towards our daughter," whispered Edward Gainsborough, the Duke of Sussex. His wife glared back silently from across the tiny dining car table that was draped in a fresh white linen tablecloth with a crystal vase containing fresh-cut yellow daisies.

"You never appreciated our daughter's talents, Edward, no, not once!" said Marguerite, growing red faced in indignation, her hands tightening into small fists under the table.

"That wasn't it at all, Marguerite. The fact that she wanted to come to America to go to school didn't bother me. What drives me insane is the school she chose to go to. MIT? I mean, really, why couldn't she have gone to Harvard and become a barrister -- err, I mean a lawyer, as they say in America, like her father? This fascination with all this technology, well, it isn't proper for someone of her royal birth. It's fine for the lower classes and their children, but she could have gone into politics and maybe even gotten herself a seat in Parliament. I had such plans," Edward sighed.

"Your plans were for your own ego," Marguerite hissed. "It's all about you, Edward, isn't it? All about how or what people think, your position in society, your parents, your profession. It's all about you and your little stuck-up world and how you are perceived by our circle of so-called mindless friends; never mind the fact that our precious daughter is in the top of her class and that today

423

she is standing on her own in front of her professors and fellow students. She needs her father's approval, Edward, not more back-handed compliments about her choice of schools or her future in this science. And by the way, dear husband, not all royals are lawyers. Some do choose technology and science and become rather successful at it!" Marguerite slammed her tea spoon down on the table for emphasis, holding a mental image of Drexel in the back of her mind as her inspiration for her last comment about royals.

Edward, leaning back, sipped his tea and looked out the window to momentarily avoid looking at his wife. He welcomed the brief silence between him and his wife as he watched the people boarding the train, hearing only the muffled sounds of Grand Central Station's loudspeakers announcing their departure in ten minutes. In the past he often would suddenly stop talking during an argument with Marguerite, especially when either her point made sense or she was right. And now, deep down, he knew that she was right, but he couldn't resist one last attempt at credibility for his version of the truth.

"I suppose by that remark you were referring to that

broken down Swedish count of yours that you almost married," Edward remarked. "What ever happened to that walking computer? I would wager he is teaching at some musty college in Sweden, eking out a living with a chemistry set and preparing his supper over a hotplate in a one-room apartment in a Stockholm slum. See what kind of life I saved you from, dear? You should be thanking me instead of arguing with me."

Marguerite bit her tongue and held back what she really wanted to say to Edward in response to his stinging insults and instead said, "Don't flatter yourself, Edward. Had you stuck around at the charity event last week instead of leaving me sitting there by myself while off chasing a barmaid..." Hesitating for emphasis, Marguerite watched her husband's face start to flush. "Oh, yes, Edward, don't think I don't know about your little escapades."

Edward, red-faced, started squirming in his chair, shocked at his wife's realization that he was indeed off chasing barmaids that evening, only returning back to the event in time to pick his wife up and drive them both home.

"I, uh, I mean, what ever do you mean, Marguerite?" asked Edward, trying to feign innocence.

Marguerite, satisfied for the moment at the frightened response by her husband, waved her hand and said, "Oh, forget it, it's not worth it. I don't want to get myself all worked up before we see Shellie. And as to my comment about not all royals become lawyers, I did see Aslund Drexel at the charity event while you were away having your fun, and he looked very successful and tall and slender and --"

"I get the point, dear," Edward said angrily, temporarily forgetting about being in the hot seat that his wife had put him in a few seconds before. All he could think about now was how jealous and self-conscious he felt at her description of Drexel being tall and slender, which Edward knew he himself was neither as he noticed his own reflection in the dining car window.

Suddenly the train lurched forward a few feet and a loud horn blew from the engineer's cabin, momentarily causing both Edward and Marguerite to put a hold on their heated conversation.

"Well, I've lost my appetite," said the Duke, getting up from the table just as the waiter showed up with their breakfast.

"Well, I haven't!" snapped Marguerite. After the waiter placed her breakfast in front of her, she motioned for the waiter to take away her husband's food.

Before leaving, Edward turned to Marguerite and said, "Maybe, dear wife, one day you can meet up again with this Count Drexel and both of you can run off together to some place far, far away, say South America, where I'm sure the two of you would be very happy together." He quickly turned his back on her before she could utter a word and slammed the train car door behind him as he left.

"Don't think that thought hasn't crossed my mind, husband dear," muttered Marguerite out loud to herself as she picked up her wheat toast and buttered it, all the while staring out the window with a wistful expression on her face.

***

The train was fully underway as Drexel and Olaf found a couple of comfortable seats in a side train compartment off the main aisle of the passenger car. Olaf was chatting away on who he thought Shellie would look like, whether she would favor their mother or Drexel or Marguerite, or maybe even their father, while Drexel remained quiet and deep in thought as he put their carry-on bags into the luggage compartments above them.

"I can't believe you are so calm about this, brother," Olaf continued. "Just think, you have an heir to your soon-to-be empire who may possibly be just as brilliant as you are. What do you want your daughter to call you? Maybe Papa, Father, or what? I know I want to be called Uncle Olaf!"

Drexel was getting perturbed at Olaf's excitement. "Listen, Olaf, I have said this before and I'll repeat it again, Shellie must not be told who we are. All I want to do is just observe her and see this daughter that I could have had in my life, but didn't. That's it. End of story."

"So you don't blame Marguerite for not telling you about your daughter those 22 years ago?" asked Olaf, yawning out loud and leaning back in his seat so he could relax.

"How could I?" responded Drexel, as he closed the luggage compartment doors. "We both were very young and somewhat scared about the future. I can only imagine what she felt at the time. And, by the way, Olaf..."

"What?" asked Olaf.

"No one, not even my own daughter, is as brilliant as me," said Drexel in a casual tone as he took a seat.

Drexel tried to copy Olaf by leaning back in his seat and relaxing, but his mind had too much going through it. Finally he sat up and asked Olaf, "Are you hungry? Because I sure am. I haven't eaten anything since we landed in our private runway at Kennedy Airport at 4:00 a.m. this morning."

Olaf opened one eye and said, "No. I just ate. You go ahead. I need a nap. Just wake me up when we get to Boston." With that, Olaf yawned and turned himself towards the train window, which by now was showing countryside rushing past them at seventy miles per hour.

"As you wish, little brother," said Drexel, stepping out of the compartment door. He could hear Olaf already snoring before he shut the door behind him.

Drexel started his walk towards the dining car, glad to be alone to his thoughts, not even conscious of his surroundings. Suddenly he felt a hard jolt, causing him to look up, finding himself being stared at by a very unpleasant-looking passenger.

"You there, watch where you're going!" snarled the short, rotund figure that had bumped into Drexel, causing them both to bounce off the metallic walls in the shallow train corridor. Before Drexel could respond, the man, who now looked more like an angry badger at that moment, continued past him without another word and ambled down the hall.

"Strange little man," Drexel thought. "I wonder why I just didn't throttle him right then and there." But his thoughts quickly reverted back to meeting his daughter and how, without revealing who he was, he could start some kind of relationship with her.

Upon entering the dining car, Drexel grabbed a complimentary newspaper and made his way to an empty table. He unknowingly sat directly behind Marguerite, who had her back to him and was engrossed in a paperback romance novel that she kept hidden in her purse so that her husband wouldn't find it. At the very sight of those books he would fly into a rage and complain about how "those books lower the IQ of any reader that finds herself so foolish as to pick one up."

Drexel, on the other hand, was casually reading the editorials and barely conscious of the waiter who was standing in front of him with a menu and coffee. Waving the man off by holding up his hand and mouthing silently the words "later, please," the waiter turned towards Marguerite and softly said, "Would you care for anything else, ma'am?" Marguerite just shook her head no and handed the waiter a ten dollar tip, which he was thrilled to get on such a skimpy meal. Thanking her profusely, he gave her a slight bow and quickly left.

Drexel couldn't keep his mind focused on what he was reading. There was an aroma in the air, a familiar scent that gave him visions of Marguerite. "I even smell her perfume around me," he said to himself, chuckling at the power his beautiful Marguerite had over his mind. Pulling the paper up to his face again, he tried to continue reading where he had left off.

Marguerite suddenly turned around, thinking her husband might come back through the cabin door with an apology for her at the way he had acted, but the only thing she saw was the back of a newspaper being held by someone whose face she couldn't see. Turning back towards her book, as hard as she tried, she couldn't hold back the tears.

Drexel, who usually could tune distressed people out, couldn't ignore the very faint and soft sobs coming from this woman in front of him. It bothered him that he was actually concerned for this creature, but something was very familiar about her and impossible to overlook.

Clearing his throat, he said, "Madame, I am sure whatever difficulty you are in can't be as bad as you are making it out to be." With that, he put down his newspaper and looked at the stranger with her back turned toward him.

There were some more sniffles from Marguerite. As she started to turn around to face the stranger who was addressing her, Marguerite said, "Thank you for your concern, sir, but I can promise you this is not a slight matter. You see, I married the wrong --" Marguerite stopped in midsentence as she stared straight into the man's ice pale blue eyes. "Aslund!" she gasped in surprise. "What? But how..." Marguerite could only sputter.

Drexel, who was in shock himself at the wonderful sight before him, became speechless. Jumping up from his table, he instinctively took Marguerite in his arms and kissed her.

"I knew you wouldn't stay away," she said, looking up into Drexel's eyes. "But Shellie can't know, Aslund! She just can't!"

"She won't, darling, I promise, but as her real father I have to see her," Drexel said.

"I know, my love, I know." Marguerite kissed Drexel again as the train entered a tunnel, where the only lights shining were those outside the speeding train, leaving the dining car illuminated briefly by staccato bits and pieces of faint luminescence coming through the windows, giving the interior of the car a strobe light effect. For a moment they both felt like they were the only ones in the universe.

Suddenly, out of the shadows, a dark silhouette of a small rotund man appeared in the doorway. "Marguerite, are you there?" asked the man, straining to see inside the dining area.

Recognizing the voice, Marguerite whispered, "My husband!" She couldn't hide the desperation in her voice, even a tinge of disappointment at Edward choosing now to come looking for her.

"Who? Him?" replied Drexel with contempt after catching a look at the man as the tunnel lights exposed Edward's profile. "Why, that's the annoying little man who bumped into me earlier. Just wait here and I'll toss that fat toad off the train head first and you'll never have to be bothered by him again!"

"Aslund, stop! Whatever he is, he is still the only father that Shellie has ever known. Just sit back down in your seat   before he comes this way!

"But, you see, I could just --"

"You'll do nothing of the sort," Marguerite interrupted, pushing down on Drexel's shoulders, causing him to obediently sit back down in his chair. She then hurried back to her chair at her own table just as the train exited the tunnel, with daylight again flooding the dining car.

"Oh, there you are," said Edward, walking toward his wife, completing ignoring Drexel who just sat there scowling at the man.

"My pills, where did you put them?" asked Edward, looking at his watch. It's already 9:45 and I am two hours past my normal time to take them.

"Sorry, Edward. I put them in one of my bags here," Marguerite answered. I'll get them for you. Just give me a minute to pay the bill and I'll be right back.

"Well, do hurry. My blood pressure is probably off the charts, no thanks to our little chat this morning, as well as these rude Americans on this train," Edward scoffed. Catching his last comment, Edward quickly looked towards Drexel, who was busy hiding himself behind his paper. Drexel really wanted to throttle the man, but didn't, for Marguerite's sake. Satisfied his remark wasn't heard by this stranger, Edward again turned his attention toward his wife who had returned and was handing him his pills.

Edward gave Marguerite a quick kiss on her forehead and exited the dining car for the second time, slamming the door behind him. There was a brief moment of silence as Marguerite and Drexel sat there in the dining car alone.

"I can't believe you have put up with that all these years," said Drexel, putting down his paper and scooting his chair towards Marguerite's table. She seemed to be ignoring his comment, and he watched as she wrote something down on a scrap piece of paper.

"Here," she said, taking Drexel's hand and stuffing the paper into it. "Our daughter has a presentation today at 3:30 in the basement of the Robotic Science building, Room 214. Don't be late. I'll save you a seat."

Marguerite stood up to put on her coat.

"But what about him?" Drexel asked, not even wanting to give the Duke the title of being her husband.

"Don't worry, Aslund. Edward will see Shellie before the presentation, but soon thereafter will pretend he has some important business somewhere and will excuse himself, being long gone before 3:30. Boston has lots of bars and, well, barmaids," Marguerite sighed. "He'll be quite content and happy for the rest of the afternoon. Now, I've got to go, love. I'll see you soon!"

Before Drexel could respond, she gave him a quick kiss on the cheek and ran out of the dining car, leaving Drexel somewhat perplexed at all that had just taken place, but satisfied all the same when he looked at the note that Marguerite had given to him. He read it again, noticing that she used a heart instead of a period at the end of the last sentence. He smiled to himself and tucked the note inside his jacket and went back to reading his newspaper, his thoughts swimming of his encounter with the beautiful Marguerite.

***

25 DREXEL'S LONG LOST DAUGHTER

The School of Robotic Science at MIT was an easy walk from the visitor parking lot to the three-story oblong, gray stone building with its high stone arches and Latin inscriptions over each archway entrance. Drexel couldn't help but look around and enjoy all the different facets of the architecture, while Olaf was sullen and upset at the fact that he couldn't introduce himself to Shellie as her Uncle Olaf. He had met Marguerite years before when his brother was dating her, but was told by Drexel that a re-introduction to her or an introduction to his newly-founded niece at this time would be too complicated and messy, and if he really wanted to observe Shellie, it would be better if he sat at the back of the small auditorium and not with Drexel or Marguerite.

As they were about to enter the school, some professors were entering ahead of them, followed by some students. A tall, striking, thin young woman stopped Drexel in his tracks. The girl was just yards ahead of them, chatting excitedly to someone who most likely was her professor. The professor was laughing at something the young girl was saying, possibly a private joke or some humorous comment they were sharing.

"Is that Shellie?" croaked Olaf, unable to hide the emotion in his voice as he talked to his brother.

Drexel could only stare at the tall blonde girl with the pink backpack. She wore a crisp white blouse, rail-thin blue jeans and tan boots, carrying what looked like rolled up charts and graphs. Finally he answered Olaf. "Yes, that is her. I'm sure of it. She looks just like her mother, except for the blonde hair."

"No!" interjected Olaf. "Look again. Look at her face, her round wire glasses, her nose and mouth. It's you twenty-two years ago. I can't believe it, brother. It's you!"

"You are romanticizing the situation, little brother. Let's follow them, but keep your distance and keep your eyes out for Marguerite," Drexel whispered.

"Marguerite may already be inside," said Olaf, as they proceeded to follow the group to the basement lecture room.

The lecture room was spacious, with stadium seating for at least two hundred. The seating rose upwards from the stage where the lectures were given. Around the room were several chalkboards with formulas written all over them, as well as a huge wall map containing many stars and constellations, possibly a prop that Shellie had earlier set up for her presentation. Drexel would know soon enough.

Sitting on the stage with a few professors was Dean Jon Anderson, Drexel's old school colleague from his days at MIT, after having graduated with a Ph.D. from Stockholm University. Dean Anderson was talking with the robotic department's chair, Professor Ogden, a cruel, self-serving man with a keen intellect that enjoyed crushing bright students' ambitions and ideas rather than encouraging them, which served to boost his own ego. Dean Anderson, a brilliant man himself, was just the opposite. He was constantly cheerful and full of fun and somehow managed to like Drexel in his youth despite the fact that Drexel never smiled very much as a young man and always preferred to be by himself rather than have any friends. But Dean Anderson managed to break through Drexel's façade and the two became fast friends, lasting up until the day they both graduated with Ph.D.'s at the age of twenty-four.

"Sulphur boy!" yelled Dean Anderson from the stage as he saw Drexel enter the room.

Drexel cringed. He had always hated the nickname his friend had bestowed on him. Drexel was the only student in the history of MIT that almost blew up the chemistry lab when he was experimenting with some sulfur compounds, stinking up the chemistry lab for weeks. The nickname stuck.

"Jon, good to see you!" said Drexel, smiling slyly while looking around the room for Marguerite, hoping she hadn't heard that awful name that Jon had given him. Fortunately, it looked like she hadn't arrived yet.

Jon Anderson bounded off the lecture stage, jumping from the podium rather than using the stairs, landing on his feet only a few steps away from his old friend. "I got your email that you were coming, but I had rather thought you would let me drive down to New York and pick you up personally. Anyway, what brings you here, old friend? Did someone tell you we may have a young genius in the robotics department and you wanted to see if it was true?"

"Something like that, Jon. I just didn't want to trouble you. I had planned to come by later and visit for a bit," said Drexel.

"Visit?" asked Jon. "Nonsense. I'm taking you out to dinner this evening where we can really visit."

Drexel had forgotten what a real friend was like and how, although not admitting it to himself, he really appreciated Jon's invitation. "Well, that sounds good, Jon." Looking towards Olaf, he continued, "And this is my brother, Olaf. We, uh, work together."

"Well, it's my pleasure," said Jon, grabbing Olaf's hand and shaking it hard. Olaf smiled weakly, still looking around for any signs of his niece. She must be backstage making some last minute preparations, he thought.

Jon escorted Drexel and Olaf to a section close to the stage and said, "Well, you two pick out some seats.

We are about to start very soon, so I'd better get back on stage. But enjoy yourselves, and I really think you'll be impressed at the type of students that we produce here."

"I'm already certain of the truth of that fact, Jon," said Drexel, shaking his friend's hand for the second time. With that, Jon left them to themselves.

Olaf noticed that Drexel was getting a bit agitated. Turning to his brother, he winked and said, "Don't worry, she'll show. I'll go ahead and take a seat up top. You stay here."

Drexel just nodded and walked a few rows up from the stage and took an aisle seat, looking for both his daughter and Marguerite. The people attending were starting to take their seats.

A few minutes passed by before Professor Ogden walked on stage, cleared his throat and announced, "This afternoon we have a young graduate student, Shellie Gainsborough..."

Drexel winced at the name Gainsborough.

"...who wishes to enlighten us here today with her

proposal on the use of robotics in space exploration and how robotics can further man's quest for space. Let me first mention, though, that any faculty and members of the audience are free to ask questions of Miss Gainsborough, but please wait until the final presentation is done. Miss Gainsborough, if you please..."

Drexel's daughter walked out onto the stage and over to the slide projector that had been put there earlier for her use. The muffled sound of polite applause from the twenty or so people that were attending could be heard. Drexel had momentarily forgotten about Marguerite not having shown up yet and was focused on his daughter, waiting to hear the sound of her voice as well as her presentation.

As Shellie quickly set up her slides, she glanced out into the audience trying to find her mother, already knowing that her father had to go back to New York on some important business. She could only see some fellow students whom she recognized and this tall, thin, strange man intently staring at her, which made her a little nervous.

Her slides were fixed and she began to talk. "If we are really to reach for the stars, mankind will have to think out of the box in order to accomplish that goal. My proposal," Shellie continued, as she started her slide presentation of scenes of outer space and very life-like robots," is that we use robotic intelligence to operate aboard any interstellar spacecraft due to the thousands of years it would take to reach the first real star system in relation to our own earth, which is Alpha Centuri."

There was some muffled laughter from Professor Ogden who was sitting behind Shellie, which made her even more nervous than she was. Her voice started to crack somewhat as she continued.

"Furthermore, we can create these robotic beings, I believe, with enough intelligence to evolve over the vast amount of time and space to eventually think for themselves and make empirically based decisions rather than make decisions based on outdated programming designed generations before."

More chuckles could be heard from Professor Ogden, turning Drexel's face red with anger. He was offended at this man's gestures while he was trying to concentrate on his daughter's presentation. Shellie went on showing more slides on how these robotic beings would evolve, drawing Drexel in more and more to her ideas. Ideas on designs she talked about that he never really thought of, but now he was making mental notes of how he would have to work on the things she was saying. He was riveted by her intelligence, totally captivated by her theories.

After fifteen minutes of Shellie enduring the rude chuckling from Professor Ogden, she ended her proposal and sat down near the podium, obviously shaken from Professor Ogden's rude taunts. Professor Ogden got up with a smirk on his face and took the microphone.

"Thank you, Miss Gainsborough, for your, uh, interesting and, may I say, entertaining comments on robotics. If the audience has any questions of this student, you may ask them now. I know I do." Then he chuckled again, trying to cover it up with a cough.

Drexel had had enough. He watched Shellie shaking in her seat, her ego in shreds. He was the first to raise his hand, which Professor Ogden acknowledged.

"I would like, first, to thank the young woman for her brilliant and refreshing comments on the science of robotics," said Drexel.

"And you are, sir?" asked Professor Ogden, who had stopped his chuckling.

"Yes, I am Aslund Drexel, with three Ph.D.'s, one of which is from this honored institute. I might add that I design and build many robotic systems used in Europe and throughout the rest of the world. And who are you, sir?" he asked, looking directly at Professor Ogden, who was starting to feel a bit nervous at the absolute confidence of this stranger.

"Well, uh, I'm dean of the robotic department, of course," answered Professor Ogden.

"And might I ask how many PhD's you have, sir?" Drexel yawning on purpose looked at his watch, waiting for the professor to answer.

"Um, I have one in mechanical engineering from this fine institution," the professor answered, now sporting a frown, thinking to himself how dare this man question him in such a manner.

Drexel, timing his next question carefully, allowed a brief period of silence to go by and then asked, "So it's safe to say you do not have one in fluid dynamics or astrophysics; is that correct, sir?

"Yes, it is," replied the professor.

"Well, then I suggest you sit down while I ask this brilliant young woman some more questions on her outstanding research," said Drexel.

Shellie was all smiles as Drexel beckoned her to walk towards him so she could take center stage. Both watched as Professor Ogden went quickly to his seat after making a few snide remarks under his breath.

Jon elbowed Professor Ogden as he sat down and said, "He sure showed you, Bob. But I guess you had it coming." Professor Ogden said nothing in response and just sat in his seat, scowling.

Drexel, fully focused on his lovely daughter now standing before him, asked question after question on robotics and space travel and listened as Shellie more than proved herself in front of him and the audience. After the question-and-answer session was over, the whole room applauded loudly. Drexel took a seat and watched as his daughter's classmates ran up to congratulate her on her grand presentation.

Olaf made his way down to his brother and took a seat beside him. "Isn't she great!" he said, admiring his niece.

"Of course she is," said Drexel. "But something is wrong. Marguerite isn't here yet."

Seconds later Shellie came down the side stairs of the stage and walked over to Drexel, extending her hand for him to shake. "Thank you for your assistance. Without it this presentation would have been a disaster, I'm afraid."

Drexel gently shook her hand, suppressing every fiber in his being not to wrap his arms around her and tell her who he really was. "No, no, young woman, you did it on your own. All I did was put down a bully. You did the rest. My congratulations on a well thought-out proposal."

"So you really thought it was good?" asked Shellie.

Before Drexel could answer, Olaf interrupted and said, "Yes! Brilliant! Just brilliant!" He was barely able to contain himself.

Drexel added, "Allow me to introduce ourselves. I am Aslund Drexel and this impetuous person to my left is my younger brother, Olaf."

Shellie laughed and shook both their hands. Shyly looking around, she said, "I wish you could have met my mother. She was supposed to be here. I guess she got lost on campus or something. Anyway, I have to get back and clean up."

"Much success, to you young woman. I can see a great future in science for you," Drexel said. Then, turning serious, Drexel handed her his card and said, "If you ever need anything, call this number. Maybe I can help."

Shellie felt strangely drawn to the kindness in this stranger's eyes. Taking the card, she smiled and said, "I will. Thank you. Goodbye."

"Goodbye," both men said at the same time, watching her run back on stage to join her classmates.

Before they could exit the building, Olaf's emergency beeper went off. Reading the message to himself, he then said, "Brother, we will have to cancel dinner with your friend. We need to return to Gotland at once. Look for yourself." Olaf handed the beeper to Drexel and let him read the entire message: "Emergency, Master. We are receiving intelligence from London that Gotland is going to be under attack within 24 hours. Please get back."

***

The rental car sat in the back parking lot of MIT near a baseball field, several minutes' walk from the School of Robotic Science. Amidst the background chatter of a few students in the baseball stands who were trying to make the batter strike out by their loud comments, Olaf and Drexel rushed back to the car, totally oblivious to anything or anyone they might have passed by. Drexel's mind was torn over not seeing Marguerite one last time, and wanting to spend more time with Shellie, versus his need to return immediately to Gotland to fend off a possible invasion.

Olaf hadn't yet figured out a way to inform his brother about a call he received several hours ago while Drexel was arguing with the rental car manager over how much he was paying for their luxury rental. He was the only one who heard the bad news about their private jet's cracked turbo engine blade from a mechanic at Kennedy Airport. He didn't want to spoil the mood for his brother after seeing his daughter for the first time, but now time was of the essence. It appears that they will have to take the first commercial flight to Stockholm, which leaves at

8:52 p.m.

Upon approaching the rental car, Drexel spotted a note attached to the windshield. Picking up the small folded, yellow note, he immediately recognized the scent of Marguerite's lilac perfume. Flipping the note open as fast as he could, he read the words, "I have finally left my husband. If you are serious about us, meet me at Times Square at Angelo's at 6:00 p.m. this evening. If you are not there, then I will assume that we just had a pleasant walk down memory lane and I will be out of your life forever."

"This is wonderful!" shouted Drexel so loud that one of the outfielders turned around in their direction to see who was making all the noise. "Hurry, Olaf, let's get going to New York as fast as possible. We can easily make Grand Central Station by 5:30, and Angelo's is a quick fifteen-minute walk from the train station. Anyway, I can explain a few things about our life together to Marguerite and we can be back in Gotland by tomorrow morning!"

Olaf, got in the driver's seat and silently motioned to his brother to get in the car and fasten his seat belt. "Brother, I don't think you realize how much time we don't have. I didn't want to upset you, but I heard from the mechanic at Kennedy that our jet has to have some engine work done. In other words, our jet won't be ready until sometime next week."

Drexel, still not losing his euphoria over Marguerite, quipped, "All right, Olaf, I can live with that. How about grabbing us a charter - money is no object - and we still get to Gotland by tomorrow morning?"

"Splendid idea, brother, and I already checked into that while we were back at the auditorium, but the only charter available immediately is here in Boston, not New York. We can go ahead and get it right now, but that means --"

"I *know* what it means. It means ruining my future with Marguerite," injected Drexel, slipping from euphoria into depression.

"Well, hear me out, brother," said Olaf. Olaf had become quite used to coming up with quick solutions for his older brother's infinite supply of problems. "Why don't I go to New York and explain to Marguerite that we had an emergency and that you had to go home and that I'll send a plane to meet her anywhere she wishes once this invasion threat works itself out?"

"Because, Olaf," said Drexel, loosening his tie, "Marguerite and I first admitted our love for each other there at Angelo's in Times Square many years ago when we ran off to New York on a whim. She would never forgive me if I didn't personally meet her there. Besides, if this is a real scenario of an invasion coming up, I'll need you by my side." Drexel glanced at his watch and knew time was slipping away. Looking at Olaf, he spilled his thoughts. "Anyway, I am not all that convinced that something is going on in England. Have you noticed that we haven't heard from our droid plants in the military, parliament, or the main part of MI5? If something is really going on, don't you think we would get wind of it from them rather than our own men on Gotland reporting some unusual chatter over various security-based radio traffic?"

At first, Olaf didn't answer his brother. He put the car into gear and drove out of the parking lot and onto the main road leading out of the campus. His mind was fixed on his brother's words about wanting him "by his side." This was the first time he had heard his brother actually come out and say that he needed him. Before, Olaf always felt he was the bumbling kid brother who always could find a way to mess things up and disappoint his older brother. His brother usually reserved the privilege of total trust for Günther Bergman. Günther was the one Drexel usually went to for advice, and Olaf knew how important that was to Günther. In fact, as the years passed, it sometimes seemed to Olaf that his brother rather enjoyed the fact that he and Günther Bergman had a competition of sorts for Drexel's attention. Now Olaf felt a shift of supreme trust was thrust in his direction and he wanted to savor the moment.

"Olaf, snap out of it and answer me. What do you think?" asked Drexel.

"Uh, yes, of course, brother," Olaf said. "Now that we're through with this little side trip, we've got to get back to Gotland. I have our men already waiting for us at Stockholm International Airport to fly us to Gotland. Besides, there's a commercial flight leaving Kennedy for Stockholm this evening that I already booked three tickets on just in case we had problems with a charter."

"Good job, little brother," said Drexel. "And, hey, wait a minute, did you say *three* tickets?"

"Yes," said Olaf, "for the on-board droid you have been tinkering with. I knew you wouldn't want to leave him on the jet to be discovered by some mechanic, so when we get into New York I'll get over to the airport and retrieve the droid while you go see Marguerite. But don't take too long. The flight leaves at 8:52 and we have to get checked in and go through security, which may be another problem we have to work out."

"You worry too much, little brother," laughed Drexel, leaning back in his seat, feeling his good mood returning. I had some plans for him anyway, but it is a good idea to take him with us. I'll explain all that later. You know," said Drexel, thinking out loud, "I almost wish we would be attacked. I need some subjects to demonstrate my new weapon systems on. Whoever is coming after us, I really pity them. Here, Olaf, give me the cell. I feel the need to arrange a little welcoming committee for our heroic guests."

"Heroic guests?" asked Olaf.

"Yes, dear brother. Don't you know all heroes die and get buried at sea?" quizzed Drexel, laughing a little too wildly for Olaf's comfort. There was the evil genius that Olaf was so familiar with. Now he watched silently as Drexel dialed his top security personnel.

26 LOVE FINDS DREXEL AND MARGUERITE IN NEW YORK CITY

It was nearly 6:00 p.m. Marguerite sat all alone in the corner of the small Italian café at exactly the same table she and Drexel had sat at and stared into each other's eyes some twenty-two years ago. The café appeared not to have changed at all. There were the ever present multi-colored, candle-dripped, dark green wine bottles sitting in the center of the table atop the same white-and-red-checkered tablecloths. An antique jukebox sat opposite her table near the bar, attempting to crank out one last record which either no one heard or cared to pay attention to, just static tunes that wafted up into the café's cigarette smoke-filled ceiling, the smoke twirling into pretzel-like shapes until they were caught and spit out by the large ceiling fan.

Two minutes past 6:00 and no sign of Drexel. Marguerite was beginning to feel a twinge of regret by acting so rashly. Separating from her husband was on her to-do list for some time, but to expose her vulnerability to a lost love was something that was totally against her cautious nature. But it was only a few minutes past 6:00.

"Maybe he got delayed by traffic and is desperately trying to get to me", she thought.

Twenty minutes past 6:00. All her being was focused on the café entrance, but no one was coming into the café but happy couples, which made the pain in her heart even more acute, contrasted with the smiling faces of those that seemed to be in love. The clock on the wall seemed to make a loud bong noise with each second that ticked by. "Had another fifteen minutes passed by?" said Marguerite to herself as she looked at the clock again.

Through the window she saw daylight had given up its role to the bright lights of Times Square. Looking at her watch one last time, she sighed and got up from the table, leaving a twenty dollar bill for her tab and tip, not wanting to engage in conversation with the waitress or any other human being for that matter. Fighting back her tears, she left the café and started walking back to her hotel that was in the opposite direction of Grand Central Station.

"I guess I am not that important to Aslund after all," she said out loud as she suddenly found herself bent over and sobbing out of control. She felt as though someone had punched her in the stomach. Her hand pressed against a storefront window, which gave her some support as the busy crowds of Time Square just streamed passed her without so much as a glance of pity or concern.

Suddenly, as if it were a dream, she heard her name faintly off in the distance from behind her. The voice was barely audible over the noises of the city and she wasn't sure she really heard anything at all. She made herself keep looking forward, thinking somehow it was her imagination or a cruel trick her own mind was trying to play on her. What a fool I've been, she thought once more to herself.

The voice cried out her name again. This time it was closer and louder, coming from someone that sounded out of breath. "Marguerite, wait!" Marguerite stopped crying, trying to listen, afraid to even breathe, waiting for the disappointment to flood her again. But she made herself turn around and look. She looked into the faces of countless strangers that seemed to be flying by her. Then she saw him, the bobbing tall frame of Drexel running towards her with his hand waving in the air.

Like a school girl let out on holiday, her joy exploded within her, but on the outside she somehow held her composure and remained calm and resolute, standing in the same spot where she had been sobbing moments before, waiting for Drexel who was dodging traffic against the light and almost getting hit by a fast moving cab, trying to reach her.

Making it across the street, Drexel stopped a couple of feet away from the love of his life, trying to catch his breath, not really knowing how to apologize, but in one of his rare moments of dealing with human beings he blurted out the truth. "We were delayed by a freight train running on the same track ahead of us. Imagine that, a freight train taking precedence over a passenger train. Only in America, huh?" said Drexel as he watched Marguerite's face for any sign of forgiveness.

Marguerite tried as hard as she could to remain aloof and mad, but that lasted only seconds. She ran and jumped in his arms, passionately kissing him below the pulsating lights of Times Square. The reunited couple, for one brief happy moment, was oblivious to anything or anyone around them. The cell phone ringing in Drexel's pocket almost went unnoticed.

Marguerite purred, "Let's go back to Angelo's, darling, and capture what we had decades ago."

Drexel, not wanting to let go of Marguerite or the romantic moment, finally made himself grab the ringing cell phone and heard himself say, "Excuse me, darling, but I have to get this."

"Yes, Olaf, what is it," hissed Drexel.

Olaf, in a panicked voice, said, "The airport is packed and the security line is much longer than I anticipated. You have to leave for the airport now or we won't get out of here until tomorrow afternoon!"

Drexel, trying not to alarm Marguerite, only could ask Olaf, "Is the droid with you?"

"Of course he is," answered Olaf. "I had to fix up his fake passport with the equipment on the plane, but I've got him activated and awake. The only thing, though, is he is not programmed for English, so as far as the outside world is concerned he's just another Swedish tourist on holiday. By the way, are you sure we can get him through American security? You know things have changed in this country lately, don't you?"

"Yes, I am well aware of that and will be there shortly," said Drexel, snapping the cell phone shut, Marguerite looking at Drexel with an expression of bewilderment and sadness.

"Who are you?" she asked as she held his face with her hands, all the while looking into his deep ice blue eyes. "I thought we were going to be together once we found each other again, but all it has been is you showing up late, and now, from what I just heard, you are leaving me here in New York to go back to your castle in Sweden? What part of leaving my husband for you don't you understand? You are my life. Why are you acting like I'm some sort of doormat that will let you come and go as you please? Aslund, again I'm asking the question, who are you and are you the one for me, because right now I'm beginning to wonder."

Drexel, feeling a little misplaced at all the emotions

between them, stood there letting her hold his face, even if she was lecturing him, all the while trying to think of a plausible excuse as to why he needed to leave immediately, an excuse that would still keep Marguerite's love for him intact and would also explain why he needed to get to the airport to get a droid through security. Those were his two primary goals that he was determined to carry out, and he could do it if he used his gifted ability to multi-task. Marguerite was the main task of course, but still he knew he could never commit his full attention to one individual, not even Marguerite. His mind's wiring at present would not allow it. But for the moment he did come up with a reasonable sounding excuse in his mind.

While gently taking her hands off his face and holding them in his, he gazed back into her soft blue eyes that looked like two separate deep pools of blue water that could easily drown all his plans and ambitions if he wasn't careful. "I can't explain right now, but if you could just trust me this one last time, I'll send for you after this is --"

"Take me with you," interrupted Marguerite.

"What?" asked Drexel, surprised at her suggestion. "How could she be so unreasonable? Couldn't she see how important his work was to him?", he thought.

"I said take me with you back to Gotland. I overheard your brother mention something about taking an android with you. Surely I am more important than one of your androids," Marguerite said, taking out her passport. "See, I have all that I need to travel. Forget my things at the hotel. I have my money with me and whatever I may need I can buy once we get to Sweden. I am ready to go to the airport now. Let's go, Aslund," she said, tugging on his sleeve, trying to turn him back towards Grand Central Station.

Drexel was amazed at her resolve and weakly followed her lead for a few steps until he spotted something across the street that brightened his spirits to the point of action. Taking her hand, he said, "Follow me!"

Marguerite let him lead on, thinking somehow she had convinced Drexel to take her with him, but when he started crossing the street in the opposite direction of the train station, she became concerned. Drexel escorted her into a fancy, high-priced jewelry store and left her standing alone while he went over to speak to the manager. Marguerite was puzzled. What could they be discussing at a time like this?

Very quickly the manager followed Drexel back to Marguerite, carrying a rather large tray of diamond rings. Drexel gestured towards the manager who was holding the tray and said, "Pick one."

"Whaa --" She couldn't finish a word due to her surprise. Looking at the store manager and then at Drexel to see if he was serious, she finally couldn't help herself and pointed to a very large blue, sparkling diamond ring that was embroidered in gold that was sitting in the very middle of the tray. The manager quickly scooped the ring up and handed it to Drexel so he could put it on her finger.

Marguerite just stood there as if in a trance as Drexel gently put the costly ring on her finger. Then he stood back a bit to watch her admire it. Before she could utter a word, he dropped to his knee like he had done almost twenty-two years ago and said, "Marguerite, will you marry me this time?"

Marguerite looked down at Drexel kneeling on the floor and without a second's hesitation she said, "Yes, of course I'll marry you, but what about --"

Drexel quickly put his fingers to her lips to stop her from talking and said, "My love, you work out the details of your divorce from your husband and plan all the details of our wedding while I'm gone. Invite whom you want and I'll fly them anywhere you wish, but may I suggest my lovely villa in South America, Argentina, to be exact, in, say, four weeks or so?"

Marguerite stood still in complete silence, letting the last few moments sink in. Finally she smiled at Drexel and said, "Yes, dear, of course! I have so much to do now, and so little time. You will call me the second you land in Sweden, won't you, love?"

"The very second," he promised, taking her hand and kissing it. "Now, forgive me, dearest, but I must be off."

"I suppose you must be, Aslund." She kissed him

one last time before he broke away and headed for the door. "I love you!" she called out to him as he ran out the door.

"I love..." But the large glass door closed before she cold hear his last words. All she could do was watch him run down the street towards the train station. She looked again at the beautiful ring that he had placed on her finger. She was finally going to marry the real love of her life. This day had turned out just wonderful, she thought.

***

Olaf was at the north terminal, furious that his brother was running so late. The droid was standing next to him, looking very much like a tall, thin, blonde Swedish businessman, holding his attaché case and waiting to go through the security check.

Suddenly Drexel appeared atop the escalator leading from the train terminal into the airport, carrying only his papers and passport. Rushing toward his brother and barely noticing the droid, he said, "Let's go get in the security line and get this over with. I'm a little nervous about these new American security techniques."

"*You're* nervous?" asked Olaf with surprise and sarcasm. "Well, me too. And have you seen that line?" Olaf turned Drexel's attention to a long line of people that was getting longer by the second. People were rushing to get in line and get through security so they didn't miss their flights. "And, by the way, the last time you mentioned getting the droid through security you said you had it under control. What happened to that no problem attitude of yours?"

"Watch and learn, little brother," said Drexel, looking cautiously around for anyone who may be surveying them. "I had planned to test this droid out anyway once we got here. The only difference is that the droid is not alone. We're going to be with him. Maybe that's not such a bad thing, since it'll give me an opportunity to see for myself any flaws or errors that might pop up in my plan."

"That's great and all, but any flaws or errors, as you say, that might come up would most likely land us in an American prison, and I don't think you or I would do very well as prisoners in America, especially federal prisoners. I've heard stories about --"

Drexel didn't let Olaf finish. "Shhhh, we're starting to move. Really, Olaf, where is your scientific curiosity?" Drexel couldn't help but tease Olaf, as he had done all his life. He knew if Olaf was really worried about his plan, he would have destroyed the droid himself before boarding.

Olaf tried to calm himself down, but couldn't escape the nervousness he felt as he watched the crowd going through the scanners which were getting closer and closer. Drexel's demeanor looked calm and in control, as did the droid's, who just looked straight ahead and moved without a sound.

The first security agent checked all the boarding passes and passports of the three men. Nothing happened but a quick smile and a nod of the head from the agent towards the direction of the scanners. Olaf let out a sigh of relief, but it was short lived. Soon the time arrived where they had to put their personal effects into a plastic case, along with their belts and shoes. The droid mechanically and masterfully mimicked everything Drexel did, right down to the way Drexel removed his watch and placed it in the tray.

Suddenly one of the agents motioned for Drexel to step into the full body scanner chamber where they ran a highly sensitive detecting wand all the way from Drexel's head down to his toes, looking for the presence of metal, wire, or chemical agents that could be hidden in his body. The machine remained silent as Drexel quickly stepped through to the other side. Olaf was next, and his body scan produced nothing as well. Then it was the droid's turn. To Olaf's shock and fear, the droid was asked to step into the body scanning chamber. The droid walked up to the scanner, but suddenly, as if on cue, the droid stopped just short of entering the chamber, making some of the security personnel put their hands on their holstered pistols.

The droid very calmly looked at the agent who was holding the wand and said something to him in Swedish. The agent leaned in closer to the droid and asked, "What did you say, mister?"

Drexel interrupted and said, "Uh, my friend doesn't speak English very well, Officer, but he is trying to say that the body scan is an affront to his personal liberty and he would prefer a full-body pat-down, which he believes is his right to do so under American law."

The agent, without any change in his expression, answered, "Yes, sir, that is true. Would you please have him step this way, behind the curtain, and we'll have two of our men pat him down and send him on his way."

"Thank you, Officer," said Drexel. Speaking a few quick words to the droid in Swedish, the droid placidly followed the agent to a concealment area behind a large curtain.

Olaf, watching the events, could no longer contain himself and started talking to his brother through the side of his mouth a bit too loudly. "Are you crazy? That's even worse than the wand!" Drexel quickly stepped on his brother's toe to quiet him down.

"Oww, that hurts!" grimaced Olaf, giving his brother a quick glare before he discreetly tried to bend his toe to see if it was broken.

"I'll do a lot worse if you don't shut up!" warned Drexel. "Look, they're all done!"

"Thank you, sir," said the agent to the droid. "And if

I may say so, sir, you are the most physically fit person to ever come through our little line here."

The droid looked blankly at the agent, but Drexel quickly stepped in and said something in Swedish, to which the droid silently walked over to the plastic tray on the other side of the scanner and picked up his belongings. Looking at the agent, Drexel said, "I must apologize for my friend. He really doesn't understand Americans very well, but I assure you he means no offense."

"Oh, none taken, sir. But just out of curiosity's sake, what do you Swedes eat over there that keeps you all in such good shape?"

Olaf, now relieved that they had passed inspection, interjected his own brand of humor into the mix by saying, "We all eat herring, lots and lots of herring."

The agent gave a quizzical half-smile and turned and went back to scanning, leaving the three men to put back on their belts and shoes.

"I can't believe our luck! How did he beat the full

body search?" whispered Olaf, motioning to the droid who was having some trouble putting his belt back through the loops of his trousers.

"Luck had nothing to do with it," Drexel said, tying his left shoe. "It was all science, just science."

"Being that I almost spent the next twenty years of my life as a probable wife to a very hairy American inmate in prison, I would appreciate a little elucidation of this science in my direction by my older brother," Olaf said.

"Don't mind at all. Glad to inform you, little brother." Looking around to see if anyone was within earshot, Drexel continued. "You see, this droid's exoskeleton is made up of an extra fibrous mesh of plastic, silicone, and soft clay, all mixed together electronically, adding firmness that feels like muscle. As I said before, I did want to try him out on his own with a passport that would never lead him back to us in case he got caught, which I doubt he ever would have gotten caught."

Olaf studied the droid and said, "So I take it he, uh, has all the usual, you know --"

"You mean is he anatomically correct?" asked Drexel.

"Yeah, that," said Olaf, a little embarrassed. "You can't really blame a guy for asking."

"Of course he is. The more real, the better he is little brother."

Olaf thought to himself for a second while putting on his belt. "Hey, wait a minute, if the droid was meant to go by himself, what would happen if he went through the full body scanner instead of the body pat-down? Wouldn't the agent's wand light up like a Christmas tree?"

"Of course not," said Drexel, getting annoyed at watching the droid trying to put on his belt. "In fact, I was hoping that he *would* go through the full body scan, but he must have detected the x-rays and considered them a threat."

"So that's why the droid said in our native language that he didn't like the wand?" asked Olaf.

"Yes. It's a good thing that Americans are notorious for not speaking any other languages than their own," laughed Drexel, "or we might not have been so lucky."

Olaf still had questions. "But wouldn't the x-rays have revealed the droid's inner workings?"

"Look," Drexel said, "just beneath the skin is a thin coat of lead that is embedded with a calcium phosphorous-based skeletal imprint into his flesh. All an x-ray would see is basically a skeleton and a gray amorphous background masking as human organs. Only a medical doctor could tell the difference."

"Brilliant! Just brilliant!" said Olaf, picking up the last of his possessions from the tray.

"Oh, you've seen nothing yet," whispered Drexel, picking up a glass of melted ice tea that someone had earlier left on the bench that they were sitting on. "Why don't you toss this onto our clumsy friend over there," said Drexel, motioning toward his droid.

"Are you crazy?" asked Olaf. "Why would you want to destroy your own creation?"

"Oh, brother," Drexel said to himself as he tossed the tea several feet into the air, watching it land on the unsuspecting droid. But nothing happened. The droid just ended up with a wet shirt and sports coat.

Olaf couldn't believe what he'd just witnessed. "You did it! You actually did it! You figured out the secret to making them waterproof!"

"Drexel, while smiling at watching his brother go into paroxysms over his achievement, calmly said, "Well, let's get to the gate. I wouldn't want to keep our guests waiting tomorrow, if and when they show up."

27 THE GATHERING STORM

All was calm at the deserted section of a private airfield, except for the few people silently scurrying around, performing various duties. The rustic wooded maintenance building that sat on the airfield was only used by MI5 and royal security personnel because it was only a two-minute flight time from the cliffs of Dover. Tom realized he was the only American present in the hideout, along with sixty crack members of the secret British MI5 top elite branch that were known as Nighthawks. Reggs, along with the rest of the men, were dressed in their black night mission uniforms, sitting below a plain wooden platform and drinking coffee. Suddenly a call came in from America. One of Reggs' men handed him the secure cell phone.

"Reggs, hi. It's Elliott."

"Elliott, you bugger, wish you could come to the party tonight, but I know you Yanks have your hands full in D.C. Did you clean up house yet?" asked Reggs.

"No, but we're making progress. The President, Bud, Jim, and I, along with some trusted Marine Corps buddies of mine, are here at the Marine barracks at 8th and I Street making sure that all the rest of our Secret Service agents get a good five-minute shower, along with key FBI and CIA personnel. You should hear the cussing from these guys," said Elliott.

Reggs burst out laughing. "When all else fails, give 'em a good bath, eh? Hope you have enough hot water."

"Yeah, really. Imagine, with all our technology, just plain old water is what does the trick. God help us if Drexel ever makes these things waterproof."

Reggs laughed again, but this time he couldn't hide his concern. "Well, mate, you can bet he will eventually figure that out if we don't take care of that bugger tonight."

"Well, good hunting, old friend," said Elliott. Tell Tom that Gravel said to bring Emily safely back and to give his regards to Drexel in lead as many times as you can."

"Actually, we all feel that way, but some of our scientist lads feel that Drexel being captured alive would be more of a use to us than dead. But we'll see," said Reggs.

"Sounds like a plan, Reggs. Until then."

"Until then," responded Reggs, hanging up.

The code words "until then" were always used by the MI5 as a sign of good fortune in a mission. To say anything more before a mission was to risk bad luck and certain failure. Elliott knew that fact and had wanted to say a whole lot more, but stayed within MI5 protocol to protect his friend.

After Reggs returned the cell phone to one of his men, he walked to the front of the briefing room and did a quick hop up onto a small wooden planked platform, standing beside two black bags that were placed there earlier. Behind him was a wall map of Gotland.

"Lads, I can't emphasize to you all enough the importance of tonight's mission. In the past we went after those that tried to hurt and destroy our country, and with our own very lives we swore to defend Britain and her people with our last breath, as we have in the past, time and time again, unwavering. But tonight we face something we have never had to face before. We face an enemy that has changed the rules, thus changing the game. He altered the perception of the sacredness of the one thing we as a people hold most dear. Reggs paused as he fought back a tear. Then he continued. "And that which we hold most dear as a nation is our Queen." The room exploded into cries of "hear! hear!" from all the men, including Tom who was sitting in the back row.

"Our Queen, who was taken weeks ago under our very noses by that bastard, Count Drexel of Sweden, now is held prisoner on an unknown island in the Baltic Sea in a castle being guarded by either his own men or his androids. This night we are going to correct that egregious crime and destroy whatever remains of his warped little empire."

"Now, I want all of you to look down at my right boot and notice the Union Jack emblem on my right foot." All the men leaned forward to see the flag painted on Reggs' right boot. "When I encounter Count Drexel, I am going to take this boot that's on my right foot and plant it, flag and all, up the good count's backside!" The room erupted again into cheers, foot stomping, and cries of "hurray, Reggs" and "God save the Queen."

Reggs held up his arms over his head to quiet the men, and then continued. "Now, many of you are wondering why we don't use a full coordinated attack with every armed service member we have, including help from the Americans. Well, lads, the answer is very simple. Most of our own people don't even believe the Queen has been taken. Her droid replacement at Buckingham has even fooled members of Her Majesty's own household staff, as well as other members of the royal family. Also, any member of MI5 outside this room as well as any trusted member of our own armed forces and government may be infected with a planted droid. We are all alone on this one, with no outside help except from young Tom here who, of course, loves our Queen and a certain young lady also being held prisoner." Many of the men started whistling and shouting, "Good on you, mate!" They patted Tom on the back or briefly rubbed his head with the palms of their hands. Tom, red-faced and embarrassed by all the attention, pulled his coat collar upwards to hide himself, but inside he was beaming with pride and excited that this elite group of men had accepted him as one of their own.

Reggs proceeded on. "Now, enough of the pep talk. Let me show you some toys our people in research, as the Americans say in their TV commercials, have made 'new and improved.'" Reggs then opened up one of the duffle bags to his left, pulling out a curious-looking wide black leather belt with dozens of odd shaped crystals set in the middle and running the whole circumference of the belt, meeting up on either side of a small metal panel with three prominent buttons, the square metal base looking like some sort of control panel.

"Now, lads, watch this as I press the green button." All eyes were on Reggs' finger as he pushed the green button. Less than half a second later Reggs, including the belt, vanished into thin air, followed by gasps from the men who were in total shock and unbelief at what they just saw. Next they heard the disembodied voice of their commander who sounded like he was walking across the stage, followed by silence. The men all started looking around, trying to see if Reggs would produce any visible trace of himself, maybe a shadow or some sort of flickering image, but nothing was to be seen. Suddenly a cigarette appeared to float off the ear of one of the men in the back of the room, followed by Reggs reappearing and holding the cigarette. Reggs handed the cigarette back to the stunned man and said, "These things will kill you, mate." The men loved the invisible act and applauded as Reggs took off the belt and threw it to Tom, who eagerly put it on and pressed the green button, causing him to disappear before everyone in the room.

"You see, mates," said Reggs, as he walked toward the front of the room again, this Drexel isn't the only genius around. We have a few of our own surprises hidden away, and here is something else that we know he hasn't got." Making his way back to the smaller black duffle bag, Reggs pulled out what looked like a heavy pair of sunglasses.

"Tom, lad, be a good sport and stay invisible and come up here and try to put a choke-hold on me," ordered Reggs.

"I'd rather not," said Tom's disembodied voice from the back of the room.

"It's okay, lad, just do it," urged Reggs while putting on the sunglasses.

"All right, Reggs, but don't say I didn't warn you." Tom, fully invisible, crept towards Reggs who was standing on the stage. All the men were so focused on what was going on that the only sound heard was their breathing. Tom crept up closer and closer, standing directly behind Reggs. Reggs seemed oblivious to Tom's presence, but when Tom was only a foot away from Reggs, Reggs pivoted on his left foot, swinging around and grabbing Tom, gently throwing him to the ground. Tom then pressed the red button on the belt and became totally visible again, to the applause of the whole group of men who were amazed at the events.

"How did you know I was there?" asked Tom, getting up off the floor and dusting himself off.

"With these, mate," said Reggs, taking off the glasses. I saw every move you made.

"Okay, gents," yelled Reggs to the rest of the men, "enough fun and games. Let's get focused on our battle plans."

28 REGGS ON HIS WAY WHILE EMILY AND THE QUEEN GO OUT ON A LEDGE

At five thousand feet, looking down below, the Baltic Sea appeared even blacker at 4:00 a.m. with no moon or stars above. Flying just below the rain and sleet-filled cloud cover was a small rescue force of fourteen British Blackhawk helicopters all moving in a V-shaped pattern, their lights out, with only the reflection of an occasional cigarette being lit by one of the pilots in the cockpit.

Reggs' helicopter was leading the V-shaped force. His main worry was what part of the castle at Gotland contained the Queen. All his men had strict orders not to fire directly on the castle until the Queen was located and rescued. Another worry he had was that Drexel might use the Queen as a hostage where her life would certainly be in danger, so that's why he set up half his force as a diversionary decoy. Upon arriving at the northern end of Gotland, he planned to land thirty members of his crack team to infiltrate the castle and secretly locate the Queen before the main assault.

Unknown to Reggs at the time was that Drexel wasn't even at the castle, having just hours before landed at Stockholm. Drexel had been picked up by some of his men in his jet helicopter that was piloted by Olaf and they were heading back to the castle at that very moment, after having radioed ahead to give the order that all his droids were to be moved out of the lab and to the underground caves below the castle "just in case there was to be any sign of trouble."

***

Back at the castle, Emily, who was in her bedroom next to the Queen's bedroom, was awakened by all the commotion below in the courtyard. Looking out through her only window, she saw a long, single line of droids making their way through a rounded opening in the courtyard wall. A string of bare light bulbs were clearly visible, highlighting a path that led to some sort of steep tunnel. Drexel's men were standing on each side of the pathway, ushering the droids downward, while some of the castle domestic staff appeared to be carrying unfinished or deactivated droids on portable carts from Drexel's lab, along with some of his equipment, all of it headed towards this same entrance. Emily's reporter instincts came alive in an instant at this strange scene unfolding before her, so, dressing quickly, she grabbed her tape recorder and headed next door to wake up the Queen.

"Betsy!" whispered Emily as she slipped into the Queen's bedroom from the unlit castle hallway. The Queen was sleeping on her side, facing the window and the lit courtyard. A Tale of Two Cities by Dickens lay open on the bed, still clutched by the sleeping Queen's left hand. Emily noticed that the book was opened at the halfway point, and she happened to remember that the Queen had just recently requested of the droid staff that same book from Drexel's private library yesterday.

"Fast reader," Emily said to herself as she tiptoed quietly over to the Queen to gently shake her shoulder, trying to wake her up. "Betsy, please wake up. This is urgent!" she said. Emily finally got a sleepy response from the monarch on the third shake.

"Is it morning already?" asked the Queen, yawning, as she stretched out her arms to prop herself up, then sat up in the bed.

"No, ma'am," whispered Emily. "It's 4:30 in the morning and I want you to see something that's happening outside in the courtyard!"

Surprisingly with little objection or comment about the time of morning or about being woke up in such a manner, the Queen got out of bed. Emily quickly helped her get her robe on as both women walked over to the window to witness the spectacle of a line of droids in orderly style quietly being ushered into some passageway off the courtyard.

"Odd," whispered the Queen, now fully awake. "What do you make of it, Emms dear?"

"I think they are expecting company," said Emily, quickly shutting the blinds when she noticed one of the staff look up towards their direction from the courtyard.

"You mean a rescue?" asked the Queen with a tinge of excitement in her voice.

"I think it's precisely that!" said Emily, taking the Queen's hand and helping her over to the armchair by the electric heater which had been put in her bedroom to help combat the damp cold of Gotland's chilly nighttime weather.

"Why, that's certainly good news, isn't it, dear?" asked the Queen, sitting down in the chair.

"Good news for us, Betsy, for sure, but --" The Queen held up her hand, silencing Emily before she could finish her sentence. "If you are going to tell me something stressing, Emms, I would better appreciate your thoughts with a warm cup of coffee and a biscuit that you will find above the coffee maker on the second shelf to the left." The Queen pointed to a cabinet above the coffee maker and microwave, items which the Queen never used but somehow now found their present availability comforting in light of the stressful circumstances that Emily was about to reveal.

"Of course, Betsy; I'll make us both a little something," Emily said, now getting up and walking over to the makeshift kitchen. Minutes later both women were sitting down together in front of the small heater, sipping coffee and eating warm butter biscuits like two old friends enjoying each other's company in the wee hours of the cold misty Gotland morning.

"All right, my dear," said the Queen, as Emily refilled both their cups, "please go ahead and finish what you wanted to say to me earlier."

"Well," began Emily, scooting her chair closer to the Queen as if she were going to share a secret that only the two of them could hear, "yes, it's true I think that someone in one of our governments has sent a rescue party to save us, but I strongly believe that this rescue mission could be turned into a hostage situation."

"You mean *me* as a hostage, don't you?" said the Queen, putting her cup down on a small end table that shared a space between the two women.

"Yes, Betsy, that is exactly what I mean," Emily answered, taking the Queen's hand to comfort her.

"Well, then," said the Queen, trying to smile, "tell me your plan, Emms. I know you have one or you wouldn't have brought the subject up."

Emily smiled and produced the small tape recorder

from her pocket, holding it out for the Queen to see. "Betsy, we both have to find some place to hide until our rescuers show up, and this," Emily said, holding up the palm-sized digital recorder, "this will buy us some time to disappear if the droid staff shows back up to grab us or you as a hostage."

"I like it!" said the Queen, smiling. "But tell me, dear, exactly how would this work?"

Emily turned on the recorder, and then made a knocking sound with her fist on the wooden table. "Okay, Betsy, I need you to say 'wait a minute, please, I'm dressing' as loud as you can."

"I beg your pardon?" gasped the Queen, taken aback at such a strange request. She was now sitting straight up in her chair with a serious frown on her face, staring at Emily.

"Betsy, trust me and just say it," begged Emily, thrusting the recorder closer towards the reluctant Queen.

The Queen sat still for a few seconds, then slowly, after losing her frown, leaned forward toward the small recorder and said in a loud clear voice, "Wait a minute, please, I am dressing and it will be a few more minutes." Before Emily could reach for the recorder to turn it off, the Queen, now smiling, gave Emily a wink and quickly continued, "And my American companion here is helping me, so you will have to give us both a little longer before we are ready." The Queen sat back in her chair, grinning at her improvisation. "I get it!" laughed the Queen. "What a clever ruse. Those silly droids will not enter our chambers without our permission, right, Emily?"

"Correct, Betsy," laughed Emily. "Those are castle droids with built-in programs on protocol. All we have to do is fast-forward the tape recorder a few times, say the same thing over and over again, and hopefully they'll just stand outside our door waiting for us to come out. That should buy us a little time."

"Emms, you have a job on my staff any time you wish," giggled the Queen. The Queen watched her new close friend as she concentrated on fast-forwarding the recorder. While she waited for her cue each time from Emily to speak again into the recorder, she practiced her lines, changing her pitch and tone until she said them the way she liked best.

After a few minutes of letting the Queen star in her new acting role and repeat her lines into the recorder, Emily interrupted her by holding her hand up and then walked over to sneak a quick look through the blinds at the courtyard below. Turning to the Queen, she said, "Betsy, we had better hurry. It looks like the last droid is going into the tunnel, and the human staff and what's left of the domestic droids are now rushing all over the courtyard. Who knows what time they will show up to get us?"

"Well, then," said the Queen calmly as she stood up and started walking toward her closet, "I guess I had better get dressed. Emms, would you please assist me?"

"Of course," said Emily. Emily took the Queen's robe, and from the closet grabbed a light blue cotton dress with pink roses embroidered on the collar that the Queen was pointing to. Then she retrieved a pair of comfortable flat-bottom leather shoes that the Count had earlier provided at the Queen's request from a local shop in small village on Gotland.

"I'm sorry you are in this mess, Betsy," said Emily, zipping up the back of the Queen's dress. "I mean, I am supposed to be this steel nerve reporter, but I am shaking like a leaf. Look at my hands tremble!"

The Queen turned around, took Emily's trembling right hand and cupped it with both of her hands. "Emms dear, sit down. I want to tell you something."

"But we have no time, Betsy! We must get out now!" Emily pleaded.

"Never mind that now, young lady," said the Queen, firmly but gently pulling Emily towards two armchairs that were close by. Then, looking straight into Emily's puzzled face, the Queen said, "Did I ever tell you what I did during World War II? As a young princess of 19, I mean."

Emily, trying to calm herself down, now became curious. She shook her head no to the Queen's question and waited for the Queen to continue with her story.

"Well," continued the Queen, "my father, King George the Sixth, and my mother, Queen Elizabeth, both wanted to keep me safe and insisted that I stick to my royal duties and learn them, but I had other ideas about royal duties and what was expected of me." The Queen paused, letting her memories catch up to her before she continued.

"So what did you do?" asked Emily. "Did they have women soldiers or something like that in England back then?"

"No, no, nothing like that," said the Queen, laughing. "We did have women in supporting roles to assist our country in its darkest time, though."

"As secretaries and office staff?" asked Emily, not really understanding where the Queen was going with their conversation.

"Well, yes, we did of course, but we had others as mechanics and truck drivers to relieve the men to go fight."

Emily's jaw dropped. "*You* were a truck driver?"

The Queen laughed. "I was both!"

"No way!" interjected Emily.

"You should have seen my parents' expressions when, after they forbade me to ever drive anything, much less a truck, weeks later I showed up at the castle gates in a camouflaged lumber truck that I had driven from our training camp at Camberley through congested London traffic, even passing through Piccadilly Circus" -- the Queen paused -- "twice!"

Both women laughed like school girls sharing a secret that no one in the world knew but them.

"The point is, my dear," continued the Queen, "that I have risen to this occasion, as you have, and I have nothing to be sorry about, nor any regrets."

Suddenly there was a knock at the door, followed by a familiar voice of one of the castle droids. "Madam, will you please come with us? Our master radioed and wants to put you in safer quarters."

"No time!" whispered Emily. "We're trapped!"

"What about the ledge?" asked the Queen in a very matter-of-fact way, nodding towards the window.

"The ledge?" responded Emily, looking at the Queen as if she had lost her mind.

"The ledge," repeated the Queen. "Does it lead anywhere?"

Emily thought about it for a second. "Well, it does go to the other rooms all around the castle's second floor. I suppose we could, uh, try, but Betsy, honestly I don't think --"

"That's the trouble with you, Emms," interrupted the Queen, "you think too much! Now go start the recorder and I'll turn off the lights and open the window and let's get out of here!"

Emily knew by the Queen's tone that it was no use to argue the point, so immediately she sprang up and placed the recorder a few feet from the door. There was a second knock, followed by a sterner voice, demanding that the Queen let them in. Emily quickly turned the recorder on and let the Queen's recorded statement play. As expected, the knocking and the droids' demands stopped.

Meanwhile, the Queen had dimmed the room lights as much as possible and had raised the blinds and opened the window. Emily tiptoed as fast as she could over to the window that the Queen was already beginning to climb through. Fortunately there was enough light from the courtyard below to make out the three-foot-wide stone ledge, but she was thankful that it wasn't daylight yet and they could mostly move about unnoticed.

"Left or right, Emms?" asked the Queen, as she casually put her right foot out onto the ledge.

"Ohhh, this is not fun," whispered Emily, as she looked back one more time at the closed door. Before she could answer, the Queen had both feet on the ledge and was standing there like she had just stepped out of her palace to walk the dogs!

"Again, Emms, left or right?"

"Uh, try right, Betsy," said Emily. "There is a room next to mine that the staff was airing out the other day while cleaning. I believe the window should still be open."

"Right is it, then," said the Queen, as she disappeared from Emily's view.

Emily breathed in deep and gingerly put her right foot onto the smooth stone ledge, daring not to look down. Trying instead to focus her attention towards the direction the Queen had gone, she could barely make out the shadowy figure of the monarch moving past her room and towards the room beyond it. Emily could see the outline of shutters thrown outwards, which, as luck would have it, meant that the windows were indeed open.

With both feet on the ledge now, Emily tried to take quick steps so she could catch up with the Queen, while at the same time hugging the rough hewn limestone castle walls. Every now and then she was able to fit her fingers into some of the open cracks between the stones, helping her to keep her balance as she made her way along the ledge. Emily paused and looked again towards the Queen's direction. Suddenly a shock went through her system. The Queen was out of sight!

"Oh, no, has she fallen?" gasped Emily out loud as she peered at the place on the dimly lit ledge where the

Queen stood just seconds before. Speeding up her gait and ignoring the safety of the castle wall completely, Emily quickly arrived at the spot on the ledge where she last saw the Queen. Mustering up as much courage as she could, she slowly leaned towards the edge of the ledge so she could get a glimpse into the courtyard. Emily's mind was racing with the thought of seeing the Queen's body lying lifeless on the ground below.

As Emily leaned over as far as she could, a head popped out of the window just a few feet away from her, almost causing her to lose her balance and fall! "Really, Emms, what's taking you so long?" whispered the Queen, staring into the shocked reporter's face.

"Whew! Thank God!" said Emily. After catching her breath, Emily climbed into the room and quickly hugged the Queen. "I thought you had fallen!"

"Fall? Me? Nonsense," said the Queen. "Now what shall we do?"

After taking a few more seconds to regain her composure, Emily, followed closely by the Queen, tiptoed to the door and cracked it open. Looking down the hallway, she could see two android figures still standing in front of the Queen's bedroom door, apparently still listening to the muffled recording of the Queen's voice. Before Emily could close the door, several more figures ran past and met up with the two androids. Shortly thereafter, all four staff members burst into the Queen's bedroom and disappeared from sight.

"We have got to move before they figure out that we escaped through the window!" Emily said, turning towards the Queen. Carefully looking back out into the hallway, Emily noticed a small passageway directly across from where they were hiding that appeared to lead down to the first floor. Emily grabbed the Queen's hand and quickly led her across the hallway into the dark passageway just as the androids and the two human staff members ran out of the Queen's bedroom and ran past Emily and the Queen, talking excitedly in Swedish amongst themselves.

Standing quietly in the dark until they could no longer hear the staff's voices, they started walking slowly down the dark stairs of the passageway. Finally the Queen asked, "Do you think we can sneak out of the castle entirely?" in a whispered voice that echoed off the ceiling of the dark and damp passageway as they walked.

"I don't think so, Betsy," Emily replied. Everyone will be looking for us. It would be best to find some out-of-the-way room perhaps near the kitchen. Only the cooks go there during meal time, and with the castle on high alert I really doubt if anyone would be in that area at all."

"Good plan!" whispered the Queen back as they continued their descent. "By the way, you never responded to my invitation about you coming back to England and being on my staff. I think you would enjoy living there very much, Emms."

"I'm flattered, Betsy," said Emily, surprised and blushing a bit, "but I have a job that I love, and of course there's Tom." Emily felt a bit of sadness at the mention of his name. It seemed like a lifetime since she'd seen him. Shaking herself out of her thoughts, she continued, "By the way, don't you have lots of people just dying to wait on you hand and foot?"

"Yes, of course, dear girl." Then the Queen paused

for a few seconds. "But, you see, I don't have many people that I would consider close friends."

Emily, stunned beyond words, at that remark just smiled in the dark while she held onto the Queen's arm to steady her as they made their way down the stairs. "Well, maybe, Betsy, I could come over for a long visit. We'll see. Come on, let's keep going."

29 A DEADLY SURPRISE AND A FREEZING SWIM

Moving within five miles of Gotland, Reggs' team was preparing to split up, one to the north of the island as planned, while the other would stay within three minutes' assault range of the castle once the all-clear was given, when suddenly Reggs heard from his north island lead team's helicopter.

"We've got a single craft coming into Gotland on radar, sir, maybe ten miles out!"

"Thanks mate," said Reggs, worried that now they may have been spotted due to the other craft's radar. "Okay, mates, carry on as planned. Maybe we'll still take them by surprise. Team Leader One out!"

As Reggs saw seven of his helicopters break away to the northern end of Gotland, a sickening feeling came over him. "I sure hope we haven't been spotted yet," he muttered to himself as he pulled his craft to the right, with the remaining six helicopters following him into the nearby fog bank.

**

Olaf, nearing Gotland, jumped in his seat when he heard the bleeps on his radar screen come alive. Studying the radar, it looked to be that there were at least fourteen aircraft headed toward Gotland. "I think we are going to be under attack any minute, brother. What do you want to do?"

Drexel, surprisingly calm, came forward to the pilot seat and looked at the radar screen, watching as the aircraft split up and headed in different directions.

Again Olaf asked, "Well, do you want us to attack them? We can out-fly and fight them as well, you know."

Drexel calmly opened a small gray metal control box that was off to the side, near the control panel, revealing one prominent red button. "No, Olaf, I don't think that will be necessary," he said, drumming the fingers of his right hand near the control box on the cabin wall. "Just tell me when any of the approaching craft get within a quarter mile of our coast and I'll do the rest."

"All right, brother, but, for the record, I disagree with your methods. There is no honor in mass slaughter with that new toy of yours."

"Honor has nothing to do with world domination. Now, are any of the craft in range yet?" Drexel asked in a casual manner as he leaned forward over Olaf's shoulder, looking again at the radar screen.

Olaf remained silent, not answering his brother on purpose, which was his way of protesting. But he knew deep down it was a futile attempt at driving home his point.

"Oh, never mind, little brother," said Drexel. "I would say our invaders are about to be reduced in half any second now." Drexel watched as the seven craft got closer and closer to the quarter mark. "Five, four, three, two, one..."

***

Tom, sitting in the co-pilot seat, riding in one of the north island team's helicopters, just happened to turn toward the pilot to ask a question about how high up they were when he saw the shock on the pilot's face as he stared at the radar screen. Hundreds of small radar blips appeared from the sea below them and were coming up toward them at a furious pace!

"Everyone bail out, bail out! Under attack! Missiles!" Before the pilot could finish yelling his warnings into the radio, dozens of loud metallic thuds hit all the helicopters at once, with no explosions. Looking at Tom, the pilot yelled, "Bail, Tom, bail! They must be magnetized mines of some sort. They are probably going to blow up any second now. Go, go, go!"

Tom needed no further prompting. He jumped out of his seat, followed closely behind by the pilot and some of the crew, when an engulfing explosion ripped through the helicopter, blowing Tom out the side of the craft, rendering him unconscious, as he fell towards the sea a mile below, his parachute unopened.

Seconds later a series of dull explosions were heard in rapid succession over the engine and propeller noise of the remaining aircraft tucked securely miles away in a fog bank not too far off the coast of Gotland.

"Did you hear that, Reggs?" asked the co-pilot.

Reggs didn't answer, but quickly checked the radar screen, only to see Drexel's jet copter set down on Gotland, with no other signs of aircraft. "It can't be! All my mates, and poor Tom!" shouted Reggs as he stared at the empty screen.

After a moment of silence, Reggs pulled himself together as best he could and took the radio mike. "All right, everyone, listen up. There is now a change in plans. These bastards must have some massive missile defense system set up all around the island which we can't penetrate, so I want all pilots to point their crafts toward the island on full speed with automatic pilots set for our present altitude. Do not open your chutes until your digital altimeters read 780 feet so that all they'll pick up is bodies falling if their radar is operational. Once we hit the water, then we'll swim in."

"Carry only your Glock Nines and your reverse holographic belts and glasses, if you can manage them, and forget the water rifles we were going to use on the droids. There's no time to drain the water out of them. Remember, the sea is extremely cold, so we have, at most, eight minutes' time to make it to the beach before hypothermia sets in. So once your chutes open, use them as an airborne sail to glide you towards the beach. Hopefully after their missiles hit our craft they'll think we are already dead and no longer a threat. Everyone respond to my orders. After that, I'll count to three and we'll begin. You mates copy?"

Like clock work, Reggs' team started responding to his orders without hesitation. "Team Two, aye, and God save the Queen! Team Three, aye, and God save the Queen!" The response continued from every craft until every surviving team member answered Reggs' orders.

"All right, then, mates, good luck to us all and, yes, God save the Queen," replied Reggs. "Now, here goes. One, two, three, go, go, go!"

Within seconds the men were all bailing out from their helicopters as their crafts flew blindly toward certain destruction. Before their parachutes could even open, all the men watched as their aircraft blew into bits one thousand feet above them as they fell out of the fogbank and into clear sky. Everyone was checking their wrist altimeters as they fell at speeds in excess of 130 miles per hour.

Reggs was watching his men as they all fell in tandem and just happened to look up to see one of the spinning helicopter rotors headed straight down towards them! He had only seconds to warn his men and no way to communicate the impending danger. Suddenly he tucked his arms into his side and streamlined his body in order to become more torpedo-shaped, increasing his speed upwards to 180 miles per hour, allowing him to get below his men and directly into their line of sight. The men, falling with open arms and legs, once seeing their commander shooting through the air like a rocket, needed no prompting; all the men at once copied Reggs by tucking in their arms and straightening their legs, increasing their speed to match their leader's, propelling the group out of the path of the falling rotor just in time as it whooshed just a few feet past the last man, who was totally unaware of how close he had gotten to sudden death. Only Reggs noticed the rotor.

Now all the men were falling at the same speed and height. "Nine hundred, eight fifty, eight hundred, seven fifty!" Reggs said to himself as he opened his parachute. Quickly his men did the same. Fortunately, the wind was blowing from the sea towards shore, so all of the team began warping their chutes by pulling on the ropes to catch as much forward pushing wind as possible. Reggs watched as some of the men even passed him as they made their way towards the rocky beach.

Minutes later, with only fifty feet of altitude left, more than half the team had made it onto sandy patches of the beach in between the jagged volcanic rocks, while the rest of them landed into the surf, suffering briefly the frigid waters of the icy cold Baltic Sea. Reggs purposely cut his chute and fell into the sea as well after noticing the last man fall into the water at least one hundred yards from shore. The man that fell behind was a superb MI5 agent, but a terrible parachutist and swimmer. Reggs knew he had only minutes to get his comrade onto dry land before hypothermia and the Baltic would take him under.

"Hang in there, Shawn!" shouted Reggs as he hit the water, feeling like thousands of icy needles were piercing into his body through his heavily soaked clothes. Throwing off his jacket, his heavy reverse holographic belt, gun, and boots, he swam towards Shawn like an Olympic champion, reaching Shawn in the nick of time. He could tell Shawn was already beginning to go into shock, but still somewhat able to respond to Reggs' commands.

"All right, mate," Reggs said, "I've got you now. Let's move together." Reggs grabbed Shawn under his arms with his left hand and, swimming with his right arm, he started propelling them both to shore and safety. "Kick, Shawn, kick!" shouted Reggs to the semi-conscious man.

Shawn kicked for a few yards and then said, "I'm so tired, sir. Just let me sleep. All I want to do is sleep." His legs quit moving in the water and his body started going limp. Reggs felt like Shawn was slipping through his grip.

"No way, mate," said Reggs, slapping Shawn's face as hard as he could to revive him. You can't leave us now. Besides, you've got to see Molly and the kids. Remember what little Sally wanted for her birthday next week?"

Hearing his daughter's name seemed to revive the man somewhat as he struggled to answer back, halfway starting to kick his feet at the same time. "She wanted, umm, something, yes. She wanted a dolly house set and, uh..." Shawn paused, not having enough strength to continue, and heading towards unconsciousness.

"Yes, yes, lad. What else? Don't stop. What else did little Sally want?" yelled Riggs, knowing he had to keep his comrade conscious. He knew they were close to shore because he could feel the currents from the backwash of the surf pulling them in.

Shawn gasped for breath and woke up. "A dolly set and, uh, a tea party set, complete with..."

Shawn didn't finish what he was trying to say, but Reggs noticed the man's legs becoming more active and kicking harder as the currents became stronger and stronger, pulling them both towards shore. A few moments later the men came within reach of some of Reggs' men who had earlier before jumped into the surf to grab the two men.

"We got him, sir. You can let go now," said one of Reggs' men.

With the last of his strength, Reggs said, "Good work, lads. Best get him warm somehow on shore."

Reggs felt extremely tired. There were clear signs of hypothermia setting in and he could feel it.

"No problem, sir," said another agent, grabbing Reggs under his arm to help him walk in the surf and onto dry land. "We have a driftwood fire in the back of one of the caves, so it's like we were never here at all."

"Excellent!" said Reggs, shivering uncontrollably. "Best get there myself, warm up, and after that we'll make a plan."

***

The jet helicopter made its landing in the main courtyard and both Drexel and Olaf jumped out. Olaf, red-faced with anger, had jumped out ahead of his brother, who still couldn't understand what all the fuss was about with him using his latest weapons on the invaders. Before Olaf could bother Drexel with another round of reasons why he didn't need to use such deadly force, the castle staff surrounded them both and started giving Drexel reports on the status of the castle.

"Really, Olaf!" shouted Drexel as he watched Olaf

storm off toward the side kitchen. "You are making a mountain out of a mole hill. Would you rather we get killed in battle, making some obscure point of honor, or would you rather win a great victory like we just did? They are all dead and gone and now the immediate threat is over. So which is right, victory or honor?"

Olaf, with his back still towards his brother, yelled back, "Yes, of course, brother, it's your victory, but their honor."

Drexel was a little puzzled at Olaf's cutting remark, but took it as just another one of the many points they would never agree upon and shrugged it off. Then he turned towards his chief of staff and asked, "Captain, are all the droids safely in the caves as I ordered?"

"Yes, sir, all are in the catacombs and accounted for."

"Good, good," said Drexel, turning his attention toward the Queen's bedroom window. He wondered how his guests were faring and if they had caused his staff any trouble while he was away. "And what is the latest report on the radio traffic out of London, Captain? Anything else unusual?"

"No, Count Drexel, no unusual voice traffic, and all of our agents now report everything is quiet. Even our MI5 plants show no unusual traffic or movement," the captain responded.

"That's good, I suppose," said Drexel, "but still something doesn't feel right." Drexel hadn't been able to take his eyes off of the Queen's window. "I'll tell you what, Captain, bring Her Highness as well as the reporter -- I mean my biographer -- upstairs to my office in ten minutes. I have a few questions I need to ask them both."

"Yes, sir, right away, sir!" the captain said, giving a stiff salute before turning away to carry out his orders.

***

High in his castle office that overlooked the front of the castle grounds, Drexel poured himself a long overdue drink as he waited for the arrival of his guests. What a great victory indeed, he thought to himself, proud of the night's accomplishments. Every weapon worked like a charm even exceeding his earlier expectations of their capability. He wished Marguerite was there with him to celebrate.

Bending over his large, green, felt-covered desk, he unrolled his building plans for the additions to his new villa in Argentina. While tracing with his finger a route around the villa that he planned to build a monorail system on, a knock came at the door. "Yes, Captain, bring them in," said Drexel, looking up over his pair of reading glasses.

The door opened, but only the captain was standing there, apparently in a state of shock. "They're gone!" he said, his voice shaking uncontrollably.

"They *who?*" asked Drexel, gritting his teeth, already knowing the answer.

"The Queen and Miss Patrick!" answered the captain with a gulp. "There is no trace of them anywhere, sir!"

Drexel slammed his fist into the soft covering of his desk. "Where are the guards? Who was responsible for -- ?"

"Sir, they had droid guards, which were all taken into the caves along with the rest of the droids, as requested, sir," the captain interrupted, still quivering.

"Idiots! Fools! Morons!" screamed Drexel, running past the captain and out onto the balcony, trying to get a glimpse at his empty helicopters on the ground below as if half expecting to see the two women escaping and running towards them. Then, turning to his frightened captain who was shivering behind him, he grabbed the poor man by the collar and yelled, just inches from his face, "Unleash the droid guards! Bring them up, I tell you, and get your men. Find them or die! Go and alert the staff now!" The count then pushed his captain backwards, causing him to stumble several times as he tried to keep from falling on the stone floor.

"Yes, sir," the captain muttered, quickly bowing and running out of the room.

Drexel's blood pressure was so high and his head spinning so hard that he walked like a drunk man back to his office couch where he collapsed, temporarily exhausted from his out-of-control behavior.

***

The fire in the cave quickly warmed and dried out all the men. Even Shawn started coming around as he sat only inches from the life-giving warmth. The other men had already recovered from their bout in the surf and the hard landings on the rocky beach and were busily checking out what was left of their equipment. Various team members were appearing and disappearing around the fire in the cave.

Reggs reached for his dried-out clothes, suddenly remembering that he and Shawn were the only two members of the team who were without their reverse holographic belts, guns, and glasses. After putting on his warm clothing, he turned his attention toward Shawn, who seemed to be almost fully awake. "How are you feeling, mate?" he asked, patting Shawn on the back.

"Fit and ready, sir," said Shawn, weakly looking up at his commander's concerned face.

"Uh-huh, that's just what I thought," laughed Reggs, patting the young commander on the back again. "You just sit here and rest. You need your strength."

Reggs looked around for his team member, John,

and gestured to him once he spotted him. "Would you step over here, please, John?" asked Reggs, pointing to a place in the cave that was out of earshot from the rest of the group. John quickly complied.

Satisfied that no one could hear them, Reggs whispered, "Um, listen, John, Shawn is in no shape to go anywhere. Someone has to stay behind and keep the fire going to make sure the boy stays warm. I guess you know what I am about to ask of you, mate, and I know it's a hard thing to do, but could you be the bloke to stay behind?"

Without a word John took off his belt, handed Reggs his glasses, and was about to take off his gun, but Reggs held up his hand to stop him. "No, mate. You will need some protection down here. I'll make do with just the belt and glasses."

John nodded and forced a smile to show that he would take one for the team, but Reggs knew better and knew deep down how disappointed John was. He also knew that was part of their training under Reggs' command to know that self-sacrifice was sometimes required even if it meant watching your friends and teammates face unknown danger while you stay back in relative safety.

Walking back towards the fire, one of the men came up to Reggs and whispered that Shawn was out cold again, but resting comfortably. Reggs told his man to leave him be and then gestured for the team to gather round.

"Well, mates," he said, testing his belt, causing it to make him disappear and reappear, "it's time to get cracking."

"Uh, sir," said one of the men, "I was thinking..."

"Go on, Jimmy," urged Reggs in an effort to encourage the boy to speak his mind. He knew Jimmy was highly intelligent and rarely spoke out loud to the group as a whole. He must have something very important to say.

"Well, sir, I was thinking that instead of scaling the tall cliffs and castle walls like we talked about in training, why couldn't we just follow the smoke from the fire through the cave. If there is a current of air flowing into the cave, that means it has to have an opening that's letting the air out somewhere maybe even below the castle, doesn't it?"

"Top-drawer planning, mate!", said Reggs grinning from ear to ear. "I was hoping one of you lads would suggest something like that. Only one problem, though," said Reggs," looking around at the group.

"What's that, sir?" asked Jimmy, still red faced from the compliment given to him by his commander in front of the group.

"Well, lad, those burning embers wouldn't make very good torches in this windy cave. Any ideas on how we would see our way through the dark?" Reggs waited for their suggestions.

Shawn, who had been going in and out of consciousness, raised himself up on his side and blurted out, "I smoke, sir." His comment was soon followed by John and three other members of the team, "Yeah, me, too," they said, holding their cigarette lighters up and tossing them to Reggs. "Can't go without our smokes, sir!" Shawn added weakly, holding his lighter up and letting John take it from him to give to Reggs.

"Blimey, these will do just perfect. Thanks, mates." Reggs took a census of how many lighters he had and then said, "All right, single file, everyone. I'll take the point with one lighter and pass out the rest to every fourth man. Remember, mates, we don't have our water rifles, so if we run into one of these droid buggers, go invisible and use any water available." After quickly scouring his team over again, he said, "All right, let's go." Looking back at Shawn and John, he said, "We'll be back, lads. Just hang tight." John and Shawn smiled at their teammates and gave a quick thumbs up as they watched their comrades slip further into the cave and disappear, one by one.

30 GOD SAVE THE QUEEN

Olaf sat alone inside the castle kitchen that was located just off the courtyard, drowning his troubles in a cup of coffee laced with rum, twirling a half-eaten Danish with a plastic fork as it sat on a paper plate. He couldn't wipe the guilt out of his mind that he felt after watching those men's dying moments earlier. They were pilots, just like himself, out on a mission, and they all died instantly, in a flash, before they knew what hit them.

"So unjust, so wrong," he muttered to himself while taking another bite of the pastry. "Has my loyalty to my brother indirectly caused the death of those men? If I had betrayed my brother long ago like I knew deep down I should have done, maybe those men would be breathing this very second." Olaf realized he was talking to himself and took a big gulp of coffee. There was no one in the room to hear his remorse or even care about his regrets.

Suddenly the hairs on the back of his neck felt like they were standing straight up. He couldn't explain it, but he felt like he was being watched. Little did he know, but two sets of frightened eyes were watching his every move from the kitchen pantry. Looking around and seeing no one, he took another sip of coffee and dismissed his sensation of not being alone. Soon he was talking out loud again. "Think, Olaf, think. Now he is even more powerful and his droids are even more unstoppable. Maybe I am just as evil as he is, but too afraid to admit it."

Just then the pantry doors swung open just three feet behind him and an elderly woman's voice, trembling with indignation, spoke. "Now, see here, young man, stop this lollygagging and wishy-washy nonsense right now!" The Queen couldn't contain herself any longer. "If you were as evil as you fear, then you wouldn't be having this conversation, albeit with yourself, right now, would you, dear?"

Jumping out of his seat and turning around all in one motion, Olaf's eyes met the Queen's eyes. "Your Majesty!" Olaf blurted out. He then gave a quick bow and then looked toward the kitchen door to make sure no one had spotted them. Looking back at the Queen, he then noticed Emily Patrick standing behind the Queen with a shocked expression on her face.

"I, um, didn't really expect her to do that. I don't know, um, what to say," Emily said, laughing nervously.

"Well, I do!" snapped the Queen. What pilots are you referring to, young man, and how many of them died doing what exactly?"

Olaf walked to the kitchen door and locked it so that no one could barge in on them. He then retrieved a chair for the Queen to sit down on and cautioned both of them to keep their voices low before he started his explanation. "Well, Your Majesty, they were what I believe to be a rogue group of men from your government. We have spies all through the various branches of your government and we really don't know who they were. From what I can tell, they are extremely well financed and well trained." Then, before continuing, he took the Queen's hand and kissed it, saying, "And I am so sorry, ma'am, but they were all killed by my brother's weapon system as they were trying to rescue you." Olaf stopped because his voice was trembling too much to go on.

The Queen's countenance quickly turned pale and took on a gray hue. For a moment Emily and Olaf both thought she would faint. One could see in her face the pain she felt as her heart grieved for the men who had tried to save her. Attempting to catch her breath, she could only speak in a whisper, like someone who had just been hit in their stomach and had no air in their lungs. "Emms, my dear, you were right last night about a rescue." Then, regaining some of her strength back, she looked straight into Olaf's eyes and said, "You must help us escape off this island today before any more lives are uselessly destroyed!"

Olaf feigned shock at the Queen's request, even though just seconds before he had decided to help the pair somehow escape from his brother's clutches, even if it meant openly betraying the only family he ever had. "I will," he said, clasping the Queen's hand. "God help me, I will."

The Queen closed her eyes for a moment, clearly in relief. Emily grabbed the opportunity to speak to Olaf, feeling that she could trust him completely since he had promised to help them escape. "You said something about your brother's droids being more unstoppable earlier when you were talking to yourself. What exactly did you mean by that?"

"Oh, that," Olaf replied in an almost matter-of-fact way. "My brother has discovered a way to make his droids completely waterproof. Already now half the droids in the castle have been converted to this new waterproofing process. The other half should be completely updated in a few weeks or so, barring any more rescue attempts or other interruptions."

"So now they are really invincible," Emily said, making herself a fresh cup of coffee and sitting down next to the Queen at the table.

"No, not totally," Olaf said. He then produced a small aerosol can from a holster that was attached to his utility belt and held it up so the two women could see it. "You see, not too long ago at a party in London we had a droid go out of control, and the only way we stopped him was to get him to ingest a pill that contained very tiny robotic creatures that disabled his entire system. It shut him down, in other words. My brother thought that was way too inefficient, so he developed a liquid formula that contained the same robotic creatures that could be easily sprayed onto the droid's skin. Once it makes contact, the creatures enter the droid's body through its synthetic pores and basically do the same thing that the pill did, except twenty times faster, rendering the droid useless. But this formula is harmless to humans. See..." Olaf then took the can and sprayed himself in the face with it.

"Amazing," said Emily, eying the small bottle of rum by Olaf's coffee cup. Olaf noticed Emily looking at the rum and handled the bottle to her. She gave an apologetic smile and then poured a shot into her coffee.

"All of the human staff now carry one of these spray cans," Olaf explained. He then tossed the can to Emily. "Here, if it makes you feel any better, you can keep it. Just remember to point and spray. I'll replace mine later on."

"Thanks," responded Emily, after she caught the can. "But don't the droids get suspicious at the humans having these cans?"

"No, of course not," said Olaf in his matter-of-fact tone. "You see, we told them it was throat spray or some such nonsense, and now they completely ignore the cans when they see them."

The Queen interjected and said, "That is all very interesting and I am very grateful for your assistance, young man, but just how do you plan to get us off the island?"

"Very easily," Olaf answered. Walking over to the kitchen window and pulling back the curtains, he gestured toward the black jet copter that was sitting in the courtyard. "There is a change in the guard in the courtyard at 9:00 p.m. tonight. It would be wise if you both stayed in the kitchen here until I return. There is a restroom just outside the hallway door, and no one patrols this area of the castle, so you should be quite safe. Just stay quiet and out of sight."

Olaf headed towards the kitchen door and said, "Anyway, I probably should get going so I can run the maintenance check on the jet copter for tonight's flight."

Trying to hide the sadness he was beginning to feel, he added, "I think once I help you escape, there is no turning back for me this time. My brother will surely know and I will lose the only family I've ever had, not to mention Drexel might try to have me killed." Olaf winked at the women before he turned to leave them, trying to lighten the mood and hide his own fearful thoughts.

Before Olaf could get out the door, the Queen stood and said, "Young man, once we get to England, you have my gratitude and, of course, my protection." Then she extended her hand to Olaf and he graciously bowed and kissed it.

"I live for that moment, Your Majesty" whispered Olaf before he disappeared into the courtyard.

***

Meanwhile, Drexel's human guards were busy in the castle basement fetching supplies for the maintenance staff when one of the men noticed an odd smell coming from an underground breezeway that ran directly off the main supply room entrance. He sniffed the air and said in Swedish, "That's odd. I smell wood smoke." The other guard then walked over to where his comrade was standing and sniffed the air as well. "You know, you are right. I smell it, too. Now, who would be down in this part of the castle making a fire?" Both men upholstered their pistols and cautiously walked over to the breezeway entrance. Before they could enter the breezeway, out of nowhere came an invisible fist, knocking the first guard unconscious. While the other guard tried to make sense out of what just happened, another invisible fist came out of thin air and hit him, knocking him out as well. Immediately the supply room came alive as Reggs and his men started appearing as if out of thin air.

"Grab their radios," whispered Reggs. "Maybe we can listen in to see what these blokes are up to."

Taking a radio from one of the unconscious guards, Reggs' man turned it on and listened. All they could hear was rapid chatter in a foreign language. "Blimey, sir, I can't understand these buggers at all. They are chit-chatting in Swedish, I think," said the agent.

"Not a problem," Reggs said. Picking up a .45 caliber pistol from one of the unconscious guards, he stuffed it in his belt and said, "Get Johnson and Ebbs up here. They're still down in the tunnel. I know one of those men speaks the lingo."

Minutes later the last of the team arrived from the caverns and stepped into the room, very surprised to see two unconscious men lying on the floor. "Aw, look, Ebbs," said Agent Johnson, "we missed the fun again."

"Here, mate," said Reggs, tossing the radio towards Johnson, who caught it with one hand. "Tell us what these blokes are squawking so much about."

Johnson turned up the volume and listened intently while the others remained quiet. "Blimey, the old girl -- I mean Her Majesty, it appears, gave these goons the slip.

The whole castle is crawling with people who are looking for her and the American woman!"

The men couldn't help themselves. A small whispered cheer went up from among them, "Huzzah!"

Johnson continued. "There's more, sir. They are saying that this Drexel chap is in his office asleep and should not be disturbed unless the Queen and the American woman is found."

"Well," said Reggs, smiling, "I think I'll go ahead and find his office and wake this Drexel chap up from his beauty sleep."

After a brief moment of subdued laughter amongst the men, Reggs turned serious again. "Okay, chaps, remember, no engagement of the enemy until Her Majesty is found and is safely off this island. I want two teams to split up once we get upstairs and into the main part of the castle.

"Johnson, since you understand their lingo, you stay with Team One and keep up with their bloody chatter. I want to know at all times what's going on. If these goons recapture the Queen, then contact Team Two by giving a wolf whistle into the radio. Maybe these goons will think it's some sort of radio interference and won't pay attention to it.

"Ebbs, you take Team Two and the other radio. If any of you find the Queen yourselves, then whistle four notes from "God Save the Queen" into the radio. Remember, our first priority is the Queen and our second priority is capturing or destroying this Drexel character. Of course, if the shooting starts, then just shout in English as loud as you want."

"But, sir," said one of the men, "you don't have a radio."

"Not a problem, mate." Reggs grinned. "I'll pick one up on the way to Drexel's office."

The men laughed again.

"Okay, lads," Reggs said, "let's move."

The men put on their vision goggles, pushed the button on their reverse holographic belts, and melted back into thin air as they climbed the winding stairway up to the main part of the castle. Once entering the main castle level, Reggs silently signaled his men to fan out. Invisible to Drexel's men or his droids, the men walked right past many of the staff as they spread out all over the castle grounds.

Reggs didn't see anything that looked like an office on the ground floor, so he made his way up to the second floor, looking in various small rooms off the outside walkway of the castle. Not too far away he noticed two guards standing outside a large door that had bold white lettering in what he assumed was Swedish. "That's got to be it," he muttered to himself as he crept very slowly towards the men. One of the guards was complaining to the other one while they leaned against the castle wall and smoked their cigarettes. All he could make out was something about not being granted leave for the upcoming weekend. The other guard didn't seem too interested in his comrade's complaint and just kept fiddling with his hand-held shortwave radio, apparently trying to tune into the latest soccer news from BBC. The guard finally found clear reception and produced a pair of tiny earphones and put them in his ears, drowning out any further complaining from his comrade. Even then the other guard kept whining and complaining, so he finally turned his back on him and continued listening to his radio.

In mid-sentence the whining guard was knocked out cold by an invisible first that came crashing down on his back, rendering him unconscious. Seconds later the other guard met the same fate. Reggs quickly took the guard's communication radio and slid it into his own back pocket.

Checking to make sure no one had heard the commotion when the guards fell, he then turned his attention to the large office door. Reggs gently turned the door knob and discovered it was unlocked, so he continued turning the knob until he heard a small click, causing him to stand still in silence and wait to see if he had been detected.

"I told you I was not to be disturbed!" growled Drexel. Yawning, he turned towards the door to see who was there, but all he caught was the door closing again. Becoming alarmed, Drexel reached over and quickly grabbed his reverse holographic belt that contained his "graben Spinnen" spray, thinking it might be a rogue droid seeking to do him harm. Talking towards the door, he said, "If you are here to hurt your master, I'll destroy you." Drexel then quickly put on his belt, pushing the button that made him invisible, while at the same time spraying the "graben Spinnen" vapor towards the door.

Reggs opened the door again just as Drexel sprayed his vapor. "Blimey, mate, I'm not a bug," said Reggs, coughing, watching the midst fall harmlessly around him. With the goggles Reggs had on he could see every move Drexel was making, but Drexel couldn't see him.

"You're not a droid or one of my men! I demand you, sir, to reveal yourself at once!" Drexel shouted into the air.

Reggs knew he was enjoying the moment too much, but couldn't help it. "You're not in a position to demand anything, you slimy bugger!" Then he purposely thrust his 45-caliber pistol out at arm's length, which was just outside the light bending influence of the reverse holographic belt, causing the gun to be revealed. All Drexel could see was part of a hand sticking out of thin air that was holding a weapon that was pointed directly at his head!

"Special branch of MI5 at your service, mate," Reggs said. "Don't move. Now, where's my Queen? You have five seconds or you'll grow a new hole between both your mangy ears."

Drexel sneered and mockingly responded, "Oh, look, the British monkey has learned how to operate one of my toys. How nice. But tell me, monkey, how many more of you are in my castle? And, by the way, just how do you expect to find your Queen if you shoot me? Hmm? One shot and this whole room will be full of my men in seconds. Then I'll have you and, oh, yes, the Queen, too."

"You may have a point, sir, but I assure you I have enough men here to take care of you and your crew, and then I'll be escorting you to justice court or at least to rot in a British jail for the rest of your life!" Reggs kept his gun trained on Drexel.

Drexel kept his mouth shut as his enemy spoke and, like a cat stalking a small mouse, started to creep toward the fireplace where there were two dueling swords that were placed criss-crossed over the mantel directly above Reggs' head. But as the count tried to creep closer, he suddenly stopped dead in his tracks because Reggs' gun was following his every move! He could only stare in disbelief at how his new opponent was able to track him so precisely!

"Whaa -- How's this possible?" asked Drexel with a gasp. For the first time, fear was welling up inside him because for the first time in his life someone besides himself had the upper hand. "Can you, uh, see --"

"Why, yes, I can, mate," responded Reggs with a smug chuckle. "Every bloody move, mate, and then some. Something our boys figured it out just last week. How about that? Now, if you could be so kind..." Reggs gestured with his gun for Drexel to start moving towards the door.

Before Drexel gave in to Reggs' order, one of the guards that had been earlier knocked out by Reggs burst into the room. Reggs spun around on one foot, while hitting the guard with his other foot directly on the side of his head, sending the man back into a state of unconscious.

This gave Drexel just enough time to run and grab one of the swords above the mantel and he quickly thrust it into Reggs' hand, causing Reggs to drop his gun. Reggs thought quickly and kicked the gun across the floor before Drexel could grab it, and they both watched as the gun slid and fell into a ventilator shaft, rattling against the tin vents as it made its way down into the boiler room a hundred feet below them.

Pulling his hand back in to his side, he became totally invisible again to Drexel, affording him a tiny moment of time to assess the damage to his hand. The pain was excruciating, but there was nothing he could do about it now. Reggs caught sight of the other sword above the mantel and managed to leap over the burgundy leather couch and reach up and grab it.

Drexel, hearing Reggs' footsteps, realized he was heading towards the fireplace and tried desperately to beat him to it. He swung his sword like a wild man, zigzagging it back and forth through the empty air, hoping to strike his invisible foe and mortally wound him. Drexel was cussing and foaming at the mouth like a man possessed, barely missing Reggs' face by an eyelash, but managed to hook the heavy goggles he wore with the tip of his blade, flinging them into a nearby wooden chair where they landed with a clump.

Drexel laughed at his accidental good luck. "Now the odds, peasant, are, shall we say, even!" he smirked. Then he thrust his sword into the air one more time, hoping to hit Reggs' chest.

"Funny thing," said Reggs, as his sword met Drexel's, stopping his opponent's wild thrust by the thrust of his own blade as they fought in the middle of the spacious office, "you royal blokes think you have a right to rule everyone's lives just because you think you can." Dodging a crashing blow from Drexel, Reggs swiped his blade again at the evil genius, tearing Drexel's shirt and drawing a small amount of blood on his left side, much to Drexel's surprise.

"Not bad for a commoner," responded Drexel in a monotone voice as he swooped his right hand down and scooped up a small brass figurine off an end table, throwing it as hard as he could in the direction of Reggs' sword, only missing Reggs' head by a mere few inches. "Tell me, Mr. MI5 hero, don't you find this ironic?"

Before Reggs could respond, Drexel thrust his sword towards where he thought Reggs' midsection would be, but he didn't draw blood. Instead the tip of his sword hit the "off" button that was on Reggs' reverse holographic belt, immediately making the wounded British agent visible! Reggs knew the vulnerable situation he was now in, especially with Drexel's lightning-fast reflexes.

Seeing his opportunity, with amazing speed Drexel sprung at the beleaguered agent, pushing him against the stone wall opposite the fireplace, right below a seventeenth century twelve-foot high hanging wall mirror, pinning Reggs down. Staring into the mirror and getting a moment's satisfaction that there was no reflection of himself, Drexel decided he would turn off his reverse holographic belt as well with the intent of invoking terror into the British agent as his blade pressed against his smaller and weaker opponent's chest.

Reggs was surprised at how strong Drexel was. With his only good hand he pressed his sword against Drexel's blade that was bearing down on him, inch by inch, as his arm started to lose strength. Drexel was pushing so hard that Reggs' lungs were gasping for air, his left arm muscles twitched in pain. No longer able to stare directly at Drexel's face, his eyes instinctively rolled upwards as he felt his own blade being pushed against him. He again pushed back with all his might, exhausting his last bit of strength.

Drexel growled into Reggs' face. "As I said, MI5 hero, don't you think it ironic that the very royalty you said plays with the lives of commoners like yourself now this very minute finds you giving your very life to rescue one of its members?"

Reggs didn't have the energy to respond. He could feel his strength leaving him. He had to think of something quick or his time to live was over. Suddenly his eyes caught sight of two small fasteners that had been drilled into the stone wall to hold the mirror up. Heavy brown twine was the only thing supporting the bulky antique fixture. An idea popped into his mind. He only hoped he had the strength left to play it out.

With his last bit of strength he thrust his left arm upwards, causing Drexel's sword and his sword to go up, and with one last forceful motion pushed both swords behind the mirror, slicing the brown twine, causing the mirror to propel forward and fall on Drexel, breaking the count's grip on the exhausted agent as he tried to protect himself from the weight of the heavy mirror.

Drexel fell backwards with the thick glass mirror landing directly on top of him, pinning him to the ground amidst a pile of shattered glass and a mangled rosewood frame. Drexel lost consciousness, letting go of his sword, and laying on the wooden plank floor in a lifeless heap, his flesh cut in a hundred places by all the tiny shards of glass.

Reggs bent over and gave himself time to catch his breath, and then he started towards Drexel with a look of satisfaction at capturing his enemy. Before he could reach the prostrate count to tie him up, more guards burst into the room with guns drawn. He didn't stand a chance against all this firepower. As fast as he could he reached down and pushed the green button on his holographic belt and vanished again into thin air, a spray of bullets flying past him as he dove for the floor.

Thinking Reggs had either escaped or was killed by all the gunfire, the guards turned their attention to Drexel who was pinned by the broken mirror. Drexel started moaning as his men helped him to his feet.

Reggs barely breathed as he made his way silently out of the path of the guards. The guards were blocking his way to the chair where his goggles landed earlier, so he gave up on getting the goggles. He had to find a way out of the room. The only avenue of escape looked to be the office window at this point. He heard Drexel weakly bark an order and watched as the guards started poking and prodding the air with their clubs, apparently trying to find him. Reggs felt safe where he was, lying on the floor off to the side of the fireplace. The guards were swinging their clubs too high above him for them to hit him.

Realizing he had only seconds to flee or he would eventually be caught, he made preparations to leap out of the window. He didn't even know how high up he was or if the window had a ledge, but he had no other choice.

Before Reggs could make a move towards the window, Drexel yelled, "We're under attack! Reggs watched as Drexel tried to maintain his balance by leaning on a guard's shoulder, while gesturing wildly with his other hand. "I want every droid and every man out fighting now! All Model One droids switch to pulsing lasers. The others use machine guns. Remember, they have belts like we do, but with goggles that allows them to see you even though you're invisible! So sound the alarm!"

Reggs didn't know what a Model One droid was or, for that matter, what a pulsing laser was, but it didn't sound good. He raised himself up into a crouching position, but stayed still. The chief guard called over his radio and seconds later he could hear a loud horn, not too unlike a freight train horn, blasting through the castle grounds.

Over the Swedish radio chatter Reggs heard the familiar voice of Johnson calling out to Ebbs' team. "It's on, mates. We've been discovered. Let's go!"

Ebbs yelled back, "What about Reggs? Have you heard from him?"

"He's a big boy and can take care of himself. Fire on, mates, fire on!" Johnson yelled, giving the code word to open fire on Drexel's men and droids.

All at once there were massive sounds of machine gun fire coming from the courtyard. Reggs knew he wasn't doing any good where he was. He had to get to the window. As Drexel's men scattered, he saw a clear pathway to the window and decided to go for it. He could still see Drexel standing in the center of the room, looking disheveled and trying to collect his thoughts. Reggs sprang up on his feet and made a dash for the stained glass window, swiping a radio from a backpack of an unsuspecting guard, dashing right past him unnoticed, and took a large leap and jumped out the window like he was diving into a swimming pool. He broke the glass and fell ten feet down and landed hard on a three-foot wide ledge that was some seventy feet above the courtyard!

Today is apparently not my day to die, Reggs said to himself. Standing up, his legs became wobbly and he almost lost his footing on the ledge, but he managed to miraculously steady himself. Immediately he started sizing up the scene below him. It was an eerie sight below. Sounds of yelling and machine gun fire could be heard everywhere, but totally invisible to the eye except for the occasional dead body becoming visible as soon as they were hit by gun fire. So far it appeared that only Drexel's men were dying. He couldn't see any of his men dying, which was a good thing.

Now he had to decide how to get off the ledge and get down to his men. Suddenly Reggs caught sight of red

laser light flashing across the courtyard. "What the --"
Reggs immediately remembered what Drexel said about
lasers. This must be one of their new secret weapons, he
thought to himself. The menacing weapon made itself
known by the presence of strong red pulses of laser light
spraying randomly below him. They appeared to be
coming from one section of the courtyard that was near a
big tunnel-like entrance. The Model One droids were
pouring out into the courtyard and firing as soon as they
stepped out into the clear!

Reggs turned on his radio and yelled, "Mates, it's me.
Listen, you've got to kill these droids that have some sort
of laser weapon. Can anyone get to water to fry those
buggers?"

Firing his pistol at the droids, Ebbs responded to
Reggs, "No, mate, no water. But you're right, bullets can't
stop these things!" Ebbs kept firing anyway, non-stop,
spraying bullets in the direction of the blasting lasers

while watching the sparks from his gun fire as they hit their invisible target, but to no effect.

Watching the droids and their lasers from the ledge, Reggs realized something. They appeared to be able to locate his men with their laser target streams! Catching sight of Ebbs again, Reggs grabbed his radio. "No, Ebbs, no! Don't stand still! They can track --" But before Reggs could finish his sentence, a red beam of laser light hit its target, blasting poor Ebbs back to visibility as it instantly killed him. Ebbs lay dead on his back on the cold stone courtyard ground.

"Damn!" yelled Reggs, in between more Swedish radio chatter.

Then Johnson broke in on the radio. "Reggs, I've found a water hose!"

"Say no more, mate. Some of these buggers understand English. Just go, baby, go!" Reggs prayed

Johnson would get every single one of these bastards that just took down Ebbs.

***

Down below, Johnson holstered his pistol and turned on the water spicket as far as he could. Fortunately, the hose had plenty of length. So, taking the hose with a high stream of water, he ran as fast as he could in the direction of what was now a line of droids firing lasers into the courtyard. So far they hadn't noticed the brave agent splashing water on the ground and running at them from the side because they were too busy concentrating their laser fire at the sounds of invisible pistol fire fifty yards away. Thankfully they were mostly missing their mark, but occasionally, if an agent stood still long enough, he was hit and would die instantly as the laser pierced his body.

Johnson was almost on the droids when he suddenly slipped on a stretch of mud and grass. Sliding on the messy ground, the hose still in his hand, he kept his presence of mind and pointed the hose towards the droids and hit them with a powerful spray of water. With his reverse holographic belt pulverized after hitting the ground, his invisibility shield quit working and he could be seen by all the droids. But he didn't care. He knew the water had hit the droids and they would be out of commission really fast.

But nothing happened. They weren't falling. The droids seemed totally immune to the water. What could have gone wrong? Before Johnson could gain his footing on the wet ground, he noticed red laser lights all around him in the grass. So between the laser lights and machine gun bullets ricocheting off the castle walls behind him, Johnson thought fast and started rolling on the ground. He managed to make it to a drainage ditch just a few feet away and quickly plopped into it. On his hands and knees he crawled through the muck and slime until he reached a large dark cement pipe opening that was used for draining waste water out of the castle. Disappearing from the sight of the droids, they quickly lost interest in him and turned their lasers on the remaining British agents in the courtyard, still firing at large.

***

Reggs needed to get to his men. Running along the ledge, he found a sturdy ivy vine that he could use to climb down. As he was starting his descent, he noticed Drexel standing near a clump of apple trees some eighty yards away. He appeared to be shouting orders at the droids and pointing in the air at invisible targets. He was wearing Reggs' goggles! "The bugger has figured out how to use the goggles. Blimey, that's why he's standing there like a blooming quarterback calling a football game" said Reggs to himself.

Holding onto the ivy vine with one hand and pressing his radio button with the other, he yelled into the mike, "Does anyone down there have a radio?" After another second or two of Swedish chatter, a voice in English answered back. "It's Sergeant Riley, sir. I apprehended one from one of Drexel's men. We are getting the stuffing kicked out of us, sir. Where are you?"

"Never mind that now, mate." Reggs didn't want to give away his location in case others were listening in. "Get a hold of everyone and tell them to retreat and find cover. That Drexel fellow has a pair of our goggles and he can see us. And forget about battling those droids with water. I just watched Johnson dowse them real good and it didn't even phase them. Just fall back. Fall back!"

As Reggs continued down the vine, a familiar voice came over the radio. "Why, there you are, you MI5 commander!" Reggs quickly looked back towards where Drexel had been standing to see if he was still there. Drexel, still wearing the goggles, casually waved at Reggs then he said, "Let me show you just how good my new droids are."

Reggs didn't give Drexel the courtesy of responding. Now that he was fully visible to Drexel, he slid down the vine at break-neck speed. Before Reggs could make it all the way down, a red laser shot whizzed by his head, barely missing his hand, and severed the vine, which caused him to drop the last twenty feet to the ground, crashing into some boxwood bushes. Scratched up and somewhat out of breath, he was still able to get up on his feet and quickly get out of sight with the rest of his men.

***

Olaf had his head inside the jet copter, checking out the instrument panel, when the gun fire let loose in the courtyard. Turning on his radio, he listened to the radio traffic for any signs of what was taking place. All he knew was that it sounded like all hell had broken loose.

He knew he had to get back to the kitchen and warn the Queen and Emily that it was time to leave.

Finding the Queen and Miss Patrick where he'd left them, he urged them to get ready to go. The Queen was reluctant to leave while her men were fighting so desperately for her.

"But, Your Majesty, if you wish to escape bodily harm, now is the time. Right now we are somewhat out of sight, but that won't last too long. All the droids are in combat mode and not even a large army could defeat them! My brother, it seems, will probably win this fight and I'm afraid your men here are doomed." Olaf waited for his argument to sink in.

"Young man," said the Queen, getting up from the table defiantly, "I will *not* run for cover while any British subject in my presence is in danger. Are you sure there is nothing we can do to help them?"

Olaf sat silent for a second, pondering her question. Then a smile crossed his face. "Well, it may be possible to disarm all the droids at once and give your men a fighting chance against my brother's human staff, but I can't promise anything."

Emily thought she was following where Olaf was going and quickly interrupted the conversation. Holding up the "graben Spinnen" spray can, she enthusiastically said, "You mean like this?"

"You are good, miss," Olaf said with a wink. "But I was thinking of something a little bit larger."

"Larger?" asked Emily, as she jerked her attention towards the window as another round of machine gun fire sounded, getting closer and closer to the kitchen. Their situation seemed to be getting rather dire.

Olaf answered, "It could be suicide, but I'll need another hand helping me and we have to act now!"

"I'm on board," Emily said without hesitation. Both her and Olaf looked at the Queen to see if she was in agreement.

"Be careful, my dear, and God speed," the Queen said, leaning over and giving Emily a kiss on the cheek. She had no other choice but to trust Olaf and hope for the best.

"Take this, Betsy," Emily said, pressing the aerosol can into the Queen's hand. "We'll be back to get you soon."

The Queen smiled at both of them, then sat back down at the table, sipping her freshly brewed tea as calmly as if she had been having her tea on a veranda back at Balfour Castle. She placed the aerosol can that Emily had given her in front of her on the table.

Olaf motioned to Emily and said, "Follow me and stay low," as he led her out the side door and past the servants' bathroom to a secret opening in the wall.

Pulling down on a lever that was disguised as a wall lamp, the wall opened, revealing a large pressurized container in a small room.

"It's heavy, miss, but I'll grab the heavier end and you grab the other end," Olaf said.

"What is this?" asked Emily as she picked up her end of the metal container. "Is this some sort of bomb?"

"Better," responded Olaf, as he got his arms around the front of the container. "It's the refill container full of the stuff that's in the aerosol can you gave the Queen. We have it hidden from the droids just in case they ever figure out what this is used for. "Now, come on and don't drop this because it is highly pressurized."

"So it is a bomb," muttered Emily under her breath as she helped carry it through a hidden part of the courtyard.

They made it out to the unguarded jet copter and loaded the large pressurized container into the middle section of the aircraft. Just as they were both boarding the helicopter, some of Drexel's men spotted them and shouted for them to stop.

"Someone's coming! Hurry!" yelled Emily to Olaf, who was already in the cockpit and revving up the engine. The slowly twirling rotors whined louder and louder as they gained more speed.

"Just a few more seconds, miss!" Olaf shouted over the noise.

"We don't *have* a few more seconds, Olaf!" Emily yelled back. Just then one of Drexel's men reached the aircraft and grabbed her leg. She instinctively kicked him directly in the face with her other leg as hard as she could, knocking the man back away from the copter and onto the ground just as it started to rise into the air. "I guess those kickboxing lessons I took last year finally came in handy," Emily muttered.

The helicopter gained more height and started to move directly over the main part of the castle, making it a clear target for anyone below to shoot at. They had to incorporate their plan fast or they both would be blown to shreds if it was discovered what they were up to.

"All right, miss, when I say go, just shove the container out the door and let gravity do the rest. Okay?" Olaf looked into her face for recognition of what he was telling her.

Emily gave him thumbs up and yelled "okay" over the roaring helicopter engine and got into position behind the container, waiting for Olaf to tell her when to push. "God, please let this work," she said to herself.

***

Drexel looked up into the air when something shiny caught his attention. There was his jet copter coming towards him. "What was Olaf doing or was it Olaf?" he said aloud. He at first thought it was Olaf because no one else on the island was capable of flying that machine. "Why would he be flying it now? Did he have a plan to help him destroy the British agents? But then again a British agent could have easily taken the craft," he thought. After a few seconds Drexel dismissed the notion that his brother could be at the controls and what he saw in the air was his craft piloted by a British agent as his jet helicopter kept coming towards him closer and closer.

***

Olaf maneuvered the craft over the courtyard like a pro. He could see the droids' red lasers flashing all over the grounds as they shot at the invisible British agents. No one seemed to be paying much attention to him and Emily yet. Once he was in the best possible position, he looked back at Emily and said, "All right, Miss Patrick, go, go, go!"

Emily didn't hesitate one second, but gave the heavy container three short shoves, the last shove putting the container right at the edge of the copter. Olaf tilted the craft on its side to make the container go over the edge, and it worked. Both watched as the bright red container fell away from the copter.

Down on the ground Drexel quickly realized what the red object was that was falling through the air. The helicopter was close enough to the ground that Drexel could see Emily's face. "You!" he screamed, just as the homemade bomb hit a patch of granite flooring and exploded, sending a large mushroom cloud into the air, filling the castle grounds. Olaf quickly steered the helicopter higher into the air, trying to get out of the affected area.

Drexel's droids immediately became visible as the contents of the container filled the air and landed on them. It instantly disintegrated them into piles of circuits and metal. It even affected the droids that were still in the castle. He watched as his creations fell from the upper windows and landed on the hard ground, barely recognizable. He looked out over the courtyard and saw nothing but melted metal.

"No, no, no, it can't be!" Drexel screamed into the air like a child who had just witnessed all his toys being destroyed. Then he ran and grabbed a machine gun from one of his staff and aimed it at the escaping helicopter, emptying the clip into the air.

"It worked! It worked!" Emily yelled. "They're all dead!" She didn't care that Drexel was firing at them. At that moment she felt invincible.

Olaf sensed the danger they were in as he heard the bullets ripping through the fuselage of the helicopter. He turned to Emily and said, "Now would be a good time to leave. Please get back up here to the cockpit, Miss Patrick, where it's safe!" Just then a strafe of bullets hit the jet turbine, sending out a large column of black smoke.

"We're hit and we're going down!" yelled Olaf, as he tried to maneuver the dying craft that had started to spin and descend at the same time.

Drexel watched the death trail of smoke coming from the helicopter as it fought to stay in the air. The craft continued to travel away from him, spinning and slowly falling, then looking like it might regain power and rise, but to no avail. Drexel wondered how the British agents found his craft and had managed to steal it. And if they had the reporter, surely they had the Queen, too. He didn't for once think it was Olaf who had betrayed him.

"Wait for it..." said Drexel to his men, holding up his hand. "Wait for it..." Suddenly there was a muffled explosion off in the distance. "Ahhh," said Drexel, relieved. "Revenge truly is sweet." Then, turning towards what was left of his men, Drexel put back on his goggles and barked an order. "All right, let's clean up this mess. No prisoners, understand?"

"Yes, sir," answered the captain of the guards as he gave the order to go after the British agents.

Drexel let his men go first and he followed in behind them. He would guide their aim since he had the goggles and the agents were still invisible. As they all started moving forward, a voice came from directly behind Drexel, only inches from the back of his neck. "Say, mate, those goggles are British property. You might want to give them back." Drexel was about to turn around and see who it was when he felt a knife's blade stick into his back.

"Who are you? asked Drexel. "One of them?"

"Yes, one of them, mate. Now, hand them over. And while you're at it, hand me your radio as well." Agent Johnson pressed the blade harder into Drexel's spine.

"All right, all right, whoever you are. Just calm down and I'll hand over what you want. Just don't get carried away." Drexel took off the goggles and handed them over his shoulder to the agent.

"Now the radio, sir," the agent demanded, but now feeling a little more nervous.

"Certainly," answered Drexel calmly as he drew his radio from his holster, silently turning it on, unbeknownst to the agent, before handing it over his shoulder to Johnson. Drexel then tried to squeeze a little more conversation out of his new assailant. "Tell me, British agent, are you going to kill me with that knife?"

Drexel's men picked up on the conversation over the radio. They were many yards ahead of him, so some of the men turned around and cautiously made their way back towards their leader, fanning out to get a good shot at the man they now saw standing behind Drexel.

Johnson responded, "No, of course not. We aren't as cut-throat as you blokes are." Johnson grabbed the radio out of the evil genius's hand, but didn't see that the radio's talk button had been activated. Prodding Drexel with the knife to start walking, he added, "No, mate, you'll be spending a long time as the guest of the British prison sys—".

Suddenly a rifle shot range out, grazing Johnson's shoulder. Realizing what was happening, he quickly dropped the goggles on the ground and stomped on them with his left foot as he turned with radio in hand to seek cover, letting Drexel escape and knowing it left him totally exposed. Two more shots rang out, one hitting the agent in the back, the other in his hip.

He knew it was all over as he felt his lungs filling with blood. As he fell to the ground, he spoke into his radio with his last breaths, "Mates, they are blind" - gasping for air - "get the bastards for old Kip. I'm done for." Then Agent Johnson went limp, the radio dropping out of his hand and rolling on the ground as he died.

Off in the distance furious cries from all the charging British agents could be heard. "Kill the bastards for old Kip! Kill Drexel now!" they shouted amidst rapid pistol and machine gun fire, spraying the whole courtyard with bullets and dropping Drexel's men like flies. Drexel's men turned visible as their bodies hit the ground dead, dozens and dozens of them.

Drexel hid in the shadows of the courtyard, trembling in terror, knowing deep down it was all over. His droids were destroyed, his men were dead or dying, and his own brother was presumed dead, captured, or missing. But he wouldn't give up without a fight. He wouldn't dare let these ordinary humans defeat him yet. He had to think of something...

Drexel turned and fled into the caverns deep below the castle. Perhaps if he could get to his secret getaway unnoticed, he'd have a good chance of escaping. Running as fast as he could, he made it to a secret five-man submarine that was hidden in an underground water-filled bay that only he, a few droids, and Olaf knew about. Reaching the gangplank, he paused to catch his breath before he stumbled on board and sealed himself inside. Then he turned on the navigation and operations computer and started giving commands.

"Computer, make way and set course for Argentina," Drexel said, feeling exhausted as he fell into his soft leather-covered captain's chair. He heard the sub's engines come to life and the controls on the panel board automatically lit up. The computer's voice, patterned in the voice of his beloved Marguerite, answered back, "All is ready, sir. Engines optimum. Life systems optimum. Course set. Ready to embark."

Before embarking, Drexel gave the computer another order. "Computer, doomsday code 4-7-5-6-2-3, alpha, omega, begin, begin!"

The computer answered back, "Computer starting doomsday sequence. Time for termination of castle set at thirty minutes, and counting."

"Very well, computer. The order to embark is given," Drexel said, readying himself for launch.

All at once the sub's turbine engines came alive and began to whine as the craft lurched forward, submerging into the black depths of the underground cave that led to an underground river that eventually would empty into the open Baltic Sea. Drexel leaned back into his chair, closed his eyes, and felt an overwhelming sadness sweep over him. Whispering to himself, he said, "Forgive me, brother; I hope your rest in death is sweet," thinking his brother was already killed by the British, as the submarine silently made its way to the open sea.

***

Reggs was standing with his men in the courtyard, surveying his wounded and the dead of his and Drexel's crew. One of his men came running up and said, "No sign of the Queen or that Drexel fellow, sir, but we can hear some woman's voice over an intercom system inside the castle speaking in Swedish, I think.

"Show me," said Reggs.

As both men ran inside the castle, upon entering the dining room hallway they could hear a woman's voice calmly repeating what sounded like the same Swedish words, over and over, in a rhythmic tone; more like a computerized voice than a live person.

"Sounds like she's counting something, sir," the sergeant said to Reggs.

Listening intently, Reggs frowned and said, "Not counting, but counting down! It's a blooming destruct signal! Get everyone out of here now" Reggs shouted, almost pushing the sergeant out of the hallway, him quickly following behind.

As the two men entered the courtyard, they stopped in their tracks, coming upon a very strange sight. In the middle of the courtyard was a small woman holding a spray can in front of her in a defense position. Around the woman were Reggs' men, some bowing their heads, some even kneeling, daring not to look directly up at her.

Quickly recognizing her Reggs, ran up to her and bowed low, "Your Majesty!" The Queen jumped back a few feet, still holding her spray can in position, and looked at Reggs somewhat suspiciously. "Are you here to rescue me?" she finally asked, still cautiously watching all the men who had gathered around her.

Reggs stood up and said, "Yes, ma'am. We are here to bring you home."

"Well," said the Queen, putting down her aerosol can, "I heard all this awful fighting, then silence, and then some woman's voice ringing in my ears, so I decided to come out and see what all the fuss was about." Looking quickly around her, she turned back to Reggs and said, "By the way, have you seen a young American woman about the age of twenty-eight? I've grown rather fond of her and I want to make sure of her safety as well as that of her Swedish male companion."

Reggs couldn't answer her about any Swedish man, but he did think he had seen a young woman in the helicopter before it was shot down. Before he could open his mouth to reply, he heard the sound of multiple helicopters coming towards them from due north. Cocking sounds from the men's pistols in the courtyard could be heard as they all turned their attention to the approaching machines, fear and suspicion still thick in the air.

Reggs started to usher the Queen out of the clearing and to safety until he recognized one of the pilots' voices over the radio as a member of the north island team! "Bloody hell, I thought they had all died by Drexel's deadly magnetic mines!" laughed Reggs, feeling a big sense of relief.

He then turned to the Queen and said, "Ma'am, I'm most happy to announce that your ride is here. Please let me escort you to the helicopter."

"Good," replied the Queen. "But do find that girl, won't you?"

"We'll do everything within our power, Your Majesty. Now, please, let's hurry," said Reggs, with the countdown very fresh in his mind.

After landing, one of the pilots jumped out of the helicopter to help Reggs escort the Queen back to the aircraft. "Your Majesty," said the man as he bowed in respect. Turning to Reggs, he said, "Hello, sir," and gave a salute.

"I am pleased to see you are alive, captain," Reggs said. I have both Shawn and John in a cave on the other side of the beach about a mile away. We need to get them as quickly as possible before this whole place blows. Reggs looked back towards the castle, walking as fast as the Queen could go towards the helicopter.

"No need, sir. We saw the smoke flying in and landed on the beach, picking up four survivors, two of which were an American woman who was slightly wounded and a tall Swedish chap who was pretty banged up. But we'll pull them through. Then of course young Shawn and John came hobbling out of their cave when they saw us land. All are in the back chopper, sir."

As they reached the first helicopter, several of the crew helped the Queen get seated. Reggs looked towards the pilot as he was climbing on board and asked, "Mate, did young Tom, the American, make it?"

The pilot didn't answer right away, but turned his attention back to the instrument panel as the helicopter started its engines. When everyone was on board and finally in the air he answered, "Yes, sir. Caught him myself falling at three thousand feet. Bloody Yank was out cold. When we landed, he came to and even helped us find these helicopters full of fuel, just sitting at Drexel's little airfield, all ready for us to fly. Clever, that Yank. I believe him and his fiancée are kissing in the last chopper as we speak!"

Reggs and the pilot both laughed and then turned their attention back to the matter at hand as they made their way across open waters. Minutes later Reggs looked at his watch, then looked back over his shoulder just in time to see a massive volcanic-type explosion blowing Drexel's beloved castle into fiery bits and pieces. One of the crew popped their head into the cabin and said, "Her

Majesty wants to know what that loud rumble was, commander."

Reggs said, "Tell Her Highness that 'loud rumble' was the sound of a better world."

- THE END -

"Drexel—the Sequel" comes out in the Fall of 2012

ABOUT THE AUTHORS

Susan Stastny is a certified court reporter for the State of Georgia, which over many years has given her a window into the workings of various professions as well as a wide range of experience in editing. Her voracious reading of all genres and her love of the arts is the driving force behind her creativity and imagination. She and her husband, John live near the beautiful Chattahoochee River in Vinings, Georgia. Contact information for Susan Stastny: susanstastny@bellsouth.net, phone 770-438-6191.

David Curry Holmes is a long-time professional Geographer with a governmental agency and has a vast understanding of computers and software. David has received a masters in geography from Georgia State University, Department of Geoscience. David and his wife Patti have three daughters, and reside and live in Marietta, Ga. David has written short stories for Public radio in Atlanta. Contact information for David Curry Holmes workingwithdave@yahoo.com

DREXEL

JC52212-2

Made in the USA
Charleston, SC
09 May 2012